Diversion of the Soul

Dawn Rowe

PublishAmerica
Baltimore

ISBN: 1-4241-3914-7
PUBLISHED BY PUBLISHAMERICA, LLLP
www.publishamerica.com
Baltimore

Printed in the United States of America

For Freddie

14 June 1959–2 February 2005

ACKNOWLEDGEMENTS

I would like to express my thanks to all of my friends who have helped and supported me with this book and to my family for their love and support.

Thanks to Megan and Max for being the brave and beautiful children who they are. Special thanks to Claire and Daz, and, of course, thanks to Ruts!

PROLOGUE

In the tranquil gardens, time held no importance. Simply the soul came to rest or reside. Yet in this moment a lonely figure waited. He stood beneath the marble arches, out of view of the two women who stood at the far end of the idyllic garden. The women were locked deep in conversation. He surveyed them with keen interest; the taller of the two in particular. The mere sight of her causing him to catch his breath with an overpowering feeling of love, it seemed impossible then, that within this same moment the deep emotion he felt became engulfed by an overriding fear, a fear which wheedled its way into his heart like a parasite. Suddenly he looked away, his body now tense.

It was paramount to him that this woman should succeed the task that was before her, for only then could they truly be together for at least one mortal lifetime and into the realms beyond and that was the one thing he so truly desired.

It was all up to her now, out of his hands, as it had been over the centuries before, when she had to his misery failed. Alas she would proceed again and she would not be alone, never alone. She would have the woman who stood with her right now, there by her side, her loyal companion her trusted spirit guide, on the treacherous journey that loomed to the place known simply as earth.

It would be quite some time before the three of them would meet again, but now was not the time to think of such things. He had said his goodbyes earlier when she had been cradled in his arms, when his eyes had met hers and there was not any need for words, when her forthcoming journey had been momentarily cast aside. He had never wanted to let her go from the fond embrace but he had and now he watched ever hopeful as she stood against the back drop of the peachy sky. A whisper of breeze gently lifting a lock of her raven hair and placing it across her cheek, she looked so vulnerable, he gave an inward sigh, clenching his hands together in a useless gesture. It was all mapped out to a point, the divine contracts drawn up, agreed by all parties. In that fleeting moment he longed to be able to change it, to rewrite the rules, so she would not leave and he would not have to wait the many earth years before he would see her again. He knew in his heart as he had done time and time before that it must be so and he was utterly useless to prevent it.

A shadow fell alongside him and he turned to acknowledge Sebastian, who smiled placing a comforting hand upon his shoulder.

"Nathanial, your lady will not fail this time." Sebastian's voice was steady as he looked into his student's eyes with a deep understanding. He knew only too well what he was feeling, for he too had experienced this pain. "We have worked harder this time, prepared her more than the last." He noted the other man's silent acknowledgement, watched as Nathanial tore his eyes from the woman for just a moment to look back at him.

Then Nathanial spoke. "I feel it in here." He clutched his hand to his heart, his eyes misting over. "Yet I am sure I felt that before and for that I feel afraid." He looked back to the woman he adored, watched her warmly embrace her companion, watched their temporary parting, for very soon she would begin and therefore have no memory of her, as she stepped through the veil of amnesia. Sebastian nodded though he remained silent.

As the women walked away from one another leaving the peaceful haven, Nathanial felt a sudden urge to stop both of them. Sebastian, sensing this, took him firmly by the wrist for his own good.

"Stay here. This is always so hard for you." He signalled across to the building at the far end of the garden. "Perhaps we should go and look in on the new arrivals. That's always very humbling. It will remind you why it has to be this way." He raised a knowing brow.

Reluctantly, Nathanial allowed Sebastian to lead him away, each step with difficulty, as each step took him further away from her final moments here.

After the serenity of the gardens, the arrival area felt oppressive, heaving with expectant relatives and noble guides, who busied themselves along the hallway and into the large welcoming rooms that led off from the great hall. He veered off left into one of the rooms, giving Sebastian the slip. He needed to be alone if only for a few moments. He strode over to the large window clutching at its wooden frame for support. He looked out on the vast space before him, his eyes focusing on the globe of golden light that had appeared as a dot on the horizon, watched entranced as it came toward him, all the while increasing in size, its light becoming more luminous, more intense, a sight that would in normal circumstance cause him to weep with happiness, a spirit returning home. He shifted his gaze, suddenly distracted by the disc of silver light that left from the top of the opposite tower. He watched as it spiralled through the air upward towards the endless sky, spears of white light radiating from its core. He watched it with a sense of knowing until it became a mere dot eventually fading from his view altogether, bowing his head he felt a pitiful emptiness, a rising panic at the sense of uselessness. Now it was too late. She was gone, soon to arrive in the chosen womb and settle to await the birthing process. Soon he would follow.

Nathanial would love others and the emptiness would for a time, be forgotten. Many earth years would come to pass before he would be reunited with her. Yet when that time arrived neither would have any recognition of the other. Somehow, he felt would know her, that something would remind him and only then would he have a sense of being complete, a step further to eternity with his beloved soul mate.

CHAPTER ONE

The serenity of the late autumn afternoon was shattered by the rooks that soared high above the countryside, cawing in perfect unison as they headed up towards the wood at the top of the hill. A cheeky rabbit paused from its unremitting munching, cocking its tiny head sideways, raising up onto its haunches and listening intently, remaining motionless as the birds circled above, then dropping back down to resume its lunch as they passed over. A few seconds later it paused again, startled by the sound of leaves softly crunching beneath approaching footsteps. Sensing it was no longer alone the rabbit careered off back towards the meadow and the safety of its warm underground burrow.

Standing back in the shadows a figure waited, anxious to see the new arrivals, it remained still with each breath becoming more drawn with expectation. The Mercedes estate car glided along the shingle driveway, just feet from where the watcher lurked, eager to view its passengers.

The car pulled up at the front of the old stone farmhouse, which stood bathed in the last of the suns amber rays. At this moment Edward's excited wails grew to fever pitch. Isobel smiled across at Jacob then turned to look back over her shoulder at her animated son. This was Edward's first glimpse of his new home, frantically he struggled to release himself from the restrictive child seat. Isobel gave an indulgent smile; the mood was the same for all of them. It had been a dream for some considerable time, now here they were sitting outside their new home, an ancient farmhouse, snuggled in the beautiful Devonshire countryside.

Jacob climbed out stretching his cramped limbs. He opened the rear door, leaning in to pull the scrabbling Edward from his seat. "Be careful!" he warned, helping him down proudly onto the soft lawn. Edward broke free from his protective clutch and then proceeded to flounder over the ornate kerb stones where he landed unceremoniously in a heap, letting out a large howl of frustration.

Incessant whines reminded Jacob with a pang of guilt, that Tarquin and Sadie their two golden retrievers, who having sat patiently on the long journey, could contain themselves no longer, and needed to explore too. He lifted the tailgate, allowing them to spill out. Joyously the dogs raced around the glum-looking child. Isobel stretched her arms gracefully above her head letting out a long happy sigh, whilst Edward huffed and puffed as his father stooped to pick him up.

"Mmm, you can almost taste the air." Isobel gazed around at the breathtaking beauty of her surroundings, finally resting her gaze on the old farmhouse and its tired façade, she took another deep breath. There had been much hard work to get here, had it been worth it? Standing there at that moment, she knew it had been the right decision. She just knew.

The shadowy figure drew in a pleasing breath, this was better than had been anticipated, the corners of its mouth creased into a satisfied smile at the sight of such a beautiful child. With one last longing gaze the figure turned reluctantly and slipped quietly back towards the lane, softly muttering beneath its breath.

Jacob strode towards his wife clutching a very red-faced Edward, whose chubby cheeks were now grass stained and wet with tears. She looked at them both lovingly; Edward would surely be every bit as handsome as his father when he grew up. She closed her eyes, holding on to the moment, it would become one she would always cherish.

"Where do we start, darling?" Jacob gave a boyish grin.

"Perhaps we should start by giving our son a tour of his new home."

She looked up at the house, surprised to see what appeared to be a face at one of the upstairs windows, in an instant it disappeared. She turned to face Edward who looked up at her expectantly. Isobel shrugged dismissing it as a trick of the light, a silly mistake. She took hold of Edward's grubby little hand. Edward followed his mother eagerly; he didn't say much but nodded his head in approval with a ridiculously cheesy grin. Isobel noted his expression with delight, as they swept from room to room of the house, their new house. Jacob left the tour to collect the flask and mugs that had been neatly packed alongside a few other necessities in a cardboard box on the rear seat of the car.

Isobel found him in the kitchen, he passed her a steaming mug which she took gratefully suddenly aware how thirsty she was, so keen were they to arrive, that they hadn't stopped once on the journey down from London to Orange Stream Farm. A name the place had held since first being built in the early 18th century. Taking their mugs of coffee out onto the terrace, they sat side by side on the stone steps that led down to the sweeping, but overgrown, lawn which fanned gracefully around the rear of the house.

"Come closer." Jacob pulled Isobel toward him. "Are you happy?"

She nodded with felicity. Their eyes held a steady gaze.

"I love you, Isobel."

"Oh, Jacob, I love you too," she said, smiling as he leant over to plant a gentle kiss on her forehead.

"I couldn't have done it without you." He looked down at her his tone sincere.

"That's not true." Isobel chuckled, tickling him playfully in the ribs.

He looked at her in astonishment, was she being modest or did she really have no idea what a help she had been to him over the years? Blissfully, Isobel snuggled closer to her husband wedging herself securely between his strong arms.

Isobel rose early that first morning at Orange Stream Farm, whilst Jacob and Edward slept soundly on. It seemed the perfect time to explore her new surroundings. Pulling on jeans and a thick sweater Isobel managed to creep downstairs, past the sleeping dogs in the hallway to slip unheard, out of the kitchen door.

Standing out on the terrace, she drew in breath, marvelling at her new home. The chill in the morning air mixed with a strong familiar woody smell, reminiscent of her childhood causing her to tremble. The landscape that spanned out before her eyes was truly spellbinding. The lawns at the rear below the terrace stretched out towards the paddocks. To her right dwarf fir trees interspersed with rose bushes divided the lawn area from the orchard that lay beyond.

Isobel headed across the lawns, she slipped under the rails into the first large paddock moving across diagonally to the far left corner. Marching purposely, pausing every now and then to look back at the house. The ground ahead of her rose gently, sweeping up towards a plateau. It was for here that she headed. Reaching the top, she climbed up onto the gate, perching herself comfortably to look back down at the farm nestled in the valley. It was beautiful. Hugging her arms around herself, she felt a rush of excitement, this was always what she had dreamed of. There was no way they could lose this place, it was meant for them, and she was undeniably already feeling a part of it. Turning her gaze away from the sleeping farm, she looked northwards to what lay to the other side of the valley. It was here that the land was less tended and had not been grazed for some time. Here was a huge meadow filled with the last of the buttercups and soft lilacs of meadow clary. The delightful scent of meadow sweet filled the air. A stream carved its way like a glittering snake right through the middle of the meadow and as she approached it, a buzzard soared overhead scanning the land below for breakfast.

At the stream's edge Isobel sat down on the dew kissed grass to admire the delicate little pink flowers of Soapwort that grew along the bank. She gave herself a sharp pinch, just in case, no, she was really here and this was now all to be a part of her life. Crossing over the stream, Isobel scrambled up the opposite bank, onto the other side of the meadow, which brought her to Orange Stream Farm's boundaries. The woods, which covered a large area, belonged to their nearest neighbours at Bramstone Hall. You couldn't see the hall from here, for beyond the wood, it lay nestled in a valley of its own. As she neared the edge of the wood the towering ancient oaks and horse chestnuts blocked the rays of the early morning sun out entirely.

Without the warmth of the sun it was cold, goose bumps rose on her skin and from the eerie depths of the wood she could hear the sharp cry of an animal, its sound haunting. As she strode from the soft meadow into the entrance of the large wood the atmosphere changed, the chill intensifying. Isobel shuddered, her mood changing, something didn't feel right.

"Don't be silly," she scolded, herself beneath her breath. "It's just a wood." But she knew it wasn't just the darkness or the towering trees, but the strange uncomfortable feeling that swept around her body like a heavy cloak. It was as if she was being watched. Isobel shivered, biting her lip in agitation, as she peered into the gloomy depths of the wood. It didn't feel as if just one person was watching but as if many pairs of eyes were piercing into her. Turning back, Isobel looked wistfully across the meadow. Feeling uneasy, she began to retrace her steps, without daring a backward glance.

Once back inside the farmhouse kitchen she found the sleeping dogs were now wide awake. They bounced excitedly at her heels, now she felt safe. Pouring two steaming mugs of coffee, she laughed at her silly behaviour. Perhaps it was all the excitement, her imagination was running away with her. She hurried upstairs to wake Jacob and tell him about their beautiful home.

It wasn't realistic for Jacob to commute to London every day. It had been decided long ago, in the days when a country property had been a mere pipe dream that he would need to remain at the helm of their export company in the city. To enable him to do this, with the minimum of fuss, he would need to spend the week at the flat in London and return home at weekends. Now dressed smartly in a suit, he climbed into the car turning to wave goodbye, a bit too enthusiastically, for Isobel's liking, at the two sorrowful figures framed in the doorway. He would miss them desperately but knew, for now; it could be no other way. In five days he would be back. Driving out of their sight, he held on to that cheery thought as he negotiated the winding lanes that led out towards the motorway.

Isobel held Edward's hand tightly as the car slid from view. Edward was alarmed that the dogs hadn't been there to see Jacob off. Isobel looked at his face, concern etched on his tiny perfect features. In fact, both dogs were dozing in their baskets enjoying the early morning sun. Tarquin raised his head briefly, thumped his tail lazily a few times then let his body slide deliriously back into his soft bed, as they passed by. Such spoilt dogs, Isobel thought to herself. Now they would have so much space in which to play and hunt. Looking at the pair of them now, it was as if even that would be too much effort.

"Can we play now, Mummy?" Edward smiled up at her. His large brown eyes glistened beneath a mop of golden hair. There was a hint of sadness within his eyes which was reflected in hers too. Neither of them had ever been without Jacob for any length of time before. Isobel sat on his bed, idly watching as he clumsily set up one of his games. Her gaze moved distractedly across to the window. She looked out over the paddocks and across the meadow where she could just make out a group of rabbits playing in the grass. A momentary feeling of foreboding weighed on her mind. She glanced down at her watch, it was nearly ten. Jacob should arrive in London by eleven; she was feeling anxious that was all. Of course, she knew she could dial his mobile phone if she really wanted to, but then she was trying to demonstrate how independent she could be. Start as you mean to go on, she thought, shrugging off the nagging feeling of doubt.

It was much later as they sat down to lunch that Jacob called to say that he had arrived safely, the traffic had been a nightmare and he supposed in future he would need to leave earlier.

"Is everything OK?" he asked. Sensing a change in the Isobel, he had left earlier that day.

"Sure it is," Isobel replied. Despite being mildly irritated that he had left it so late in the day to call. Edward noticed a tear fall from his mother's eye and wondered why on earth there was any need for that. Daddy would be home soon and he had said that he would bring a present with him. Mums could be really silly. He was a bright child and as a sudden afterthought wondered if perhaps there was something that they hadn't told him before resuming his ham sandwich.

Isobel put Edward to bed a little later than usual that evening, glad of his company and the endless questions about rabbits. Isobel was surprised that he hadn't asked after his father. Now as she sat alone in the sitting room, it didn't seem quite as cosy as it had earlier, when Edward had been giggling and playing happily by the fire with the dogs.

The flagstone floor felt cold beneath her feet as she padded through to the study to pour a large brandy from the crystal decanter. Isobel returned to the living room, sinking back on to the sofa where she curled her feet up beneath her. Lonely nights, they would take some getting used to, but she was sure that this first would be the hardest. Glancing across at the roaring fire, Isobel felt a laughable sense of achievement, one that only a real townie would appreciate. It was the first real fire she had ever lit. Now watching the dancing flames which licked hungrily into the air, with a gentle roar, she smiled with contentment. Despite the intense chill which had swept in uninvited and settled heavily in the air around her. There was a sudden loud rattle at the window, which caused her to jump, the brandy glass still poised at her lips. Hardly daring to breathe she waited, glancing down at the dogs who did not stir. It rattled again, followed by the whistling wind. How silly, she thought, before turning her attention to the glowing fire once more.

Olivia Pearson checked her reflection in the mirror. With a grunt, she rearranged a few straying strands from her otherwise neat, shoulder length, blonde hair. Outside in the distance, Ruffles, her German shepherd, could be heard barking.

"Dratted dog!" she cursed. "He is a pain in the arse. Damn thing." Well there was no way she was going out to look for him now. Neatly applying a frosted pink lipstick, she admired herself one last time. Then she checked her watch before taking her jacket down from the peg in the hallway. Climbing into the Range Rover, she pulled the sunroof back to feel the evening sun comfortingly warm on her head. Placing her Chanel sunglasses meticulously on the bridge of her nose, she sneaked a final image check in the rearview mirror before she drove into the village.

The village of Peterbridge was a typical chocolate box affair. A row of rose swathed cottages in duck egg blue and candyfloss pink, a large duck pond, on its surface floated a variety of wild ducks and in the best of village tradition, there was plenty of local gossip. Olivia loathed the place, almost as much as she loathed herself. Grabbing the few bits she needed from the shelves, she hastily paid before anyone could dare to make polite conversation. Not that for one minute she considered any of the locals would have anything interesting to say. Life within Peterbridge was notoriously dull.

The drive back to Bramstone Hall was far more relaxed than the speedy journey there had been, now that her chores were complete for the day. On the way back along the windy lane that led to the hall, she passed the entrance to Orange Stream Farm, craning her neck as she passed by for any sign of life from within the farm's rusty gates. Recently she had been quite tempted to drive in and introduce herself, as new neighbours usually do, not to be particularly friendly, more darn right nosey. After all Bramstone Hall was only another mile along the lane, that made herself and Graham their nearest neighbours and their first port of call in an emergency.

When she reached home, Olivia was irritated to find that Graham was back.

"Shit, he's early!" she muttered. In fact he seemed to be making a habit of it these days. Oh well, if that was the case he certainly couldn't be screwing his secretary anymore. Graham stood waiting at the door looking marginally apologetic.

"Sorry forgot my damned key." He smiled, revealing a row of uneven yellow teeth. Olivia returned a forced smile.

"Not a problem, early day again I see?"

Graham smoothed his brow accompanying it with a huge yawn, showing all of his less than perfect teeth.

"Yes, love, it's a bit quiet, but nothing to worry about."

Olivia took the groceries through to the kitchen, hauling the bags on to the worktop; she opened the fridge, and poured herself a large glass of Chablis. Graham appeared at her side, with a disapproving glance.

"Bit early for that, eh, darling?" Tossing her head back, Olivia gave him a defiant glare.

"Balls," she retorted. Turning on her heel, she marched purposefully through to the drawing room without a backward glance. Graham shook his head, letting out a deep sigh. It seemed as if he could do nothing right these days. He went upstairs to change, keen to take Solvent out for a ride. He hadn't ridden him for the last few days and the horse needed regular exercise if he was to remain anything near manageable. He had considered riding up to the western boundary of their land, to the point where it linked up with the Jackmans' old place, and then he could be nosey and see who had moved in, surprised that Olivia had not already been round to investigate. She had always been a nosey bitch. But he had to admit it, he was rather intrigued himself. They had paid through the nose, if the largely inflated sum that was being bandied about was to be believed and for what exactly? In his expert opinion the place needed complete renovation, after all he should know, being in the business. Besides he was still smarting that he hadn't been asked to market the property, oh well, the place had an unpleasant history. No, personally he wouldn't have touched it with a barge pole.

Olivia meanwhile had drained her glass, she returned to the kitchen for a refill just as Graham shimmied off through the back door.

"No doubt off to ride your disgusting beast of a horse?" she yelled after him. "Well I hope you get bloody well thrown off it!"

Graham showed no response as he shuffled up to the stables, glad to escape for a bit, the atmosphere decidedly claustrophobic. Olivia's pensive gaze followed him. She wondered where it had all gone wrong; most probably before they had even married. All she felt for him was hate pure hate.

Graham was from a wealthy family and able to offer Olivia the lifestyle that she sought. He was relatively good-looking and certainly had an abundance of charm, but she doubted that they had ever really loved each other. Not real grown up love, at times Olivia had to ask herself did that kind of love really exist. However, if she was honest, she had come very close to knowing a few years ago with Stephen.

Stephen had been a junior negotiator within Graham's firm, Pearson's prestigious Property Agents, specialists in the sale of large country houses. Just the thought of him gave Olivia goose bumps. It had all been so very passionate, quite unlike anything ever with Graham. Yet Olivia had known in her heart that she was just a tiny part of Stephen's life, a stepping-stone in the days when it was fashionable to shag the boss' wife. He had been just twenty-three when he joined the business; she had been thirty-four. Feeling bored and very unattractive Stephen had been the most welcome distraction from the monotony of everyday life. The intimacy with Stephen had been a whole new experience, unleashing powerful feelings Olivia had never known existed. Fifteen months their affair had lasted, during this time, Graham had been an unpleasant afterthought. Who he was with and what he was doing hadn't mattered in the least.

When Stephen had made the decision to move to a more prestigious office in Worcester, it had been the end of their relationship. Shortly afterwards, Olivia hadn't been surprised at all to see him with a beautiful, much younger woman. Although this had saddened her greatly, it had been expected, and she had grieved nonetheless. Wine had become the medicine she needed.

In the following years, Olivia had slowly reverted back to her old self, the life before Stephen self. These days the only passionate encounters with Graham would be after she had drank enough wine to totally distort his face and mask his rough abrasive touch.

Olivia sat staring out of the French windows. She could see Graham, ready for the off on his wild-eyed horse, there was a stab of jealousy. Graham had a unique way of letting everything go way above his head. Graham knew she was hurting, but he didn't seem to care or to be bothered by it in the least. She gave a deep resentful sigh, right now life really sucked and she couldn't, as hard as she looked, see any way out of her dull existence.

Later that evening, after a solemn dinner, accompanied by three further bottles of white wine, mostly consumed by Olivia, she lay restlessly bronzing under the solarium wondering what life had in store, apart from the increasingly attractive prospect of taking a gun to her head, she heard Graham enter the room, heard his rasping breath. As he approached where she lay, her body began to knot. Olivia swallowed, hard; she may as well get it this over with. After all it was why he had appeared; just think of Stephen, she told herself, that's right think of him, anything to make it more bearable.

Jacob fell exhausted into the armchair, looking around at the half empty flat. He had the bare necessities; everything else was down in Devon along with his beloved Isobel and Edward. Jacob thought about phoning but it was far too late. It had been such a busy day and the time had seemed to disappear. He would give them a call early before he left for the office. After all he felt confident that Isobel would cope, even though she had never liked being left alone. Their marriage was strong and now how strange it felt for them to be apart. It was that feeling that bothered him and he wondered how she was coping down there alone. It was as if you had forgotten something, and the rest of the day it nagged and preyed on your mind. Except this was far more intense, it made him feel anxious and restless. He had to keep reminding himself that it would pass. The week had flown, tomorrow would be Friday and at around six he would leave London for the journey back to the tranquillity of the farm and those he loved dearly. With that in mind, he drifted into a peaceful sleep.

CHAPTER TWO

Slowly the car's engine spluttered into life. Isobel reversed the battered old Ford out of the garage. Edward gazed warily across at her.

"Why do you look cross, Mummy?"

"I'm not cross, darling." Isobel turned to smile at her son. "It's just that this is not the most reliable of cars. I am just trying to get to grips with it."

"Where's your car, Mummy?"

Grinding the gears into place, Isobel explained the best she could to a four-year-old, that this was now to be Mummy's car, as the smart BMW had been sold to enable them to manage the hefty mortgage. Edward seemed to be happy with this explanation even though he really didn't have a clue what his mother meant and settled back to enjoy the view as they headed into town.

As they walked along the high street Edward marched happily at her side. Shopping could be fun; it nearly always meant a new toy of some description. Today he would be good, besides he had picked up on his mother's air of frustration and didn't fancy her stern tongue.

After a reasonably successful outing, followed by a tantrum free lunch, Isobel sent Edward out to play with the dogs in the garden. As she kept watch from the kitchen window, the phone ringing interrupted Isobel. It was Jacob.

"You sound harassed, are you OK?"

"It's these bloody idiots that work with me, well, with the exception of Gloria," he added gently. "The bank has been breathing down my neck. I am sure they think the farm is a mistake. Shit, sorry, honey." His tone softened, he didn't want to alarm Isobel unnecessarily. "It's been a busy day I'm tired and, boy, I have missed you."

"I know. I have missed you too."

"I hope to be with you around nine this evening," he added brightly. Isobel replaced the receiver. Jacob had always been under pressure. The export company he ran was a strain. The business had been handed down from his father; it would be terrible for Jacob if it were to fail. Isobel didn't intend to worry, instead she moved nearer to the window looking out across the countryside. In the distance she thought that she could hear shouting, but their nearest neighbours were a considerable distance, maybe she had imagined it.

It would be great when Jacob's parents could come down to see their new home. They were both retired but still incredibly active. They now lived in north Essex. Both were avid gardeners, keen members of every horticultural association and Isobel would value their ideas. She had no doubt at all that they would fall in love with the cosy stone farmhouse; the surrounding countryside; and be entranced by the beautiful stream and the dramatic views up towards the wood. Isobel felt herself shudder at the thought of the wood where she had felt so uneasy that first morning; she hadn't returned there since. Isobel was suddenly aware that was Edward waving to someone from the garden, alarmed she hurried outside. There she saw an older woman with swept back grey hair and a wrinkled but kindly face, appear at the side gate. Obviously a local, she decided looking at her weathered appearance. The woman was carrying a large wicker basket.

"I am very sorry to trouble you, my dear." Her voice was gentle and warm, dripping with a broad West Country accent. Isobel opened the gate smiling politely, her eyes drawn to the basket that was crammed full of jars along with several small muslin tied parcels. Following Isobel's interested gaze the woman offered the basket towards her invitingly.

"Rita Mallins. I live the other side of the village. I was wondering whether I could tempt you with any of my homemade produce." She placed the basket down extending her hand warmly toward Isobel. "Oh, and not forgetting of course to welcome you to the village."

"Thank you." Isobel smiled back, delighted to meet someone at last. "Please do come in and have a cup of tea, it's nice to meet you. In fact it's great to see someone!"

Rita nodded accepting the invitation with a smile. As Isobel set out two cups, Rita explained that she had been friends of the previous owners of the farm. To Isobel's delight, Rita was an extensive source of information. Perhaps, Isobel thought, as she poured in the milk that some would even call Rita a bit of a busybody but on first impression she appeared to be much too nice for that. It emerged that jams, marmalade and cookies weren't Rita's only talent. She was in fact a very influential person in the village. Isobel, starved of some company, devoured the gossip hungrily, especially that about her nearest neighbours at Bramstone Hall. Apparently they were a ghastly couple, not very well liked. In fact, Rita described them as rude and arrogant persons.

"Of course Olivia, the wife, hits the bottle but then I expect she has good reason. I have heard that her husband Graham can't keep his eyes off other women and it doesn't stop there, if you get my drift." Rita took a sip of her tea. "Best make your own mind up on that one, love. Don't expect it will be long before you run into them."

Maybe that was who Isobel had heard shouting earlier, it would certainly explain it. Eager to hear more, Isobel couldn't help leaning in closer. At that exact moment Edward leapt onto Rita's basket, sending jars of jam and pickle catapulting across the kitchen floor. Rita merely laughed, as Isobel leapt to her feet, cheeks flushed to retrieve the jars. At which point Edward had spotted the cookies with an excited squeal and scrabbled toward them like an excitable puppy. Rita chuckled, passing him some with a delighted smile, and waving Isobel's apology away.

"How old is he?" She gazed across at Edward who sat munching contently.

"Four," Isobel replied, looking at her son. "He is a perfect bundle of mischief."

"He is simply adorable," Rita cooed, leaning across to pat Edward's head affectionately.

When Rita stood to leave, she took Isobel's hand warmly in her own.

"I hope that you and your family will be very happy here." There was genuine warmth in her eyes. She looked up at the house. "Just what this place needs, my love, a young vibrant family to chase away the shadows." Isobel looked at her quizzically. She didn't respond, instead turning to smile at Edward and pass him another cookie. Isobel decided there and then that she liked Rita and standing with Edward watching the old woman leave, she gave a happy sigh.

Later, that evening when Edward was sound asleep in bed, Isobel prepared a chicken casserole, placing it in the ancient Aga, which she was still trying to get the hang of, hoping that tonight it wouldn't result in another charred offering at the base of the pot. Leaving it to simmer, she went upstairs to run a bath. Carefully she added a few drops of patchouli and lavender to enhance her mood, relaxing but with a promise of passion. Undressing in front of the mirror she studied her reflection with a critical eye. It would be her 30th birthday next spring. Her body was well toned and had miraculously escaped any stretch marks during her pregnancy. If anything, her breasts were on the small side, but at least they remained firm and rounded. Her belly, however, was a lot more rounded than she would have liked, she gave it a gentle stroke as she pulled in its muscles. "Oh that looks better," she murmured, as she flicked a tendril of chestnut hair back across her olive shoulder. Nevertheless, her deep brown eyes glistened with dissatisfaction; she had put on a few pounds. She turned away.

Reclining back into the warm scented water, she gave a deep sigh. Despite her not being as slim as she would have liked it seemed as if she had everything else her heart could desire. Jacob was due home and she let the worries that had haunted her earlier in the day subside. On a positive note she had made a friend, and survived her first week alone, what could possibly go wrong?

The sound of a car its tyres scrunching on the gravel outside, made her leap up with excitement from the bath, pausing only momentarily to grab her robe and hastily wipe her feet on the bath mat. Isobel's heart thumped at each step she descended. Jacob stood at the foot of the stairs, looking she thought, incredibly handsome. He grinned broadly up at her. Then catching her in his arms as she leapt toward him. He tugged playfully at her hair as he bent to kiss her slender neck.

"God you smell wonderful." He breathed in her scent, squeezing her buttocks playfully. "It is great to be home. Nightmares drive, but so worth it, I haven't had this sort of welcome for a long time."

"Oh, darling, I have missed you so much, you just wouldn't believe how much." She kissed his cheek feverishly. "How was the journey home, it wasn't too hellish, was it?" She led him toward the kitchen. "Let me fix you a drink, darling."

"Great I could murder one but first I would like to go and freshen up and look in on my son. I won't be long, honey."

Isobel opened a bottle of wine. She took two crystal glasses from the dresser and set them down on the table. The crystal only surfaced for special occasions but this evening certainly classified; she decided filling them both to the top. Shortly Jacob appeared, a large towel wrapped around his waist, his hair damp and glistening. Isobel handed him the glass of wine. He took it and gazed at her searchingly.

"So how has it been for you, darling? Did you cope alright and more importantly did you miss me lots?"

Gently entwining her arms around his neck she kissed him hard on the lips. "It is so good to have you back." She clung tightly to him, glad he was back home at last and suddenly painfully aware of just how much she had missed him. "I missed you so much more than lots."

As she fetched the casserole, she looked across at him sat at the table with a sense of longing that she had not felt for quite some time.

"Did you go out at all?" she asked, serving up their dinner.

"No, far too tired for that."

"Not even for a drink after work?"

"Not even for a drink after work!" He crammed in a fork full of chicken. "Why, did you think I might?"

"It had crossed my mind." Feeling a bit guilty, she changed the subject.

"Do you have to go to London every week?" A little taken back, Jacob leant across the table to take her hand, giving it a gentle squeeze.

"You know I have to, but hopefully after a while I will be able to do a shorter week."

"Yes, I suppose that is a possibility, let's see." Isobel forced a smile. "Anyway, Edward and I have met somebody today."

Jacob looked across at her curiously. "Really, sounds interesting, who?"

"A sweet lady from the village, called Rita." She paused to take a sip of wine. "Oh and apparently our neighbours are frightful according to Rita."

"Really, that will be something to look forward to then." Noticing her shiver, he fetched a throw from the living room and draped it around her shoulders. "So, this Rita what's she like?" he asked.

"She seems to be really nice, about late sixties at a guess. Edward was very taken with her or it could have been her cookies."

Jacob looked puzzled.

Isobel laughed. "Never mind, it's a long story."

"It wasn't too awful down here, just you and Edward, was it?" Jacob asked tentatively.

Isobel stood up and began to clear the plates. "No not at all, actually it's been very peaceful." She averted her eyes from his enquiring gaze. "And amazingly I've been chopping logs and I'm becoming a dab hand at lighting the fire."

"Really." His eyes sparkled with admiration. "Turning into a proper little country girl then."

When they finally went up to bed, he took her gently. He needed for it to be tender, to savour what he had missed all week. She clung to him, thankful of his gentleness, afraid she may cry as emotion welled up within her. Afterwards Isobel fell immediately into a deep, contented sleep. Hardly passionate but she was exhausted and he understood. Jacob lay restlessly.

Isobel's statement earlier had worried him. It appeared that she was already feeling apprehensive after just one week. He looked across at her, her fragility deceiving, he knew how strong she was beneath her delicate facade, it would just take time for her to adjust that was all, he told himself.

Turning over on to his side, he became aware of a strong smell, it drifted into his nostrils, enticing a sneeze. It smelt herbal not unlike sage, whatever it was, it didn't agree with him. He guessed it was an air freshener he would tell Isobel in the morning. He didn't want to flare up his allergy; whatever new fragrance she was using it would have to go. The smell seemed to intensify, becoming almost unbearable, making him feel quite nauseous. He pulled the sheet to his face covering his nose. It was ghastly, he looked across at Isobel who slept soundly on but he noted the silver glow emanating from Isobel's body. Gosh, he thought with horror, it's been a long hard week, he was far more exhausted than he had realised. Thumping his pillow, he laid back his head trying to get comfortable and ignore the smell which had become quite overpowering.

Sombre rain laden clouds gathered overhead. The brisk eastern wind picked up, whirling the leaves into miniature tornadoes, across the impeccable lawns of Bramstone Hall. The rooks circling high above the wood flew in perfect synchronisation into its dark depths, to escape the imminent soaking. Olivia watched from the kitchen window, listening to the rain as it gathered momentum against the glass. Well that's written off the notion of a healthy walk, she sighed. There was no way she would venture out in this, even if she did have a full-length Barbour and Wellingtons from Harrods. Better stick with the backup plan, she mused, a smile spreading across her face. A glass of wine and her new classical compact disc, indulgently she spent the rest of the day, tucked away safely inside the walls of the hall.

Graham walked through the door at seven, tired and hungry; he was looking forward to dinner. Instead of the comforting aroma of shepherd's pie or perhaps the excellent lasagne that Olivia had sometimes been known on a rare occasion to make, he found his wife out cold on the sofa, a glass of wine spilt on the floor beside her. His immediate reaction was to drag her from her drunken slumber and hurl her against the wall. Instead he took a deep breath to dissolve the fierce growl that was surfacing in his throat. Good god the woman was becoming an alcoholic. It hadn't escaped his notice how much wine was missing from the cellar, it was worrying and it damn well couldn't continue. Mumbling witlessly, he made a sandwich with the last two slices of stale bread and hard lump of cheddar. There was no mineral water and he had specifically asked Olivia to get some in. He scratched his head, god who did she think paid for all this lot, was it really too much to ask. The doorbell rang, the growl surfaced. "Who the bloody hell is that?"

Graham stormed down the hallway prepared to tell whoever it was to piss off, before he remembered. Oh shit, he had asked Carmen to call round and Christ the place was a state. Carmen Franklin ran the local riding stables, a very colourful character, yakked too much for Graham's liking though. Graham had found her property for her, a couple of years back and now he required a favour in return. He hadn't let on to Olivia but he was having a few problems with Solvent. In fact a bit more than that, he couldn't control the wilful beast and had damn near had a nasty tumble on their last outing. In his opinion Carmen was the right woman to sort him out. Smiling broadly he opened the door. Carman stood cold and shivering on the doorstep, her red curls clinging to her damp ruddy cheeks.

"Sorry, I'm dripping wet. I was running late and had to dash straight from feeding the horses." With a limp, apologetic grin she stepped inside.

"No apology needed." He signalled for her to go on through to the kitchen, avoiding the shameless Olivia in her drunken stupor. Graham poured them both a beer; he explained what had been happening, keen for Carmen to be away before Olivia surfaced. Carmen sensed the urgency, rapidly draining every last drop from the glass in her hand.

"Well I can certainly take a look at him, how about if I pop in tomorrow?"

"Doubt I will be here, but I will ask Olivia to be around and point you in the right direction. I expect she will be glad of some company."

Graham saw her out in to the blustery night, thankful that Olivia had not roused. Switching out the lights, he made his way wearily to bed.

The following morning he found Olivia sat at the kitchen table, looking remarkably fresh, a glass of juice in one hand, an oatcake in the other.

"Sore head, my dear?" Olivia ignored his comment, taking another nibble of her breakfast. "Well I won't hang around, you are obviously occupied. By the way, a lady called Carmen will be dropping by later to look at the horse. Would you be so kind to show her up to the stables?"

Olivia wrinkled her nose in disgust. "That's a joke, right? I mean you want me to hang around all day to show some airhead bimbo where your horse lives. You know I don't go up there and I hate horses."

"Olivia, my dear. Yes I do." Graham arched his brows until they became lost in his furrowed forehead. "Not for one minute that I think you have anything more useful to do." He left without saying goodbye. Jesus he could barely look at her these days, without wanting to throttle her. A man of his calibre needed a strong respectful wife. Someone he could depend on. She never asked how he was or what he was doing, but she was more than happy to spend his cash. What a sucker he was. He started up the engine and flattened his foot to the throttle; things were going to change from here on.

One thing Olivia had always been good at was gardening, self-taught from an early age. She had taken great pleasure in transforming her mother's wild flower beds into an oasis of vibrant colours. These days the garden had become her safe haven, a special place to sit alone and admire her handiwork, why even Graham had complimented her on the unusually shaped borders, with their sharp contrast of colours. She stood on the patio looking at the dying roses, so fitting. The sound of footsteps at the side gate made her spin round 90 degrees. A short red-haired woman stood sheepishly grinning across at her. Olivia looked her up and down rather haughtily then sauntered casually over. "I guess." She drew in breath, looking at the fresh-faced chubby woman squeezed into ridiculously tight tatty jodhpurs. "That you are Carmen."

"Yes. Carmen Franklin. I do hope your husband told you that I would be calling by."

Secretly relieved that Carmen was plain and plump, Olivia extended her hand warmly across the closed gate.

"So, you're the brave soul who has volunteered to sort out my husband's brutish mule?"

"Really is he that bad! Eh," Carmen gave a nervous snort.

"Worse." Olivia shook her head. "The animal has no manners at all."

"May I take a look?" Carmen asked brightly, unperturbed by Olivia's dismal view. Olivia led the way gingerly up to the stables, pausing by the first stable door.

"This is the tack room. Graham seems to have every horsy gadget imaginable in there, so no doubt you will find whatever it is you need."

"You don't share his passion for horses then?"

"Good god no, do I look like the type?"

Carmen smiled to herself; Olivia really was the most frightful snob. They continued along to the next door.

"There you go, the beast himself, otherwise known as Solvent." Olivia stood, hands firmly on her hips staring triumphantly at the wild-eyed stallion. "Leave you to it then."

"That's great, thanks, Olivia." Carmen gave a courteous smile.

Solvent had shuffled to the back of his box, where he was munching on his hay net, eyeing Carmen suspiciously as she entered.

"There's a good fella," she soothed. Calmly she walked up to him and slipped on his halter. Olivia watched how she approached him in a kind, sensitive way. Deciding at that moment that she may like to stay and watch, it could turn out to be interesting. Without any fuss and howling, as Graham would normally do, Carmen brushed and saddled Solvent, he in turn stood patiently rather enjoying the kindly female attention. Carmen led him out into the sunshine, preparing to mount and pausing to look at Olivia, she held up two crossed fingers. Once Carmen had swung effortlessly into the saddle Solvent began to wiggle and jiggle beneath her.

"He's certainly feeling fresh," she said with a cackle.

Olivia took a large step back, out of the way of the stallion's large swaying quarters.

"Would you like me to open the gate for you?"

"That would be great," Carmen panted, breathlessly.

Olivia leapt forward helpfully, the bigger distance she could put between herself and the snorting beast the better. She swung the gate wide open for Solvent to leap through, dangerously close.

"I'm going to take him into the paddock and work him for a bit," Carmen shouted over her shoulder. Olivia leant lazily against the fence to watch Solvent be put through his paces. Olivia had no experience in matters of horsemanship but even to her untrained eye she could see what Carmen was achieving, by riding Solvent in large circles which she increased and decreased regularly, changing direction. It became apparent that Solvent began to relax.

"You see!" Carmen looked across triumphantly. "He's beginning to relax, notice the way he is dropping his head and relaxing his jaw."

"Well yes, I can see a difference, whenever I've seen Graham on him he is always gazing at the stars."

"His mouth is beautifully light and he responds to the aids," Carmen sang joyously.

Absently Olivia shook her head, this was all becoming much too technical, instead she concentrated on how Carmen's podgy little calves seemed to wiggle endlessly at Solvent's shiny sides and she couldn't help but notice how Carmen's huge bosoms flopped up and down, it made her small pert breasts hurt just watching. Carmen was like a weeble, she was as short as she was round. Ankle to knee couldn't be much longer than her own little finger, she thought with distaste. Twenty minutes later flushed and breathless, Carmen brought the stallion to a standstill and turned to face Olivia.

"That's enough schooling for one day. I think I will give him a walk down the lane now to cool him off."

"Be my guest." Olivia watched Carmen and Solvent disappear down the drive and out of view then went back to her gardening. She liked Carmen, most unusual as Olivia didn't like many people at all, but there was something about her, maybe she would even invite her in for a drink when she had finished with Graham's brute. Maybe Graham had done something right after all, a bit of good company wouldn't be bad at all. She looked like she was up for a good drink, she would certainly need it after hauling Solvent around that paddock. Even better she wasn't Graham's sort, no far too big.

Jacob put the phone down to Isobel, took a quick slurp of coffee and rushed towards his office for a meeting with the new Yorkshire suppliers. Gloria, his trusted personal assistant, intercepted him en route.

"Have you got five minutes, Jacob? I would like you to meet Stella's replacement."

Stella had left the week earlier after being with the firm for the last six years, heavily pregnant and not planning to return. This had been quite a blow for Jacob; he had always been able to rely on Stella who was ultra efficient and more importantly he liked her a lot. Gloria, on the other hand, was irreplaceable. Any problem and Gloria would sort it out; he could always rely on her no matter what. An immaculate, silver-haired woman in her mid-fifties, with the rare ability to remain calm in a crisis. Gloria equally admired Isobel and Jacob. She saw they had a good strong marriage, rather like her own. In fact she often thought of them as a younger version of herself and Martin. Gloria propelled Jacob to the front office, ignoring his halfhearted protests.

"Jacob, this is Elizabeth Hilliard, I have hired her this morning."

A slim, pale woman, held her hand weakly out to Jacob. "Welcome to the team." Jacob took her hand with an enthusiastic shake. "Hope you settle in well, any problems let Gloria know, she is our resident problem solver."

"I'm sure I will settle in just fine." Elizabeth smiled at him. Gloria watched Jacob stride from the office then turned back to Elizabeth who was watching her new boss leave with great interest. "Well any problems see me; don't bother Mr Kadeer. He has enough on his plate, OK, love?"

"Yes fine," she replied, turning to look back at the woman who watched her closely.

Gloria gave her a friendly wink then headed back to her own desk. Elizabeth had been charmed; it was hardly surprising Jacob was a good-looking man. She would keep an eye on her. Gloria had a nose for trouble and could spot that sort of thing a mile off. Elizabeth was highly qualified with glowing references but she was young and attractive and single. Of course as much as Gloria loved Jacob, he was a man, a man separated from his wife for the best part of a week, nothing should be left to chance.

Jacob finished up in the office and went down to the workshop to see Olan, the workshop manager.

"Did we get all the orders out OK today?"

"Sure did, things have gone well today, makes a change, eh?" Olan scratched his balding head.

"Great, I know how much pressure you are all under down here. I want to take on a new contract. I just hope we can manage."

"No worries, son, we will get there."

"Knew I could rely on you." He punched Olan's arm playfully. "Anyway there was something else I wanted to ask you. How do you fancy coming down to Devon and spending Christmas with us?"

"Hey that would be grand, Maria will be made up. We have really missed you guys since you moved off into the wilds. Especially your lovely lady, Maria was asking after her just this morning."

"Great, so you can. Isobel will be pleased." She would too, he thought. Olan and his Italian wife Maria had been good friends of theirs, often meeting up for a bite to eat or stepping in to baby-sit when Jacob's parents were not available.

"You heading back to the flat now, mate?"

"Yes, going to call it a day here." Jacob grimaced. Enough was enough.

"Well you can come back to ours, you know my wife, she will have made enough for an army and we can't have you starving."

Jacob thought for a moment. Olan was right; he hadn't been relishing the thought of going back to the empty flat. The temptation of one of Maria's hearty meals made his mouth water. It wasn't a mistake and he found himself a few hours later, flopped out on the battered sofa in their sitting room after a huge feed of veal casserole and a very generous helping of trifle.

"That was fantastic as usual, Maria."

30

"Oh, don't mention it, darling. You know you are always welcome here." Maria leant forward, tapping him gently on the back of the hand, her large ruby lips forming a knowing smile. Then she tilted her head sideways with a look of concern. "How is Devon, everything OK, is it?"

"Yeah it's great, the travelling is a bit of a pain but I expect I will get used to it very quickly."

"Isobel likes it?"

"Isobel loves it, misses me, but again it's just a matter of adjusting."

"Great," Maria relaxed back in her chair, "and of course we shall love to be with you at Christmas. Tell Isobel I am really looking forward to it."

Jacob arrived back at the flat a little after ten, feeling uncomfortably full and completely shattered. He was missing Isobel like mad and couldn't wait for the weekend. He dialled her number, waiting impatiently for Isobel to answer. Much to his annoyance there was no reply; he replaced the receiver somewhat anxious. Deciding to take a shower and try again later, where on earth would she go at this time, he wondered.

Isobel found herself laughing, really laughing for what seemed like the first time in ages. Was it Rita's wicked sense of humour or quite possibly the effect of the very moreish and potent rhubarb wine? Her cheeks felt positively flushed. Edward seemed blissfully happy surrounded by Rita's menagerie of animals, two ancient dogs, three fluffy kittens; two lop eared rabbits and a tortoise all of which had free run of the house. Isobel had learnt a lot about Rita during the evening, apart from what she had heard earlier in the week, from folk in the village. For starters she was extremely popular and well respected amongst the local community, always willing to step in and lend a hand. Isobel watched as she untangled a playful kitten from Edward's shoelace, age had taken its toll on Rita's face but you could tell that she must have been a really attractive lady in her youth; her deep blue eyes sparkled out from sunken sockets. Physically she appeared tireless, in fact Isobel felt very unfit in comparison. Isobel prepared to leave just before eleven, as Edward finally began to tire.

"Thank you, Rita. I have really enjoyed this evening."

"Oh don't mention it, I am glad of the company and I just love having little Edward here."

"Well thank you all the same. We have both had a really nice time."

"You're most welcome." Rita patted Isobel's shoulder affectionately. "Mind how you go now, that wine is stronger than you think, my love."

Isobel took the quick route home, a little quicker than was advisable she thought after all that wine but the chances of seeing a policeman on these lanes seemed pretty remote. Turning into the drive, the lights of Orange Stream Farm shone out ahead to welcome them. Isobel opened the front door, Tarquin and Sadie galloped up the hallway, their tails thudding against the wall as they raced excitedly to greet them. Edward had now succumbed entirely to tiredness and insisted that Isobel carry him on the last leg of his journey to bed. The minute his head hit the pillow he was out. Isobel realised how tired she was feeling, even a bit drunk. The telephone began to ring. She rushed to the bedroom to answer it before it woke Edward.

"Thank god, you're there at last." Jacob's voice echoed with relief. "Where have you been? I have been worried about you."

"Sorry, have you been calling all evening?"

"I was missing you and I wanted to say good night."

"Sorry." Isobel kicked off her shoes, lying back on the bed. "We went over to Rita's house."

"You could have thought to let me know."

"Jacob, that's not very fair. I called earlier today at the office you were in a meeting. You never returned my call."

"You could have left a message, honey." He was becoming irritated by her mood.

"I did, presumably with the new woman, Elizabeth, I think, who is she anyway?"

"Oh right." Jacob's tone softened. "You're right, the new girl, don't know much about her really, left it to Gloria to organise, she is a replacement for Stella."

"Right, OK then." Isobel struggled to keep the phone wedged under her chin as she tried to remove her jeans with one hand. "Pretty, is she?"

"Nothing special, pretty average I guess, very thin and scrawny."

Isobel, free of her jeans, began to wiggle free of her top, dropping the receiver as she did so.

"Good night then." There was an irritated edge to Jacob's voice.

"OK, Jacob, night, speak tomorrow." Isobel replaced the receiver. Scrambling free of the rest of her clothes, she dived beneath the sheets, glad to be home and chuffed that she had actually achieved an evening out, the first since moving to Devon. God she hoped she hadn't sounded too drunk Jacob would be livid if he knew, especially as she had driven home even worse with Edward in the car.

Isobel leant across to switch off the bedside lamp, plunging the room from a warm glow to cold sinister darkness. Exhausted she closed her eyes, lying motionless as she listened to the rain outside, finding it mildly soothing as it lulled her toward sleep. The room grew chilly, dampness crept through the air and settled above her but she didn't notice under the warm cosy duvet.

The consistent drum of the rain against the window turned to the rhythmic beat of horse's hooves that approached along the muddy sodden track. Hardly daring to breathe she waited motionless, catching her breath as the solitary horseman appeared before her, the hood of his cloak concealing his identity. The horse pulled up at her side with a snort, she could smell the putrid scent rising from its heaving sides, and the horseman drew back his hood, to smile down at her. She felt her pulse quicken, at his rugged good looks. Holding his hand out toward her, he hoisted her up onto the horse and she huddled up behind him. Holding on tightly, her arms circled his warm musky body as they headed further along the track. He pushed the tired animal on, faster and harder across the stony uneven ground before swerving violently into the dark circle of trees. Pressing on more still, as the branches tore at their clothes and scratched at her skin beneath, she didn't dare to look up, instead keeping her face pressed into the back of his cloak, while they continued into the darkness. Finally he slowed the breathless steed before coming to a sudden halt. Climbing down, he offered her his hand as she slid from the animal's sweating back. Feverishly he took her into his arms, kissing her lips urgently with his warm searching tongue and she melted beneath his touch.

He broke away to look at her face, his eyes searching hers as the heavy cloud overhead parted, allowing a shaft of moonlight to spill into the darkness, bathing the trees around them in a silvery glow. She looked longingly in to his dark eyes and he gave an anxious smile. "Tell me," he asked. "How much longer must I wait? My heart is breaking, when, my love, can we be one?"

The clouds thickened and the rain began again, the moonlight was gone in a second. He held her close and the veil of darkness concealed his face. Where was her voice? Why could she not talk, a hard lump had lodged in her throat, why was it so painful? The rainfall became heavier, large drops fell on to the leaves that lay at her feet with loud echoing splashes. Darkness prevailed and she clung to him her cheek pressed against his, the falling rain masked her tears. He was the love of her life, nothing mattered but this man that held her in his arms, she would not make him wait much longer, it would surely kill her if she did. She reached out to him, the hot tears stung at her eyes, soon they would be together. Stretching her fingers toward his face, she traced his jaw, felt the rough unshaven skin and felt a shiver ripple through her body. There wasn't much time she must tell him her plan, he must know she had decided he had waited far too long.

Isobel opened her eyes in the darkness, unsure for a moment if she was still in the forest. Feeling out in the darkness, she found the bedside lamp, flicking the switch to bathe the icy room with the warming light. Slowly the temperature began to rise. He had seemed so real as if he had been there in the room with her, she could still smell the animal's sweating flanks and the damp air on her skin. Isobel dabbed at her bloodshot eyes, a quick glance at the bedside clock told her it was a little past 1 a.m. She turned off the lamp, willing herself to go back to the dream, desperate to feel him, to taste him once more, but he had gone, he was she thought, sadly lost forever.

Isobel awoke emotionally drained. Not only from the over-indulgence of wine at Rita's, but from the disturbing dream which had appeared so real. Wearily she went downstairs, needing to shake the memory of the dream from her mind and come back to the real world. Sat at the kitchen table she sipped fresh coffee, slowly the grogginess lifted. With a lighter head she dialled Jacob, he hadn't seemed in the best of moods last night.

"Darling, glad you answered. Sorry I was tired last night."

"What were you thinking, you little minx, making me worry."

"It wasn't intentional, it was just nice being at Rita's and chatting."

"It's OK no need to explain, darling. Is everything else OK?"

"Yes fine, except, well while I was at Rita's—something she said, something that I have been thinking about the last few days."

"Go on."

Isobel got straight to the point. "We have all this land and we're not doing anything with it. I thought perhaps I might get a horse!"

"A horse!" Jacob screeched. It was just about the last thing he had expected Isobel to want.

"Don't sound so shocked, lots of people around here have them you know."

"Yes I know, but well it's at least ten years since you have ridden, I mean, don't you have to get back in to practise first?"

"Sure, but I don't mean like now, some friends of Rita's have stables nearby. She said she would have a word on my behalf."

"Great, well see how you get on, but what about Edward, who will look after him when you're hacking your nag around the countryside?"

"Rita has kindly offered to have him. He loves it there, Jacob, and she is so good with him fussing round like mother hen. It would be good for both of us."

"Okay, I guess so." There was little else he could say really, when Isobel made her mind up he couldn't change it, no doubt she would grow bored with the idea anyway. Jacob put the phone down, he looked across at Gloria.

"Isobel wants to get a horse, can you believe that?"

Gloria smiled. "Sounds like a great idea, bet they all have horses down in the country." Jacob tapped his fingers lightly on the desk. "Best get to work, I hear horses can be very expensive creatures indeed."

As soon as they were dressed, Isobel and a sleepy-eyed Edward headed to Rita's house. Rita was out collecting the eggs; she looked up on hearing the car.

"You're out and about early, my darlings." Edward ran straight to her, arms outstretched.

"Wanted to catch you before I change my mind. We talked about your friends with the stables," Isobel shouted, climbing out of the car.

"Oh, yes we did, didn't we?" Rita ushered them into the house and through to the kitchen. "Have a seat, love, so you're serious about going for a ride, it wasn't the wine talking?"

"Yes, I used to really enjoy it. Don't know why I gave up, must have become more interested in boys or something."

"That's what usually happens." Rita chuckled as she transferred the eggs from the basket to the larder. "Boys no end of trouble, should have stuck with the horses, love." Rita closed the larder door and bustled over to scan her busy diary. "How about, if I collect you around ten tomorrow morning, take you over to the stables, that way I can introduce you to Brad and Marina, great couple, 'bout your age as well. I will call them and check it will be OK."

"Brilliant." Isobel rubbed her hands together, her face lighting up at the thought. "I will look forward to that. Come on then, Edward; let us get out of Auntie Rita's way." She placed a guiding hand on his shoulder, before he could protest. "That's right, wave goodbye to Auntie Rita," she said, propelling him towards the car.

As they drove away, Rita smiled to herself. Isobel had definitely referred to her as "Auntie Rita" that had made her very happy indeed.

After a tiresome lunch where Edward had whinged and whined and thrown a spectacular toddler tantrum and Isobel had decided that she would be booking Jacob for a vasectomy ASAP, she sat flicking through a copy of *Horse and Hound* that she had picked up on the way back from Rita's. Edward was now taking a much-needed nap upstairs. Tarquin and Sadie, much to their delight, lay stretched out on the rug before her in the living room. Closing the magazine, she lay back with a smug grin. She was looking forward to tomorrow, her mind full of the next day. She pondered over Brad and Marina. What would they be like? Rita could not speak more highly of them. Her eyelids began to feel heavy, Rita's wine and lack of sleep was starting to catch up with her, slowly she gave way to her tiredness, snuggling back onto the cushion behind her to sleep off the last of the hangover and definitely no wine tonight.

The silence broken by a high-pitched screech, causing Isobel to sit up in alarm she listened for a moment, disgruntled, before she got up. It certainly hadn't sounded like Edward but she had better check in on him. Edward, much to Isobel's relief, was still sound asleep. Gently she closed the door and tiptoed back downstairs.

Halfway down there was a clatter from the kitchen preceded by another screech, clutching the handrail a chill crept across her body. Hugging her arms around herself, she tiptoed on down. It had been an eerie sound, not unlike the sound she had heard coming from the wood on that first morning. Then a terrible thought struck her, what if a fox had got into the house? After all it was a possibility, wasn't it? Picking the umbrella out of the stand by the door, she headed to the kitchen, her jaw set, legs feeling like jelly. Cautiously she opened the door, tentatively looking around but to her dismay, there was nothing. Placing the umbrella down Isobel was relieved. Scolding her own stupid behaviour, for becoming paranoid and ridiculous, she filled the kettle then leaning against the pine dresser, she looked out of the window at the charcoal sky, where rapidly, assembling clouds brewed, threatening a storm. She turned instinctively to scan the now peaceful kitchen once more. It must have come from outside. Maybe a bird, there was a logical reason she was sure, but as her eyes swept across the table, she gave a small whimper. The magazine that earlier she had been reading lay open and on its surface, was something else; something quite small and shiny perched on top of the glossy pages. Now she could have sworn she had left the magazine on the sofa. Edging towards the table, she gave a gasp, hardly daring to believe what she saw there. Her own wedding ring, no it wasn't possible. A quick glance to her left hand confirmed it was. Possible or not it was sitting there right in front of her eyes, and how, was a complete mystery. With a shaking hand she reached out to scoop it gently up, almost afraid that it would fly from its resting place and spin uncontrollably through the air. Triumphantly she placed it back on her finger only then noticing how loose it had become; nonetheless if it had fallen it would hardly end up here, she considered.

Shaking her head in disbelief, she went back to lie on the sofa. She definitely needed sleep, her mind was jumbled, she was becoming alarmingly forgetful; she didn't even know what she was doing anymore. Eventually after endless tossing and turning she fell into a restless sleep.

CHAPTER THREE

Even the persistent rain slanting in from the west couldn't dampen Isobel's spirits. However magnificent Orange Stream Farm was, and she loved it dearly, Isobel felt a great loss. All her friends had been left behind in London. They had been here nearly two months now and she was feeling lonely. Meeting Rita was a major breakthrough. Right now Rita was the person keeping her sane, but she was a lot older and Isobel craved the company of someone her own age. Isobel broke from her thoughts, as she turned the next bend and a filthy Range Rover careered towards her, swerving at the very last minute, narrowly avoiding a head-on collision. Isobel pulled in tight to the hedge, abruptly screeching to a halt and stalling the car, her heart thumped wildly. The Range Rover hurtled past regardless of their near miss. Isobel watched in her rearview mirror, as a few hundred yards further along the road, the vehicle slowed down, pulling up on to the sodden verge. Concerned for the driver's safety, Isobel took a few deep breaths then restarted the engine, backing up to the next gateway. The Range Rover remained stationary; a woman jumped out and looked intently at each tyre. Seething Isobel walked back towards her.

"Are you OK?" Isobel asked politely.

The woman spun around looking at Isobel quizzically, almost surprised that she should be there at all.

"Yes, of course. What's the matter?" she snapped.

Isobel taken back by her rudeness was not surprised as the woman drew alongside her to smell alcohol on her breath.

"You swerved across in front of me, I was actually more worried about you," she replied through gritted teeth, keen to avoid a confrontation with the woman, who was now looking totally bemused.

"Blasted little rabbit in the lane back there, didn't see the little blighter till the last moment." She extended her hand coldly. "You're new around here, aren't you?"

"Relatively," Isobel stammered, unsure what to make of her.

The woman frowned questioningly.

"Olivia Pearson, pleased to bump in to you." She proceeded to hoot with laughter.

"Ah!" Isobel couldn't hide the surprise in her voice. "Isobel Kadeer pleased to meet you too."

"Ah ha." Olivia looked delighted. "That means we must be neighbours, does it not? I live at Bramstone Hall. I recognise your name, heard you had brought the place." She gave a knowing nod. "Pop in some time, we can get to know one another, a coffee perhaps."

Isobel doubted she meant it and even if she did, she was certain they would have very little in common.

"That would be nice." Isobel nodded.

Olivia held up her hand briefly as she climbed back into the Range Rover and without a backward glance sped off down the lane leaving Isobel open-mouthed in disbelief at her sheer arrogance.

Olivia sped back home, dived in the front door and checked her appearance in the mirror, aghast at the dishevelled image that frowned back at her. Therefore, it turned out that their new neighbour was a bit of a looker. What an utter blow, she thought. Well she would have to make sure that Graham didn't bloody well get his arse round there; he would be sure to be smitten. Olivia went through to the kitchen and poured herself a large drink, breaking her own rather silly promise; after all, it was an emergency, she reminded herself. Standing by the sink glancing absently out of the window, she caught a quick glimpse of Carmen, leading Solvent out of his box. Draining the remainder of her drink in one large gulp, she dragged on her wellies and hurried up to the stables.

"Morning," she called, breathlessly. "So how's it going with the mule?"

"Great." Carmen glanced across at Solvent. "Actually I don't think that there was ever much of a problem really."

"How do you mean?"

Carmen pointed to the steel bar in Solvent's frothy mouth. "I have swapped him into a snaffle. Your hubby had him in a Pelham," she drew in breath, "he never really needed it." Looking at Solvent sympathetically, she shook her head. "He has been fighting it. In fact it has been most uncomfortable for him. You know," Carmen paused to look brightly at Olivia, "he has a lot of talent this horse."

"Oh really do you think so?" Olivia looked at her in surprise. Solvent had always seemed so out of control and wild to her mind, so very different to the gentle giant that Carmen seemed keen to portray.

Carmen rubbed his forehead affectionately. "Yeah, he's a real old softie."

Olivia watched entranced as Carmen schooled Solvent in the front paddock, as she eased the horse into each fluent movement with the minimum of fuss. Solvent had his ears pricked forward, he seemed keen and there was a definite twinkle in his big brown eyes. In fact, he was positively showing off. Carmen rode him over to where Olivia stood, giving him a long relaxing rein, allowing him to stretch his neck.

"He looked beautiful, almost dancing across the grass," Olivia commented.

"Yes we were doing some dressage. He has been well trained in the past. Do you think Graham would be offended if I gave him a bit of tuition with Solvent? It would help them to find each other a bit."

Olivia knew Graham would be mortified by Carmen's suggestion, after all he considered himself the next Olympic gold medallist. Smiling sweetly up at Carmen, she dared to lean across and stroke Solvent's damp sweaty neck.

"I'm sure he would be delighted! In fact, why don't you call round this evening and have a drink with us both to discuss it. Let's say about eight."

Graham arrived home around six-thirty, pleasantly surprised as he opened the front door to find Olivia looking rather seductive in a burnt orange shift dress. There was a hot meal of lamb and onion casserole with minted new potatoes and a generous stock of mineral water in the refrigerator. Things were certainly looking up, he decided as he chomped on the lamb. Olivia was being positively friendly, chatting about the garden while he ate his meal. Gradually he began to relax; no doubt, she had come to her senses at last.

Olivia chose her moment carefully, casually slipping in to the conversation. "Carmen mentioned she would call round later."

Graham looked pleased. "Really, perhaps she wants to update me on Solvent's progress."

"Yes, she did say that. As soon as you have eaten perhaps you should go upstairs and change."

As Graham changed out of his work suit, he wondered if Olivia's sudden change of heart wasn't quite odd, in fact rather unnerving. There had to be an ulterior motive. However, for now, he wasn't going to question it, he was enjoying her attention far too much.

When Carmen arrived, it was plainly obvious that she had made rather an effort as well. The unruly red curls had been swept back from her plump face and were held in place by a large onyx clip. Her normally blotchy skin dusted lightly with powder and there was the slightest hint that a mascara wand had touched her short red lashes. Squeezed into a pair of stonewash jeans she was looking rather casual in a cotton open necked shirt, which was left enticingly unbuttoned to show her plump freckly cleavage. She swept in the front door past Graham, who stood open-mouthed, his sense of smell totally overpowered by her cheap perfume, which hung heavily in the air as she passed by.

"On time, that's most unusual for me." She giggled.

"You will fit in nicely tonight then." Graham winked. "It seems there are a lot of unusual things happening around here tonight."

Olivia fixed them all a drink, which they took through to the drawing room. Carmen was the first to break the ice. "I'm really surprised that you don't ride, Olivia, what with having all this land and Graham having such a keen interest?"

Graham burst out laughing. "Olivia on a horse, perish the thought."

Carmen glanced over at Olivia who was hurriedly draining her glass of wine. She couldn't help but feel sorry for her. Carmen swiftly changed the subject. "Well, to business, I am very pleased with Solvent, he is going really nicely." She cleared her throat. "But I have to say, Graham, he doesn't need half the equipment that you had him in."

"What do you mean?" Graham glared, his mottled complexion softly reddening as he did so. Olivia knew the glorious moment was arriving and leant over to top up everybody's glasses.

"Well for starters the Pelham is far too severe, I have put him into an egg butt snaffle, which he seems to be far happier with. I have taken off the martingale, this he definitely does not need!" Carmen emphasised her words dramatically, then taking a deep breath she continued. "I think that if you are in agreement, that perhaps it would be a good idea for me to give you some tuition with Solvent." Carmen watched his expression. Graham sat very still the only movement, was a nervous flicking of his tongue across his front teeth.

"You really think there's a need?" he replied finally, questioning her expertise.

He chose to ignore the malicious snigger from Olivia's direction. Sensing his embarrassment, Carmen turned toward Olivia choosing to address Graham through her, feeling awkward and wondering if she should have said anything at all.

"Of course it's not essential. I just thought it would be a benefit to you both."

Graham shot Olivia a steely glare across the room. "Why ever not?" he replied, with an air of amusement. "There is no harm in it. Perhaps I am a wee bit rusty, if I am honest." He smiled broadly across at Carmen. "So when do we start?"

Olivia felt herself stiffen as she listened to Carmen suggesting to Graham that he may like to take Solvent to her yard, so that they could use the indoor school. Graham was readily agreeing, knowing that it would be safer and far less humiliating away from Olivia's scornful gaze.

"Promise not to work me too hard though," he said saucily, glad that it was now making Olivia far more uncomfortable. He had no doubt that this arrangement would not sit comfortably with her ladyship.

Jacob navigated the Mercedes through the abominable London traffic and the driving rain, back toward the empty flat. It was one of those nondescript evenings in the city. He pulled up outside the off licence; tonight he would find a little solace in a bottle of wine, perhaps even a vintage, he thought. As he came out of the shop into the blustery night, pulling his collar up protectively against the damp evening air, a young woman walking towards him smiled. Vaguely he recognised her face and as she drew closer he recognised his new work colleague. "Oh hi, Elizabeth, isn't it?"

"Yes, you remembered." She looked across at the shop from which he had emerged. "Fancied a nightcap by the look of it?" She pointed toward the shop and then at the tissue wrapped bottle clutched to his chest.

"Yes nice vintage claret to be precise." He forced a smile, wondering if she may think he was an alcoholic. Elizabeth looked freezing; the tip of her nose was scarlet and her hair hung soaking and dripping down her shoulders. "Have you just left the office?"

"Yes on my way to the tube, such a ghastly night, isn't it?"

"Where are you heading then?" he asked, with keen interest.

"Back home. Palladium Drive to be exact."

"I know it. Come on, hop in let me drive you there, it's too ghastly a night to walk."

"Oh no, Mr Kadeer, I don't want to send you out of your way, you must have plans?" She looked hopefully up at him, then lowered her eyes bashfully, a movement well rehearsed.

"Jacob, please, and it's absolutely no trouble at all," he said, opening the door for her. "Besides, I drive right past there." He smiled reassuringly.

Elizabeth settled back in her seat shaking her dripping mane, hoping desperately that her mascara wasn't halfway down her cheeks as they trawled through the evening traffic.

"So what exciting plans do you have for this evening, Elizabeth?" Jacob asked, lighting a cigarette and offering her one.

Elizabeth shook her head. "An early night. My social life has been hectic and I have some beauty sleep to catch up on."

Jacob smiled. "I thought perhaps we had been working you too hard?" He looked out at the fresh onslaught of rain as he pulled up outside Elizabeth's house.

"Thanks, Jacob, I appreciate the lift."

"As I said, it's not a problem. In fact it seems silly you getting the tube when you're right on my doorstep, you know you're always welcome to a lift." Elizabeth nodded, getting out of the car and wrinkling her nose in disgust as the rain grew even heavier.

"I may just do that. Good night, Jacob."

Jacob arrived back at the flat; he poured a large glass of the wine, after giving the bottle an appreciating sniff, then kicked off his shoes and sprawled across the sofa. He skipped through the TV channels but there was little of any interest, so he reached for the phone and dialled Devon. Edward answered in a high-pitched squeak, ignoring Jacob's request to speak with his mother, as he proceeded to gabble on about Auntie Rita and each of her animals, one by one and in irritatingly and precise detail. "That's great, darling, but where's Mummy. Please?" Jacob asked mildly irritated.

"Bath, she's in the bath," he replied, indignant at his father's obvious lack of interest.

Jacob ate his microwave meal, drank the rest of the wine, then absolutely shattered fell asleep on the sofa oblivious of the fact that he had not yet spoken with Isobel.

Edward had hurried through to tell Isobel, who was sat at the dressing table applying moisturiser and when she had tried to call back there had been no answer. Guessing that Jacob must have fallen asleep, she decided to leave it until the morning, besides she was feeling totally shattered herself.

That night the dream came again. This time more detailed. The lines etched on his face, the worry more pronounced. His breath was warm against the coldness of her cheek and the gentle pleading in his voice more haunting. Once again, they were in the moonlit glade and the rains relentless, fell from the sombre sky. There was the same numbness and inability to speak, a great urgency consumed her body but she was unable to communicate what she was feeling to him. As she slept tears crept from her eyes, why could she not answer him, why did it always end this way, she needed to know what it meant and who he was? What was it that she had decided, that he needed so desperately to know?

Graham Pearson lay in bed unable to sleep, in nervous anticipation of his public humiliation, a situation which Olivia had enjoyed putting him in immensely. What a first-class bitch! It all began to fit now, the meal, her civil manner, what did she stand to gain from her cruelty? He couldn't believe Carmen had anything to do with it, after all the lessons she suggested were quite justified and it pained him to admit it but his skills of horsemanship were not what they used to be. Solvent could be a difficult bugger, but what Carmen failed to realise was that he didn't get enough exercise because Graham had to work so dammed hard to keep Olivia in the style to which she was accustomed. He gave a sigh, women they were all the same!

He sneaked a sideways glance at Olivia wondering whether to initiate sex, but then thought better of it. It was sure to be a knock-back, there again, he mused, she was rather inebriated and most probably would be too out of it to bother putting up a fight. He looked at her now with distaste and thought no, definitely not, she had enjoyed humiliating him too much earlier. No damn the woman if she ever wanted sex with him again she would have to beg for it. There were plenty of women out there more than willing to participate, and no doubt it would be a lot more fun too. He gave a churlish grin as he snuggled beneath the covers. He rather fancied a younger model this time, and preferably one who shared his love of fellatio.

Isobel was pleased, the following day dawned brighter than had been forecast. As she dressed, last night's dream was fading, as watching Edward tackle his boiled egg and soldiers she waited eagerly for Rita to arrive.

"Good day for it?" Rita declared. She stood back, hands on hips watching Isobel strap Edward safely in the back seat.

"Yes it's been a few years since I've sat on a horse. I hope it will all come back to me and that I won't make a complete and utter idiot of myself."

"Like riding a bike, they say you never forget, but you will ache for England tomorrow, mind."

They arrived at Meadow Brook, which far exceeded anything Isobel could have imagined.

"This place is awesome. Why do I suddenly feel like I want to go home?" Isobel wailed, winding down the window to admire the house and its grounds as they crawled along the driveway.

"Nonsense, you couldn't wish to meet a nicer couple, you'll see," Rita clucked, as she parked the car. She leant across to pat Isobel's knee comfortingly. "Trust me, love, they aren't snobbish at all."

Rita led them down towards the stables. "Besides if it makes you feel any better all this is thanks to a very generous divorce settlement."

"Really, go on," Isobel asked, with interest.

"Yes, married to a multi millionaire, something to do with yachts. They had a daughter but she doesn't ever seem to be around much, spends most of her time in South Africa with her father and his new wife."

A strikingly pretty woman appeared from the large barn, which Rita duly informed Isobel was the indoor school, Olympic size no less. The woman smiling welcomingly approached them. Her sleek, champagne coloured hair fell smoothly just below her shoulders, her skin was bronzed, obviously she had just returned from some tropical hideaway. Isobel felt most inferior, she tried to control the sudden flutter of nerves, as the lady strode confidently toward them. Sickeningly her figure was amazing, long, gazelle legs, ensconced in expensive looking suede chaps, she wore a tight black, tunic top which enhanced her curves. The most striking feature her amazing aqua marine eyes which glimmered, welcomingly as she stood before them. With great warmness she offered a slender hand towards Isobel.

"Isobel, wonderful to meet you at last, darling. Rita has told us so much about you, it's really good to meet you." She bent down to greet the boy. "And you must be Edward. We've heard a lot about you, young man." Isobel stood open-mouthed. It hadn't occurred to her that this was Marina, she looked far too young. Isobel had imagined her to be more mature, perhaps a little weathered and possibly bow legged from all her riding, certainly not a glamour puss.

Finally she found her voice. "It's great to meet you too. Thank you for inviting me. It's really very kind of you."

"Nonsense, come on let me show you around." She smiled. "We are very proud of what we have here and I love an excuse to show it all off."

"Gosh I can see why, it is ever so beautiful," Isobel breathed.

Marina led them along the cobbled driveway which ran between two fenced paddocks. Large wooden pots sat every few metres planted with baby firs and trailing ivy. The paddock to the right was the smaller of the two and ran uphill to the hedgerow which bordered the lane. This, she explained was where the older mares grazed in the summer.

The paddock to the left was enormous; it undulated gently and ran as far as the eye could see down to a copse. From where they were standing they could see high above the copse towards the hills and countryside beyond.

Marina stopped to rest on the fence. "It's a fantastic view, isn't it? I never tire of looking at it, you can see for miles." Isobel nodded in agreement. It was a magnificent view, the sort that gave one a sense of freedom, and you never felt that in London.

Marina looked across at her as if reading her mind. "Do you miss London?"

"I did a bit at first, but since I've met Rita," she turned to look at Rita with a warm smile squeezing her arm affectionately, "I feel differently. I realise now that this is where I belong." She took a deep breath, before turning back to Marina with a smile. "To be honest I don't relish the thought of going back to London now, not even for a weekend."

Marina laughed. "Come on, let me show you the rest of this place."

Edward was getting cold and bored by the time their guided tour had brought them back to the stables. Rita decided it was best to take him home, arranging to call back in a couple of hours to collect Isobel.

"Let me show you inside the stables now." Marina swung open the large sliding door to the internal stables. They stopped at the first stall. "Take a look at our new arrival. She is only eight weeks old, born very late in the season." A pretty chestnut foal wobbled precariously by its mother's side. "Beautiful, isn't she?"

"Beautiful," Isobel sighed. "How many horses do you have?"

Marina turned to face her. "Well let's see, 15 of my own and ten liveries either hunters or broodmares."

"They must keep you really busy?"

"Yes they do, but of course my husband Brad helps and we have Amber, she's a godsend, works like a trooper." Bang on cue, Amber emerged from one of the stables, with a friendly nod in their direction. "Now come and meet the star of Meadow Brook." Marina signalled to the far right-hand corner stable. "This is our stallion, Lizard, as he is affectionately known." Marina patted his muscular neck proudly as she explained that she had bred the stallion herself.

He was truly magnificent but his temperament didn't match, he pushed his ears flat back, baring his teeth at Isobel, who took a nervous step back.

"We're hoping to compete him in the spring; he's still very green at the moment."

"Very green indeed," a deep mellow voice interjected. "And a miserable sod in the stable, as you can see."

Isobel spun round and somehow wasn't surprised to see an extremely attractive guy with equally bronzed skin and dazzling white teeth like a film star. Marina slipped her arm around his waist and proudly introduced him. "This is my husband, Brad." It seemed to Isobel that everything about the Cobbetts was beautiful. One thing was for sure, she would never forget her first meeting with them. The only thing that stopped Isobel from turning emerald green was the fact that they appeared to be so exceptionally nice.

Rita pulled up outside her house and chuckled at Edward who had already unbuckled his seatbelt and was trying to open the car door. She looked across at him. "Now what would you like to do, young man? Now that Mummy is getting a chance to enjoy herself?"

Edward looked up at her and asked in excitement, "Can we feed all the animals?"

"What all of them?"

He giggled. "All of them!"

Rita watched entranced, as he dashed around after the hens throwing handfuls of corn. He was such a happy little soul. She would have loved to have a child herself, but sadly it was not to be. God knows she had tried everything. When the doctors had failed she had turned to nature. Everything she could possibly do had been done, every lotion, potion or spell had been exhausted. Her powers as a white witch had failed her for the one thing that she had so desperately wanted. She had never given up hope, despite the fact that her power of being able to see into the future had shown her quite clearly that it was not meant to be. But Edward, she looked at the child lovingly now as he dashed past her, he had been foreseen a long time ago.

She took his hand protectively. "Shall we go in now; I have a surprise indoors for you."

With an excited squeal he broke free to run ahead of her up to the house. Rita gave an indulgent grin. She hadn't been able to sleep last night looking forward to today. She quickened her step, eager to catch up with him; she didn't want to miss a moment.

Brad placed a firm hand on Isobel's shoulder, making her blush. "Now for the bad news. I'm afraid you've drawn the short straw, you'll be riding with me today." He steered her towards the next stable. "Now meet your partner, Jasmine." A slender grey mare stood dozing. Isobel gave a sigh of relief, she looked harmless enough. As if reading her mind, Brad reassured her, "She's a nice sort, just right for easing you back in the saddle. Don't worry, she'll look after you, Rita told us it's been awhile."

Isobel gently rubbed the little mare's nose, which she seemed to enjoy, closing her eyes sleepily as Brad saddled her up. Then he led the mare out into the yard, where the sun had crept from behind the clouds with reassuring warmth.

"Are you okay to mount or shall I give you a leg up?"

"I think I can manage," she replied, whilst scrabbling up into the saddle. Jasmine wasn't particularly tall but it seemed a very long way up. They started with large circles at one end of the school, slowly it came back to her. Fortunately Jasmine was very responsive and Isobel didn't have to work to hard.

"You're doing great," Brad enthused. "I think we will give you another twenty minutes work, concentrate on your posture, we won't push it today." Finally they came to a halt in the centre of the school. "Well done, you." Brad smiled up at her. "That was a great start. Still feeling so keen?" Isobel, somewhat out of breath, dismounted her legs decidedly wobbly as they touched the ground. Giving a sigh of relief that she hadn't made a fool of herself, she smiled up at Brad.

"I really enjoyed it, but I had forgotten how tiring it can be."

"Another few sessions and you'll be away," he said comfortingly.

Isobel unsaddled Jasmine under Brad's guidance. Marina stood by the door watching them. "How was it then?"

"She did great." Brad winked across at Isobel. "Didn't you?"

"Not as bad as I thought, at least I stayed on!" She giggled. "So tell me, how much do I owe you both for your time?" Brad laughed, his eyes twinkling beneath a mop of blonde hair that glinted in the sunlight.

"Well if you're serious about this and we haven't put you off, then nothing. Rita said you wanted to buy a horse eventually?" Isobel looked from one to the other quizzically.

"That's right, although I shouldn't imagine it will be for a while yet," Isobel replied.

"You're going to need some experience, lots more lessons. Perhaps you would consider helping out around here, in exchange for some tuition, would that suit you?"

"Well if you're sure that would be OK?" She looked dubiously across at Marina, who smiled back warmly with an agreeable nod.

Brad shook her hand. "That's decided then, so how about twice a week, whichever days suit you. Let's say, nine-thirty until two, and of course during that time you get to have a lesson."

"Thank you both so much, I really do appreciate it, this is just what I need and so kind of you both."

"Fancy a coffee?" Marina asked brightly. "I could murder a cup, don't know about you two. Come up when you're done here, it'll be ready and waiting."

Isobel barely had time to down the rich velvet coffee, as she admired the elegant, state-of-the-art kitchen, when Rita arrived to collect her. Disappointed to leave, but ever so pleased with herself, Isobel left Meadow Brook on a high. Rita listened to her excited chatter all the way home, giving a satisfied smile it was so good she decided to see the young lass looking so vibrant and happy.

Adam Docherty refolded a pair of trousers and hung them meticulously back onto the rail. It annoyed him that the customers would come in and rifle through the clothes, and then leave them strewn across the shop. He sat wearily down behind the till, took a slurp of coffee from an ancient chipped mug, that had been a birthday present from his mother. Coffee didn't seem to taste the same from anything else.

For three years he had owned Docherty's, a trendy clothes shop tucked down one of the pretty cobbled streets, just off the main square. He believed in quality, and would only sell clothes that had been designed and finished well, a far cry from his early days in a well-known high street chain. He hadn't done badly for himself. The cramped family home in Southern Ireland seemed a long time ago; mind you it was Nelson Black who had helped him on his way. He laughed to himself, good old Nelson, a real Londoner; bit of a boy in his day no doubt. Adam had managed one of his little earners for him, a "tienda exclusivo" at the quayside in Puerto Banus. He took a gulp of coffee, they were good days, hard work but good, but he had soon tired of the relentless sun, endless girls and Nelson's special sangria.

He remembered back to the first year he had opened Docherty's. It had been hard, there were times when he thought it may have been a terrible mistake, but the exodus from London was the making of him. He gave a satisfied grin as he looked around the shop and its tasteful décor.

Naturally handsome, Adam's long dark hair framed a strong masculine jawline, his crooked nose only added to his appeal. The only thing that seemed to elude him was a good woman and god knows he had dated enough. He hadn't come across one woman in his thirty years that he could have taken to his heart. He had dated plenty of pretty leggy fillies with golden manes, he had turned to the dark smouldering voluptuous type. He had even tried the arty bohemians, and educated well-to-do upper-class females and that had been a mistake. None of them could give him all that he desired, if they had beauty they didn't have a brain or vice versa. On the odd occasion where he thought he had managed to find the complete package they had disappointed him terribly with their flaming tempers and egoistic demeanours. He shook his head sadly as he sat down. She was out there somewhere and hopefully if he was lucky one day he would find her.

He bent down to stroke the little greyhound bitch that lay at his feet. "Good girl," he murmured with a twinkle in his eye, she was all the company he needed right now. He opened the paper with a sigh of frustration and sat back to see what had been going on in the world.

The door swung open, Graham Pearson literally fell into the shop, panting heavily, his face red and blotchy. Adam looked up at him in amusement. "Morning, Mr Pearson, you're rushing around a bit today. You want to take it easy or you'll give yourself a heart attack."

"I know, but I'm parked on double yellows, so I can't hang around. I trust my trousers are ready?" Adam took a parcel from beneath the till, he handed it to Graham.

"Don't worry about paying me now; we can sort it out later."

"Right you are." He gave a thankful nod, turning on his heel then paused to look back over his shoulder as he reached the door. "We really must go for a beer some time, lad. I keep saying it and we never do. One lunchtime, next week, I'll drop in." He closed the door behind him, pausing to put his thumb up at Adam. The little hound lifted her head up with a wistful gaze, as the door banged shut.

"You know, girl, I reckon that sounds like a good idea. Think we should call it a day. Come on, let's go and get a pint, I could murder one."

CHAPTER FOUR

Christmas was only a few weeks away, for the first time since she could remember Isobel wasn't excited, or more to the point the least bit organised. In previous years by this time everything but the last grocery shop for the big day would have been taken care of. Life at Meadow Brook with the Cobbets was proving to be far more exciting. She could barely drag herself away from the place these days, preferring Brad and Marina's vibrant banter to Jacob, who had been sulky and moody recently. It hadn't taken long for her to feel at one with country life. London seemed a distant memory to think she had even thought of going back! It seemed that the weekends and the tales of city life were becoming rather a bore nowadays. Friday nights had begun to form a tedious pattern for Isobel. Jacob would arrive home around ten, they would make love and then eat and Jacob would crash out on the sofa exhausted. Yet Isobel found herself bursting with tales of her week, but he could never stay awake long enough to hear them, leaving her frustrated and feeling very resentful. Jacob was beginning to spend more time catching up on sleep during their precious time together, tired by the week's work and the tiresome drive. Isobel was tired of creeping around the house, trying not to disturb him and reassuring Edward that Daddy wasn't actually ill. It had become a relief to wave him off, back to London, on a Monday morning.

She thought about the coming weekend, as briskly she swept the main yard at Meadow Brook. Her marriage was crashing around her ears, not what she had envisaged when they had left London; in fact, it was all going pear shaped. Pausing to rest on the broom, her eyes wandered up to the sky following the path of a jet as it disappeared into cloud then re-emerged, until finally it was out of view altogether. Was that how her marriage would end up? Disappearing from her altogether? They had certainly entered the clouds, she thought.

"Penny for your thoughts!" Marina emerged with a grin, from one of the fillies' boxes a little further along.

"They're not worth a penny." Isobel laughed, as she fell in step alongside Marina. "Anyway, how do you manage to look so goddamn good in this freezing weather? I don't see you sporting a bright red nose or blue lips, unlike me."

"Thermal knickers, vest, socks the lot. You've got to dress for the occasion, and you city girls obviously need to learn a trick or two. Besides you'll soon warm up we're going out for a ride."

"Oh, fantastic, are we really?" Isobel's face lit up, as promptly she dropped the broom with a clatter. "I've been looking forward to going out, and I've finally progressed from the sand school. Yippee."

"Better than that, honey." Marina smiled mischievously, placing her hands on Isobel's shoulders and looking her in the eye. "No longer are you confined to the saddle of our very gorgeous little Jasmine."

Isobel could hardly contain her excitement, jumping up and down on the spot. "Go on, go on."

"I do hope you will like my choice. After all there is such a wide choice here and if that isn't a clue." She threw back her head and laughed aloud at Isobel's foxed expression, jumping up and down with sheer frustration. "Oh, Isobel, it's easy, I thought you would guess, why it's Questionable Choice."

"Really, Quest, are you sure?" she asked hesitantly, a grin rapidly spreading across her face.

"Why do you have a problem with that?"

"It's just that—" She shifted uneasily from one foot to the other. "Well isn't he a little bit lively for me, and not only that, but he is a livery, maybe the owners wouldn't like it and—" She gave an anxious grin. Marina cut in.

"Nonsense, you're more than capable. As for his owners, they haven't been anywhere near him for six months." She paused, a wicked gleam in her eye, and then smiled broadly at Isobel. "I decide what goes around here, so saddle up. Meet you up by the gate in ten minutes."

Hands trembling with a mix of apprehension and excitement, Isobel fetched the saddle and bridle; she hurried to the last stable. Quest, as he was affectionately known around the yard, stood around sixteen hands high; a handsome horse with a deep mahogany coat, ebony mane and tail and a delightful white blob on the upper part of his left nostril. He was reasonably bred too, Cleveland bay cross thoroughbred, home produced by Brad and Marina, then sold on as a four-year-old to a lady in Somerset, for her junior daughter to compete; however, he was to remain at Meadow Brook for further schooling and to mature a bit more.

Feeling slightly apprehensive, Isobel climbed into the saddle, tightened her girth and headed up to meet Marina who was ready and waiting with a very excitable lizard. Quest jogged in eager anticipation, as they set off down the lane. Isobel was immediately smitten, he felt so alive, ears pricked forward, taking an eager interest in all that was around him.

"Let's head down the lane, then I think we should branch off onto the bridle way and hopefully it'll be dry enough for a canter," Marina instructed. The cold wind whipped at Isobel's cheeks, as they cantered side by side along the edge of the five-acre wood. Isobel leant forward to pat Quest's sweaty neck, as they turned for home. This was living, never had she felt so alive.

Isobel finally tore herself away from Meadow Brook, Quest now a firm favourite. She drove hell for leather to Rita's to collect Edward, where she found him stood on a chair in the kitchen, helping Rita to make chocolate chip cookies. He was not pleased to see her, turning up to spoil his fun; he gave a look of complete disapproval at her arrival.

"You look better, love." Rita signalled to Isobel to sit down as she wiped her floury hands on the front of her apron.

"Do you think so really?"

"Yes you do, you looked really cheesed off this morning, what's been bothering you, love?" Isobel glanced across at Edward, who was far too busy rolling out dough, to notice what she was doing. Right or wrong, Isobel wanted to confide in Rita, as she was feeling so guilty about her feelings, it didn't take long to pour her heart out whilst keeping her eyes awkwardly fixed on the glass of barley wine, that Rita somehow unnoticed had thrust into her hand.

"Do you know, love?" Rita poured herself a glass, eyes slightly misting over as she did so. "I loved my late husband, dearly. God rest his soul." She paused to take a sip of wine. "We had more than our fair share of off days with each other, weeks sometimes but it wouldn't have been natural if we didn't, no relationship is that perfect." Rita topped up Isobel's glass. "You have found yourself an interest and there is absolutely nothing wrong with that, why just imagine if you hadn't, where would you be then? Miserable most likely and far less tolerant of Jacob being tired all the time."

"Most probably back in London," Isobel said ruefully.

"Exactly, so don't worry. You're a caring person, that's a good thing but never sacrifice yourself, love, remember that."

"Well I'm glad I didn't hot foot it back to the city, and it's all thanks to you, Rita." Isobel raised her glass to the other woman, who modestly waved it away.

"Nonsense, you're a spirited young lady, saw it in you the first time we met. You would be getting on with it, with or without my help."

"I don't think I can agree with that."

"Yes you can, not many lasses would stay in that big house all week, alone and in the middle of nowhere." She raised an eyebrow. "I've seen quite a few come and go."

"But it was always our dream!"

"Sure, but remember dreams don't always work out the way we hope they will, don't punish yourself. Enjoy it, love." Rita was right, Isobel loved Orange Stream Farm, perhaps it would be better to think of this as a temporary hiccup, and hope things would soon be back to normal. She couldn't envisage going back to London, not now. Rita watched the younger woman's thoughtful expression with interest. "What's running through your mind is there something else you're not telling me?"

Isobel was hesitant. "Do you believe that we all have a soul mate?"

"Yes, as a matter of fact I do, I believe we all have a soul mate out there somewhere. Sometimes it takes us a long time to realise exactly who it is, sometimes many lifetimes, when they may have been right under our nose all the time." She winked with a knowing smile.

"So you do believe in reincarnation then?"

"Of course, there has to be more to it than this. I mean you're born, you die. No, there's much more to it than that. Think of it like going to school, it's what you learn in each lifetime that really matters." She shook her head. "Come on drink up, it must be time for another."

Later that evening when Isobel spoke to Jacob on the phone, she told him excitedly about her ride out with Marina, Edward's cookie making, and Rita's barley wine, avoiding her conversation with Rita and the doubts she was having about their future. Jacob tried to sound enthusiastic, but she could tell he was tired and not really the least bit interested.

"Home in two days, can't wait." Finally, his tone brightened. Isobel sounded pleased though her heart was saying otherwise.

She ran a deep bath. Slowly the soothing water ebbed away any niggling doubts, it seemed Orange Stream was most beneficial for her and doing absolutely nothing for poor Jacob. As she lay peacefully in the warm waters, relaxing and trying to adopt a positive frame of mind, encouraged by something Rita had said about getting things right, she heard her name being called. Feeling her body tense, she listened intently. It was so quiet now, nothing stirred she must have imagined it. A few minutes later as she softly patted her skin dry, she heard it again this time louder and with a sense of urgency. A chill crept up her spine; she shivered as she climbed in between the bed sheets, her heart hammering in her chest. It was impossible, nobody was here except Edward, and this had been distinctly a woman's voice. It was strange yet it didn't really surprise her, it took a long time for her to fall asleep, her imagination running riot. Scolding herself, she tried to quieten her overactive mind.

Graham found himself enjoying the little escapade at Briars Lodge immensely, oddly finding some perverse enjoyment in trotting around the ménage, whilst Carmen jogged alongside, her huge breasts bouncing up and down, as she screamed breathless instructions to him.

Solvent was beginning to respond much better for him, after just a few lessons and there was the added bonus that Olivia was hopping mad at him disappearing off for training.

"We're losing the light now," Carmen screeched. "Better wrap it up for today." Feeling a little worn out but trying to hide it, Graham took Solvent back to the stable. His backside ached from 20 minutes trotting without stirrups and his lower regions were suffering too. Carmen peered over the door. "Give yourself a huge pat on the back, Graham, you did really well today."

"Thanks, Madame." Graham saluted her.

Carmen fell about laughing. "Oh, Graham, I'm not that bossy, am I?" Her puffy cheeks turned crimson.

"No you're worse!" Graham chuckled, as he slapped Solvent's neck affectionately. "Actually, I am very impressed, you're a very good instructress, are you like that in all areas?" He winked suggestively, sending Carmen even more crimson.

"Oh, you cheeky beggar, come in to the house, we deserve a drink. I'll have none of your nonsense mind."

"Sounds like a good idea, you go on ahead. I'll just rug this lad up, then be up to join you."

"Should I give Olivia a call, tell her you're stopping for a quick whisky?"

"Are you bloody joking?" Graham spluttered, looking at her in disbelief. He frowned. "I'm not ten, besides Olivia and I do our own thing." He shrugged. "Anyway it might be a couple of quick whiskies!"

Stepping inside Carmen's snug little kitchen, Graham couldn't help but smile to himself; it reflected her most aptly. Very cramped, bulging everywhere yet warm and inviting. A week's worth of washing up stood piled high on the drainer, copies of *Horse and Hound* spilled out from beneath the coffee table, across the stone floor. Over by the fridge, scattered across the floor were dirty cat bowls, encrusted with several days' remnants of food. A collection of butter dishes stood on a pine shelf, all from various parts of Cornwall or Devon. Obviously well travelled, he mused. A vast vat of linseed stood on the dining table which Carmen hastily removed, to make space to set out two tumblers along with a bottle of vintage malt. Graham was suitably impressed. He planted himself on one of the rickety wooden chairs, discreetly trying to dislodge the resident fat tabby, with a sharp elbow nudge. Carmen picked up each tumbler in turn holding them up to the light, scrutinising them for a moment, then hastily rubbing the rim of each glass with the cuff of her sweater, she poured a rather generous measure in to each glass.

"Cheers." She held up her glass briefly, and then downed it without batting an eyelid, eyeing Graham quizzically as he merely sipped his. "I had you down as a whisky drinker."

"Yes very much so, this is fabulous vintage you know." He paused to take another sip. Sluicing it tentatively around his palate, Carmen watched in amusement. Whisky was whisky, it all tasted the same to her; she poured another and polished it off in the same way. At that moment, it occurred to Graham, even though Carmen and Olivia were poles apart, both loved their booze, and could easily drink him under the table. He watched Carmen pour herself yet another.

"Sorry about the state of the place." Carmen followed Graham's bemused gaze, around the room. "You must think I am a right one?"

"Not at all, there's nothing wrong with being relaxed about one's domestic duties," he replied pompously. Then he winked putting her at ease. If she wanted to live like a pig well that was up to her, if however she was his wife, he would be seriously kicking her into touch. Carmen got up to clear the dirty cat dishes, throwing them in with the other backload of washing up in the sink. Graham pretended not to notice. She moved on to the pile of magazines bending to stuff them back up beneath the table. Seizing his golden opportunity, Graham was quick behind her; he just couldn't help himself really, his hands circling her plump body, edging forwards and up beneath her sweater to her large breasts which fell heavily into the palm of his hands as he managed to negotiate her extra support bra and its multitude of clasps. Beads of perspiration had collected beneath her breasts, which strained like two wild animals, aroused beneath his touch, straining to be free.

Graham had been right; there was no resistance, only little moans as he gently kneaded her clammy skin. Carmen's short stocky legs began to buckle, she fell forward unceremoniously on to the floor, unzipping her muddy jods and wiggling free of them, to expose a billowy, pink pair of buttocks. Graham couldn't wait to plummet between them, grabbing a fist full of matted red curls; he drove into her, gasping through gritted teeth.

"Now it's my turn to give the riding lesson." His face grew purple with exertion.

Brad lay feet up, head supported by a large satin cushion on the sofa in the drawing room; Marina appeared from the kitchen with two glass mugs of steaming Irish coffee, placing them down on the Edwardian table, she snuggled up next to Brad.

"Isobel is quite taken with Quest, don't you think?"

"Yeah, they certainly seemed to hit it off; though he can be a little shit when he wants to."

"Mmm." Marina turned on her side to look up at Brad, her blue eyes gleaming. "I really like her."

"Yes me to, nice lady." He tried to appear interested whilst watching the TV. Marina scooped up the remote control, flicking off the television.

"Who am I talking about?"

Brad looked blank; he circled his arms around her body, leaning forward to kiss her forehead. "Isobel, of course, see I can do two things at the same time." He grinned smugly.

"Of course she is very attractive too." Marina took a sip of her coffee.

Brad thought for a while. "Yes suppose she is fairly."

"Bet she gets lonely as well."

"Bound to, what with her hubby away all week, yes I expect she does."

Brad reclaimed the remote, switching the TV back on. "Do you mind, love, if I just finish this programme there's only five minutes left."

Pouting, Marina got up. "OK but I have an idea, a pre Christmas party." Marina smiled mischievously to herself. "Say next Friday."

Brad gave a deep sigh. "No matchmaking, she's married."

"No, silly, just invite all the gang, make Isobel feel welcome."

He grinned. "Whatever you say, honey."

Marina headed off to the kitchen for pen and paper. There was nothing she liked better than a party, a grand one at that.

"So what did you want to tell me?" he asked on her return.

"Oh that was an age ago, now, how many canapés do you think we will need?"

Brad had no doubt that the small welcoming party would turn into a rather lavish affair. Marina didn't do things any other way. He felt a stab of guilt, he should be financing things like this, but he didn't have that sort of cash. Marina had heaps, which was apparent she just couldn't resist spending, supplied by her ex. It really pissed him off sometimes, but as he watched Marina excitedly planning her do, he shrugged it off, as he always did, there wasn't really anything else he could do.

Jacob watched as Elizabeth approached his office, she paused to tap lightly before entering.

"Any idea what time you're leaving?"

"Nearly done now." He signalled for her to take a seat. "Give me ten minutes then we can leave, just stay right there." He strode off to the other office with an arm full of papers. Elizabeth nestled back into the leather-padded chair, gazing with interest around his office, particularly at the photos on the shelf, positioned to gaze down at Jacob as he sat at his desk. There were two small photographs of Edward: one as a baby sat proudly in his pram, and the other which she guessed was fairly recent. The attractive child stood at the top of some stone steps, flanked at either side by two doe-eyed golden retrievers; then there was a large framed picture. Jacob was standing arms encircled around a raven-haired woman, who smiled adoringly up at him, she looked divine in a low cut black evening dress. Jacob returned, "See you're admiring my family, lucky man, aren't I?"

"Sure looks that way." Elizabeth smiled sweetly across at him.

They drove back through the drizzle. "Anything the matter?" He glanced across at Elizabeth.

"No sorry. I was miles away." She licked her lips. "Dismal night again."

"Are you happy working for me?"

"Yes I am, why is there a problem, is my work not up to scratch?" There was no concealing the note of alarm in her voice.

Jacob slowed the car a little so he could turn to face her. "Quite the contrary, I have received glowing reports from Gloria, in fact she is really impressed with your work."

Elizabeth felt herself relax. "As I have said before I take my work very seriously, there is no room for error." She paused. "It was how I was brought up."

Jacob smiled across at her approvingly. Elizabeth felt her pulse quicken, he was so damn handsome, yet he didn't seem to realise it. The more she saw of him the more she was falling.

"You're doing it again," he remarked.

"Sorry bad habit of mine, daydreaming."

Jacob fished in his pocket for some cigarettes.

"I didn't know you smoked, well that's a lie that first night you gave me a lift."

"Sshhh I don't, well the odd one but nobody knows, can you keep a secret?" He laughed. "I used to smoke like a chimney, but Isobel made me quit when Edward was born." He inhaled deeply. "I keep the odd packet but it really isn't a habit." He turned to look at her, his expression seemed to ask: have I convinced you?

Elizabeth twisted her hands nervously in her lap. "Why do you feel the urge to have a cigarette now?" she enquired, looking into his eyes for a clue.

"Special occasion I suppose." He winked, adding to her profuse disappointment. "It's Friday tomorrow and I am going home." He smiled, contentedly at the thought. Elizabeth's heart sank.

"Jacob, you've just missed my turning." Her head turned violently round, as they sailed past.

"So I have, well I guess that means you will have to join me for dinner tonight, would that be permissible?"

Elizabeth's jaw fell open in amazement. "I well…I don't think I'm really dressed for dinner."

"So you will join me then?" He shot her a cheeky grin. "Relax, nowhere fancy, it would be great to have some company though."

"I would love to." Elizabeth suddenly felt very shy, even though inside she was bursting with happiness at the invitation. Jacob took a detour to a trendy Italian on the outskirts of town, it didn't matter any more to Elizabeth that she was still dressed for the office she would damn well enjoy it come what may.

They ate leisurely, sharing a bottle of chilled white; Elizabeth had left the ordering to Jacob who had deliberated for some time before deciding on tender fillet steaks stuffed with docellate, which had been divine. Jacob was charming and witty; Elizabeth found she didn't want the evening to end.

Later as they pulled up outside Elizabeth's home there was no peck on the cheek, in fact no physical contact at all, she found it hard to conceal her disappointment. Jacob kept the car running. "Thanks for keeping me company, Elizabeth, and we must do it again sometime. I hope you enjoyed it too?"

"Very much, thanks, it was a great meal." Elizabeth let herself quietly into her parents' home. Resting against the door for support, she let out a long contented sigh. She had to remain positive, and tonight she decided was definitely a good start.

CHAPTER FIVE

"Wow very smart, Mr Kadeer, but far too formal." Isobel fell back onto the bed laughing. "Look Brad and Marina are very rich, but they're not stuffy, that would be out of place."

Exasperated Jacob flopped down onto the bed next to her.

"Why don't you just pick me something, then the job's done?"

On command, Isobel leapt from the bed to fetch a pair of jeans and a casual shirt. "These will do just fine."

Jacob's eyes twinkled up at her mischievously. "Do we have time for a quick—" He broke off interrupted by the doorbell.

"Definitely not, that will be Rita. Get dressed and see you downstairs."

Jacob found Isobel sitting in the kitchen, chatting to Rita; he looked across at Isobel, she looked stunning, so much more relaxed than she had in London.

Rita stood up. "Oh, Jacob, I finally get to meet you at long last." She held on to his hand warmly ignoring the shiver that ran through her body. Jacob liked her immediately, taken by her genuine warmth.

"Terrible that we haven't met until now. I feel so rude and you have been so kind to my family."

Rita blushed. "You have a beautiful family, you must be very proud." She hugged Edward, who nestled into her, smiling. Rita wouldn't hear of them waiting to settle Edward into bed. "Be off with you both, we are fine. Edward has at least a dozen story books lined up for me to read. Just you make sure you have a wonderful time."

Rita closed the door behind them then looked around the empty hallway, pulling her cardigan tighter around her shoulders, she gave a shudder. She had sensed it when she first walked in, the spirits were still present and she wasn't imagining it, they had grown stronger. Some were harmless but there was a very unusual presence as well.

Isobel drove to Meadow Brook, Jacob had done enough driving. "Jesus Christ," Jacob exclaimed, sitting up. "Is this it?"

Isobel gave a girlish giggle. "Just you wait till you see inside, it's really something."

Brad met them at the door with a welcoming smile. "Hey, Jacob, it's great to meet you at last, let you out for once, did she?" Then he winked at Isobel, leaning over to plant a kiss on her cheek.

He ushered them through to the kitchen and fixed them both with drinks. They were joined a few moments later by Marina. She looked incredible. Jacob was taken aback as she threw her arms firstly around him in a warm welcome and then rushed to hug Isobel. Marina and Brad then enthused to a rather dazed Jacob how well Isobel was doing, which made Isobel blush. Marina drew Isobel to one side whilst the guys discussed Formula One which was of no interest to her, whispering, "You kept that rather quiet, he's really cute."

"Jacob?"

"Yes Jacob. Don't look surprised he is really good-looking." Marina linked arms with Isobel's, as they sauntered through to the drawing room. "Come on, guys, dinner's ready."

They took their seats, as Marina heaped their plates, with huge mounds of spaghetti tossed in a delicate basil and shrimp sauce. A large plate piled high with homemade garlic bread stood in the centre of the table alongside a bowl of freshly grated Italian cheese.

Brad opened a bottle of Dom Perignon, pouring them each a glass. "I propose a toast, to Jacob and Isobel, to welcome you both officially to Devon and to the start of a wonderful new friendship." They tucked into the delicious food, with the exception of Marina, who toyed irritatingly with hers, twirling the spaghetti endlessly around her fork.

"Actually there was another reason I asked you both tonight, apart from meeting your charming husband." She winked at Isobel, then turned to smile coyly across at Jacob. "We're having a party next week and would love you both to come if you can make it?"

"Gosh we'd love to." Isobel clapped her hands together in delight. "It is ages since we've been to a party."

Marina gave a smug smile. "Brilliant, we can introduce you to some of our friends."

Edward had fallen asleep shortly after the second story; Rita kissed his forehead, smiling down at his sweet, angelic face. Leaving his door slightly ajar, she tiptoed downstairs, where, hauling her bag up on to the sofa beside her, she began to unpack some of its contents. Candles, herbs and oils she set them all out on the table, she glanced up at the clock. There was plenty of time, spreading the purple silk cloth before her; she began to recite the protection spell whilst anointing the candles. Carefully her fingers worked. Her voice not faltering, she focused on the task before her. Last time she had been disturbed, this time she must complete her work. The room began to grow cold, but she took no notice. The whole procedure took less than ten minutes and with hands clasped, she smiled; satisfied that she had achieved peace for a while.

Isobel gave Marina a hand to wash up before they joined the guys in the lounge, along with Belgian chocolates and a tray of liqueurs. Brad leant across Marina's lap to squinting through bleary eyes at his guests. "Sorry, I have to ask. Is it true that Orange Stream Farm is haunted?"

Isobel looked across at Jacob, suddenly lost for words.

Jacob took charge. "It's the first we've heard of it. We certainly haven't seen anything. If it was true, then perhaps we've scared the spooks away."

Brad leant back on the sofa disappointed. "Oh I never believed it anyway."

Marina stood up. "Coffee, anyone?" Jacob nodded but Isobel was still interested in the supposed haunting.

"So who said it was haunted?"

Brad looked up, his speech now slightly slurred. "I don't recall, but I know that the owner before you, well his wife died there and supposedly—" He stopped to hiccup. "She wasn't the first person to die there. No apparently over a hundred years ago, a couple lived there and the wife was having a torrid affair, so the old man understandably pissed off at his wife shot her lover, then turned the gun on her, as well as blasting himself, terrible, eh?"

Marina glared at him from the kitchen doorway. He stood up, sensing Marina's distaste.

"Think I'll give Marina a hand. Like I said it's no doubt a load of rubbish and if it was true you would have found out by now."

Jacob agreed, he didn't want Isobel's head full of that sort of rubbish.

They left shortly after midnight to relieve Rita, who would no doubt be keen to get home and not wanting to take advantage of her kindness. Isobel drove slowly back along the winding lanes.

"Wow, that was some gaff!" Jacob let out a long, low whistle. "Bet it will be some party, eh?" He squeezed Isobel's thigh. "In fact I think you'd better slip into Redwood this week and get me something decent to wear."

"Only, if I can have a new dress," Isobel teased.

"Sure you only live once. Let's splurge out a bit. Never fear we won't be outdone." They both exploded into fits of laughter. Isobel felt her heart skip; it was just like old times.

Graham thought about Carmen, she was most unlike any of the women he had ever had before. He was enjoying the change, besides it was a secret, nobody would ever know. He was still in the doghouse for being late home. There had been no dinner for a week; it hadn't even bothered him, especially not this evening, as he was slipping out to meet Carmen. He made his escape, relieved that as usual, Olivia was rather tipsy and didn't really seem interested in what he was doing.

He arrived at Carmen's a little after nine, she had pushed the boat out tonight, and the place was immaculate. After a lot of tidying up, the first she had done for months, she had taken a long hot soak, then prepared a steak and kidney pudding for their supper.

Now opening the door with a huge grin and glowing from head to foot, she kissed Graham warmly on the cheek. Graham closed the door behind him; he didn't wait for a welcome drink, fumbling wildly with her tight jeans, then unbuttoning her shirt as fast as his fingers could work. He quivered at the sight of her nakedness, as she stood before him. She was a wholesome woman, her breasts heaved up and down, and he couldn't wait to plummet between them.

Olivia had not drunk as much as she had made out to Graham. As soon as he had shut the front door behind him, she pulled on a jacket and set about following him. Not sure where they were heading, she maintained a reasonable distance. Ignorant until Graham finally pulled off into a driveway. Olivia pulled off the road into the next lay by, slipped out of the car and headed back to the driveway where Graham had disappeared. It was obviously a shag he was going for, why else had he been in such high spirits all week? If she could see with her own eyes, then she would feel strong enough to do something about it, what, she wasn't quite sure. It wasn't until she got to the house and saw the sign, "Briars Lodge" that it twigged.

Perhaps it was all quite innocent. Her heart rate increased dramatically. As she crept along the frost-covered grassy bank, it felt crisp beneath her step. Leaning against the cold stone wall for support, she swallowed hard, pausing to take a few deep breaths. There was the sound of muffled voices from somewhere inside. Lurking amongst the shadows, Olivia took a step back and looked up at the dark house, there was a dull light from the room above her head. Cautiously she went to the door, on trying the handle it swung open. The sound of laughter filtered into her ears. Taking another deep breath, she crept in to the darkness, only pausing to slip off her shoes. Nerve-racking, inch-by-inch she headed towards the stairs, groping along the wall with her hand; she tried to find her bearings, as she began to climb. At each step, her mouth grew drier, her throat a little tighter.

The adulterers, in their obvious haste, had not closed the door properly, a small crack remained, enough for her to see, if she inched carefully forward. Holding on to the doorframe for support and squinting through the crack, she stifled a gasp, hastily she covered her mouth with the other hand. Carmen lay spread-eagled across the bed. Graham, her Graham, had his head buried between her breasts, as he licked like a lapping kitten and stroked them. Olivia felt insanely jealous and inexplicably mad. Should she march in to confront them? It seemed doubtful as her legs wouldn't move! Olivia began to tremble, losing some of the earlier bravado, as her eyes followed the gentle movements of Graham's fingers across Carmen's seal-like body. Olivia's anger began to dissolve, now turning to deep regret. Graham had never delighted or indulged in foreplay like this with her. What was the fascination with this woman before him? Suddenly it didn't matter, she felt sick to the core and useless.

Graham gathered speed, as he then entered Carmen hungrily, causing Carmen to howl out like a snared rabbit. Olivia gave a horrified groan, causing her to clutch the doorframe even tighter. Carmen's podgy calves were entwined around Graham's milky white flabby body, just as they had been around Solvent's gleaming chestnut hide. Olivia turned she could take no more, gagging as she reached the top of the stairs, relentless she fled pausing only to collect her shoes by the door, but not bothering to put them on, in her haste to flee. As she reached the car, she doubled over, retching fiercely on the verge. Finally exhausted, she climbed back in the car, locking the doors, cradling her thumping head in her hands; big sobs wracked her shivering body. Feeling very empty and somehow emotionless, she drove back to the twinkling lights of Bramstone Hall.

Wearily Olivia undressed, she climbed in to bed, her mind racing. This was a situation that could be turned to her advantage perhaps? Is that what she wanted, had he crossed the line for the final time?

She tossed this way and that, sleep evasive but thoughts of her revenge, eased her troubled mind.

"Mummy, I don't want to go the shops, please can I go to Auntie Rita's?" Edward's legs stiffened, as Isobel marched him briskly onwards towards the shops.

"Not today. We must get you some new shoes. Now be a good boy please." Edward began to wail, tears sprang from his blazing eyes. Isobel gritted her teeth and dragged him along relentless to the shoe shop. He was behaving as if a spoilt brat today. Used to unwilling small people, the shop assistant produced a lollipop, which never failed to work. Preoccupied Edward sat motionless while shoes were selected and fitted. They left the shop on a much happier note than they had entered. Edward bucked up no end, as they entered the department store, adorned with twinkling Christmas decorations and Christmas carols being played merrily in the background.

Christmas was the last thing on Isobel's mind, as she headed to the dress department, only to be waylaid by Santa himself, at women's hosiery. Quite what he was doing there she wasn't sure, but it was most welcome as Edward had a present thrust in to his hands. Thankfully, this kept him amused as she tried on several outfits, finally settling for the age-old little black dress, nothing flash, rather plain but a perfect fit.

As they left the store, Edward was beginning to lose interest in Santa's present, dragging his feet and pulling faces. Then the whingeing began, there was still Jacob's outfit to buy. Cursing softly under her breath, Isobel swore she would never have another child. The good lord must have been looking down on her at that moment, despite her selfish demeanour. As a familiar voice from behind them called out, "Is that my little Edward I hear crying?" They both wheeled round at the same time.

"Rita!" Edward shrieked, breaking free of Isobel's grasp and launching himself at Rita with passion.

"Sounds like you have a rather stroppy Edward with you today."

"I certainly do. I think he is tired and it's not much fun being dragged around the shops."

"Well good job we met, I am all done, got all I needed today. Shall I take him back with me; you can collect him on the way home."

"Rita, you're an angel. That would be great."

Isobel couldn't believe her luck, as with a sense of relief she watched Edward stride off joyfully, at Rita's side.

Isobel fished her shopping list from her jacket pocket. Despite the distraction of Edward, she had managed to grab a few Christmas prezzies along the way: one for Jacob, also an exquisite set of china farm animals for Rita which would sit nicely on her kitchen dresser. It was time for a coffee break, she needed to revive her energy and found a seat in the Italian coffee bar. She ordered a cappuccino then took a long hard look at the remainder of things on her list. There were still a couple of presents she should really pick up today, time was running out. Isobel pulled a pen from her bag then started jotting ideas down. The waitress shuffled over to enquire if she might like anything else. "Actually you could help me, are there any men's clothes shops in town? I am not really that familiar with the area yet."

The dowdy waitress, seeing the chance to be of some use, other than to serve up beverages or Danish pastries, shuffled closer.

"What sort of thing are you looking for, love?"

"Well something a bit different."

"Now have you tried Docherty's, bit pricey mind? Not far from here either."

The waitress looked pleased, when Isobel replied she hadn't. She gave Isobel detailed directions. much to her supervisor's annoyance, who stood by the till, tapping her foot impatiently, table 49 needed clearing and table five obviously needed a refill and it wasn't her job to do it.

In the hope of finding something for Jacob to wear to the party, Isobel set off for Docherty's. The display in the window screamed expensive. Deciding what the hell, she went on in. It was a small shop, rather pokey; an ancient looking greyhound on arthritic legs came to greet her. Isobel paused to stroke its bony head, before browsing absently along the rails. A pair of fawn trousers caught her eye, she pulled them down to take a closer look, then catching sight of the price tag, embarrassedly replaced them, the waitress had warned her it was pricey. She checked the tag on a shirt hanging overhead, again well over two hundred pounds, Isobel turned to leave.

"Ahh now I see you have good taste." The soft Irish voice startled her. She turned to face an incredibly handsome man, as she blushed; his eye searched hers. "Or is that not the case?"

"Well I—" Isobel lowered her eyes. He stared intently back, and she felt faintly uneasy. "It's a fair bit more, to be honest with you, than I was looking to pay," Isobel tucked her hair back behind her ear, distracting his enquiring gaze. "You know with it being Christmas as well."

The man watched her face with interest; he extended a strong hand. "Adam Docherty."

Blushing furiously, Isobel returned the handshake. "Isobel Kadeer, nice to meet you."

Softly Adam took hold of her left hand. "May I?"

"Mm, yes," she murmured entranced, as he took her hand masterfully in his own.

"So is this a present for your husband? I see you're married." He glanced down at her rings. Placing her hand down on to the trousers, which she had been admiring just a few moments before, he asked, "Now tell me what do you feel?" He watched her expression. Isobel felt weird, how surreal, what was she supposed to say; even if she had known the words wouldn't surface. He manoeuvred her hand gently in a gliding motion along the material.

"Can you feel it?" His voice grew husky. Isobel felt giddy. Feeling vulnerable, she let her hand be swept gently, back and forth along the cloth.

"They feel expensive." She giggled at her silly statement.

Adam winked at her. "Yes go on."

"They also feel luxurious." She looked up at him hopefully. Softly he released her hand. Immediately she missed its warmth.

"So think about what you have said." He smiled broadly and took a step back.

Isobel felt incredibly foolish, he was some salesman.

Adam's eyes twinkled merrily. "You know what I'm saying don't you?" he teased.

Indeed she did. Shifting uneasily from one foot to the other as the exotic, spicy smell of his aftershave wafted into her nostrils, awakening her senses. Isobel was beginning to fear he may have sent her into some hypnotic trance and that maybe the waitress was his accomplice.

Adam replaced the trousers "Are you local?" he asked. He stooped to lovingly pat the dog's head, putting Isobel slightly more at ease.

"Bramstone way," she replied, purposefully vague.

"Ah know it well. Where about?"

Isobel took a deep breath. "Orange Stream Farm and yes I will take the trousers." Adam lifted them carefully back down.

"You won't regret this, in fact—" he gazed at her longingly before continuing, "I am willing to take a bet that your husband will be back to buy some more."

She nodded. "Perhaps you will be right."

Isobel left the shop with a warm glow from deep inside. She had no doubt that every lady customer received Adam's well-crafted sales pitch, but if she was honest she had never experienced anything like it, smiling to herself, she picked up pace and headed back to the car.

Isobel arrived back at Orange Stream to find a handwritten note from Rita, informing her that they had gone to the market; she would drop Edward home around five. It was ten past two that would give her a few hours, so changing into jodhpurs and sweater she let the dogs out for a pee then headed off to the Cobbets'.

Marina was out in the school lunging one of the youngsters.

"Hi, you're late today. Where have you been hiding?"

"Just been in to town, to do a bit of Christmas shopping, not very organised."

Bringing the young grey to a halt, Marina patted its gleaming neck enthusiastically. "Good girl," she crooned, as she led her over to where Isobel was standing. "You've missed all the action this morning."

"Really, like what!"

"Well I am not sure you're going to like it, Quest's owners turned up with some guy. Who has subsequently gone and brought him, can you believe it?"

"Oh, no. Really!" Isobel's heart sank. "I didn't even know that he was up for sale."

"Neither did we." Marina cocked her head to one side. "They just turned up out of the blue, Brad was livid. Anyhow he'll be staying with us until Christmas Eve that's when they have arranged to collect him." Marina knew that Isobel had a soft spot for the horse. "Look, Brad's gone to the saddlers why don't we go out for a ride?"

Marina decided it best if they didn't use Quest; it wasn't worth risking an injury. She handed Isobel Packard's tack. "To make it fair," she said. "I'll take Brazen."

Isobel tacked up Packard who fidgeted restlessly nipping at her, as she tightened his girths. He was a fairly attractive horse but temperamental and certainly no comparison to Quest.

They rode along the lane both women admiring the countryside. Packard spooked into the road as a small robin flew from the hedgerow, irritating Isobel. Quest wouldn't have been so idiotic, she thought.

"I'm really looking forward to the party." Marina looked across at Isobel.

"Oh me to, do you need a hand with anything?"

"To be honest I have called in caterers, now that the numbers have ballooned from thirty to sixty."

"It's going to be a big party then?"

"You bet." Marina slipped off her hat to rake her long crimson nails through her hair. "Do you mind if I ask you something, Isobel?"

"Fire away."

"Be honest with me, won't you? How do you see me as a person?"

"I admire you," Isobel replied, simply and with no explanation.

"Admire, but why! Is it because I am fortunate to have so much, like the big house and a stable full of horses?"

"No not at all." Isobel blushed. "I admit it would be very easy to be envious of all that, but it's your vigour for life, you always seem to be so happy. You are always smiling, you always look stunning and you just seem to take everything in your stride."

"You reckon?" Marina replied.

Isobel went on. "Besides all that, you have the perfect marriage, you seem to be made for each other." Isobel noticed Marina's jaws tighten. "Surely you're not going to shatter my ideals and tell me I am wrong?"

"Well, no, not about me and Brad we love each other very much, but he is younger than me and I worry constantly if he will still love me when I am old and wrinkly."

"But you're beautiful!" Isobel shrieked astonished.

Marina shortened up her reins as Brazen began to jog throwing his head wildly in the air, she settled him back to a walk.

"I am going to shock you now, Isobel," Marina said, laughing. "The real reason I manage to look so good is the simple fact that I can afford to. Cosmetic surgery is a wonderful thing. You don't believe for one moment that I was born with such perfect breasts, do you?"

"You've got to be kidding!" Isobel's eyes widened, she was at a loss for words.

"Told you. Shocked, aren't you?"

"Not shocked, surprised, you look so good, besides what does it matter? You certainly don't look false."

"I suppose I just don't feel real any more. Trying to hold back the years."

"That's being a bit harsh, don't you think? You're only in your thirties."

"Well that's just it, you see, I lie about my age and I'm actually forty-three." Isobel couldn't hide her disbelief.

"See, told you you'd be shocked and I expect you're thinking that I'm really vain and sad. There are sixteen years between myself and Brad."

"No I don't think you're vain, all I can say is you jolly well don't look it."

"Please though, Isobel; don't tell any one, will you?"

"Of course not, Marina, you can trust me. I won't breathe a word."

"It's just that Brad, well he kind of thinks that I'm thirty-two as well."

"How on earth have you managed to keep the truth from him? I mean you're both so close."

Marina fidgeted restlessly in the saddle. "It's easy really. Brad has always given me free rein." She drew in breath. "I handle any papers or documents; I make sure he never sees my passport!"

"But why did you tell me?" Isobel interrupted, panic-stricken!

"I trust you. I know we haven't been friends for that long but I really like you, Isobel."

In that moment Isobel realised just how lonely and frightened Marina actually was. Living a lie must be exhausting for her, especially deceiving the person she loved the most.

Marina gave an awkward cough. "Anyhow enough of me, what are you guys up to for Christmas?"

"Oh really rather boring, Jacob took it upon himself to invite some friends of ours down from London. I would have preferred to spend it alone really. What about you?"

"Molly, my daughter, will be spending time with us. First time in two years. I know it sounds awful but I think it will be quite a strain all round." They turned onto the bridle path, at the edge of the village; it was a thick bog, the horses' hooves squelched through the thick brown mud, which splattered up their legs like melted chocolate.

"You and Molly aren't that close then?"

"Molly is a daddy's girl. He remarried a South African woman 'Maddie.' Molly adores her; she's the mother I could never be. I sometimes think that Molly must really despise me."

"That's a real shame."

Marina nodded in agreement. "Isn't it just?" She gave a nonchalant shrug. "Come on, let's have a canter along this bit, the ground appears to be a lot drier," she said, glad to change the subject, feeling decidedly uncomfortable on the subject of Molly.

They turned back into the drive at Meadow Brook, spattered from head to foot in mud. Isobel's hands felt numb from the cold. Marina was glad to see Brad's car was back.

"Oh goodie, hope he managed to get my dressage saddle," she shrieked.

Isobel un-tacked then washed off Packard's muddy legs, lost deep in thought. Brad appeared looking in at her over the stable door. "Did you girls have a good ride?"

"Yes, we did thanks."

"Marina told you about Quest?" he asked, Isobel tentatively. She nodded her head.

"Yes such a shame, I really liked riding him."

"Yes, suppose we're all gutted. Never mind we'll have some foals arriving in the spring, they'll keep us all busy." He patted Isobel's shoulder sympathetically. "Don't worry, we won't lumber you with Packard." Isobel looked at the horse's miserable face as he tore greedily at his hay net.

"I sincerely hope not." She gave a half hearted grin.

CHAPTER SIX

Gloria was not surprised by the dismal weather forecast on the radio. Heavy snow was due to hit much of the country; her aching hip was a sure a sign as any. She hurried in to Jacob's office to let him know, but was sidetracked by a very irate Olan, whose normally placid face was red with rage.

"Gloria, please can you sort out that bloody dimwit on reception. Five calls have been cut off to my office this morning and she doesn't pass on any messages." He relaxed his jaw a little. "We're all under a lot of pressure down there at the moment, and she isn't helping."

Madeline usually ran reception, but she was off sick with influenza, the agency had sent a temp who was far from competent.

"Okay, Olan. I'll get on to the agency. Leave it with me."

Disgruntled, he turned and ambled back downstairs. Gloria called across to Elizabeth, who was on the computer. "Could you please give Jacob a message? Tell him that heavy snow is forecast, he may want to leave for Devon this evening. I meanwhile have to go and sort out our lovely receptionist."

Elizabeth went in to see Jacob; he was tied up on the phone. It would keep, she decided; besides it must be time for a coffee.

Gloria spent the rest of the day in a spin; everything seemed to be spiralling out of her normal meticulous control. Getting the orders out on the road was becoming a problem, what with the snow arriving and the extra Christmas orders.

Jacob left for a lunch date. He hated this time of year, all the good will wining and dining with clients, particularly today when faced with John Wood, a thin faced nuisance of a man, a pair of spectacles perched at the end of his crooked nose. John was an assessor for one of the large insurance companies he was finicky and full of self-importance. Jacob yawned his way through three boring hours spent in an exclusive Chinese restaurant, restlessly watching John as he picked painfully, at morsels of food with his chopsticks.

Arriving back at the office frustrated, Jacob called Joanne in to go through his diary; it was of utmost importance that she kept a few hours spare for him to go Christmas shopping. Isobel had given him a large list of things to get for Edward, things that she wouldn't find easily in Devon. Then he sent Joanne out with a couple of hundred quid to get all of the office staff a gift, it kept morale high.

Jacob finished the day, sharing a good quarter of the bottle of his best malt with Olan in his office. When they finally emerged outside to the car park, they were astonished at the weather, everything including Jacob's car, covered by a large blanket of snow.

"Shit where did this lot come from? It's going to be crap for business, eh?" Olan shook his head, looking across at Jacob.

"Yeah looks a bit grim for getting down to Devon too. Oh, well, let's hope it stops soon."

"You would be a fool to drive down in this, mate, reckon we will all be sledging in to work tomorrow."

Jacob shrugged peering up at the sky before turning to wave goodbye to Olan over his shoulder.

He walked over to the Mercedes. A figure lurked in the shadows and he peered through the veil of falling snow. Elizabeth stepped out from behind the car.

"Elizabeth, are you OK? Gosh, you look freezing. Here take this, love." Jacob handed her his jacket. "Have you been waiting for me long?"

Elizabeth seemed edgy. "I haven't been waiting for a lift. I feel so awful about—"

"Look, get in!" Jacob interrupted her. "It's freezing," he said, through chattering teeth as he opened the door and bundled her inside. He hauled himself into the seat besides her, rubbing his hands briskly together. "Now what's this about feeling awful?" he asked. Starting the engine, Jacob turned the heater to maximum then turned to look across at Elizabeth, noticing for the first time her dishevelled appearance. "Oh, God, Elizabeth, you have been crying. What ever is the matter?"

"I feel terrible, Jacob," she sobbed. "I was supposed to pass on the message about the snow. Gloria specifically asked me to, but it slipped my mind." She pulled out a handkerchief, dabbing fiercely at her bloodshot eyes. "I was supposed to let you know so you could leave earlier for Devon."

Jacob lit a cigarette; he listened intently as she went on. "Gosh, I feel so awful. I know how important getting home is to you. The weather is forecast for a couple of days and I have really ruined your chances of making it back."

Jacob ground the cigarette in the ashtray, then taking the handkerchief from Elizabeth's trembling hands wiped gently at her eyes. "Poor Elizabeth, I couldn't have left earlier, even if I had wanted to." He paused to smile at her. "How sweet of you to be so concerned, but please don't feel bad it's just one of those things, certainly nothing for you to worry about." Jacob handed her the handkerchief back.

She smiled nervously. "I haven't been sleeping well lately, my mind's all over the place."

"Is there anything I can help you with? Perhaps you're working too hard?" he added helpfully.

"No really I'm fine. Sorry, Jacob."

Jacob drove her home; she was quiet during the journey. He felt embarrassed, the poor girl had worried herself to death. It was good to know how considerate she was, but he had, he reminded himself, known that ever since he had taken her for that meal. There was something intriguing about her; she really threw herself in to everything. Not unlike him, when he had first started working for his father, keen to make a good impression. Elizabeth was probably wasted working for him. She appeared to be capable of far greater things. Perhaps in the New Year, he would be able to offer her a better position.

Jacob arrived back at the flat and the phone was ringing. It was Edward. "Daddy, we have got loads and loads of snow, can we make a sledge when you come home and—" He was cut short as Isobel prised the phone from him, her tone frantic.

"Jacob, have you got snow there too?"

"Oh, boy." He gave a low whistle. "Have we got snow, I haven't seen snow like this for years."

Isobel was hopping mad when it dawned on her that Jacob would be unable to make the party. She had been adamant she wouldn't go alone, but after much bullying from Jacob, she finally caved in. Perhaps it would be OK, she thought. It would just be a bit daunting arriving alone. *You can do it*, she told herself sternly. Isobel called Marina to let her know. "Oh, darling, you must be gutted, you hardly see each other as it is and I expect Jacob is feeling pretty lousy about it too."

"Yep, he's really pissed off. We have both been looking forward to it so much."

"Well never mind," Marina said, brightly. "There'll be plenty of good-looking chaps to give you a whirl around the dance floor." She gave an excited shriek. "Hey, how about the sexy Graham Pearson, for starters? Now that would be a hoot."

"Ugh, mm, thanks, but no thanks I am not that desperate."

"Well just make sure you wear something incredibly sexy, keep the men on their toes. There's a few people dying to meet you, and dare I say they are mostly male."

Isobel put the phone down. Now with an acute attack of butterflies, perhaps she should ask Rita to bring a bottle of rhubarb wine, and then she could down a few glasses before leaving. For a little Dutch courage, she thought.

The day seemed endless. After clearing the snow from the steps and pathway—Edward tried to help where he could, but soon got cold and bored—they took the dogs out over the fields. Edward collapsed in fits of laughter as Tarquin stuck his head deeply into the wet snow, then gave an inquisitive snort, showering snow in all directions, which proceeded to excite him more, as he began to furiously dig with both paws.

"They are so funny, Mummy."

"Aren't they just, the daft beggars." Isobel giggled. "It's been a long time since they have seen snow, and it's just too exciting."

Isobel stood back to watch Edward and the dogs play, until a loud bark from behind made her jump. A large German shepherd came bounding across the field. Sadie scampered back to Isobel's side with a pitiful whimper but Tarquin charged across to greet the newcomer, tail held high. Edward turned to follow. "No, Edward, come back, we're not sure if it's friendly."

"Where has that doggie come from, Mummy?" Edward asked concerned.

"I'm not sure, there doesn't appear to be anybody with him, does there?" Isobel suspected he had come across from Bramstone Hall. It was getting cold. With a shiver, she took hold of Edward's hand. "Come on, let's go back, Ed, your nose is bright red."

"But, Mummy, we can't leave Tarquin?" Tarquin was galloping off with the other dog, blissfully ignorant of Isobel's frantic calls.

"Don't worry he will follow, let's go," she placated Edward. Sadie bombed off ahead of them, glad to be getting away from the intruder who had stolen her playmate. Isobel gripped Edward's small-gloved hand tighter; the snow was so deep. She could hardly make out the width of the bridge, as they cautiously tiptoed across it. Isobel looked over her shoulder; Tarquin wasn't following, far too busy playing to notice they had even left. They climbed over the fence which led to the home paddock, from here, it was all downhill and if Tarquin didn't look up soon they would be out of his view. Isobel tried to whistle but her limp attempt carried on the wind in the opposite direction. She hesitated then climbed back up onto the fence. "Tarquin, Tarquin," she screeched, as loud as she could. Finally, he pricked up his ears; she could see he was torn, home or new friend. The German shepherd sensed his apprehension and began to play more aggressively. "Oh, shit," Isobel swore aloud.

"What is it, Mummy?" Edward tugged at her jacket sleeve. Isobel couldn't decide whether to continue on walking downhill or try to retrieve Tarquin, it was the other dog that worried her, it looked as if it was becoming hostile. Then much to her relief a person could be seen in the distance. They were calling out presumably for the dog. Obviously not the time for polite neighbourly conversation in this atrocious weather, they continued back towards home. Sadie was sitting on the terrace waiting for them, looking very pleased with herself. Isobel smiled as she turned to see Tarquin gambling through the snow, head bowed against the brisk wind which was gathering in strength.

Olivia however was not so pleased. "There you are, you dratted animal, it's not my idea of fun you know ploughing through this snow in the freezing cold." Ruffles looked suitably ashamed, as he trotted back to Olivia's side, tail tucked firmly between his legs. Olivia had spotted the Kadeer woman with her young son. Muttering under her breath, she grabbed hold of Raffles' collar and hauled him round for the trek back to Bramstone Hall, skirting past the dark wood which always gave her the jitters. She pulled up the zip on her coat as far as it would go. How rude was that woman, she didn't even wave. Well if she was at the party tonight she would bloody well ignore her. In fact more importantly, thinking of the party, what in hell's name would she wear? Marina would be done up to the nines as usual and Graham had indicated it was to be a big affair. It would have to be something quite classy; of course it would be the usual farce arriving on Graham's arm pretending to be the happy couple, whilst watching the best of Devon's jet set, knocking back champagne and filling their faces on exquisite little titbits, that looked far too good to eat. The most sickening thing of course would be watching the hosts, Mr and Mrs Perfect, floating around in unison, socialising with their guests. Olivia probably wouldn't have bothered to go, given their current situation, which was at an all-time low. However, curiosity had the better of her, as she was just dying to meet Mr Kadeer, who so far had managed to keep himself well-hidden and dodged most of the village. He could be an interesting proposition, after all he plainly had a stuck-up wife, and maybe he too was aching for some excitement.

Two hours later after a deep soak, Olivia threw a handful of crushed ice into a glass with a generous measure of Baileys. "Cheers," she toasted her reflection in the mirror. "The first, of many."

Ten to five, Brad checked the clock. Marina was already upstairs getting ready whilst he had spent the last hour helping the caterers bring all the food in, along with fetching up bottles of vintage champagne from the cellar. All that remained for him to do now was bed down and feed all the horses. There was no way he would be ready for eight, he ran his fingers frantically through his hair.

"Oh, I am really looking forward to this. What do you think?" Carmen looked at her reflection in the mirror.

"Great!" Graham tried to sound convincing, nodding his head mechanically, in approval.

"You know it was worth splashing out a hundred pounds on this outfit," Carmen squealed. The beautiful satin dress hung loosely around her waist, falling in soft pleats just below the knee, the long sleeves tightened at the wrist and the neck of course plunged daringly between her breasts, it was so her. To compliment the outfit, her hair had been swept back tightly into a bun, held securely with a diamante clip. Graham raised his eyebrows, what a shame that his wife didn't derive so much pleasure from an outfit that cost a mere hundred quid. Suddenly he became aware of the time, which flashed accusingly on the bedside clock.

"Jesus I must fly." He kissed her quickly on the back of the neck. "Hey, you look stunning. See you later, love." Graham paused at the door to look back at Carmen who was having a final twirl. "Remember don't make it too obvious tonight." He bit his lip. "I mean let's be discreet."

"Don't worry." Carmen chuckled. "Olivia won't suspect a thing." She leapt across the floorboards planting a big kiss on his sweaty forehead. "Go on, shoo!" she ushered him hastily out of the door.

Isobel bathed, she smothered herself in scented body balm and music played softly in the background. Edward was deliriously happy because Rita was coming; he lay sprawled across Isobel's bed piecing together a jigsaw, ignoring his mother totally.

"There what do you reckon?" Isobel stood in front of Edward.

"Wow, Mummy, you look like Cinderella." The child gazed up at her. Isobel, more than delighted with his response, threw her head back and laughed happily. The sound of a car outside sent Edward bolting full pelt downstairs, screeching, "Rita!" as he raced to greet her. Isobel followed more sedately, Edward couldn't reach the catch and he jumped up and down excitedly as Isobel opened the door for him.

"Why, Isobel, you look fantastic!" Rita looked her up and down. "Well, you will be the belle of the ball tonight."

Edward ran excitedly around her singing, "Cinderella, Cinderella."

"Well." Rita held up a bottle of rhubarb wine. "You won't need this; you look a million dollars, that's all the courage you need, my girl."

"Oh yes I do." Isobel grabbed the bottle from her. "I am as nervous as hell."

Isobel marched through to the kitchen to grab two glasses; she sat down at the table signalling for Rita to do the same.

"God I wish Jacob was here." She took a large gulp of the wine, and then wiping her mouth with the back of her hand rather unfittingly, she looked across at Rita. "Gosh, I'm glad that stuff's so strong," she said, then poured another glass. Rita had merely taken a sip of hers. Rita had planned to stay the night so that Isobel didn't have to rush home; Isobel took her upstairs to show her where she would be sleeping.

"Bet you have to fight them all off tonight."

Isobel felt herself blush. "Oh I really don't think so. I mean. I expect Marina will look absolutely amazing."

"Yes without a doubt she will, but I tell you, Isobel, you will give her a run for her money tonight."

Edward appeared from his bedroom, carrying a stack of books.

"Look, Rita, look. I have all these stories for us to read."

"Wow, I think that lot will take us forever, young man." Rita stooped to tickle Edward; he giggled dropping the books and rolled around the floor, laughing.

Isobel watched their warm exchange; Rita was like a surrogate grandmother. Jacob's mother was good with Edward but her life was so busy he never got to see much of her. As for her own mother God rest her soul, Edward had never known her, she had died long before he was born. It was a shame, but she doubted that even Evelyn would have come close to Rita. Rita spied Isobel's empty glass. "Come on just time for a quick refill and then we had better get you there before you fall over."

Isobel stood shivering. Alone on the imposing doorstep, she watched as Rita and Edward drove away. She took a deep breath and rang the doorbell. Brad swung open the door. He took one look at Isobel and drew in breath. "Wow you look amazing." He threw his arms around her waist, squeezing her tightly and kissing her firmly on each cheek.

They went through to the kitchen, where Brad thrust a glass of Cristal into her hand; he leant forwards to whisper in her ear. "Marina was a bit upset earlier; see if you can cheer her up, darling." Surprised, Isobel murmured she would try, wondering if it could have anything to do with their conversation while out riding. Brad spotted the tense expression on her face. "Relax, come on, there's quite a few here already, let me take you through and introduce you."

Isobel found herself gasping; the drawing room through to the indoor pool looked wonderful, swags of holly and mistletoe hung decoratively around the room. White sparkling lights adorned the ceiling, like a star filled night. The band had set up in the far hand corner, where a temporary dance floor had been laid, surrounded by large bunches of gold and silver balloons. More balloons hung in a large net, suspended above the swimming pool, and to top it all, a gigantic Christmas tree decorated simply with white lights and a large solitary gold star at the top stood over by the French doors, which led out to the terrace. There was a large gazebo made entirely from holly and fir which housed a gigantic table, topped with the most magical array of food.

Marina crept up behind her. "Hey, darling, you look great. What do you think of the house?"

"Thank you. Wow, you look marvellous, and the house what can I say, it's," she drew in breath, "...magical, simply magical."

Marina linked her arm beneath Isobel's, waving Brad away. "Come and meet my friends," she said, then whisked Isobel headlong, into the throbbing crowd, over near the dance floor.

Isobel recognised Olivia immediately; she was stood near the edge of the dance floor, deep in conversation, she broke off as they approached.

"I think you have all met before." Marina smiled, sweetly, propelling Isobel forward. Graham lurched forward beaming.

"No, I don't believe I have had the honour yet." He took Isobel's hand grazing the back of it with his lips. "I had no idea how beautiful our neighbour was, or I would surely have been round to visit."

Olivia forced a smile. "Nice to meet you again, oh, how rude of me, sorry, I am hopeless with names."

Before Isobel had chance to reply, Marina had pushed her further forward still, whispering, "You don't want to get stuck with those boring old farts."

Olivia eyed Isobel as she went past; she even had a bloody good figure. Was there no God, and where was her elusive husband? Surely, he hadn't tired of the country already. Olivia took a large gulp of her champagne. It may well be a vintage but it lacked power to her taste, she thought grimly.

A pale woman with short blonde hair leapt out in to their path.

"You're needed, Marina darling, Brad is hunting for you." She looked across at Isobel. "Don't worry I'll take care of your guest."

Marina shot off to rescue Brad from whatever crisis was happening. The pale woman introduced herself. "Judy Matthews, friend of Marina's. We have known each other for years and you are most defiantly Isobel."

"Correct, it's good to meet you, Judy." It turned out that Judy was another equestrian expert. She had stables in Surrey, where she bred show jumpers, world class no less. Isobel was very impressed as she reeled off her list of successes. As she spoke, she became very animated throwing her arms around, then cackling at her own little jokes. Isobel smiled sweetly and nodded between her frantic sentences, but it was becoming rather boring. Eventually Isobel excused herself by pretending to recognise someone at the other side of the room and bid Judy farewell for the time being at least, she hoped.

A large group of guys exploded into the drawing room, most of them appeared fairly drunk. A mousy woman standing to Isobel's left quickly explained they were Brad's friends from public school. A rowdy drunken lot, as she put it. "All total womanisers. Give them a wide berth if I was you, love, they have been known to get very boisterous." She raised a knowing, fuzzy, in need of a trim brow. Isobel took a few moments to look around at the other guests. Mostly under fifty, she decided. There were a few older couples, who seemed to know each other and were loitering together, in their own exclusive gathering. Judy caught up with her again. "See the gang have arrived," she signalled to Brad's rowdy friends. "They will probably be stripped off and in the pool before the night's out, well let's hope so," she added, bursting into a deep throaty cackle.

"Who's that talking to Graham?"

"Now that is Carmen Franklin, surprised you haven't met already, wicked sense of humour that one."

"As a matter of fact I have, briefly," she replied, watching as Carmen, who stood chatting to Graham Pearson, literally bounced on the spot in front of him. "Nice girl goes on a bit though. Take you over to say hello if you like?" Politely Isobel declined, and then made a second getaway.

The band had eased tempo, Brad grabbed hold of Isobel's wrist. "Fancy a dance, honey?" Isobel nodded it was much more preferable smooching with Brad, than being caught up with Judy.

"Bet your old man was gutted that he couldn't be here."

Isobel nodded. "Yes, I feel a bit guilty to be honest."

"Don't be you—" Brad didn't get chance to finish his sentence, as one of his mates crept in between him and Isobel, sweeping her off in the opposite direction. Brad shrugged; admitting defeat then went off in search of his dear wife who seemed to be very good at avoiding him this evening.

Isobel managed a couple of dances with Geoff, whom she had managed to find out a fair bit about in a very short space of time. He seemed a really nice guy, liked to talk about himself a lot though. She was just beginning to relax when Graham appeared and very reluctantly, she found herself being pressed into his eager clutch. It was certainly an experience, and not a pleasant one. The overpowering smell of garlic on his breath, made her want to retch. Graham tried his hardest in the short time he had her to extract as much information as he could, but she managed to skirt most questions or offered very brief answers. Much to her relief Carmen appeared to claim him, as the music livened up once more.

Isobel parched, and with aching calf muscles, headed off in search of a drink. At the bar she downed a large vodka. John Jacobs, an owner of one of the horses, came and stood by her chatting about how wonderful Marina and Brad were, how they had saved his marriage, not only that, but his prize mare as well. Isobel knew the mare, Bustinette; she also knew that Brad and Marina had done nothing to calm the mare's fiery temperament other than to remove her from John's hellish stables, where his heavy handed groom had taken much of her spirit.

Isobel escaped to the toilet. Heading down the hallway she bumped into Carmen, who had emerged from the bathroom, her lobster pink cheeks, all aglow. Isobel jumped in surprise, just as she was about to enter the bathroom, Graham emerged hastily tucking in his shirt-tails, winking as he hurried past her. As Isobel sat down on the loo she let out a giggle, guess it wouldn't be a proper party without somebody nipping off for shag.

Olivia found herself a quiet corner where she could line up a chaser of drinks, and survey the action from the shadows. Graham had been missing for some time now, it wasn't hard to guess whom he was with, but hey, her time would come. When she did set eyes on him again he was removing his jacket to join a group of Brad's trendies, dancing to some favourite seventies hits, Olivia outwardly groaned with embarrassment. Carmen however had made her way to the food; Olivia thought she might join her even though she wasn't the least bit peckish. She found Carmen heaping dollops of everything onto her plate.

"Looks tasty, how about leaving some for everyone else," Olivia said, haughtily.

"Oh hi, Olivia, how are you enjoying the party?"

"Yes, very nice. Can you really eat all of that?" Olivia looked at the overloaded plate Carmen balanced on her arm, with distaste. Carmen didn't take offence, merely handed a clean plate to Olivia. She waved it away screwing up her nose.

"Thanks, but no thanks I am not as lucky as you, darling. I eat it, I wear it if you know what I mean." Then cupping her hand to her mouth, she feigned a look of horror.

"Sorry, how rude, you're the last person I should have said that to." She beamed at Carmen and everyone else in earshot. Carmen, who was positively squirming, gave a faint smile then made a rapid retreat out to the garden, to polish off her nosh in private.

Isobel was feeling rather tipsy, her vision was beginning to blur. The tall of Brad's mates asked her to dance. Jason as it turned out seemed quite a pleasant guy. He owned an antiques shop in Salcombe. He wasn't around long, much to Isobel's annoyance. Carmen came and poached him from under her nose. "Must be my turn," she shrilled, hopping from one foot to another.

Isobel slid away from the dance floor, food is what she needed now, to soak up the alcohol a bit. As she manoeuvred carefully past the pool an arm slid around her waist. Perturbed she spun round with an angry glare, expecting to see Graham grinning at her. Instead a sexy, familiar voice, whispered in her ear, "What would be my chances of a dance with the most beautiful woman here tonight?" Deep brown eyes, flecked with gold, gazed down at her seductively. Despite the glut of alcohol coursing through her veins Isobel felt a sudden panic; it was him.

"You do remember me, don't you?" He pulled her towards him, out of the path of other guests heading towards the food. Isobel was staring, she knew she was, but that was all she could do.

"So how did he like the trousers?" Speechless Isobel managed to nod, as he skilfully led her through the crowd on to the dance floor.

Slipping his strong arms firmly around her waist, he pulled her in closer, gently moulding his body against hers. Dancing was easy with him he even seemed to guide her clumsy feet in the right direction. Adam's body was warming, somehow sensual against hers, his breath smelt sweet, it was warm against her flushed cheek. As they danced Adam's hands slid comfortably down to her buttocks, where he let them rest lightly. Isobel gazed wildly around, nobody seemed to notice, they were all too busy enjoying themselves. There was the teeniest feeling of guilt, yet it wasn't uncomfortable, quite the contrary. Hesitantly, she began to relax slowly letting go. There was a natural urge to place her head on his shoulder, instead she looked up above, where the lights twinkled down at her and the balloons swayed in the gentle breeze that blew in through the French window. *I will never forget this moment*, she thought dreamily; *it's so romantic*. What was it with this guy? Marriage and motherhood seemed a million miles away. The music changed, Isobel drew back with a sudden air of reluctance. "Shall we get a drink?" She led the way to the bar, turning to speak to Adam but he had been collared by Brad who was dragging him off towards the kitchen.

Marina appeared looking slightly dishevelled but smiling. "Hey you're looking a bit pensive." She nudged Isobel playfully.

Isobel laughed. "You always seem to be saying that to me."

"Well you are, anyway saw you dancing with the rather yummy Adam Docherty."

"Yes, I was rather enjoying it too. How well do you know him?" she enquired.

"I don't really, more a friend of Brad's; he buys a lot of clothes from Adam's shop."

"I know." Isobel took a gulp of champagne." That's where I met him, when I went to buy Jacob some trousers for tonight."

Marina laughed. "You seem to be getting very well acquainted." She drained her glass of punch. "God that's strong." She grimaced at the taste. "Well, Adam's certainly a bit of a dish."

Smiling thoughtfully, Isobel peered over the rim of her glass at her, replying, "He most certainly is." Then she giggled. "Gosh don't tell anyone I said that."

Isobel scolded herself for feeling disappointment at Adam being hogged by the lads. Graham appeared at her side, in a fluster. "We are leaving shortly," he informed her. "Can we offer you a lift?" Isobel supposed she should accept and found Brad and Marina to thank them both for a great party then reluctantly she left with the delightful Pearsons.

Perched uncomfortably on the back seat of Graham's car, she sat silently as they sped along the winding lanes. Isobel watched Olivia, who sat stony faced for the entire journey, while Graham sang very loudly and out of tune to the Rolling Stones CD that was playing. Every so often he would grin at Isobel in the rearview mirror, making her feel even more nauseous than she already was.

With great relief, Isobel climbed out, glad that she hadn't thrown up in their posh car. They dropped her at the front door, she slipped in quietly, undressed in the darkness then wearily climbed into bed but she couldn't sleep. Tossing and turning restlessly, she struggled to come to terms with how she had felt earlier. She loved Jacob with all her heart, so how could such powerful feelings unleash within her. She and Jacob hadn't spent much time together lately, but then surely that would make them grow stronger and long for the times that they were together. Isobel knew only to well that she wasn't feeling that way, in fact rather the opposite. She was, she thought, with a sickening realisation, beginning to detach herself from the situation. Making a new life, one in which it seemed that Jacob didn't figure much anymore.

Brad was horrified when he struggled out of bed at six a.m. after only three hours sleep.

The mess downstairs was unbelievable; it must have been one hell of a party. There were glasses everywhere, ashtrays overflowing; the pool was full of debris. Marina softly padded up behind him as he stood scratching his head wondering where to start.

"Don't worry, I have sorted the caterers to come back and deal with this lot."

Brad looked back at her bleary eyed. "That cheers me up no end." He pulled Marina in towards him and resting his head on her shoulder said, "But I still have to go out and feed all those hungry horses."

"It won't hurt if you leave it a bit longer." She looked up at him eyes twinkling.

"Well I am up now, so." He gave a weary sigh. "I may as well get my skates on."

"Perhaps I have a better offer." Marina let her silk wrap, slip to the ground then leant forward kissing Brad passionately. As knackered as he felt there was no way he could resist her.

"I drank a fair bit last night and I haven't had much sleep, I think I'm going to need a hand." Gently he pushed her down towards his crotch. Willingly she leant down taking him in her mouth; it didn't take long to arouse him. As Marina sat astride her husband bouncing blissfully up and down she was totally unaware that some of the caterers had arrived to clear up. Surprised by the early morning rumpus, they stood back in the shadows watching the display with great interest.

CHAPTER SEVEN

All that remained of the heavy snowfall was the odd icy patch that lurked beneath the hedgerows, along the lane. The farm was looking particularly bleak; the fields parched by the heavy frost. Christmas Day dawned cloudy and grey. Olan and Maria had arrived late Christmas Eve and after sharing several bottles of very good red, were now sleeping soundly in the guest room.

Edward was the first awake, eager to see what Santa had brought for him. Excitedly he bounded into Isobel and Jacob's room with a stocking full of presents. They watched, sleepily, as Edward tore open the beautifully wrapped parcels squealing with delight at their contents. It didn't take more than 5 minutes for him to have them all open and a large pile of paper lay strewn across the floor.

Jacob went downstairs to make hot drinks. He returned carrying a large tray with warm croissants, a pot of coffee and two glasses of Bucks Fizz not forgetting chocolate milk for Edward. Isobel sipped her coffee, propped up on her pillow she watched Edward play. The wonderful thing about Christmas Day was that everybody would be in high spirits. Isobel pulled two parcels from her bedside drawer and handed them to Jacob.

"Wow what's this?" He kissed Isobel's cheek, before tearing at the brightly coloured paper. The first was a solid silver photo frame with a beautiful picture of Edward in it. Edward was sat on a sledge with Tarquin and Sadie holding the rope in their mouths pulling him along.

"Hey that's great, how did you get them to do that?"

"With great difficulty!" she declared. "Come on open the other one," she urged. Jacob arched his brow in surprise, as he opened the lid of the velvet box, to reveal an exquisite pair of platinum cuff links. He placed them delicately in the palm of his hand.

"Thanks, honey, just what I needed." He looked across at Isobel. "We can afford them, can't we?" he said, jokingly, and festively grinned from ear to ear.

"I found them at this wonderful little jeweller, which I discovered in Marchton, on the way to the Equine clinic, with Marina."

"I love them, thank you, Isobel."

Isobel wondered if there was a present for her, obviously not, as Jacob suggested that they should get dressed and wait for Olan and Maria to get up. He headed off downstairs, muttering about lighting the fire. Isobel drained her coffee and climbed into the shower. It wasn't until the powerful jet of water pounded her body, that she began to feel properly awake and able to fully embrace the first Christmas Day at Orange Stream.

Jacob would be cooking Christmas lunch, it was a family tradition, Maria had insisted on helping. Isobel didn't mind in the least, it would be a relaxing day for her. However she had insisted that they take a pre lunch stroll across the fields, to really build up their appetites. Neither Jacob, nor Olan was very keen on walking, reluctantly they had agreed. Edward appeared pulling back the shower curtain, a buttery piece of toast wedged between he's fingers.

"Daddy, wants you to hurry up."

"Oh does he now. Tell him I'll be down in ten minutes." Edward hurried off, two salivating dogs in tow.

Carmen awoke with a sore head, parched throat and furry tongue. Christmas Eve had been spent with a group of mates in the only wine bar in Marchton. Yawning, she turned over to face the sleeping mass to her left. It was all drifting back. Gareth Faulkes, they had dated a few years back. That was until he had dropped her for a surprisingly older model, one that conveniently had a lot of cash. They had, she recalled, consumed countless bottles of house red and plates of smelly French cheese. They must have got back to hers some time around two, very drunk, but amazingly not so that they couldn't spend two hours indulging in some rather mucky sex, which had included various props, in the main, a tub of cream cheese and a rather limp carrot, fished from the depths of her overcrowded fridge.

Carmen prodded him sharply in the back. "Come on, superman. Wake up!" She tickled him under the ribs. "I'm going to make a brew and then we can finish what we started," she cackled. "As I recall I never got all the way and I'm feeling rather cheated." She flounced off to the kitchen. There was a muffled groan from beneath the bed covers.

"Don't forget the bacon butties, love, it is Christmas."

"For Christ sake, get up, woman, it's Christmas Day!" Graham shouted through the bedroom doorway at Olivia who was choosing to ignore him.

Why the hell should she, what the hell was so special about it anyway? Olivia managed to lift her head briefly and glance at the bedside clock. It was ten to eleven. Ten more minutes, she thought to herself, and then snuggled indulgently back beneath the covers.

Graham came bashing back up the stairs he stormed into the room. "I just went to put the turkey in."

Olivia buried her head deeper in to the pillow. Insistent, Graham moved up the side of the bed.

"Did you hear me, Olivia?" His voice rang with anger.

"What, dear?" Olivia managed to croak.

"Turkey, dear, except it appears no turkey in this case," Graham screeched at her. "Tell me that I'm wrong, that you've put it some place else, in the cellar perhaps?"

Wearily Olivia sat up; her cold blue eyes met his, which were rampant with rage. "Yes, you're right," she said, calmly. "There is no fucking turkey, so there." She stuck her tongue out at him then settled back down. Graham slammed the door as he left, cursing loudly as he went crashing downstairs.

Although Olivia had behaved with defiance, her bottom lip began to tremble. There was nothing merry about today, but then there wasn't about any other day. She could pretend to everybody else that it didn't hurt, but right now it did, it hurt like hell.

"Coats on, everybody, wrap up warm, it's freezing out." Jacob jollied everyone along, he was becoming impatient. Like sheep they followed him out of the front door, into the icy morning. At Jacob's insistence they walked around the back of the house, along the drive, even though, as Isobel pointed out, it would have been far quicker to slip through the back fence.

"No follow me. I want to show Olan and Maria the barn and stables." He spoke with a bossy air, daring her to challenge him. Edward clenched Isobel's hand on one side and Maria's on the other. You could hardly see his little face, as his coat was zipped up past his chin and his woolly hat was pulled down past his forehead. Jacob sauntered ahead stopping at the stables, babbling at Olan, who didn't seem to be too enthusiastic about the history of the old buildings. Isobel caught up, Olan was smiling, at her with a questioning gaze, she smiled back blankly.

"Sorry did I miss something?" she asked.

"Yes, darling, you did," Jacob snapped, impatient. "Olan was I believe asking you a question."

Isobel smiled apologetically. "So sorry, Olan, I didn't catch that."

Olan puffed into his cupped hands, rubbing them together briskly.

"I was just wondering what you call the horse."

She looked across at Jacob puzzled, he smiled back at her through chattering blue lips, and confused she looked back at Olan, who took a step to the side. Isobel found herself gawping in astonishment. The stables were not shut up, as they normally were, but even more surprisingly a familiar horse's head hung over one door looking at them expectantly, a beautiful bay, with an unmistakeable white blob on the left side of his nose. "It's Quest," she squealed in excitement, then paused to look back at Jacob with a huge grin.

"Happy Christmas, darling, I hope you were serious when you said that you adored him."

Disbelief followed by utter joy surged through her frozen limbs as she flung herself into Jacob's arms.

"Thank you, darling, oh thank you so much," she sobbed. Smothering Jacob's frozen mouth, with warm, grateful kisses.

"He's probably hungry, I haven't fed him this morning, just chucked some more hay in, before I came up to bed last night." He smiled. "You know, I think he likes me."

Isobel rushed in to the stable flinging her arms around Quest's silky neck, planting kisses on his soft muzzle.

Jacob appeared at the doorway. "The surprise doesn't end here, come and look, love." The whole of the tack room had been kitted out, a saddle rack had been fitted which held all Quest's gleaming tack. Feed bins had been installed which were full of food, there were new shiny buckets, a grooming kit and a wooden rail with new rugs folded neatly over them. "Apparently everything you need is here; I left it all pretty much to Marina." Jacob smiled smugly.

"How in lord's name, have you managed to do all this, without me finding out?" Isobel asked incredulous.

"Yesterday morning when you slipped into town, Brad bought the whole lot over. We were amazed that you didn't suss us, fortunately young Quest here remained quiet. We thought that he would give the game away." He patted his neck proudly.

Isobel threw her head back laughing. "Oh, Jacob, you're the best."

Isobel gave quest a feed, straightened his rug, added more hay to the rack and fetched a fresh bucket of water. Then after a few more kisses prised herself away to continue on their walk. They walked across the fields, Jacob linked arms with her. "Oh and another thing, darling, Brad, Marina and Molly will be joining us for Christmas lunch. So you can say your thank yous then. Is that OK?"

Isobel punched Jacob's arm playfully. "You bet it is!"

After downing a few scotches from the comfort of the old faded armchair, Graham gave up waiting for Olivia to surface. He pulled on his boots and Rutland jacket, left the house and climbed into the Jag. As Olivia didn't seem to want to offer any sort of company, he would seek solace somewhere else. Carmen would be bound to be feeling lonely on a day like this; he would give her a nice surprise.

Carmen opened the door her usual smiling self. "Hi there, didn't expect to see you today, love." She took Graham's coat and hung it on the peg, pausing to catch her breath. Gareth had only been gone 15 minutes. Thank goodness, she had had the foresight to dive straight in to the shower.

"Something smells good." Graham's mouth watered, he was starving.

"You haven't eaten yet then?"

"No. Not by choice though, I hasten to add."

"Well it's nothing much, I have a duck roasting, a few spuds and some veggies."

"Sounds delicious!" Graham salivated, as he placed a couple of bottles of wine on the table that he had brought along with him. "There," he gave a satisfied grin, "something nice, to wash it down with."

"Yummy." Carmen passed him the corkscrew. "Dinner will be another hour, shall we have a glass?"

"Excellent idea!" Graham slapped Carmen's bottom as she passed by.

She patted the space on the sofa next to her. "Come on sit down and relax, we can have a cosy afternoon together."

Carmen's simple Christmas dinner was surprisingly good. When the two bottles of wine had been drunk, Carmen came up trumps, fishing out a magnum of Moet which had been gathering dust in a cupboard beneath the stairs.

"Won this last year in a show jumping competition." She held it up triumphantly for him to see. "I knew the perfect occasion would come along, in which to demolish it." She gave a devilish laugh.

Graham prised the bottle from her clutch. "Oh it's fairly cool, that's good, nothing worse than warm champagne." He grabbed two glasses from the dresser. "Fancy drinking this in bed?"

Giggling wildly, Carmen followed him upstairs.

Graham placed the bottle down on the bedside table, next to the tub of cream cheese, which he looked at curiously. "Shouldn't that be in the fridge?"

"Midnight snacks." Carmen removed it, sheepishly.

"Hang on not so fast." Graham chuckled. I might find a good use for that in a bit." He winked suggestively.

Carmen groaned. She had only just cleansed herself from the smell of the last basting.

Olivia rose from her sweaty bed sheets, a little after five. Graham was out; it was not hard to imagine where he had gone. Olivia took a shower then dressed in a sweater and casual trousers, she went down to the cellar to fetch a bottle of wine, observing that supplies were becoming dangerously low. Olivia hoped Graham hadn't been down recently, he would be livid.

What a great Christmas Day it had been, the phone had rung several times but she had chosen to ignore it. It was most probably her mother, ringing from her sun bed by the pool in the Caribbean. Perhaps, she mused, that she would have fared better to join her, rather than be under Graham's feet, whom it seemed detested her, as much as she detested herself. Mind you she bloody well hated him too. Olivia stopped abruptly as she poured the Krug into her glass. Did she really hate him? Or was it the agonies that were forced upon her? It was amazing but somewhere inside Olivia wished that she could find the energy to try to make a go of her marriage. Olivia's hands began to shake, her throat tightened, if she hadn't spent the day wallowing in self-pity, and put in a bit of effort, the day may have been reasonably civilised.

Olivia put the bottle firmly down, if it was possible to try again the last thing she needed was to start drinking. Instead Olivia put on her jacket, grabbed the car keys and headed out in to the cold evening.

At Orange Stream Farm a serious game of Pictionary was under way. Marina was getting very excited, as she had guessed every one of Brad's sketches and they were firmly in the lead.

"You're too slow." Isobel wailed at Jacob. "We are trailing badly."

"Maybe that's because I am tired, that's my excuse anyway. It's all that toiling over a hot stove." He winked at Maria. "It was tough, eh?" Maria smiled back, nodding in agreement. It was true they had surpassed themselves with the delicate crab and avocado mousses, followed by the traditional turkey dinner and for those that couldn't manage the sticky

Christmas pudding with extra brandy there were dark chocolate baskets, filled with ginger syllabub.

Marina's daughter Molly was quite charming; nothing like Isobel had imagined her to be. Anyone could see that there was no closeness between mother and daughter, but they both seemed to be trying hard, for everybody else's sake. In her own right Molly was a charming and helpful thirteen-year-old, it appeared that she would never be as beautiful as her mother, but there was that same genuine warmth. Isobel found her very easy to get along with. Edward was very taken with her; Isobel had had to tell him off, he didn't give the poor girl a moment's peace, pulling at her arm and insisting that she help him set up all his new games. Molly was more than happy, despite all of this, to go up and read him a bedtime story. As Edward finally slept they sat comfortably around the fire chatting and sipping warmed brandy. Isobel may have had some misgivings about their first Christmas in Devon, but this one had proved to be truly magical.

It was a little after midnight Isobel lay awake, Jacob slept soundly beside her. She looked across at him lovingly, how she could have thought that they were distancing, and he had made every effort to impress, to make their first Christmas here truly wonderful. How selfish she had been.

Olivia drove sedately along the lanes that led to Carmen's, gathering her thoughts as she did so. Perhaps it was better to forgive all the infidelities, wipe the slate clean. After all it had been very bearable, once, a long, long time ago. Graham wasn't incapable of being tender and loving, if she handled the situation correctly, if he could forgive her, for acting such a bitch. As she drew ever nearer to Briars Lodge, her confidence began to fail her. Was she having a complete moment of madness? As she pulled up outside, the beam of her headlights illuminated Graham's Jag, there was no turning back now. Olivia switched off the engine; she sat motionless, for a few moments. It was deadly quiet, how foolish she had been, expecting Graham to emerge sheepishly, on hearing her car. Olivia got out, on shaky legs. Swallowing hard, she headed to the front door. Whatever else happened she must not lose her cool.

Graham and Carmen frolicked passionately on the old dilapidated bed, blissfully unaware of their impending visitor. Olivia knocked but there was no answer, it was easy this time having been here before. Calmly she went upstairs to the open doorway; somewhat detached she saw her husband's naked body snaking rhythmically along Carmen's.

93

Carmen was the first to notice Olivia, standing there in the shadows a painfully haunting expression cast across her face.

"Oh, my God, it's Olivia." Carmen quickly tried to hide her nakedness, scrabbling at the sheets. Graham's eyes followed Carmen's horrified stare, the rosy glow on his cheeks bought about by sexual assertion, drained to leave him pale and ghostly.

Olivia stepped in to the room, twisting her locked hands nervously in front of her. Carmen darted for the wardrobe desperate for something to sling on, leaving Graham with the crumpled sheet as his only defence. At that moment Olivia felt immensely powerful, the sheer terror in both of their faces, it was almost, laughable really.

Graham spoke first. "It's not what you—"

Olivia held up both hands. "Please, Graham, spare me, I have known for ages." She paused to smile wryly across at Carmen. "It doesn't hurt anymore; you're not the first you see." She glared at Carmen. "If you don't mind, I would like a word, alone, with my husband."

Carmen scurried off in her dressing gown, in need of a stiff drink, her eyes lowered to the floor as she passed by Olivia.

"Look, Olivia." Graham's face was scarlet and Olivia could tell by his tone that he was brewing for a fight.

Olivia stood her ground. "We can make a big deal of this but I'd rather we didn't." She ran her fingers through her silky hair and then looked deeply into Graham's wary eyes. "I suppose from the way I have been behaving lately, that this was to be expected."

Graham nodded his head in agreement, watching her suspiciously, as she came over to sit wearily beside him on the bed. She seemed so calm, considering he had been caught in the act.

"I would like to try and start afresh." Olivia looked across at him almost pleadingly. "You don't have to answer now, just get dressed, then come home and we can talk." Graham bowed his head; this was the last thing he had expected. Olivia stood up, smoothing her hands down her trousers. "So you will meet me back at home then?"

Silently, he nodded. For the first time he saw the immense sadness in Olivia's eyes and felt overcome with guilt.

"Come on, Elizabeth, we'll have a right laugh."

"No, but it was really kind of you to ask."

"OK. Suit yourself but if you change your mind call." Elizabeth put down the telephone then sat for a while, staring into space. Elizabeth had never been very sociable, her main interest was the man in her life, and Elizabeth centred her world on partnerships. Dominic had broken her heart in two when he walked out of their flat in Clapham after living together for ten months. They had been planning to wed; their relationship was perfect or so she had thought. That was until he dropped the bombshell that he was leaving her for another woman, another woman who in fact turned out to be Elizabeth's boss, Analise Richmond.

Analise was fifteen years older than Elizabeth and for the life of her Elizabeth couldn't fathom out what Dominic saw in her. In fact there could only have been one thing, money, it was the only thing she had. Within twelve weeks of him leaving, Elizabeth had heard via a friend that he and Analise had married. This had been a few weeks before Christmas and needless to say it had been a miserable time for her.

Jonathan Hilliard looked anxiously at his daughter. "Anything the matter, love?"

"No." Elizabeth looked up at her father. "I'm fine, just thinking that's all."

"Your mother and I are having a glass of wine out in the conservatory, would you like to join us?"

Elizabeth smiled and followed her father through. *They must fear that they will never be free of me*, she thought, as she sat opposite them sipping warm wine.

Later she lay on her bed, glad to escape her parents' pitiful glances. Daydreaming about Jacob, she wondered, what he would be doing right now. Elizabeth wanted Jacob badly; she had made her mind up that she would seduce him, after the Christmas holidays. Yes it was wrong but she couldn't deny her feelings, nobody would find out, she would be discreet, Jacob's perfect mistress. She would offer him all the things that Isobel couldn't. She turned onto her side and looked out of the window; whatever he was doing, she would be willing to bet he had thought about her too. He felt it too she was sure, one could tell, she thought, licking her lips.

CHAPTER EIGHT

"Would you like to go out for a ride now, Molly?" Marina asked, casually.

"Mother, you know I don't ride too well, but don't let me stop you." Molly glared at her mother. Marina shifted uneasily. Molly always did this to her, made her feel stupid and a totally inadequate mother.

Marina seized her opportunity. "Well if you don't mind, you know we have a tradition of riding to the pub."

Molly looked at her in exasperation. "There's no need to explain, just go ahead."

Marina found Brad in the kitchen. "Molly won't join us, but she's happy for us to go."

"I don't know. She's just a kid perhaps I should stay here with her."

"Nonsense," Marina retorted. "She will be fine." She pulled on her riding boots. "Come on or we'll be late."

Brad watched Marina saunter across the lawn in the direction of the stables. He felt sorry for poor Molly; it was difficult not having your parents together, even harder when your stepmother treated you better than your natural mother. Molly didn't love Marina, Brad was sure of that; even so Molly was very loyal to her mother. Marina, on the other hand, did love Molly, even if she did try to deny it. Brad had noticed the way she looked at her child and he knew that it ripped her apart. Brad knew this because he knew Marina like the back of his hand; he could read her like a book.

Olivia awoke on Boxing Day with a sense of purpose. Graham had returned from Carmen's shortly after her and they had spent all night talking. Olivia wasn't sure if it would work but she was really going to try, Graham had certainly seemed keen to give it a try. Graham sat up in bed, leaning on one elbow and gazing across at her, Olivia smiled back at him.

"Darling, this is truly what you want, isn't it?"

"In the past, you treated me badly, I became frigid and uptight," she sighed. "We never talked about it, did we?"

"I know I behaved badly, but I always felt like you despised me, then I found out about you and Steve."

Olivia gasped in surprise. "You knew about that?"

"I thought you knew that I did. That surprises me. I felt you did it to get even and there wasn't a lot I could do, was there?" Graham watched Olivia's face closely as her eyes began to well with tears. "Please don't drink anymore, Olivia, it doesn't suit you, darling. If we try hard we can make this work," he begged. Gently he took her hand in his own. "We are worth the effort, we just need to put the past behind us." Softly he pressed his lips to hers; kissing her gingerly and somewhat cautiously, then he wrapped his arms protectively around her fragile body.

Olivia found herself overwhelmed by a deep sense of longing, a need to be held. Gently she removed the satin nightgown holding Graham's gaze as she did so.

"We need to make love." It was barely a whisper. It had been a long time, Olivia gave herself completely to Graham's soft exploring lips and fingertips and it was like beginning again. She had forgotten how good it could feel, she just needed to relax and forget all about Carmen.

Blowing out through his nostrils, Quest scraped restlessly at the tarmac while Isobel struggled to tighten the girths. Maria and Olan watched from a safe distance.

Maria laughed. "He looks keen to be off."

Isobel looked down at them all; gritting her teeth as she gave one last tug and managed to get the girth securely fastened another hole.

"So, I'll meet you all at the pub, about twelve." She looked across to Jacob who stood grinning back at her.

"You are OK with this?" she asked, sheepishly. "I feel really bad going off on this ride and deserting you all for the morning. I mean it is Boxing Day after all."

"Don't be daft, I didn't buy you the horse to stand in the stable all day. You have a good ride, love." Jacob patted Quest's neck. "You look after my girl, young man, and bring her home safely."

Isobel waved, as she set off at a brisk walk down the drive, Jacob stood watching proudly.

"You know, Olan, I am damn pleased with myself, she looks really happy, don't you think?"

"Certainly does, I don't profess to know much about horses but that sure as hell is a good-looking animal."

Jacob kicked idly at the gravel. "Isn't he just! Come on, folks, let's get back in the warm. Large whiskies all round, I think."

Isobel had allowed herself plenty of time to arrive at the designated meeting point, the old rail road where they would all join up for the leisurely ride to the Friars Inn. There was always a large turn out, she had been told. Marina had warned her about the return journey, when after too much champagne it turned into Peterbridges equivalent of the Grand National. In fact last year there had been three casualties. Isobel wasn't sure if she was up to it, it sounded pretty hairy. She rode Quest along on a fairly loose rein, she wanted him to fully stretch out and relax before meeting up with the others, they rode along a large field, then turned out on to the lane. Quest pricked up his ears at the sound of hooves clattering along the lane towards them. He began to jog in eager anticipation, Isobel gathered up her reins. There were two horses approaching, one of the riders cried out to her. "Hold on a minute, mind if we ride along with you?" As they drew nearer, Isobel recognised Carmen Franklin; the other rider was hanging slightly further back.

Isobel smiled. "Yes, that's fine, would be glad of some company," she said, looking over her shoulder as Carmen's horse trotted up alongside her. Carmen sat rosy cheeked and puffing, in the saddle.

"Hi, Isobel." She turned in her saddle to look back at her companion. "Have you met Adam, not sure if you have yet?"

"Oh I don't think so."

Adam, looking rather smug, caught up with them. "We most certainly have met, but I had no idea you rode, Isobel." He manoeuvred his horse, sharply in between Carmen's and Isobel's, forcing Carmen up on to the verge. Isobel felt her pulse quicken and tried not to appear too flustered.

"I never had you down as a rider either." She twiddled nervously with her reins, feeling suddenly self-conscious, focusing on Quest's black silky mane in front of her.

"Come on, guys." Carmen dug her heels into her sweaty chestnut's side. "We are going to be late if we don't get a move on." Carmen gave her mount an encouraging clucking sound, as she pushed on in to a trot. Isobel and Adam followed behind.

"This isn't my nag you know." Adam looked down at the handsome grey he rode. "Borrowed him from Carmen, bless her, for the ride today." He looked across at Quest. "Handsome horse, is he yours?"

"Yes, I just brought him," Isobel heard herself say.

Carmen yelled back to them, from her lead way ahead.

"Think we're in trouble." Adam winked at Isobel.

Isobel gave an inward groan. Jacob and the others would be waiting. It was awful, she wished that they wouldn't be there and she hated herself for thinking it. Gathering up her reins, she squeezed Quest forward, to catch up with Carmen, who was shouting obscenities over her shoulder at them. Adam held back a little so that he could observe Isobel, he noticed how firm she sat in the saddle, and to think he nearly didn't come along today. Oh how very glad he was that he had.

"Lee, you pompous bastard." Graham dug his shiny spurs, deep into Solvent's sides, steering him towards a fair-haired guy, sat astride an old-fashioned dapple-grey cob. Carmen watched from the trees. Poor Solvent, he was so hard on him. Graham hadn't learnt a thing, now poor Solvent would suffer. The cheeky git had left yesterday without saying a single solitary word, Carmen was not amused.

Brad and Marina arrived impeccably dressed on the best looking mounts. Marina spotted Isobel waving madly, she rode over to her. "Hi, darling, how's your head today? Mine is exploding after all that booze up at your place." Marina grinned. "Your husband's got a lot to answer for, getting me so pissed."

Isobel giggled. "Jacob's good at that, I think Olan's feeling pretty rough this morning too."

Marina straightened the black bowler on her head. She winked at Isobel. "Not too many drinkies here, it's the charge of the light brigade on the way home."

Isobel rode the last few hundred yards to the pub alongside Marina. Adam had disappeared much to Isobel's relief. Brad was caught up in conversation with a pretty young woman on a delicately limbed Palomino. The pub car park was packed, Isobel spotted Jacob with Olan and Maria, sandwiched between layers of warm clothing and leaning on the Mercedes. Olivia was parked next to them in the Range Rover; she was staying in the warmth of the car. Isobel halted Quest by the car and slid down into Jacob's arms where he gave her a big hug.

"God ,you're freezing and this is meant to be fun, is it?" He looked around at the other riders with their teeth chattering and bright red noses.

Olivia appeared beside them. "Hey, that's a beautiful horse."

Isobel looked at her in surprise. "Thank you, Olivia, Jacob brought him for me for Christmas."

The Friars Arms car park was filled with the sounds of raucous laughter, snorting horses and the warming smell of brandy, which was being brought round on trays and offered free to all the riders. The brandy warmed Isobel's tummy, gradually returning some life to her frozen body. Olivia stayed with them smiling warmly at everybody; Isobel couldn't believe the difference in the woman since their last meeting. Carmen was most surprised, as she passed by Olivia, who smiled sweetly up at her and said, "You look cold, love." Olivia whipped a glass of brandy from a passing tray, and pushed it firmly in to Carmen's hand. "There that will bring you back to life." Carmen accepted with a limp smile then made a hasty retreat back from where she had come from.

"Don't have too much of that, eh, love?" Jacob signaled to the large glass in Isobel's hand. "You have to make it back yet."

Isobel pulled a sarcastic face. "Whatever you say, honey."

The hour at the pub passed quickly. Marina helped a red faced, jovial Brad back into the saddle.

"Hey, Isobel, everybody's coming back to ours for some more booze later, you will too, won't you?" Isobel shook her head, she rode up alongside him. "I really would love to but Maria is cooking lunch for all of us, I daren't." Isobel turned to wave to Jacob, then she followed the others in to the field opposite the pub.

Marina had disappeared to the front of the field; Isobel found herself jostling along at the rear with people she hadn't met before. A silver-haired lady on a small bay smiled, reining her horse across, she leant forward. "In my experience this is the best place to be, let all the loonies bomb off." She gave a frantic, clucking sound, aimed at her mount, who she was trying to keep alongside Quest, her horse flattened its ears, making a beastly face in protest. Ignoring it, the woman went on.

"I will warn you now, once we reach the bottom of this hill it's let loose time." She tapped her nose. "Stay well back, there will be ousted riders littering the hillside on your descent, and you've just got to try and dodge them." She let out a rapturous laugh. "Good luck!"

Isobel's eyes widened, her stomach churned. The woman smiled. "It's your first time?"

Isobel nodded anxiously.

"Don't be alarmed. I'm willing to take a bet you will be here next year, it is most exciting."

Isobel looked down the hill ahead of her, the riders had dispersed into smaller groups and you could cut the air with a knife. The horses sensed it too, especially those that had been there before. They began to tremble, jogging on the spot, restless to be off. Quest began to sweat; he threw his head violently in the air, chomping at the bit. Carmen was bouncing along at the edge of the field towards the front, excitement hung heavily in the air of the cold winter morning. Isobel shortened her reins, checked her helmet was secure, and then broke into a gentle canter, instinctively scanning the riders ahead for any sign of Adam. It took a while but her heart leapt as she spotted him up ahead, a couple of horses behind Brad.

Suddenly like bullets fired from a gun the horses at the front were away, the thundering of hooves on the hard ground quite deafening as it broke the restless calm. Quest began to snake sideways, fighting Isobel's firm hold. It took all of her strength to keep a hold of him, as she looked ahead, taking in sharp gulps of icy air. The leaders were already at the base of the hill, heading on towards the dark shroud of trees. A loose horse was amongst them, the wind stinging at her eyes meant that she failed to see the deposited rider and galloped on past oblivious.

Horses galloped either side of her, she couldn't hold Quest any longer, letting him have more of his head he surged powerfully beneath her, and the sheer force of him took her breath away. Free from restraint, he stuck his head out, powerfully buckling his rear quarters beneath himself as he propelled them forwards. They approached the wood where a few rider-less horses stood, their reins dangling to the floor, blowing heavily through flared nostrils. Isobel took a deep breath of pine scented air, sticky beads of sweat clung between her breasts.

Following the sandy pathway, which began to narrow, she brought Quest back to a slower pace; he didn't fight her this time after the exertion of the hillside. There was a large fallen tree across the pathway, Quest approached it gallantly and she scrunched her fingers into his mane for extra support as he sailed effortlessly over. Ecstatic Isobel clapped his warm sweaty neck. The path continued, eventually widening out in to a large field, enclosed by a hawthorn hedge on the right hand side. Isobel followed the horses ahead, gaining on them all the time as she did so; it was hard to stop the broad grin spreading across her face. Brad was on foot a couple of yards ahead he waved cheerfully as she passed.

"Are you OK?" Isobel's voice was lost on the wind.

Brad smiled indicating all was OK. Following along the hedge which curved right handed the ground seemed more rutted, reluctantly Isobel slowed up, she didn't want to damage her horse's legs. The final run was now in sight, below her at the bottom of the gently shelving field, there was a large meadow which ran up towards Peterbridge. It rose gently for about a mile to a plateau, it was here that the entrance to the lane would be and the first rider to the plateau would be declared the winner. Isobel was quite aware that there was no chance of her winning, but if she pushed on now she could hope to be in the first twenty, unscathed at least. Isobel softened her hands, squeezing Quest's sides encouragingly. Obliging he powered on ahead, joyously devouring the rock hard December earth. The rustic fencing flew past the corner of her eye as a brown streak, watching the ground ahead for ruts she steered him on up the incline to home. Each horse and rider had adopted their own route across this final field. Her jaw set in grim determination she drummed her heels lightly against Quest's now foamy sides. The waiting riders were so close now, with a final drain of effort they flew to the top of the plateau to a round of applause. It took a while to pull him up, Isobel circled around by the trees, slowly coming back to a walk, she kept him circling to cool down as he blew heavily from his exertions.

Marina trotted over laughing. "Oh well done, I counted you in, you were eleventh."

"Really, I can't believe it." She looked around at the others, sat astride their heaving horses, every time a rider came in there was a lot of whooping and clapping.

"You haven't seen Brad anywhere, Isobel?" There was a note of concern in Marina's voice as she pulled alongside her.

"Oh yeah, he's fine but he has lost his mount."

"Oh, bloody idiot, too much champagne, I knew he would come off."

"Where did you come in?" she asked.

Marina took off her bowler to give her scalp a good itch. "Fourth!"

"Hey brilliant, bet you're pleased."

"Not really, one down on last year. But guess what, Carmen Franklin came second; her face is so red it looks like she may explode at any moment. Max Greenfield won again third year running. He's a point to pointer, so a bit unfair." She pulled a face.

"What about Adam?" Isobel feigned vague interest.

"Oh, he was about sixth, him and Carmen have gone back to see to their horses." She paused to scan the field for Brad. "I believe they're coming back to ours though for drinks."

Isobel brought Quest to a halt, thoughtful for a while. "Maybe I could come back, if it would be alright to leave Quest at yours for the night?"

"Course you can, darling." Marina smiled. "You can call Jacob from our place. He won't mind if you stay a bit, will he?"

Isobel wasn't quite so sure, but the lure of Adam was far too strong to resist, it would be worth getting into trouble, just this once she decided.

"Look, Brad may have decided to head home. Let's go on, it's bitterly cold," Marina said. They rode back steadily letting their horses have full rein to stretch their aching muscles. They arrived back, and immediately attended to their loyal mounts. Isobel wiped Quest down, then borrowed a rug, to keep him warm, she gave him some water and filled a large hay net for him to munch on, pleased with their joint effort.

Back up at the house, the young blonde was waiting with her husband, Isobel later found out, that they were Lillian and Simon Mantalla, city slickers who came down to the country when work would allow. Carmen and Adam were there too, along with Dick Waters, the local huntsman. Molly was taking good care of everyone supplying drinks and making endless rounds of salmon sarnies.

Molly smiled up at Isobel. "Good ride?"

"Oh yes thanks, Molly, I really enjoyed it, any sign of Brad yet?"

Molly looked alarmed. "No." Her face paled. "Is he OK?"

"Oh sure, don't panic, he fell off, so he's leading his horse back, just takes a while on foot that's all."

Brad finally made it home leading a badly lame Bronson. Marina left the gathering to check on her husband. Isobel found her self alone in the kitchen washing up; Adam joined her at the sink. "Hear you had a great ride."

"Yes, I did it was great fun."

"Not bad for a first timer," he teased. "Not bad at all." He took a slug of whisky. "In fact I think the first time I went I landed on my arse rather unceremoniously."

Isobel giggled. "Thank god that didn't happen to me." Turning to smile up at him, she felt instantly weak at the knees.

"Brad and Marina are taking a long time. Do you think everything's OK?" He looked concerned.

Isobel nodded. "He thinks a lot of that old horse; I think he was rather brave to risk him in the first place." She finished her brandy. "I think I better go and check my horse, I have to leave soon."

Adam took her arm. "Hang on I'll come with you, and see what's happening with Brad."

Isobel walked alongside him, down to the stables, stealing a glance in his direction, every now and then. It was strange to see him in riding gear, and not done up, like she had seen him at the shop and then again at the party. Brad was in the barn hosing Bronson's leg; he looked up as they entered.

Brad shook his head. "God it's bloody swollen, reckon I might have to get the vet out in the morning."

"Ouch, it looks bad." Isobel crouched down to inspect Bronson's right fore.

"Are you waiting to get off?" Brad looked helplessly up at Adam.

"Yeah sorry, mate, have an engagement you know how it is."

Carmen appeared with a cold poultice from the tack room.

Brad looked up at her. "Better let you go, Adam's got to be somewhere."

"OK, just let me give you a hand with this, Marina's had to go and check on everyone up at the house."

Isobel cleared her throat and asked, "Carmen, would you mind dropping me off on your way."

"Course I can, give me ten minutes and we can go."

"Thanks, I'll just go and say goodbye to my trusty steed."

Isobel refilled Quest's hay net. He was standing dozing at the back of the stable. She ran her hands down his legs. Good, she breathed, there was no sign of any heat or swelling.

"Thank you for giving me such a wonderful ride." She kissed his velvet muzzle scratching him affectionately behind the ears.

"Lucky creature, I am insanely jealous." Isobel whirled around. Adam was watching her across the stable door.

"May I?" He signaled to come in. Silently she nodded; he came over and stroked Quest's neck. "He is a beautiful specimen, bet he cost you a small fortune."

Isobel shrugged. "Yes a fair bit."

"Probably a bit more than a pair of my trousers," he joked.

Isobel blushed. "Just a little bit." She held two fingers a short distance apart.

Adam's gaze softened as he looked at Isobel. "You are very beautiful too."

Isobel felt herself blush, she looked away.

"Sorry did that offend you."

Nervously Isobel found her voice. "No it's a compliment, thank you."

He watched her intently. "Sorry." He shrugged, lowering his gaze. "I am just one of those people that blurt out exactly what they are thinking. Is that good or bad, I don't know?"

Isobel cleared her throat not daring to look up at Adam, she asked, "So what's on your mind right now?"

"Do you really want to know?"

"Actually yes, I'm curious." She averted her gaze for a moment.

"I want to hold you close to me. I want to smell your hair and skin, but then I don't want to offend you," he said gently.

"Perhaps you wouldn't."

Adam moved closer towards her, pushing a stray tendril of hair back from her rather serious face. "Are you sure about that?"

Isobel took a step closer until she could feel the warmth of his breath upon her face.

"Not entirely," she whispered.

Adam raised a brow. "I had you down as the sort of lady that knows what she wants." He looked directly in to her eyes as he said it.

Isobel's palms began to tingle; her heart was hammering, she lifted her chin instinctively up towards him, searching for his lips which came down to meet hers. Closing her eyes, she tasted his mouth it was slightly sour; it tasted of whisky, but his lips were soft and seemed to fit hers, just so. Isobel felt as if she was falling, falling back through space everything appeared weightless; she entwined her arms around his neck for support, as gently Adam rubbed his strong hands up and down her spine. Then without warning, he pulled away. Isobel lowered her eyes to the floor, suddenly ashamed of her response. "Sorry."

Adam tilted her chin up toward him. "I hardly know you and yet I am falling in love with you. What's happening, Isobel? It's the weirdest thing."

"We were kissing, just kissing." Isobel's eyes blazed, was he fooling with her, it appeared he had a habit of that.

"A kiss is never just a kiss." Adam's eyes glazed; he was saddened by her flippancy. "You are married, let me remind you."

"Oh really," she retorted haughtily.

"No I mean."

"What exactly do you mean?" Isobel struggled free of his arms. She paced around the stable, she felt foolish.

Adam's eyes glistened as he watched her indignant and wild, exciting him more. "Maybe you're just in need of some excitement." He studied her face.

"Certainly not," she exploded.

At that moment Carmen's cheery face appeared at the door. "I'm ready now, folks, shall we leave?"

"Yes," they snapped in unison.

Isobel gave Quest a final pat then followed Carmen silently to the car.

Neither Adam nor Isobel spoke on the short journey, Isobel made a point not to even look at him as she got out and waved goodbye specifically to Carmen.

Jacob flung the front door open. "Well done, darling, eleventh that's brilliant. You must be starving, Maria's just dishing up." In truth Isobel didn't feel starving, just sick, and hideously sick with guilt.

Isobel didn't want to offend Maria, she managed to eat a little of the food she had prepared. Afterwards she sat on the sofa, the warmth of the fire and the gentle hum of conversation made her drowsy. Before she knew it she was asleep. Jacob covered her with a rug and tiptoed out to the kitchen to join the others for dessert.

CHAPTER NINE

Isobel and Jacob along with Edward, who was cold and whingeing profusely, stood on the doorstep, in the pouring rain. Olan and Maria were returning to London. Olan had tried his hardest to entice them to London for the New Year, but Jacob remained insistent that they should stay at home. Isobel, on the other hand, wasn't exactly sure where she would like to spend it. She was still full of remorse about the kiss. She guessed in the circumstances she would agree with Jacob whatever he wanted. It ended up being just the three of them at home. For the best, Isobel thought, as Jacob prepared a seafood meal, accompanied by the last of the champagne.

Edward lasted until eleven o'clock; Jacob carried him up to bed. When the clock struck midnight, Isobel was horizontal in front of the fire, on the woollen rug, with Jacob.

"I love you, darling," he whispered in her ear.

"I love you too," Isobel replied. Unsure if she meant it and feeling totally confused. It was a New Year, and depressingly she didn't even know her own mind.

The day dawned frosty. The hedgerows sparkled, kissed by an icy wand during the early hours. Jacob had indulged in too much champagne. He awoke with a sore head. Edward was happy playing with his toys and didn't want to accompany Isobel on a walk so she decided to set off alone. Wrapping up warm with gloves and a scarf, she set off at a brisk pace across the fields. The water in the stream was frozen; the banks were slippery underfoot as she scrambled down to prod the ice with a large stick, leaning forward she gazed in the hole she had made. Reminding her of when she was seven and they had gone to her mother's friend's house. She had done much the same thing then, but decided to see what happened if she stood on the ice, it hadn't been a small stream but a large pond. Isobel had been petrified as the ice had cracked beneath her feet. It was fortunate for her that a kind man, out walking his dogs had spotted what she was doing and had raced over to haul her out before she had disappeared forever. Her mother had given her a good ticking off and she wasn't allowed to have tea. It had been her favourite as well. Isobel smiled at the memory. That was the thing about Orange Stream Farm; it reminded her of her childhood in so many ways.

Isobel stood up, and with the help of the stick, which she wedged into the frozen earth, made her way back up the slippery bank. The wood stood before her, dazzling in the early sun. She stood still, to study it. From here, it didn't seem eerie at all. It looked pretty and inviting, mesmerised she walked towards its edge. It was without doubt a very cold morning but as she neared the edge of the wood the temperature dropped further still. Isobel stopped. What was it about this place? Why was it always so cold and sinister, why did she feel as if she wasn't alone here?

Hugging her arms tightly around herself, she waited to see if there was a change in the atmosphere, daring herself, just this once to be brave. As she stood staring in between the trees, she felt a wave of emotion for no apparent reason, it wasn't even as if in that moment she had anything particular on her mind. A picture formed in her mind's eye. It was almost as if she had been propelled into a daydream, one over which she had no control.

The sound of horses' hooves drumming on solid earth in the distance, followed by an urgent shout from behind, startled her; she turned to see a man. It was he appeared beckoning for her to join him. He looked pained if she was not mistaken even afraid. Slowly she turned to go to him; he smiled now, pleased at her decision and held his arms out welcomingly toward her. It didn't feel strange, she was not afraid in fact it seemed to be the most natural thing in the world. She quickened pace with a sudden desperate urge to throw herself at him. Just as she reached him and held out her hands, a shot pierced the silence. He gasped, the sound unpleasant before plunging forward heavily in to her arms. It was bitterly cold, she felt the warmth of his blood as it seeped through hers clothes and on to her skin. She screamed, sickened by the realisation of what had happened and then releasing her hold, he fell to the ground with a soft thud. Weeping uncontrollably, she leant across his lifeless body as his face grew paler and paler, a trickle of blood escaped his frozen lips. Then there was the sound of laughter. She swept around and her gaze met with a pair of cold, calculating eyes. This man was familiar, too familiar, it was then she realised with horror that it was Jacob. Yet, this was not the Jacob that she knew, as he looked beyond her and smugly down at the dying man in her arms. Blinded by tears, she gazed down at the ashen face cradled in her lap and with a terrible jolt; she knew exactly who he was.

"Adam," she breathed, softly she released her hold. Horrified she looked up at Jacob. "Why?" she screamed the words at him.

He didn't reply, his smile sickening. She felt nothing but pure hatred spear through her heart.

Why had he done this, why? She pressed her face into her hands too numb now to even sob. When she looked up, she did so with a start. Everything around her was still, not even the branches of the trees in the wood stirred. There was nobody there, no lifeless body lay before her and no blood stained her skin. When her breath rose, it surfaced in shuddering gasp. Hot tears pricked at her eyes, goose bumps rose on her flesh; she shivered despite the layers of warm clothing. Isobel rose to her feet and looked around. What had happened, had that all been a figment of her imagination? She wasn't sure, but she needed to get home. It wasn't safe here. Stumbling across the open field, her eyes watered from the cold air, her limbs felt heavy, she needed to focus on each step if she was going to make it back. Her mind raced, was it the wood, or had she glimpsed something from the past, a past she could not remember?

There was no way to explain it, she must be still drunk from last night. As she reached the house she fell breathless in to the kitchen. Jacob was at the sink filling the kettle. He looked up with a smile.

"Hey, you're in a hurry. What's going on?" He raised a questioning eyebrow.

Isobel stared back at him her eyes wide with terror. She took a deep breath; it seemed so ridiculous now, standing here in the kitchen, looking at her husband or the man who had just shot Adam, almost laughable. Isobel gave a wry smile, how ridiculous would that sound, if she dared to tell him, besides she couldn't mention Adam. Whatever had just happened, out there on the borders of their land, would have to stay with her, for now at least, she thought grimly.

"I just fancied a bit of exercise that's all." She shrugged, sitting down to pull off her boots. "Is that OK?"

Jacob was still feeling hung over and fragile, he wasn't in the mood for a row, and instead he took another mug down from the cupboard. "Fancy a cuppa?"

Isobel smiled. "I sure do it's freezing out there." She bit her bottom lip and took a deep breath, it was all in her mind, it had to be and she must keep it together if Jacob wasn't to think she had really lost the plot.

The following Tuesday Jacob returned to London. Isobel was glad of the breathing space. The picture locked in her mind, of Jacob standing over

Adam's dead body, still sent chills up her spine. Isobel hadn't told a soul. She doubted anyone would believe her if she did. In fact she didn't really believe it herself. It had seemed real, in some inexplicable way it had happened but there was no rational way she could explain it.

Edward sat at the kitchen table toying with his bowl of cereal, Isobel sat opposite him cross legged on the bench thumbing through the local directory, then placed a large circle around the only two nurseries in their area. She had decided to put a card in the local store advertising her typing skills. Jacob wouldn't like it, he was too proud to want her working but Isobel needed to do something, there was an incredible urge, to be a bit more independent. Jacob didn't need to know, not yet and putting Edward in to nursery would be good for him, besides she couldn't always rely on Rita it wasn't fair.

Olivia crept in to the bedroom with a large tray, there was orange juice, boiled eggs and a rack of toast, she placed it down on the bedside table.

"Breakfast, darling."

Graham groaned and rolled over to face her. "Oh, no, back to work today. Where did the holidays go?"

"Graham, you can't wait to get back to the office normally."

Graham smiled to himself. "It's not really normal though, is it?" He took her hand. "Things have changed and I am rather enjoying it all at the moment."

Olivia smiled at him then looked out of the window. "I am sorry about last night."

Graham lifted the breakfast tray on to his lap. He took a sip of the juice and said in a soothing tone. "Please don't worry about it, darling, it will take awhile for you to relax, that's all."

It did worry her though; she bit her lip then squeezed Graham's hand tighter. "You are satisfying me, darling, please don't think that you're not, it's just—" She tailed off.

Graham was cramming egg in to his mouth and spoke between hurried mouthfuls. "Really, Olivia. Don't worry about it."

Graham placed the tray back on the table and pulled Olivia into his chest kissing the top of her head. "Stop trying so hard, we're happy. Now tell me what you're going to get up to while I am at work today."

Olivia took a deep breath, and then smiled meekly. "To be honest I hadn't thought about it."

Marina held Brad close. In all their time together she had never seen him sob like this. Brad sat hunched over the table, his face ashen. He sobbed pitifully for the loss of Bronson.

Bronson had been special; Brad had owned him from a yearling, before he met Marina. In fact it was, kind of due to Bronson that they had met in the first place. Brad wept from guilt as well; he never should have taken him for the ride, he was too old, and it had all been too much for the old fella. Marina knew all the reasons why Brad was so heartbroken, but she felt helpless, there was nothing she could say to make it better, just support him while he grieved.

Molly was in her room, deeply saddened by the news. It was awful to see Brad so upset, he was usually so happy. Silently she packed her case, stifled sobs filtered from the room below her. Molly was due to fly back to South Africa that afternoon; Brad was supposed to be driving her to Heathrow. Molly wondered if she should call a taxi, but she was afraid that she wouldn't have enough cash. Then she remembered Isobel, she was always so kind, perhaps Molly should give her a call. Molly found her mother's phone book and dialled Isobel's number. Isobel was very upset about Bronson, and insisted that of course she take Molly to the airport. Molly hoped her mother wouldn't be too mad; after all she was only trying to help.

Adam was busy packing a case; he was due in Paris for a meeting at six. He was staying on for a big fashion show in the city and perhaps look up an old girlfriend. Sean his pal was going to look after the shop and Bitz his beloved greyhound. He sped along the M5 and out onto the M4. Isobel entered his mind yet again; he couldn't stop thinking about her, try as he might. Adam wondered for the hundredth time what she was doing. He strummed his fingers in time to the music on the steering wheel. He had to push her out of his thoughts, somehow. It was playing on his mind that her husband would be back in the city by now and that she would be alone at the house. Adam bit firmly down on his lip, he was tormenting himself. Christine had been calling him a lot lately, normally he would have taken her out, shagged her brains out by now, but he didn't want to, he didn't want all that meaningless shit anymore. He was getting older he needed more in his life. He had worked so hard with the business, he needed somebody to share it with, somebody who made him feel alive, someone like Isobel, Isobel, who just happened to be married to another man and have a son, God life sucked sometimes. He pushed his foot down harder on the accelerator; it was just as well he would be out of the country for a while.

"Morning, Jacob, there's a stack of stuff on your desk. I'll get you a coffee." Gloria bustled off to get the coffee; Elizabeth followed him in to the office.

"Did you have a good Christmas, Elizabeth?"

"Hectic to tell the truth, too many parties, too much eating and drinking, you know how it is."

"Actually, it was all quite tame for me this year, but we had a good time. In fact I feel pretty fresh to start off the New Year." Elizabeth had to agree, Jacob was looking really well, very relaxed.

That wasn't a good sign, she noted. Obviously, meaning, his marriage was blissfully on track and there wouldn't be a chance of her getting a look in. She retreated solemnly back to her desk, to sit staring at the pile of invoices, in front of her.

"They won't get done by looking at them, love!" Gloria clucked, her tongue in cheek as she swept past.

"Everything packed, darling?" Molly looked up at her mother. Marina's face was a picture, she looked too happy in the wake of Bronson's death. Molly couldn't help but think this was because she would be leaving today.

"Yes, all done, are you glad? I will be out of your hair soon?"

"Don't say that, Molly, it's most unfair, besides I thought you must be missing your father." Choosing to ignore her mother's remark, Molly did up the zipper on her brown leather suitcase.

"By the way. Isobel has very kindly offered to take me to the airport."

"What do you mean?" Marina spun round in the doorway.

"Yes, I called Isobel to ask her. I didn't want to disturb Brad at this time." Molly saw her mother's jaw clench, the anger which blazed in her eyes. "Well I thought with the death of Bronson and all tha—" She stopped short, at her mother's explosive outburst.

"How dare you call up my friends like some taxi service, that's the last thing Isobel needs."

Molly stood her ground. "No, she didn't mind at all; in fact, considering the circumstances, she was only too glad to help."

Marina ran her fingers through her hair twisting it in to knots at the ends. "Call her back; tell her that I will be taking you."

"No."

"Why ever not, child?"

"Because, Mother, I don't want to go with you."

Marina stormed out of the room seething. Brad was in the kitchen making a cup of tea, he looked up as Marina marched in "That bloody annoying little cow, she is so spoilt!"

"Who?" Brad looked across at her in surprise.

"Molly spoilt brat." Marina spat her name with a venomous snarl.

"OK, calm down, have you had a fight?"

"She's only gone and asked Isobel to take her to the airport, I mean how bloody rude. I asked her to change it but she won't."

"Oh, dear, I see, well." Brad went over to Marina slipping his arms around her waist.

"Poor you, it's not personal. I expect she was trying to be helpful." He shrugged his shoulders. "Besides Isobel wouldn't have offered if she didn't mean it. Relax, honey, let her go with Isobel and don't part on bad terms."

Marina opened her mouth to protest then thought better of it. "I suppose so," she said sulkily.

"Besides the poor lass probably thought you were upset about all this too."

"Well of course I am."

"No, Marina, you're not really. Let Isobel take her, that's what Molly wants and you have to respect her decision."

"You bastard, exactly whose side are you on?" Marina stormed off into the other room.

Brad had never stood his ground with Marina before or dared to voice his opinion. It felt good; besides Marina would get over it. Molly appeared in the doorway, looking decidedly uncomfortable.

"Isobel is coming up the drive, would you mind lifting my case out? It's rather heavy."

"Of course, honey." Brad carried the case out to the hallway, placed it down then turned to her. "Thanks for being so considerate. I am sorry that I am not up to driving you." Feeling embarrassed Molly focused her gaze on the old battered suitcase.

"I should say goodbye to Mother, but she's in one of her moods."

Brad shrugged. "She gets like that." He grinned at the child. "And moody as hell with me sometimes, Molly, so you're not the only one."

Molly looked up at Brad, she held his gaze. "Yes but she loves you."

"Oh, Molly, sweet Molly, she loves you too, very very much. It's just that she finds it hard to show it at times."

Molly managed a fainthearted smile. "Thanks, Brad, for a lovely Christmas. Please tell Mother goodbye."

Brad leant forward kissing her forehead. "Safe journey, you know you're always welcome."

Molly glanced back over her shoulder down the hall; there was no sign of her mother. Swallowing hard, she stepped out in to the cold air. Nothing would ever change, no matter how much she hoped it would.

Isobel shifted the old Escort in to fourth gear, and then settled into the middle lane on the motorway. Rita had very kindly offered to look after Edward, much to his delight, as he didn't travel too well. Molly had scarcely said a word since leaving Devon. Isobel glanced across at her.

"You alright, love?"

"Yes thank you." Molly smiled back politely, and then added in a faint voice, "I'm sorry if I have messed up your plans."

"You haven't in the least; I didn't have anything on at all. Did you enjoy your stay?"

Molly replied that she had but her tone was unconvincing.

They arrived at Heathrow around two. Isobel went into the departures lounge to check Molly in, she was flying unaccompanied first class, oh the things money could buy.

"What time does your flight leave?"

"About four-thirty, if it's on time, but it's pretty cool they have great movies."

"Oh good that should make the flight go a bit quicker then."

Isobel couldn't remember the last time she had been on a plane, a few years before Edward was born at least. "Well I shall be thinking of you when I drive back, flying high in the sky on your way to sunnier climes."

Molly sniffed hard. "Yes but I think I have caught a cold since I have been here."

Isobel left Molly in the capable hands of a young stewardess who would be responsible for Molly from now on until handing her over to her father at the other end. Isobel watched as she disappeared from view.

Molly was a good kid, Isobel wondered if she would ever have a daughter herself. Somehow, she couldn't imagine having any more children; Edward was just starting to get easier why she should want to go back to all those sleepless nights and nappies. She hurried back to the car, pulling her collar up protectively against the bitter wind; she should make it back before dusk if she hurried.

CHAPTER TEN

April arrived with dreamy azure skies. England basked in endless sunshine, promising a sizzling summer.

Quest grazed peacefully in the meadow, the sunlight creating strobes of gold to collide across his hide. Isobel pulled into the driveway and as she made her way up the path, she looked down with a satisfied smile at the colourful array of flowers which seemed to be appearing daily. Edward safely deposited at nursery, which thankfully he adored, was out of the way until lunchtime. Humming softly she clutched the paperwork, which she had collected from Rita on the way back. Rita had decided to share some of her famed recipes with the rest of the world and amongst all the other hundred and one things she had to do, was in the throes of writing her first recipe book, which naturally Isobel had been very happy to offer to type up for her.

In fact, after placing her advert in the local shop, Isobel had been inundated with requests for her secretarial skills, ranging from Pony Club schedules, to monthly church meetings and correspondence for an American businessman who was living in Devon until the summer, and who always tipped her extremely well. Carmen Franklin had also given her quite a bit of work to do, since she had started taking in working pupils, who needed various extracts copied from horse manuals then photocopied endless amount of times. In fact, she had gleaned a fair bit of information from these books along the way.

Rita's book was by far the biggest job; the hardest part was sorting it all into the right order. Isobel sat in the study sifting through the endless papers when the telephone rang. It was Marina.

"Hi, honey, fancy popping to the pub for a bite to eat?"

Reluctantly Isobel declined, she really needed to crack on, as she didn't intend to charge Rita, how could she, and the quicker her work was typed, the more effort she could put in to actually earning something. "Perhaps we could meet up on Friday, instead," she suggested.

"OK if you can drag yourself away from that wretched computer."

"Promise, I'll pick you up about one."

"Good, I have something else up my sleeve as well, how does going to see a tarot reader, grab you?"

"Oh I don't know if that's really my thing."

"Well have a think about it, I'm certainly game. Speak soon."

Isobel replaced the receiver and gave a satisfied smile; she was going to enjoy her first summer here.

Marina was disappointed; she really fancied a few drinks. It had been a long morning. Most of the horses were out now, but the youngsters still had to be worked. Marina had been up at six, everything was done, she fidgeted restlessly, feeling bored. Brad had gone down to Cornwall to look at a horse for himself, something to replace Bronson. He wouldn't be home much before four. She wished she had gone with him now. One thing she wasn't good at was amusing herself.

They hadn't been getting on that well since Christmas, Marina seemed to spend each day becoming increasingly wary of Brad, he was becoming quite hard on her and she wasn't sure how much longer she could cope with it. Marina went out into the sunshine, stripping naked she lay down on the sun lounger. Slowly, beneath the sun's warmth she began to relax. The doorbell rudely interrupted her, with a start she sat up. Wrapping a large towel around her naked body, she padded through the house to the front door.

Half expecting to see Isobel who had changed her mind, she was flabbergasted to see Howard standing there. Howard looked her up and down. "Guess I've called at a bad time, sorry I should have phoned first."

"Well you're here now; you may as well come in." She led her ex-husband, through to the kitchen.

"Well I am pretty sure you didn't just happen to be passing, so what is the problem?" she snapped.

Howard gave a casual smile. "There's really no need to be so defensive."

Marina grunted. "Well, can I get you something to drink, coffee perhaps."

"Mmm something stronger would be nice." He found himself staring.

"Should have guessed, some things never change, you never really were a coffee drinker," she said haughtily.

Marina fixed a large gin and tonic for them both, silently relieved that Brad was out; he would be absolutely livid. She was amazed that Howard had just turned up out of the blue. She flopped down on to the chair opposite him, he was here now and something told her his visit spelt trouble.

"Well I fancied a drink this afternoon; but I never dreamed it would be with you," she said, popping on her sunglasses.

"Always full of surprises, Marina, or had you forgotten?"

"Hardly, but we're ancient history. I'm not sure I care to remember." She looked across with a defiant glare.

Howard took a sip of his drink. "You still fix a good drink."

"I had lots of practise, didn't I?" Marina pulled the towel protectively around her body. "So, Howard, what's this all about?"

"In a nutshell, Molly. You're breaking her heart. What happened here? She came home so unhappy from her visit at Christmas."

"I have no idea why that should be." Marina got up to fix another drink, taking Howard's glass from him even though it was still half full.

"Stop being so bloody selfish for once, you do know; your expression tells me you do."

Marina ignored him, handing him another gin, she slumped back down on the chair.

"Marina, please for God's sake you're her mother." Howard's eyes pleaded with her.

"I thought Maddie was her mother now."

"Don't be silly."

Marina drained her glass. "Do you want another?"

"Marina, listen please. Molly is upset, I can't stand that. It kills me, she's innocent in all of this."

Marina leapt defensively from her chair, letting the towel slip from her body, and went inside.

Her eyes filled with tears, she hated being put on the spot about Molly, especially by Howard of all people. Howard averted his gaze from her nakedness, she was trying to shock him he knew her so well. It had been five years since they had last seen each other. She still looked amazing, but she was still as stubborn as a mule and he guessed always would be. Marina seemed to be taking an age with the drinks he went through to the kitchen. Marina stood at the sink her head in her hands. Gingerly Howard placed his fingertips on her bare shoulders. He turned her around to face him.

"What is it, what's the matter?"

"I am sorry, Howard. I just don't know how to be a good mother to her. Nothing that I do is right." She sobbed.

Howard held her close. "Where's all that fighting spirit?"

Marina managed a faint smile. "I've calmed down a lot; guess I am finally growing up."

Howard looked down at her she appeared so fragile. Marina looked up in to his eyes. Slowly Howard released her, afraid of the feelings that began to surface.

"Look, honey, I didn't mean to dump all this on you. I'm here on business, looking at a yacht for a mate down in Salcombe, I just thought maybe you would have some idea, I hate for her to be unhappy." He took a step back. "I'm staying at the Imperial. Have a think about it. I don't want to pressure you. I'm here until Friday morning, I just think the poor kid needs more time with her mother."

Marina shrugged, he handed her the towel. "Forget that drink, honey, take care of yourself."

Marina watched Howard's rental car disappear from view. The old bugger had aged but he still had that charm. She went upstairs to dress. She would take Lizard out for a ride to clear the cobwebs away. She needed time to think, he was right of course it was unfair for Molly to be so unhappy but then life wasn't really fair was it she mused.

Olivia knelt on a cushion in the garden tugging at the weeds in the border. The garden was looking beautiful; it was a full-time job. It was so nice to feel some happiness in her life again. Graham seemed really pleased; he had booked them a trip to the Caribbean to visit her mother. Everything would be perfect, if only she could get over her inability to climax when they had sex. Graham didn't seem at all perturbed by it, but it didn't feel natural to her, incomplete somehow. It puzzled her more than anything, it should be so natural, he was her husband, but her body would tighten and it wouldn't happen. It would be better if she could have a bloody drink, but she had kept to her promise and hadn't touched a drop since Christmas. It haunted her how Carmen had delighted in her husband's touch, Graham had been so rough and ready with Carmen, yet he treated her more tenderly as if she would break. She wouldn't be afraid to try something new; she just didn't know how to ask. Maybe the break away would improve matters.

She stood up, to gaze proudly around her garden. It would look better this year than it ever had. A bench was what it needed, she wiped her earthy hands on the front of her apron, if she hurried, she would catch the garden centre before it closed.

Brad arrived home around three-thirty; he had missed his wife a lot today. He dialled the Italian restaurant in Redwood, reserved a table for two at eight, then he went down to the stables. Lizard's box was empty she had obviously gone out riding, how crafty, when it was time to bring the mares in, she could have saved him the trouble just this once.

Marina arrived back as he put the last mare in her stable. Lizard began to screech in excitement at the passing mare, pawing the ground restlessly, arching his neck. "Look at me," he screamed.

"He's feeling horny, know the feeling." Brad winked at her.

Marina laughed. "Just hurry up and get that mare in before he climbs the gate."

"I've booked a table tonight. A little surprise, as I have been such a miserable shit these last few weeks."

Thank god, she breathed; at last, she was forgiven.

As Marina climbed into the Jacuzzi, she thought about Molly. She would meet Howard, it was about time she got over her feelings of inadequacy and started to put a bit more effort in to being a mum.

Brad joined her. A glass of wine in each hand, he passed her one.

"Brad, Howard called by today." Marina took a sip of her wine.

"Howard, you mean as in your ex, Howard?"

Marina giggled. "Yes, I know I was pretty shocked too."

Brad felt a stab of jealousy. "What the fuck did he want?"

"He wanted to talk about Molly; she's been upset since Christmas."

"What a surprise, I wonder why." Brad looked at her in dismay.

"I know, I know." She held her hands up. "That's why I went out riding earlier, to think." She paused taking a deep breath. "If you're agreeable, I have an idea."

"Go on then." He moved closer, interested as to what hair brain idea she would come up with next, if it involved Howard she could forget it.

"I thought I might take her away, perhaps to Disneyland for Easter."

"Just the two of you do you mean?"

"Yes, you're not offended, are you?"

Brad shifted uneasily. "No course not, but what about Howard?"

Marina screwed up her face. "What about Howard?"

"Well where does he fit in?" He looked questioningly at her.

Marina slid her arms around his neck. "Howard's just trying to be peacemaker. He was in Salcombe on business, and he called by to do his fatherly bit."

Brad could not suppress his anger, he gave an irritated sigh, and it annoyed him. Marina had been gently manipulated by Howard today. Yet, whenever he had brought the subject up, it had been thrown right back in his face. Marina noticed the sudden tension in Brad's body.

"Look, I know I've been a right bitch, it's been playing on my mind. It was you that really made me think about all this."

Brad relaxed a little. "Are you sure you want to do this, you can't build up her hopes only to let her down you know."

"I know, I have thought it all through, we need some quality time together."

Marina rose from the bubbling waters. Brad handed her a towel.

"Don't worry about Howard; he'll be on his way back to South Africa by now." She gave him a reassuring glance.

Isobel hadn't spoken to Jacob at all yesterday, he had left a message with Edward but Edward had failed to pass it on, until now. Isobel dialled his number at the flat, there was no answer, it was late, and on the off chance she tried the office.

"Hi, darling, you just caught me, did you get my message."

"No not really, Edward was very vague."

"I'm coming home first thing in the morning, that's why I am still here now, Elizabeth kindly offered to stay and help so I can set off early."

"Oh did she?"

"Yeah you know, they're all keen for a bit of overtime."

"I bet they are."

Jacob laughed it wasn't like Isobel to show a bit of jealousy, it was quite flattering.

"So what time shall I expect you?"

"Hope to be with you about eight. Bye, darling."

Isobel replaced the receiver; she didn't like the sound of this Elizabeth, only too eager to help, at this time of night as well. In fact on reflection, Jacob always seemed to be harping on about Elizabeth, perhaps there was something in it. Isobel shook her head, no Jacob wouldn't do that, he wasn't the type for some cheesy affair; she pushed the thought firmly from her mind.

Edward was fast asleep in bed, it was quarter to ten. Isobel would have to cancel lunch on Friday with Marina, if Jacob was going to be home. It was a bit late to call now, she would tell her in the morning, they seemed to see less and less of each other these days and she missed her company.

Wearily Isobel got in to bed, pressing her cheek hard against the pillow; she wondered what Jacob would be doing. He might have stopped on the way home with Elizabeth for a drink, it made her feel strange, angry, by the time she fell in to a restless sleep she had convinced herself that Jacob was having a torrid affair with Elizabeth. Maybe she would go up to London, to get a look at Elizabeth; cunningly, she could combine it with a visit to Jacob's parents, restlessly she fidgeted beneath the cotton sheets.

The owl's sharp cry faded into the distance. She felt safe here, as he held her close. Looking into his eyes, she saw the sadness, the same sadness she always saw. It was her fault; she was the solitary cause of his sorrow. A tear trailed down her cheek she wiped it fiercely away. Her heart weighed heavily in her otherwise empty chest. Oh how she loved this man, loved him with all her heart.

Isobel opened her eyes, she dabbed at her damp cheeks. It was only a dream she told herself sleepily, rolling over. It was always the same, he was always there.

That smell it was here again, the same smell that followed the dream. It didn't scare her anymore but it made her sad. What did it mean? She gave a sleepy shrug. Perhaps, she should accompany Marina to have her cards read, but there again, she may hear something she rather wouldn't. The words "Your husband is having an affair" resounded in her ears.

Marina wasn't bothered about Isobel cancelling lunch; she had other matters to attend to.

Marina dialled Howard at the Imperial. "Howard Lavantte's room please."

"One moment." The operator put her on hold. Nervously she twisted the telephone cord between her fingers.

"I'm very sorry, madam, there's no reply at the moment. May I take a message?"

"Yes, would you please tell him that Marina Cobbet will be calling at noon today? Thank you." Marina put the phone down, she had done it now. It was awful she was being deceitful to Brad; nonetheless there were things they had to sort out. What he didn't know wouldn't hurt him. As far as Brad was concerned she was going shopping, and it wasn't a total lie, she would be, straight after she had been to see Howard.

Marina wasn't sure what to wear, the Imperial was very upmarket, but she didn't want Howard to get the wrong impression. Despite her doubts, she dressed in her timeless Chanel suit, and then stood staring at herself in the mirror. Marina tried to tell herself it was because she had looked such a wreck on their last meeting, but that was foolish she wanted to wow Howard, it was in her nature. She left a note for Brad on the kitchen table, signed "with lots of kisses."

Graham peered with bemusement over the top of the *Financial Times*, at Olivia. She stood in her marigolds, scrubbing a dirty pan in the kitchen sink with all the gusto she could muster.

"Perhaps it would be easier to get a new pan?" he chuckled.

"No, see, all done, you can see your face in that now." She looked across at him triumphantly.

"You have changed so much, Olivia, it's spooky. In fact, is that really you?"

"Hey, cheeky, I have scrubbed a fair few pans in my time."

Graham put the paper down, striding over to give her a big hug. "This time next week, darling, we'll be lying on the beach, are you excited?"

"Yes, I can't wait."

"Did you ask Isobel about looking after Solvent while we are away?"

"No, but I will go over this morning." In truth it had totally slipped her mind. She pulled off her gloves. Graham pecked her cheek and left.

Olivia stood staring out of the kitchen window, across the gardens. Toying with the idea which had just struck her and wondering whether it was viable. It didn't seem fair to ask Isobel, especially as they didn't know her that well. Besides, Solvent could be a nasty sod when he wanted to be, he needed firm handling. Olivia smiled thoughtfully, to be honest there was nobody better than Carmen for the job. Carmen wouldn't dare decline after all that had happened. There was no time like the present, after a quick peek in the mirror and a dab of lipstick she set off to Briars Lodge.

Olivia was surprised; the stables were a hive of activity. She managed to seize a passing stable girl who directed her straight to Carmen, giving a demonstration in the arena.

Carmen nearly dropped her lunging whip when she spotted Olivia leaning on the gatepost observing her from behind dark glasses. Carmen handed the reins to Jade, one of the young girls, and set off to see what Olivia wanted, hoping she wasn't brewing for a fight. Olivia observed Carmen pitifully as she trudged through the sand toward her. Olivia spoke first.

"Sorry to interrupt, I can see you're busy." Olivia removed her glasses. "I'll get straight to the point; I'm here to beg a favour, actually."

Carmen could feel an uncomfortable heat, which crept up her body. Fiercely she wiped her grubby hands down her jodhpurs waiting nervously for Olivia to continue.

"Graham's booked us a week in Barbados, darling, and we're a bit stuck with the animals."

Carmen gulped. Olivia noticed the relief in her eyes. Carmen smiled meekly, there had to be a catch. "You get on so well with Solvent. I thought you would be the best person to ask."

Carmen glanced back at her students, who had all stopped what they were doing and were standing open-mouthed, eavesdropping on their conversation.

"Sure, Olivia, no problem, but it would be far easier if I could have them both here."

"Of course whatever is easiest for you." Olivia replaced her glasses, smoothing her hair meticulously. "Thank you, Carmen. Perhaps you could collect them both Thursday evening?"

Olivia turned; she walked back to her car, without even waiting for her reply. Carmen watched her leave; there was no end to the woman's cheek. Graham had obviously won her round, as long as she didn't give her any drama what did it matter. Olivia certainly looked better. Carmen looked down at herself, scruffy as usual. It wasn't surprising that Graham had gone back, there was no comparison. Olivia had to be playing a game; she had a reputation for being a nasty piece of work. Carmen couldn't believe for one minute that forgiveness was on her agenda, no, she must have a trick up her sleeve somewhere, she thought.

Isobel cleared the mass of papers from her desk as she set about tidying the place up a bit. The last week had flown; there had been little time for the domestic chores. Edward was tired, he whinged incessantly at Isobel as she cleaned, he didn't want to help and he didn't want to play with his toys either.

"Come on, Edward. Daddy will be home shortly let me just finish this then I will cook you some breakfast."

Isobel had decided to pack a picnic, they hadn't been out as a family for quite some time and the weather was so nice. Edward deserved a treat, and there was the added bonus that it would cheer Jacob up too.

Jacob arrived home in good spirits; Edward filled him in on the last few days, while Isobel finished preparing the hamper for their day at the beach. It was only a fifteen-minute drive to the beach, but somehow, they never managed to go very often. Isobel was looking forward to it; they would take the dogs as well, it would be a nice treat for them. Jacob made coffee for them both which they took out on to the terrace in the warm early morning sun. It seemed ages ago, that first day at Orange Stream Farm, when they had sat, much the same as now. She had met so many people since then and if she was honest it hadn't all panned out as she had planned, but then life rarely did. Would she change any of it, she thought to herself, maybe some of it. Isobel took a large gulp of coffee, unaware that Jacob was watching her closely.

"You look a bit serious, love. Is anything the matter?"

"No. I was just thinking that we have been here six months already."

"Any regrets?"

"No. How about you? Do you have any?"

"Darling, as long as you're happy. Well, then so am I."

Isobel shrugged, that just about said it all really.

CHAPTER ELEVEN

The Imperial Hotel stood imposingly at the edge of the cliff, overlooking the Sandy Bay and the cove. Small fishing boats bobbed alongside ocean going yachts on the relatively calm, green water. Holidaymakers poured in an endless stream into the many gift shops, selling post cards and sticks of crumbling rock. People flocked to the little inn and the trendy cafes, to bag the best tables, for cream tea and scones, whilst watching the cove and its inhabitants go about their day.

Marina parked her car to the rear of the hotel. You never knew who might be around, the last thing she needed was Brad getting wind of this meeting. The reception area in the hotel was gratefully cool. The staff, dressed smartly in navy suits with shiny name badges, smiled helpfully as she approached the main desk.

Marina was informed that Howard had moved and was now occupying the Somerset Suite; she was given directions from the elevator. She began to feel quite nervous as she approached the door to the suite. No doubt, Howard would be surprised at her visit, especially as she had been decidedly offish with him at their last meeting. Marina paused at the door, to straighten her skirt and rake her fingers hastily through her hair. Taking a deep breath, she gave two light taps on the door.

"It's open, come on in." Howard was walking towards the door as she entered. He smiled warmly, instantly putting her at ease. "Hi, Marina, I'm glad you decided to come and talk, can I get you a drink?"

"A Martini if you have any?" She slung her bag down on to the sofa then went across to the window to admire the view, which as expected from the most expensive room in the hotel, was amazing.

"I can fix you a Martini, if that's what you'd really like but I took the liberty of ordering some champagne." He signalled to the bottle of Cristal, standing in the ice bucket on the table.

"It was always your favourite." He gave a knowing grin.

"It still is." She licked her lips. "Yes, Howard, I would adore some."

Marina slipped off her shoes, settling back in the large armchair by the window. "Great room, it must be costing a small fortune?"

"Enough, but as you can see, the view alone is worth it."

She nodded her head in agreement. Howard handed her the champagne.

"Cheers." Marina let the cool crisp bubbles trickle gently down the back of her throat, she glanced out to the sea, it was so calm today, most serene.

"So how was the yacht?"

"Very nice, I have advised him to buy it. I will get to use it whenever I am here. Not that I am here much these days. Well, not as much as I would like to be."

"Would you then? I thought South Africa was the best place on earth or that's what Molly tells me."

Howard gave a deep throaty laugh. "I think Molly is trying to wind you up. Yes she loves South Africa, but she also told me that Devon feels like home, real home."

Marina was surprised by this comment; trying not to let it show. The last thing she had made it feel to Molly was like home; still, it gave her some hope.

Howard noticed how good Marina looked today, her scent filled the room. He sat watching her as she surveyed the view below and he smiled. There was no one quite like Marina. She possessed an aura that no other woman, that he had ever encountered, could match. Marina had grace, genuine grace; it was the way she was. Today as he watched her, he was reminded of their first meeting. It had been at a party in Sloane Square. Confident, so self-assured she had stood out like a sore thumb. Howard like a magnet had weaved his way across the dance floor to become acquainted. Marina had spent the rest of the evening with him ignoring the many other admiring glances, instead enjoying his flirtatious behaviour. The following evening he had taken her to dinner at The Ivy.

Marina had been suitably impressed at the choice of restaurant and the ever-flowing vintage champagne. Howard had been horrified, when he escorted her home to a damp dismal two bed flat that she shared with two rowdy art students. He wanted to rescue her at once, a woman with such class deserved so much better. A year later she finally accepted his offer of marriage, making him the happiest man on earth.

Marina fidgeted awkwardly in her seat. "Brad isn't aware that I am here today."

"Why ever not!" he asked surprised.

"To be honest I don't think he would approve, besides I don't think it really matters."

A shadow fell across Howard's tanned, leathery, complexion. "We have been divorced over five years now; surely he does not consider me a threat?"

She shrugged nonchalantly and smiled. "He's a bit insecure, that's all."

Howard knew that feeling too well, it was part of the package with Marina. "I suppose it's the fact that we were together eleven years and have Molly." Howard ran his fingers along his chin. "How come you and Brad never had a child?"

Marina, taken aback, frowned, it seemed a strange thing for Howard to ask. She sipped her champagne looking out of the window, focusing on a small red boat that was being loaded by two weatherbeaten fishermen. "I would have thought that was self-explanatory, after all, was it not you that reminded me just what sort of mother I've been to the one child I have."

Howard stood up, walked over and pulled the champagne bottle from the bucket of ice; slowly he walked back stopping to refill Marina's glass. "Sorry, that was most insensitive of me. Anyhow enough of that. You look beautiful today."

Marina smiled, her eyes lighting up. "Thank you, Howard."

Howard joined her at the window. He needed some air, the air in the room was heavy with Marina's scent and thoughts of what had been. He needed to breathe.

"Are you happy, Howard?"

Howard held firmly on to the balcony railings, staring straight ahead, out to sea. "Yes, in my own way. Life's not perfect, but it keeps me ticking."

"I think I can relate to that. You know it's funny." She cocked her head to one side. "People think that if you're rich. Well that life should be perfect, don't they?"

"Tell me about it."

Marina turned towards him, a soft breeze blew in through the open window, and she shivered.

"Would you hold me, Howard?" Instinctively, without a word he took her into his arms, they felt strong and protective. Marina allowed herself be enveloped by them, warm and safe.

Howard remembered how it had felt before. Like this, every time. He shuddered then, remembering how she had done the dirty on him, it had nearly killed him at the time. He had felt sure he would never recover. Then there had been Maddie, sweet, patient Maddie. He thought of her now, so trustworthy and reliable, yet boring and completely predictable.

Softly Howard cradled Marina against him, intoxicated by her smell, awakening old feelings. Marina lifted her head to look up at him. "It feels nice."

He looked down at her, as he stroked her hair and nodded in agreement. "It feels right." Howard pulled away from her, he studied her face, his eyes glistened. "Are you sure this is what you want?"

"To be honest, I am not sure, but it feels right. You feel it too I know you do."

Howard nodded, he bent kissing her forehead lightly, and gently he slipped her jacket from her shoulders. Marina shivered.

"Are you cold?" he asked.

"No." She gave a wry grin. "Maybe a little bit."

Howard went over to the window; struggling with the lock, he closed them. He turned to face Marina, she stood in her underwear, looking vulnerable and smiling, shyly. Howard led her silently to the bed. It was a great advantage; he knew her body every inch of it. He could never forget it. Sex with Marina was awesome.

Afterwards, lying comfortably in each other's arms, there was guilt. The lust had elapsed. Howard spoke first. "I don't expect this will ever happen again."

He felt Marina stiffen in his arms. Marina realised with a sickening feeling what she had done. Howard was so emotional, she had unleashed powerful feelings and brought back all of his old hurt. Then surprising herself she pulled back pushing herself up on to one elbow.

"I suppose the answer to that should be no, it won't. But I don't know why, Howard, I can't say that!"

Howard pulled her close, pushing her hair softly back behind one ear. "I love you, Marina, I always have." He gave a weary sigh. "I know you can't say the same."

Marina bit her lip. "What is love, are you sure that you really know?" She looked earnest. "I want to be safe again, away from all the pretence but—" She stopped, doubtful of her next words.

"Go on," Howard encouraged, as he gently stroked her hair.

"And now I don't know," she said finally.

Howard let out a sigh. He could cope with that. Maybe in her words, there was some sort of hope, very distant, but there nonetheless.

"Are you hungry?"

"Starving!" Marina suddenly realised she hadn't eaten a thing all day.

"So what do you fancy?"

Marina smiled. "You decide, while I take a quick shower."

Howard watched her walk to the bathroom. When they had eaten she would leave. A dismal feeling swept over him, he closed his eyes. Marina would leave him and go home to Brad. He pushed the thought from his mind. It hurt too much.

Isobel sat on the stripy picnic rug watching Jacob and Edward play football. She watched the dogs sniffing along the banks further up along the cliff. On Sunday she would tell Jacob that she intended to return to London with him to see his parents. Since she had begun to feel wary of this Elizabeth, jealousy had gnawed at her stomach. Jacob appeared smiling the words from his mouth taken on the breeze.

"Sorry what did you say?"

Jacob sat down beside her and asked. "Are you OK, darling? You have been distracted all day."

"Really? Well I'm fine honestly." She forced a smile.

Jacob wasn't sure that he believed her.

"So how is Quest? Have you been out riding a lot?"

"Yes. He's lovely." Smiling, she placed her hand over his. "I have been busy typing this week, so I haven't ridden that much."

Jacob raised his eyebrows. "You know there is no need to do all this typing."

"I want to," Isobel snapped.

"Sorry." Jacob held up his hands in defence and then he winked.

Isobel softened slightly.

"I know how much your newfound independence means to you." She ignored the hint of sarcasm in his voice; it was a male pride thing, she told herself.

Edward collapsed exhausted when they arrived home. After a hot bath and some warm milk, Jacob took him up to bed.

They sat in front of the fire watching the flickering flames. Jacob opened a bottle of wine but he hardly touched his, as he sat gazing thoughtfully into the fire. When Jacob led her up to the bedroom, she let him undress her and make love to her. Her heart wasn't in it. Jacob knew and it hurt him. He lay awake staring into the dark, long after Isobel had fallen asleep. Carefully he leant out of bed, feeling for his trousers then hauling them up on to the bed he fished in the pocket for his cigarettes and lighter, he lit a cigarette, inhaling the acrid smoke, deep into his lungs.

"Jacob, whatever are you doing?" Isobel screeched as the smoke filtered into her nostrils.

Jacob jumped from the bed then looked at her with genuine shock and at the cigarette in between his fingers. "God, sorry I forgot where I was."

Isobel shot him an icy glare, she felt sick inside, unsure what that meant. "Well where exactly did you think you were and with whom may I add?"

Jacob threw the cigarette out of the window then turned to face Isobel with a sheepish grin. "That's not what I meant, it was more a case of being alone. I should have told you." He lowered his eyes to the floor.

"How long have you been doing that?" Her voice echoed in the quietness of the room.

"I'm not going to lie, about five months now." He climbed back in to bed beside her.

Hastily she climbed out. She grabbed her dressing gown, put it on and paced up and down the room, agitated.

"I had no idea, is there anything else I should know?" She directed her gaze at him.

"Oh, don't be silly. It's a cigarette, hardly crime of the year."

"Do as you please." Isobel shrugged then left the room.

Jacob's immediate thought was to follow her, fight his corner but he was tired. Too tired even for this, instead he thumped at his pillow and laid his head wearily down.

Isobel sat alone in the dark lounge the only light was from the embers of the dying fire. She was mad. Her throat was tight and her mind racing, she finished the last of the wine. Why hadn't he told her? Isobel tried to contain her active mind. Maybe she had overreacted, all this Elizabeth nonsense was getting to her, and it was making her paranoid.

Isobel got up, she stoked the fire, there was a faint crackle. There were no more logs in the basket; it was far too cold to go out at this hour. Instead she lay down on the floor and curled into a ball. She must go to London if only to satisfy her own curiosity.

Brad sat in the kitchen. He had been contemplating another cup of coffee or moving the muck heap, a challenge he had been putting off for weeks. He heard Marina's car pull up outside. It was nearly six, he switched the kettle on. Marina swept through the front door laden with shopping bags. Brad grinned at her. "You didn't get much then?"

"You know me, never could resist a bargain."

Brad raised an eyebrow. They certainly had different ideas on what exactly a bargain was. Marina looked sheepish. "Sorry I'm a bit late."

"Maybe you could go and slip that lot on, love?" he looked suggestively at her.

Marina felt a sudden panic; she couldn't possibly after her day. "To be honest, love, I am feeling rather drained my period is due anytime."

"Oh." He tried to hide his disappointment. "Fancy a cupper then?"

Marina rose early the next morning. Softly she tiptoed to the bathroom, studying her face in the mirror. Solemnly it looked back at her. For someone with a hell of a lot to smile about, boy did she look miserable. Wracked with guilt, she didn't fancy facing Brad. What had he done to deserve being treated like this?

Vigorously she brushed her teeth until her gums bled. She told herself it was a mistake it was easy now that she was here, back at home.

Marina dressed then hurried down to the stables, the least she could do was see to all the horses. Lizard whinnied gently, greeting his mistress eager for an early breakfast. Marina rubbed his long ears affectionately and kissed his velvet muzzle. She strode along the yard looking in on all the others. The first of the mares was standing asleep at the back of her stable; her pale grey coat looked ghostly in the early morning light, which seeped through the rafters. Marina stopped in horror at the next stable, Royal Gala, one of the older mares who was heavy with foal, lay motionless, her huge ripe belly, lifeless against the golden straw. Nervously Marina unbolted the door, the mare did not stir, Marina's heart hammered against her rib cage.

"Oh please God, don't let her be dead."

She crept to her head; the mare's eyes were rolled upward. Marina gasped, frantically feeling the mare's swollen belly she was still warm. Marina fled the stables screaming for Brad at the top of her voice. She began to sob as she ran breathlessly toward the house.

The vet shook his head as he looked up, apologetically. "She was a good mare, what a terrible blow for you both. Sorry."

Marina was devastated; the mare had not been due for another month. It appeared she had gone into premature labour and died of a heart attack in the early hours. Brad kicked savagely at a nearby bale of hay. "It's not bloody fair, she was so fit."

The vet bolted the door behind them. "Sometimes there is no explanation." He shrugged. "It just happens unfortunately."

Marina, sitting on an upturned bucket, watched the vet leave; it was part of everyday life for him, yet she couldn't help wondering if God was punishing her for yesterday. She smiled meekly at Brad. "You go put the kettle on. I better feed this lot; I'll be up in awhile, we just have to accept it." He squeezed her arm, giving a sad nod.

This was her fault she was being punished. She had loved that mare. Sod Howard, why the hell had he shown up after all this time?

Adam's trip to Paris in January had proved to be worthwhile. The addition of a new young designer had been a shrewd move and business was booming. Despite being busy he had managed to find time to unwind with Vanessa Coombes. Old acquaintances, they had run into each other at Heathrow, on his return trip from Paris. Vanessa was the ex girlfriend of Jerry Hampton, who had been one of Adam's best customers. Jerry had left the country twelve months ago in favour of the States, a bitter blow for Adam at the time, as he was a trusted regular who thought nothing of spending five grand a month in the shop. A real flash bloke, pots of money, fast car and he had Vanessa, who never failed to turn heads. He was a real rogue into this and that. Unbeknown to Vanessa, he had several other women on the go as well. Adam had always felt quite sorry for her. When Jerry left, Vanessa opted to stay in London, which hadn't gone down too well. It was rumoured that he had no choice, but to leave, it wasn't hard to imagine why. She however had declined to accompany him. Adam guessed that it had finally dawned on her what kind of guy he really was.

Vanessa was tall and slim, her pale, porcelain complexion brought alive by her deep-set, green eyes. Egyptian in her look she was of impeccable English breeding, her father an Earl. After their chance meeting, they had begun to meet up on regular occasions, first for drinks, then for meals and finally sex. If Adam was honest it wasn't earth shattering, more comfortable. It suited them both, she wasn't keen to get too serious and he certainly wasn't. Adam was pleased that they were meeting tonight. He drove home in high spirits. It was a beautiful evening; he sat out on the balcony with a glass of malt awaiting her arrival. A few minutes later he watched her car roll up the drive. He watched as she climbed out, long slender legs first. He felt a twinge in his loins; he hadn't seen her for over a week. He pondered if they should make love before they went to dinner. Vanessa was having none of it, brushing aside his amorous advances and suggesting they leave right away, even skip the pre-dinner drink on the balcony.

On Sunday evening, Isobel was feeling anxious, suffering a bout of last minute nerves, as she duly informed Jacob that she would be returning to London with him. To her amazement, he was thrilled at her news.

"Great, that's fantastic. Mum and Dad will be over the moon."

"Do you think so?" She smiled at his obvious delight.

"Oh, God, yes and, Gloria, I'm sure they all think you've turned in to some country bumpkin." Isobel winced, did that mean they all thought she was now a complete bore.

"So when did you decide this?"

"Just now," she lied. "Besides, it's ages since Edward and I have seen your parents, he will have forgotten who they are."

"Well it's terrific. Don't be too appalled at the flat though, I haven't cleaned or anything for ages."

Isobel gave a hearty laugh that really was the least of her worries.

Carmen gave Solvent one last polish, with a soft cloth. His coat was gleaming. It was paramount that he looked perfect when she deposited him back to his owners. Ruffles had made himself extremely at home during his visit, all the cats, were now too scared to come any where near the house and Carmen had had to resort to feeding them out in the back shed. Ruffles too had been bathed and groomed, and smelt pleasantly of Lavender. There was no way that Carmen would allow Olivia to find any fault in the condition of her animals, whilst they had been in her care. It was quite the reverse; she went in to raptures of how well they looked. Graham shifted uneasily, positively embarrassed by the whole farce. He hadn't been pleased when Olivia had told him. Now all he could do was smile politely.

Carmen left in the horse box, Olivia waved her off, Graham dived back inside, in search of the Bacardi he had brought back with him. Wistfully Olivia watched as the box disappeared from view. It was odd but she liked Carmen. She should invite her over for a meal as a thank you. Just once would be OK. It would prove there were no hard feelings.

Jacob and Isobel called in to see Brad and Marina, before leaving for London. Edward chattered excitedly in the back of the car. Brad looked across the yard at them with a broad grin then came striding over. He patted Jacob on the back.

"Hello, stranger, haven't seen you for ages."

"Work, you know how it is."

"I suppose you heard about Royal Gala?" He looked across at Isobel.

"No, what did she have?"

He turned to face them. "She died, Isobel. Sorry I thought Marina would have told you."

She shook her head sadly. "No, sorry, Brad, I didn't know. How terrible, when?"

Marina appeared smiling brightly. "Hi, guys." She kissed Jacob on each cheek.

"So sorry about Royal Gala, how beastly the poor thing," Isobel said.

Marina sniffed. "Yes it is, sorry I should have rung and told you."

They went up to the house; Edward looked longingly at the inviting pool.

"Can we go swimming, Mummy?" he asked. All ready to strip off his clothes and dive in.

Marina laughed. "Don't think you're really dressed for it, sweetie, perhaps another day."

"Actually, Marina, we're on our way to London. We called by to let you know. Just for a few days."

"Hey, great, half tempted to come with you. Better not though, we really need to keep an eye on these mares."

Brad came through with the coffee. "I don't know, seems every one's whizzing off, except me." He grinned. Isobel looked expectantly up at him. "She hasn't told you that either, I'm shocked."

"Told me what?" Isobel looked across at Marina. "Come on, spill the beans."

"I'm off to Disneyland next week, with Molly."

"Wow lucky you. I bet Molly is pleased?"

"Over the moon, we are both really looking forward to it. I think it's time I made amends for ruining her Christmas." She held up a quietening hand. "I don't expect you to answer that, I know what a perfectly selfish moo I have been."

Edward slept the entire journey to London. Isobel looked out of the window with distaste. Once this had seemed heaven, now all the high-rise buildings and lack of sky made her feel claustrophobic. As she stepped out of the car, the air felt heavy in her lungs, dirty and unclean.

Jacob had not exaggerated about the flat, it was a tip. Isobel looked around, with a pained expression, as Jacob hurriedly gathered up dirty plates and kicked scattered magazines beneath the sofa.

"Don't panic, Jacob. I can take care of this later, why don't we go into the office? I can walk to your parents' apartment from there."

She had to get it over with, it was screwing her up. She had to put a face to this tormentor, then she would escape to the safety of his parents, they were up from Essex for a break. When the country got a bit boring they would whiz up to their city home. They would make freshly brewed coffee and fuss round her and Edward; it would be nice to be spoilt for a while.

They arrived at the office, Jacob strode up the stairs ahead of them, leaving Isobel to hold Edward's hand and assist him up the steep flight of steps. Gloria broke in to a huge grin when they finally made it to the top, into the large open plan office.

"Isobel, Edward, how wonderful to see you," she shrieked. Galloping over to hug them both, Jacob watched proudly from his office doorway.

Gloria bombarded Isobel with questions, smiling down at Edward and squeezing his hand tightly as she did so. Isobel was pleased to see her, but she found herself looking past Gloria, so she could scan the office for any sign of Elizabeth. Dreading the type of woman she may be. Jacob had certainly made her seem plain and boring. Jacob kissed her cheek lightly. "Better crack on, love, I'll be in my office."

Isobel nodded. She would hang around for a while. Gloria wasn't keen to let her go. Pulling up a chair, she was insistent that Isobel have a coffee and then she wanted to hear all about the new house, new horse and all the new friends she had made. There was still no sign of Elizabeth.

"I thought that Jacob said you had a new lady. He hasn't burdened you with everything again, has he?"

"Oh no, Elizabeth does a lot. Of course I'm forgetting you haven't met. She should be in soon; I believe she had the dentist first thing."

Isobel left Edward chatting with Gloria; he was giving her a detailed account of Rita's house. Slowly she extracted herself and went to see Jacob. He waved her in. He was on the phone. It seemed strange, she felt like an intruder. It was if she didn't belong here anymore, it wasn't her imagination. It was different the atmosphere wasn't as pleasant as it had been once. It was fraught, brisk and hectic. The other line rang, she jumped. Normally she would have answered it without a second thought, she let it ring on. Jacob finished his call. "Sorry Monday mornings they are always so manic. So what are your plans for the day?" It almost appeared that he was keen to be shot of her. She mumbled about seeing his parents and cleaning the flat. He leant forward pressing a fifty-pound note in her hand.

"For a taxi, bet you've forgotten how expensive London can be." She took the money stuffing it in to her pocket, as she stood up.

"I'd better go, what time will you be back to the flat?"

"Fingers crossed, as you're here—" he paused. "I will try for five, darling."

"OK. Whatever." Leaning across, she gave him a quick peck on the cheek.

Edward was sat on Gloria's lap, drawing a picture. Gloria looked up and smiled. "He is such a poppet, you will call in again before you leave won't you, love?"

"Of course, Gloria, perhaps we could meet for lunch?"

"Yes, that would be nice. Wednesday would be good."

Isobel smiled. "Wednesday it is then."

Aware of somebody behind her Isobel turned. A dark-haired woman smiled back at her.

"Hi, you must be, Isobel." She held out her hand and then glanced across at Edward, a huge grin spread across her face. "Definitely Edward." She leant forward to tickle him between the ribs. "Why, you look just like your daddy!"

Gloria intervened. "Sorry, Isobel, forgetting my manners. This is Elizabeth, our new secretary. Well, not so new but it's the first time you have met. She has settled in nicely, part of the team."

"I can see that," Isobel whispered between gritted teeth.

Isobel took a big gasp of air as they made it downstairs and out in to the street. She put her hand against the wall for support and took a few seconds to regain her composure. She shuddered. It was awful up there; it was awful here. The place was stifling and she couldn't wait to leave. In fact, she didn't think she could last the next couple of days. Clutching Edward's hand, she headed towards Brooke Street, her mind racing. As for Elizabeth, she wouldn't trust her an inch. Her intuition had been correct, and it wasn't pleasing.

CHAPTER TWELVE

Olivia loved the month of May. It was, for her personally, the best month of the year. The sun shone in a brilliant arc across the gardens at Bramstone Hall, enhancing the vibrant shades of Flora.

"Well as I was saying." Olivia topped up her own glass of white wine and passed across a plate of sandwiches to a rather dazed Carmen, whose lobster pink cheeks were rapidly changing to a sinister shade of deep cherry in the warm sunshine. "You really need to think about this before you give me an answer, I understand that." Olivia stifled a giggle. "And I expect that this has come as a bit of shock."

Carmen bit slowly into the smoked salmon sandwich, mulling over Olivia's proposition. Slowly, she munched on the finest Salmon which by now had become tasteless. Olivia leant across to fill Carmen's glass, watching her closely through narrowed eyes. She sipped a little more from her own glass, she daren't have another if Graham found out he would not be impressed. "Whatever you decide, please remember that this is strictly confidential. I don't want the entire population of Redwood finding out about this."

"I understand." Carmen shook her head then took a large gulp of wine. She stood up stiffly, looking across at Olivia with a forced smile. "I'll sleep on it. Oh and thanks for lunch."

Isobel rubbed down Quest's hot sweaty coat. They had been out for an early ride across the fields. Isobel had given him his head, to gallop across the large meadow. Now he stood with heaving sides and a sweaty, matted coat from his exertions. Greedily snatching mouthfuls of wispy hay from the net, which Isobel had soaked earlier but that had already dried in the heat. Isobel was tense and the horse could sense it. As she rubbed distractedly at his coat, she thought back to the way Elizabeth had looked at her son. It was weird, it had unnerved her. It had also shocked her how she had felt so uncomfortable in London. Once her home a place she had loved; now it seemed like her enemy and she had no desire whatsoever to return. Elizabeth Hilliard had got under her skin; if that woman had any idea at all she would be smiling in glee. Jacob was Isobel's life, if he was to tire of the country and maybe even Isobel herself it, it didn't bear thinking about, did it?

She shuddered. It was there though, a woman's instinct, the expression "No smoke without fire," came to mind. Isobel couldn't face the fact that Jacob may possibly be sleeping with another woman, it cut like a knife but what seemed far worse was the fact that they were possibly plotting behind her back. That they were laughing, laughing at her. That's what disturbed her the most. The fact that she, herself, hadn't exactly been an angel, at this moment escaped her mind.

Marina hadn't told her exactly who she had been with, when she was supposed to have been with her. It was obvious that it was with someone she shouldn't have been with. Isobel didn't want to know, she wanted no part in the deceit. In fact Marina couldn't have picked a worse time, a time when Isobel's brain was in utter turmoil. It was Brad she felt for, he was nothing short of perfect, he simply idolised Marina.

With a sharp jerk of the lead rope, Isobel pulled Quest in to the cool shelter of the stable away from the swarm of flies which buzzed irritatingly around his head.

Later that morning when Isobel went to collect Edward from Rita's, she found herself staring aimlessly into her cup of green tea. Rita observed how quiet she was and sent Edward off to collect the eggs. It didn't take long for Isobel to unburden once again. Rita sat patiently nodding her head with a sympathetic smile.

"You know, that Jacob adores you. You maybe don't see it the way us others do." She paused thoughtful for a moment. "We tend to stop noticing these things after a while. I don't believe for one moment he would cheat on you."

Solemnly Isobel shook her head. Rita was living in the past. Everyone seemed to be at it these days. Besides Rita would probably say the same about Marina, and Isobel knew better.

Later that Evening as Isobel tucked Edward in to bed after two very long bedtime stories, which she thought would never end, she found herself saying a prayer. Isobel wasn't religious but she would often resort to prayer in times of despair, she asked for a nice weekend, a weekend where Jacob wouldn't ask every five minutes "Have I done something wrong?" She climbed into bed and closed her eyes. *Please let us get along, please.*

Marina stood resting with her foot up on the fence watching the gangly-legged grey colt, as he wobbled precariously around his mother who was ignoring her inquisitive son and tearing ravenously at the lush spring grass. Brad joined her. "Wow he is a real little stunner, a colt at last."

Marina smiled indulgently. "We will keep him, won't we?"

Brad shook his head. "Doubt it, after losing the old mare and her foal, this one will have to be sold." Brad watched the leggy foal skip around to the other side of his mother. "Seeing that this is the sire's first colt as well, I would say that makes him rather valuable."

"I know but—" she protested half-heartedly.

"No buts, this is a business after all." He looked across at the other new foal alongside its mother. A small chestnut filly, she didn't have the same stunning features of the colt.

"Even the filly will have to go. The stud needs a good income this year."

Marina gave a non-committal shrug. Brad was being awkward, trying to take the upper hand and the control out of her hands.

They walked back toward the house. "Well, darling, the foals are all here safe and sound. I think it's time you and Molly took that holiday, it has been delayed for long enough."

"Really!" she shrieked.

"Really, go and call Molly before I change my mind."

Graham drove home early; it had been a sultry day in town, close and rather uncomfortable. He drove the Jag into the driveway pulling up by the front door. He let himself in, calling out to Olivia. There was nobody home, the house was empty. He went up to change. From the bedroom window he spotted Olivia crouched out in the garden amongst the Rosemary and Basil, a pink polka dot scarf tied at her neck which had drawn his attention. Graham tapped the window she looked up and waved. Graham splashed his face with cold water, and then he joined her in the garden.

"Do you mind if I go riding, love. I'm feeling a little tense, need to relax a little."

Olivia stood up wiping away beads of perspiration with the back of her one ungloved hand.

"Sure, go ahead I still have a fair bit to do here."

Graham smiled. "You have been busy."

Olivia pulled savagely at the mint, grabbing a large handful." For our new potatoes this evening." She grinned.

Graham looked across at the sun which was descending behind the hill to the west then back to Olivia. "I will be about an hour I guess." He leant forward, over the fragrant thyme to kiss Olivia on the lips then headed up to the stables.

Marina was feeling apprehensive, as she dialled Molly at home in South Africa. She wondered if Molly actually believed that she meant it, after Marina had to postpone twice already. Molly was pleased to hear her mother's voice she seemed in good spirits. Marina was devastated when Molly informed her that it would not be convenient for her the following week. "So when can we go!"

"I'm sorry, Mother, it's just I have some important exams coming up. I don't think I can leave until I have finished them all."

"Oh, I see and when will that be?" Marina tried to hide the disappointment in her voice.

"To be honest, three weeks at the earliest, in fact we could coincide this with Daddy's visit to the States," she asked hopefully.

Marina was a little taken back; she had no idea that Howard may be brought in on it.

"Well I don't know we're—"

"Oh, please say yes, please, Mother."

Molly seemed desperate. Before she realised it, she had agreed. When she replaced the receiver she began to wonder if Howard had set it all up. Surely not, after all it was her fault that the plans had been changed so many times.

Marina went down to tell Brad that it was all arranged. He was mixing the evening feeds. "Bet you both have a great time." He smiled boyishly at her. "I'm insanely jealous."

Marina smiled back; she gazed into the mash of bran and barley he was stirring. She could look any where at that moment, except into Brad's captivating eyes.

Jacob arrived back from London a lot earlier than usual, he was feeling rather pleased with himself, for managing an early getaway. Plonking his case down in the hallway, he called out, but there was no welcome, the house was deserted. He slipped off his sweaty shoes, then headed for the kitchen and the heady smell of rosemary.

Propped up against the empty fruit bowl on the kitchen side was a note from Isobel. Informing him that Edward was with Rita, who would be dropping him home around seven and that she had gone out riding and not to worry because the dogs had gone with her.

Jacob switched on the radio. He opened a bottle of Chablis which was chilling in the fridge. He took it through to the living room where he stretched out on the sofa.

The house seemed strange without anybody else around, he had never been here alone before, and the sound of silence was most unnerving. Isobel had been acting strangely lately. This just confirmed it. He wondered as he sipped the wine if they were growing apart. It certainly appeared that way. They hadn't made love for weeks there had never been any problem in that department before. Then there was the way she had been behaving towards him, he had noticed she seemed fine with everybody else, yet offhand and moody with him. Jacob fished in his pocket for a cigarette. He found he was smoking more and more these days. Elizabeth seemed to think he was stressed, he was inclined to agree.

Slowly he let the smoke uncurl from his lungs. He smiled to himself, Isobel would be horrified; it was against her rules. Rules, rules, he hated them. Come to that he was beginning to dislike this house; he blamed it for their unhappiness. It was pulling them apart. He looked around, it always felt hostile and it always smelt strange.

Graham clucked his tongue encouragingly at Solvent, digging his heels firmly into his sides, urging him up the steep incline towards the wood. Feeling lazy in the heat, Solvent ambled along at a slow unexciting canter. As they neared the top he veered violently beneath Graham, swerving out to the right. Graham lost his stirrups lurching forward on to Solvent's neck. Solvent wriggled energetically beneath him, depositing Graham into a large patch of stinging nettles. Graham's head hit the ground with a thud. It took a while for him to focus, through the grey fog, as he saw Solvent's big shiny rump disappear at a rate of knots and out of view.

"Bloody animal," he cursed aloud, then let out a howl of pain as he realised where he had landed.

Breathlessly he stood up, scratching profusely at his bare, swelling arms. Huffing and puffing, he followed in the direction in which Solvent had fled. Searching the ground as he did so, for any sign of a rather large doc leaf to ease his agony.

"Hi, it's OK I've caught him," a voice called out helpfully.

Graham looked up with relief, to see Isobel perched on her horse, leading a shamefaced Solvent his snapped reins in her hand.

Isobel tried hard to stifle a giggle. "Oh, Graham, I'm sorry I fear it was my fault. I think we made poor Solvent jump."

Graham took off his hat and waved it courteously at her forcing a smile through clenched teeth. "Thanks, I'm glad you caught the old bugger. It's a long walk back to the hall."

"Are you OK? It looks like you have been stung everywhere."

"Don't I bloody know it." Graham began to scratch again.

"Look, if we ride over to the stream you can cool off and dock leaves are plentiful there."

"That sounds like a very good idea." Graham puffed, as he hauled himself back into the saddle. Normally he used a mounting block to assist him but he wasn't going to show himself up in front of Isobel. They both dismounted when they reached the stream. Isobel held the horses, while Graham scrambled down the bank to plunge his arms into the soothing water. Then he grabbed a large handful of leaves and rubbed gently at his mottled arms. Isobel diverted her attention to the rooks which were flying high above the wood.

"Noisy beasts, aren't they?" Graham huffed, as he scrambled back up to join her.

"Yes." Isobel nodded her head in agreement. "It's an eerie sort of place. I went to the edge once but I didn't fancy going in."

"That's because it's haunted," Graham replied.

Isobel frowned. "Really and do you believe that?"

Graham sat wearily down on the bank taking Solvent's reins from her with a small impish whimper.

"As a matter of fact I do. Legend has it that a young servant girl was murdered in its depths some time in the seventeenth century. Apparently, or so I have heard she was believed to be taking cover from the young master, who was after her virginity no less."

Isobel listened intently then shivered. "Did they find the murderer?"

"I am told not, makes you wonder if it was the master himself. They got away with that sort of thing in those days." Graham chuckled. "Now there are those that would have you believe the young girl was a witch and that the wood was a meeting place for worshipping the devil."

Isobel hugged herself. "That's made me go all cold and goose bumpy."

Graham smiled he was enjoying this. "Well I have never ventured in there and I certainly don't intend to." He looked thoughtful. "In fact even the dog won't enter and Solvent gets jittery, if we ride anywhere near the edge."

Isobel glanced across at the wood; it was only the Rooks who seemed to be able to enter it.

"Come on, enough fairy tales." He signalled to Isobel to mount.

"If you don't mind I will ride back with you, and then take a short cut via your land."

"Yes that would be nice; in fact, why don't you stop in and have a drink with us, there is a stable to put your horse in."

Graham's face lit up at the prospect. "Yes indeed, that would be most kind."

Isobel knew that Jacob would be home by now. He wouldn't much welcome company. It didn't matter, she was angry with him. There would be no pussy footing around tonight.

Carmen Franklin was incredibly tired. She left it to the other stable girls to finish up. After peeling off her dirty clothes, she took a bath and as she soaked, she pondered Olivia's strange offer.

To her utter amazement Olivia was frantic to learn to ride. She was very keen to be able to accompany Graham. It would be a task, seeing that she had never even sat on a horse. If Carmen agreed to it, she was supposed to teach her in record time and without another soul finding out. For Carmen it would mean giving up several hours a week at least. It would mean a lot of hard work. Would it be worth it? Olivia had promised to reward her well for the effort. Carmen couldn't help wondering if there was an ulterior motive Revenge being the favourite.

She climbed dripping from the bath, rubbing roughly at her skin, she had arrived to the conclusion that perhaps, it would be better to stay on the right side of Olivia, she really didn't want to piss her off.

Jacob heard a car; he went to the window and saw it was Rita, returning Edward.

He went out. Edward had fallen asleep in the back of the car. Rita got out chuckling to herself.

"Think I've tired the poor little mite out. He's been helping me do some fencing." She placed a comforting hand on Jacob's shoulder. "You must be working too hard, you're looking tired, love."

"Yes, I am, Rita. It's more from the drive down though I think."

He leant to kiss Rita's cheek. "Anyway, how are you?"

"I'm fine. I love having this little boy to look after. He makes me laugh, so he does."

Jacob scooped Edward in to his arms.

"He had some tea with me, so he's all fed. Reckon he needs his bed now."

Edward didn't stir. Jacob nodded.

"Think you're right. Can I offer you in for a drink?"

"No thanks. I'll be off now, tell Isobel I'll give her a call on Monday."

Jacob struggled upstairs with Edward. He couldn't believe how heavy his son had become. As he pulled the curtains he saw Isobel riding back across the field, there was another rider alongside her. Softly he cursed under his breath. With Edward out for the count, he would have liked to make love, attempted to get close to his wife; it appeared that wouldn't be happening now.

Graham stayed for ages it was only as the light began to fade and Jacob's best brandy was finished that he decided to make a move. With Isobel's assistance he managed to crawl up on to Solvent's back. Isobel watched as they ambled off in the direction of home. As soon as Graham was out of sight, Jacob slid his arms around Isobel's waist drawing her towards him. Isobel wriggled free from his embrace, mumbling about being absolutely knackered and disappeared upstairs.

"For Christ sake," Jacob exploded. He was becoming sick of her frosty attitude. He strode to the kitchen, fished another bottle of wine from the fridge and taking it through to the lounge, and changed his mind. He needed a cigarette and took a detour to the terrace at the back of the house, the dogs bounced along behind him.

Isobel took a quick shower pausing only a minute or two under the powerful jets of water. She dressed in her pyjamas then tiptoed downstairs for a glass of water. Cautiously she peered around to see where Jacob was, the back door was ajar. Isobel could see him sat out on the terrace. A glass of wine in one hand, a cigarette in the other.

Isobel felt every muscle in her body twitch, shaking her head she stomped back up to the bedroom got into bed and turned out the lamp. He was being an arsehole on purpose, well what did she care, he would die of cancer and it wouldn't be her fault. Restlessly she fell asleep. When she awoke in the morning Jacob was not beside her.

Brad watched Marina pack her case for the big trip to America. He raised a doubtful eyebrow with a silent wince at what she was packing.

"Are you really going to need all that posh stuff for traipsing around theme parks?"

"You never know." She shook her head disapprovingly at him. "Besides, it's a very posh hotel. I'll need outfits for the evenings."

Marina shut the case triumphantly. "There all done." She walked toward him, placing her hands on his shoulders and looking him square in the eyes. "Stop worrying, I can take care of what I will, and won't need."

"Quite right, but have you forgotten that I won't be there to carry it all, as I usually do."

Marina placed a silencing finger against his lips, then pulling down the straps of her summer dress, she wiggled free of it, to stand naked in front of him. "We'd better say our goodbyes. I'll be gone for two whole weeks," she purred.

Olivia had been delighted when Carmen rang to say she would be happy to teach her. After the first lesson she wasn't quite so sure. Every single muscle ached and it felt as if there was still a horse between her thighs. It was an immense challenge. She had to bite her lip when Carmen screeched at her from the centre of the ménage. No doubt, it would all be worth it in the end, she thought.

After that evening's lesson Olivia was feeling very proud of herself. Carmen joined her in the stable to supervise removing Gypsy's tack.

"You're doing extremely well, Olivia; in fact I would say you're a natural." Olivia smiled smugly to herself, as she slid Gypsy's saddle from her back.

"Thanks, Carmen. Graham will be so proud of me." Without thinking she threw her free arm around Carmen's neck to give her a grateful hug. Flustered, Carmen turned crimson. Mumbling, she went off in search of some hay.

As Brad hugged Marina goodbye at international departures he struggled not to cry. He hated being apart from her. "Now you're sure you have everything?" He looked across at her, much like a father would his daughter. Marina appeared like a child, small and vulnerable. Molly looked drained from her earlier flight. Brad hugged the wide-eyed child.

"Take care of your mum, won't you, Molls?"

Molly nodded, it was a strange thing to ask, and after all, she was the child. Molly knew Brad meant it sincerely. Brad watched sadly as they went through passport control and out of view. They looked more like two sisters, rather than mother and daughter. He hoped that this trip would work out for them both. Molly needed her mother to behave like a mother so desperately. Marina needed to be able to love her daughter. He crossed his fingers as he walked back to the car.

Jacob left for London. Isobel looked out from the bedroom window, while Edward watched sadly from the front door step with the dogs. Turning away from the window Isobel hugged herself, as a little shiver coursed her spine. It was going to be a hot day, but Isobel felt coldness. She fixed some breakfast for Edward, fed the dogs then went out to the stables. She brought Quest in from the field putting him in to the stable where he could stay shielded from the hot sun and ravenous flies until evening. As she fetched him some hay and topped up the water buckets, she wondered if Marina had made it away, OK. Rita appeared looking very fresh.

"Morning, Isobel, what are you up to today?"

"Well nothing really, why?" She smiled curiously at Rita.

"Well thought you might like a break?" Rita asked.

"Oh yes and what exactly did you have mind?"

"Well I want to kidnap your son. I have a friend coming down from Wiltshire, who is just dying to meet him. Thought you could have a day off from the computer, perhaps go shopping."

Isobel's face lit up. "Bless you, Rita. I would love to, you're an angel, do you know that?"

Chuckling to herself, Rita went off in search of Edward. Isobel knew he would be simply delighted. Five minutes later right on cue she heard his whoop of joy. With Edward safely packed off with Rita for the day, Isobel stood beneath the shower, letting the jets of water pummel her skin and wash away the misery of the weekend. A whole day to do as she pleased, she smiled indulgently to herself, as she dressed and pinned up her hair.

Isobel had worked hard over the last few weeks. It would be great to spend some of her hard-earned cash. It was time for a splurge. She hurried in and out of several trendy shops trying on different outfits. It was time, she decided, for a change of image. After bagging a few outfits that weren't her normal sort of thing and feeling heady with excitement of her daring new look she thought she would treat herself to something expensive to wear beneath them. She headed down one of the small side streets and found herself, staring into a small boutique, at the expensive lingerie displayed in the window.

"Now that would definitely suit you, though personally I prefer it in white."

Isobel spun around to look straight into the eyes of Adam Docherty.

"You reckon," she replied casually. As if reading her mind, he went on. "Sure do, but I expect you're standing there wondering if you should blow that sort of money on a bra and panties."

Isobel felt herself stiffen at his comment. "You have no idea, what I would look like in it. And indeed if I can afford to blow money on a bra and panties." Haughtily she strode in to the shop leaving Adam standing open-mouthed on the pavement.

Isobel paid the assistant. Picking up the beautifully wrapped parcel, she went back out in to the street. Adam was waiting for her. He smiled broadly at her return.

"Start again, shall I? Morning, Isobel, how are you, haven't seen you around?"

Isobel grinned. "Very well, thank you, Adam, and how about you?"

"Business is manic, otherwise good. So how is life treating you?"

"Oh, I guess, much the same." Isobel shrugged. "I suppose you know that Marina has gone to the States for a couple of weeks. Oh, and they lost one of their mares."

"Didn't know that she was away, heard about the mare though. Carmen told me, very sad." Adam's face brightened. "Will you join me for a drink? Be nice to have some company on my lunch break, for a change."

Isobel was thoughtful for a moment. There really didn't seem to be any harm in a drink.

"Sure that would be nice," she replied.

Adam steered her along a few streets, then on to a footpath which led to a green. Here they found a small round shaped building, a pub called Spellbinders. A rather unique little place, filled with pictures of witches and wizards. Cauldrons and Crystal balls adorned the shelves which ran along the walls, dried lavender and other fragrant herbs tied with brightly coloured ribbon hung at intervals from the ceiling. The menu, Isobel noted, followed the same theme with bubbling cauldron broth and garlic infused frogs legs. It was hardly the most appetising. Each table sat in its own quaint inglenook, around the circular bar. Much to Isobel's relief, they offered much more privacy than the normal arrangement.

Adam guided her to a table, pulling out a stool for her. "So what's your poison?" He gave her a reassuring wink, along with a quizzical smile.

"Orange juice please."

"Oh come on, I mean a proper drink," he said exasperated. "It's not often

I get a beautiful woman accompanying me on my dinner break. Surely that deserves a more celebratory tipple."

Isobel smiled meekly, feeling her cheeks flush. "OK, white wine and soda please."

Adam bit his lip and then smiled. "That's a bit better."

Isobel watched him walk up to the bar. She gazed around at the other people who were mainly in their twenties and thirties, most of them looked like they were out on a break from the office. There was one couple that took her interest. They were sitting, chatting excitedly to each other at the bar, oblivious of anyone around them. Definitely having an affair, she decided. The bloke was far too attentive to the woman. She felt her jaw drop; maybe this was how it was for Jacob and Elizabeth, at lunchtime in the city, all sweetness and light. Laughing at each other's witty conversation, why even sharing a cigarette. Then Jacob would have to come home to his sad boring wife at the weekend. Isobel pushed the thought firmly from her mind. She gave Adam a grin, as he returned to their table with a bottle of champagne and two glasses, which he placed down on the table with a sheepish grin.

"I know." He held his hands submissively in the air. "They didn't have any soda, next best thing I believe."

Isobel grinned back. He was so gorgeous there was no way, she would protest. It hadn't escaped her notice the admiring glances that Adam was receiving, from just about every female in the pub. Self assured, strikingly handsome, Isobel felt very comfortable being there with him. Adam seemed keen to learn as much as he could about her. Isobel wasn't quite so keen to disclose, choosing her words carefully. The more Isobel drank of the champagne the more relaxed she became, perhaps a little too relaxed, thanks, no doubt, to not having eaten anything for the last twenty hours. Thanks to her nonchalant mood, she didn't protest when Adam went to the bar for another bottle. Right at this moment she didn't want the afternoon to end. Adam returned with the second bottle. He grinned down at her.

"You're amazing."

"Me?" She looked up at him in surprise.

"Don't look so shocked. I've noticed the way you're always putting yourself down. Not only are you beautiful and incredibly sexy but you're really interesting." He cocked his head to one side. "Believe me that's a rare combination in my experience. You're very sensitive, aren't you?"

"Yes I suppose I am." Isobel looked away and took a sip of the champagne. She looked back he was staring at her. "You're embarrassing me, Adam."

"Sorry I didn't mean to. I just wanted you to know what I was thinking, that's all."

"What about you then, Adam? I mean you haven't said much about yourself?" Isobel looked with interest, in to his dreamy eyes.

"Where do you want to start?"

Isobel shuffled softly back on her seat, her eyes firmly focused on Adam's.

"Perhaps the beginning would be a good place."

When the second bottle was empty, Adam took a break from his life history, to look at Isobel questioningly. "Ten minutes to closing, fancy another drink. Brandy perhaps?"

Because Adam had been talking more than drinking, Isobel realised she had consumed most of the champagne and was feeling quite drunk. "I really couldn't, God knows how I will drive home as it is." Adam wagged his finger at her across the table. "There's no way you can drive. I'll have to give you a lift."

Isobel stood up. "I'm fine honestly, after all it's not really that far."

Adam thought she looked a bit unsteady. Taking her arm, he guided her outside into the warm afternoon air. Immediately, Isobel felt dizzy. "Maybe I will accept that lift after all."

"I think that would be best." Taking her hand, Adam led her back to his shop. "Just need to set the alarms and collect my mutt." He signalled to the ecstatic greyhound.

Isobel stroked the animal's sleek head. "She's a real little sweetie, isn't she?"

"Sure is and I love her to bits," Adam replied. Proudly kissing the dog's head. "Now are you ready?"

Isobel nodded, as Adam led the way out the back of the shop and to his car.

"What shall we do about your car?" He looked across at her as he fastened his seatbelt.

Isobel chuckled. "Wouldn't worry, it's only a beat up old Escort, no one will want to steal it. I'll collect it in the morning."

Satisfied, Adam gave a nod, then shifting the car into gear, he headed east. Isobel leant back looking out of the window at the passing country side. She'd really gone and done it now. She was very drunk, had left her car in town and was now accepting a lift home with the most excruciatingly handsome guy ever. It was fun though. The prospect of going home seemed suddenly boring, and she said so.

Adam chuckled. "Really now, what would your husband have to say about that?"

Isobel threw her head back laughing. "Right now I don't really care, he'll be out with his friends anyway," she added, trying to justify her statement. She watched Adam's face for a reaction; he merely smiled back at her. She looked so vibrant and alive.

"I think you've had too much champagne," he said finally.

"And whose fault is that?" She giggled, turning up the stereo and shouting to be heard above it. "So where are we going now?"

"I think coffee somewhere would be good right now."

"We're heading towards home," Isobel wailed.

Adam looked at her pleading eyes. "I know, your son will be home soon and you need to sober up," he said.

"Spoilsport!" Isobel pulled a face at him. "Oh come on, one coffee, just one little cup."

Adam grinned back at her. "OK, Isobel, you win. I was trying to be a proper gentleman but if you insist."

"I most definitely do." She leant across, smiling.

"Well I'll have to drop my dog off; it's too hot for her to be left in the car."

"Sure." Isobel nodded her head in agreement.

Isobel hadn't really given any thought to what sort of home Adam lived in. Her jaw fell open as they pulled up in front of the electronic gates.

"Holy Moses, this is some place, isn't it?" Isobel gasped looking up toward the house they were approaching.

"Well don't get too excited. I only own a small part of it."

"Still just the same, it's awesome. So which part do you own?"

He grinned. "Oh, just the top floor."

"Of course, what else," she murmured dreamily.

He pulled the car around to the rear of the large Victorian mansion. Isobel took off her seatbelt and slid rather ungracefully out of the car. She followed Adam round to a small wrought iron gate, which he held open for her. The little greyhound bounded off for a much needed pee.

"Just follow the path round, be with you in a moment." He signalled the direction in which she should follow. The path led to a large oak door which Adam unlocked.

"Follow the stairs up to the top." He whistled to the dog and then followed her up.

At the top of the stairs, there was a large landing with a huge window, looking out across the front lawns and lake. A very old looking marble table stood to her left, on it stood a large vase of water lilies. Their scent filled the air, she lingered, to smell them.

He smiled at her. "Mrs Rogers. She arranges all the flowers around here, they're her passion." Adam went ahead and opened his front door. Isobel smiled then followed him in. The apartment was open plan, an elective mix of antique and contemporary. A large picture window looked out to the rear and across the countryside beyond, letting in a wealth of light. The curtains at the window were made from a stunning heavy aged looking material draped back with wrought iron hooks. There wasn't a great deal of furniture in the room; two very worn but comfortable looking sofas; a bronze-legged glass coffee table and, in stark contrast, a very state of the art music centre. There were a few old photos in frames dotted here and there. The Kitchen area, reminded Isobel of a New York kitchen, straight from the set of an American sit com, complete with a bright red fridge.

"Please, take a seat." Adam banged the back of one of the sofas. "I just want to feed her before we leave."

The little greyhound looked at Isobel apologetically, as if she knew what her master was saying. Isobel looked thoughtfully around her. Adam was busy in the kitchen, the little dog at his heels. She listened as Adam spoke in soft tones to the dog, patting her lovingly every so often. Then he stood back to watch as she ate delicately from her china bowl. Isobel admired the sensitivity he showed the small hound. As she watched the warm exchange from the sofa, intense warmth swept her body, followed by a cascade of butterflies deep in her stomach. Feeling marginally strange, she went over to the window, taking a deep breath as she did so. The feeling was still there. This was a new sensation that enveloped her body. Isobel placed a comforting hand on her belly which was beginning to somersault.

Adam joined her. "Are you OK? You don't feel sick, do you?"

"No, nothing like that." She smiled back at him. "My mouth has gone incredibly dry though."

"Argh well that will be the effects of two bottles of bubbly. You're starting to become dehydrated. Would you like a glass of water?"

Isobel followed him to the kitchen. "If I start to sober up I'm going to feel worse, aren't I?"

"You are for sure." Adam laughed. "Best to keep drinking, but then I think you would be out for the count."

Isobel pulled a face. "Maybe I should be the judge of that."

Adam raised an eyebrow. "Let's go and get that coffee then?" He watched as her eyes flitted furtively around his apartment, before settling back on him.

Isobel folded her arms protectively across her chest. She spoke directly with defiance in her tone. "No let's stay here, and then we can have a proper drink."

"What like a whisky you mean?"

Isobel screwed her nose up. "No I've never been keen on the stuff."

"Well, what would you like?" He couldn't hide the amusement in his voice. For somebody who hadn't wanted a drink in the first place she was doing pretty well.

"How about some red wine?" She looked at him hopefully.

Adam shuffled nervously from one foot to another. "Red wine that's great. You realise however that if we stay here drinking, we will be tempting fate."

Isobel plonked back down on the sofa. She sensed his uneasiness. It only urged her on, enjoying the power. "Perhaps some things are best left to fate." She nestled back with a coy smile, rather surprising herself.

Brad arrived back to the empty house. He poured himself a large scotch and strode across to the window to look out at the paddocks. He could see most of the horses, they all looked OK. He gave a small sigh, Marina had only been gone a little over five hours but it felt like a lifetime already. He supposed he should try and eat something, but he couldn't face it. Instead he picked up one of Marina's magazines from the table and sat down to flick through it. It was mostly a load of shit, he decided. That was until a four-page article on women's extra marital affairs caught his eye. With avid interest he read it. The article pointed out favourite alibis, why it was most likely to happen and where. If the article was to be believed they were all up to it. With a sick feeling, he put the magazine down. He would go mad left alone here all night; he checked his watch then grabbed a jacket. This was the perfect time to catch up with some old mates down the local. Brad drained the last drop of scotch from his glass then set out to the car, whistling softly.

CHAPTER THIRTEEN

Jacob sat at his desk, stressed and angry which wasn't like him at all. Gloria had been off the last few days with an upset stomach. Olan seemed to be having a major crisis on a daily basis. There was a ridiculous amount of petty squabbling on the workshop floor and the orders were not getting out anywhere near as fast as he had hoped. In fact it appeared that Elizabeth was the only sane person among his staff at the moment. He called her into the office.

"Look, Izzy, I'm up to my neck at the moment. May I put you temporarily in charge until Gloria gets back?"

Elizabeth's face lit up at the prospect. "Most definitely, I would be delighted, Jacob." She sat down opposite him. "Whatever you need, just let me know, I'll help out wherever I can?"

Restlessly Jacob scraped his fingers through his hair. "If you can just keep some sort of order out there." He signalled through to the other office. "Then that would be great, something less for me to worry about." He gave a wry smile. "I have a lunch meeting today and another tomorrow, with new suppliers. It's a very important meeting."

"Don't worry." Elizabeth smiled broadly. "I'll make sure everything is running smoothly here."

Jacob grinned then reached for his cigarettes and lighter. "I knew I could rely on you." He paused to light his cigarette. "Another thing," he said gently. "When you go out to lunch, will you grab me another packet of ciggies?"

Elizabeth stood to leave. "Consider it done."

Jacob watched her leave. He knew he had been right about her, she was totally reliable. Without even being aware, his eyes followed the soft contours of her bottom as she left his office.

"Well done. Keep it going, that's excellent?" Carmen shrieked at Olivia, who sat firmly in the saddle. As she tried to perfect a twenty-metre circle and keep a light contact with the mare's mouth. "More leg, more leg," Carmen enthused, just a little too late, as the mare fell off the circle then dwindled in pace to a walk.

"Sorry!" Olivia puffed. "I'm getting tired and my legs are really starting to ache now."

"No that's OK." Carmen signalled for her to turn in. "Let's call it a day, you've done really well."

Olivia slid carefully down from the mares back; patting her neck enthusiastically, she looked across at Carmen. "I'm sorry I find it so very exhausting."

"Yes it is, but in time your legs will grow stronger."

She took the reins from Olivia to lead the mare in. "You know you are doing remarkably well. In fact I reckon another month and you would be up to Solvent."

Olivia beamed with delight. What would Graham say; he would be so proud of her?

Olivia un-tacked and sponged her mount down. Graham would be home soon and after saying thank you to Carmen, she hurried off home, feeling rather triumphant. In fact she wondered how Graham would react if she suggested sharing a bottle of wine with their evening meal. She really ought to celebrate.

A ray of sunshine slanted in through a small gap in the curtains, causing a gleam of startling bright light to fall across Isobel's face, which was nestled into the pillow. Opening her eyes, she blinked against the brightness and held her hand protectively across her face. She lay for a moment staring at the ceiling. With a sudden jolt she sat up and looked at the bedside clock, it was nine thirty.

"Edward!" she screeched aloud. The strong scent of sage filled the air as she pulled the sheets tightly, around her. There was something different about this morning; despite the fact that she had overslept, there was warmth. As much as she loved, the house, and she did love it so very much, it had never seemed that warm, there had always been dampness in the air. This morning it felt warm and inviting, as shafts of light created a rainbow across the room. She gave her eyes a fierce rub, Edward appeared in the doorway looking puzzled.

"Yes, Mummy?" he asked. He was eating a pot of chocolate yoghurt, most of which was plastered over his face and dripping down his chin onto his pyjamas. Tarquin and Sadie stood hopefully, either side of him, saliva dripping from the corners of their mouths. Weakly Isobel beckoned for him to come over to the bed. The memories were flooding back now. God she had spent the afternoon with Adam. Worst of all she had drunk far too much. It was alarming; she could not recall how she had made it back home. Isobel jumped out of bed giving Edward a big hug. At least he was safe. She looked out of the bedroom window for her car and then she remembered that it was still in town.

"How did you reach that yoghurt, darling?" She gave Edward a disapproving glance, it was hardly a hearty breakfast.

He pulled away from the looming flannel. "The lady helped me get it."

"What lady? Oh, did Rita stay?"

"No the other lady, she is nice I like her." He smiled, and then went back to the yoghurt.

"Don't tell lies please." Isobel wiped the chocolate from his face as he struggled backwards, out of her reach.

"Now you go and get dressed while I take a shower." She had no time for his fairytales this morning.

How terrible, as hard as she tried to remember, she couldn't fathom out how she had got home from Adam's place. They hadn't done anything she was sure of that. Or was she? Her mind wandered to Adam, she drew in breath. Her feelings had been very strong at Adam's apartment, that much she could remember, she was disappointed that she couldn't remember very much else.

Having got dressed she found Edward watching TV in the living room.

"Darling, did Rita drop you home last night?" she asked casually.

Edward giggled. "Oh, Mummy, you are a silly sausage."

Isobel raised an eyebrow, looking sternly at her son.

"She put me to bed, don't you remember." He looked at her with sadness in his eyes.

Isobel softened. "Oh of course that's right." She gave him a gentle squeeze. "Would you like some proper breakfast now?" she asked, taking a carton of milk out of the refrigerator.

After swallowing two aspirins, Isobel dialled Rita. How bloody irresponsible of her. God only knows what Rita would make of it.

"And how are you feeling today, love?" Rita enquired, brightly.

"Embarrassed, I feel terrible, Rita."

"Oh don't be daft. You said you had a great time, that's all that matters. It was so nice for you to bump into old friends. I expect you want a lift in to town to collect your car?"

"Oh would you? That would be great help."

So as it stood she had come home alone, he must have dropped her off before Rita got back. Well that was something; Rita believed she had met up with old friends.

Carrying a bowl of cereal through to Edward, she managed to smile. It was as if a great weight had been lifted from her shoulders. Adam had obviously been a perfect gentleman.

Isobel went out to fetch Quest in from the paddock. Edward, with the two salivating dogs in tow, followed her.

Brad called the Farrier and arranged for him to come and trim all the mares' feet, a week on Friday. Jasmine also needed a new set of shoes. Her owners had instructed him to sell her, as their daughter had lost interest. Her once daily visits having now fizzled out to never. It would be sad to see the little mare go and he was determined to find her a first class home.

Only the two stallions stayed in, now that the warmer weather was here. Brad was glad as he removed his sweater and began to muck out their stables. As he forked fresh straw into the stable he wondered how Marina would be getting on. With the time difference she would most probably be asleep right now. He would give her a call later.

Brad finished the stables by eleven. After a shower he headed in to town. Old Charlie had given him a tip. Never being able to resist a flutter he set off. The house was too quiet and too empty to stick around.

Isobel tried to appear brighter than she actually felt, as she sat next to Rita on the drive to town. Much relieved when they pulled alongside her car, thankfully still in one piece. "Thank you so much." She squeezed Rita's arm affectionately. "Come on, Eds." She signalled to her frowning son. "Let's go!"

Edward dropped his bottom lip.

"Come on please," Isobel said, briskly.

Edward began to wail. Obviously the sad look wasn't enough. He needed to make some noise for a more dramatic effect. He gave it his best shot. It worked. Rita looked sympathetically at him. "Oh, come on, sweetie, no tears now, darling."

Isobel felt pathetically weak herself. "Please don't do this, Edward. Auntie Rita was stuck with you all day yesterday. Now come on there's a good boy."

Rita gave Isobel a faint smile feeling rather embarrassed. Edward would prefer to stay with her, but secretly she was delighted. Isobel looked grimly at her child's red blotchy face. He was being a complete brat.

"Look I don't want to sound condescending, but I have a few deliveries to make, why don't you leave him where he is, maybe he'll have a bit of a nap while I'm driving round. I'll drop him off on the way back; it might be easier in the long run?"

Isobel never liked to give in but today she didn't have the energy, she nodded her head in agreement. She watched them drive off, glad that Rita had saved the day, yet again!

Isobel climbed into her car checking her appearance in the rearview mirror. She looked pale and drawn, she thought. It would probably be wise to go home but Adam's shop was just there and she would love to verify what happened last night. She hovered in her seat for a moment then decided she couldn't resist. Locking the car, she marched round to the front of the shop. Adam, sat at his desk, had his head bowed to his work. He looked up as she came in and flashed his most dazzling smile. "Bet you've got a sore head today?"

"Correct!" She sat down on one of the faded leather armchairs, with a sheepish grin. "So was I totally amazing?" A questioning frown clouded her pretty features.

"I wish I could have found out. Not to be, I am afraid," he replied. "We went out to grab another bottle of red and you fell asleep. I decided to take you home, being the gentleman that I am." He shrugged his shoulders. "Foolish decision really."

"How, utterly, embarrassing." Isobel squirmed in her seat. "I am such a lightweight."

"Were you ill? You looked quite green when you got out of the car."

"No. well I don't think so, not that I remember." Isobel held up her hands in despair. "Thanks for taking me home and not taking advantage of me. Please don't tell me anymore, I'm feeling ashamed enough as it is."

"Wouldn't dream of it, anyhow I suppose it was my fault. I rather encouraged it." He got up from his chair and came toward her. "Despite that, I really enjoyed your company." He looked down at her. "You still look beautiful, apparently even with a raging hangover."

Isobel felt his warm breath against her neck. Instinctively she moved toward him. Their lips met, lightly at first as he grazed his lips against her but then with more urgency. Isobel felt the warmth in her tummy, as the kiss grew in intensity. She stood up interlocking her wrists around his neck, intensifying the kiss further. He felt so familiar as if their lips had locked a thousand times before.

She broke away to look questioningly into his eyes. "This feels right, doesn't it, Adam?"

He nodded silently, and then went to bolt the front door, turning the sign to, closed. Isobel watched, as he walked back to her, taking her hand in his. She followed him through to the back room which was bare apart from a small table, two rickety chairs and a few rolls of cloth. Adam kicked the chairs roughly away from the table; with a sweep of his arm he cleared its surface. Then pushing Isobel back, he began kissing her neck. "You are so beautiful. I have been dreaming about this moment," he murmured, taking her hand. He placed it to the left side of his chest. "Do you feel that?" he asked.

She nodded, she was aware that his whole body trembled.

"This," he said, looking at her, "has never happened to me before—never." She knew instinctively how he felt because she felt it too. She held his gaze, aware that she could lose herself in his eyes forever. He smiled down at her and in that instant she knew, she gave a whimper of surprise. The powerful surge of recognition rocked her body and stirred her soul. It was him, God it was him. Now she was confused what did this mean? Suddenly, overwhelmed, tears pricked at her eyes. He kissed her lips gently, and then frowned, looking down at her in dismay. "Isobel, what is it, what is the matter?" He drew back uncertain, afraid that he may have overstepped the mark. He had thought that this was what she wanted.

She sat up, wiping at her eyes with the back of her hand. "Oh, Adam, I don't know where to begin."

"It's okay if you've changed your mind." He looked embarrassed, slightly uncomfortable. Isobel stood up and wrapped her arms around him tightly. "No, Adam, it's not that, not that at all. I have to ask you this, and I know it seems a strange thing to ask you, now, but have you ever seen me before?"

He was still for a moment.

"I'm not really making myself very clear, am I? Before that first day I came into the shop and bought the trousers, had you ever seen me before?" She looked at him questioningly, a sense of urgency to her tone.

He sat down on the table and rubbed fiercely at his temples, looking across to where she stood, poised for his answer. "Well, it's going to seem kind of daft, but I knew before that. I knew that you were coming. I have pictured your face. I've seen it in my mind a thousand times." He took her hands in his, pulling her closer where he looked into her eyes. "Does that sound like a complete madman?" He watched her eyes light up and a knowing smile caress her lips.

"It won't sound half as mad as what I've got to tell you, believe me."

Adam placed a silencing finger to her lips. "Isobel, I want you to tell me everything, every last detail, and I promise I won't think you're mad, but first I have to kiss you." He pressed his lips against hers and felt her surrender; he caught her as she fell into his arms. She gave a deep shuddery breath as his hands slid beneath her blouse and his fingertips traced her bare flesh. She unbuttoned her blouse, eager for him to touch her more, watching him closely as he looked down at her body.

"God, you're so beautiful!" he breathed, sliding his hands along the contours of her body. Anxious for their flesh to touch, Isobel frantically removed his sweater. She lowered herself back on to the cool surface of the bare table, writhed beneath his tongue as he traced a line from her throat down across her belly and back up to circle each nipple. She ran her fingers restlessly across his back, her body trembling. He had only just begun to delight her, but she wanted to explode, her mind was racing. Taking his time, he ran his fingers lightly along the inside of each thigh. Isobel fought the emotion that tore at her heart, she felt helpless, and overwhelmed with longing that it actually pained her.

As he entered her, she could fight it no longer, a torrent of sensations rippled through her body. She had never felt like this before, her body jolted violently beneath his. Adam gave a heady gasp as the bolt of emotion ripped through his body for a moment lost in the throes of ecstasy.

Resting his head against her bosom, he looked up at her with a satisfied smile. "I think we have just opened the door to something quite amazing."

Isobel nodded smiling back at him. He kissed her forehead tenderly then taking her face in his hands, he asked her. "Tell me now, about your dream."

She gave him a puzzled look. "Yes, the dream," he said. "I thought I was going crazy and that it was only happening to me. Now I can't stop thinking about it and what it means. I think you have the answer."

Isobel sat up hugging her arms around herself. "Yes you're right, Adam, it is a dream, and in it we're together, and you want me to be with you." She paused; she couldn't tell him about her vision at the wood. "I know it sounds odd, Adam, but I think we have known each other in a previous lifetime, and I think that's what our dreams are trying to tell us. You know, we have loved each other before."

He looked thoughtful for a moment, then gave a quiet laugh. "I don't know if I can believe that or not. Maybe if it's true, we have unfinished business."

Isobel nodded in agreement, taking his hand. "I don't understand it either, yet I feel sure we were destined to meet. It's exciting but somehow scary too."

Wrapping his arms around her, Adam pressed his face into Isobel's hair which smelt sweetly. "I think maybe you're right; I could have done this with you thousands of times before. Don't let's worry about it, I just thank God that I have found you, I'm so in love with you."

She felt her pulse quicken as she clung to him more tightly, almost scared to let go.

Marina got up with a thumping head, last night's cocktail party had been a real bash and it had left her feeling like a zombie this morning. There was a knock at the interconnecting door, Molly burst through excitedly.

"I think we should do Animal Kingdom today." She thrust the guidebook at Marina.

"Great, love. Whatever you want, I'll leave the organising to you."

"Oh, Mum, you look pale. Did you drink too much?"

"I just need a shower, wake me up a bit."

She left Molly sprawled across the bed scouring the guide, only to return thirty minutes later to find her sprawled in just the same way. There was a second knock at the door. Molly bolted past her.

"I'll get it."

A friendly looking waiter appeared with a trolley. Molly handed him a few screwed up dollar bills from her back pocket. He departed with the ever cheerful. "Have a nice day."

Molly looked across at her bewildered mother. "Breakfast," she announced, proudly.

"I couldn't." Marina held her stomach. "I never eat breakfast."

Molly shot her a disapproving grin. "You don't eat anywhere near enough, Mother, no wonder you're so skinny."

"Skinny, you think I'm skinny?"

"Just a little bit, Mother," Molly chortled, whilst heaping her plate with pancakes and maple syrup.

Marina went over to inspect the trolley. "Couldn't you have ordered something a little healthier?"

"What's the point? You wouldn't eat it anyway," she retorted, through a mouthful of pancake.

The phone rang. Lazily Marina stretched across the bed to answer it, it was Brad.

"Yes we're fine." She paused to look across at Molly who was on seconds. "Yes, Brad, Molly's really enjoying herself."

Jacob stood outside to wave off his client before going back to his office. Elizabeth appeared a few moments later carrying a tray with two steaming mugs of coffee and a plate of warm Danish pastries.

"Phew it's warm today!" Jacob loosened his tie. He checked his watch. "Come on, sod the coffee. It's too hot. Let me treat you to a drink down the pub."

Elizabeth's heart leapt. She was out to collect her bag in seconds. They strode briskly down to The Trumpeter, three streets away. It was already starting to get busy, there was only one bench left outside in the small cobbled back terrace. Jacob ordered himself a pint and a glass of chardonnay for Elizabeth; they sat watching the London traffic idle by.

Elizabeth spoke first. "It must be nice to get out of the city at weekends?"

"Sure is." Jacob took a gulp of his lager. "It's a brilliant chance to unwind. Only trouble is it goes too quickly."

"Your wife must really miss you during the week though?"

Jacob tapped the side of his pint in a strumming motion. "One would think so." He looked up and smiled at her before asking, "Fancy another?"

Elizabeth watched him walk to the bar. She smiled to herself. She had definitely struck a nerve, so there was a glimmer of hope. He came back with the drinks and she deliberately stayed away from the subject of family and Devon. He needed bringing out of himself. He seemed so withdrawn lately. They finished their drinks and headed back to the office. Jacob had to fly off to a meeting and the office was quiet for a change. Elizabeth spent most of the afternoon plotting how to get Jacob to fall in love with her. It was much clearer now she had sensed there might be a problem. It would make things a lot easier for her.

The first week in America went quickly, theme park after theme park and hot dog after hot dog for Molly. Marina watched now as they took respite from the strong midday sun under a tree, as Molly tucked in to yet another hot dog. She was as thin as a rake and yet she ate like a horse. Marina wished that she had been so lucky at that age or indeed even now.

Molly was excited at the prospect of her father arriving and Marina wasn't sure how she felt about it. She knew she felt awful about lying to Brad and wished she had told the truth, but it was too late now. She was missing Brad so much, much more than she had anticipated. Molly interrupted her thoughts. "Come on." She looked up with excitement. "We'd better get a move on, there's still so much to see."

Marina was exhausted when they finally fell back in to the hotel room, she headed straight for the mini bar despite Molly's disapproving glare. A loud knock sent Molly scampering towards the door and Marina prayed it wouldn't be more food.

"Daddy!" Molly shrieked, in delight. Howard stood smiling, in the doorway.

Marina smiled warmly. "Come on in, Howard."

"I didn't want to disturb you both."

"You haven't," Marina said casually. "Can I get you a drink?"

"I will." Molly squeezed by her. "Whisky, is it, Dad?"

Howard nodded. "Okay, only a quick one then…thanks." He took the glass from Molly with a grateful nod. "I was wondering if you ladies would like to join me for dinner tonight."

"Oh you bet, Dad." Then Molly looked across at Marina and added hesitantly, "I mean would that be OK with you, Mum?"

Marina smiled at Molly. "Of course, that would be nice. What time, Howard?"

He downed the whisky and gave the empty glass to Molly. "About eight. Shall we meet in the bar?"

Molly hummed gaily to herself as she got ready. It would be the first family meal since she was quite small. It was hard not to be excited.

Marina spent ages getting ready despite her apprehension, aware that Molly would be watching both her and Howard's every move.

As they sat in the restaurant, sharing an exquisite meal, the three of them, it felt odd. It was like having a double life, one that ran parallel to your own. This is how it would have been if they had never parted. Yet they had, and there was another man and another life. It was just too strange, Marina tried to relax. Molly's constant chatter at least, helped to ease the tension. Later they all went back to the hotel bar. Molly stayed awhile but after an hour announced that she was exhausted and needed to get to bed. After arranging to meet with Howard the next day, she kissed them both good night and went up to her room. Marina and Howard watched as she stepped into the elevator.

"She loves being with you," Howard commented, wistfully.

Marina swallowed hard, she knew that herself. It was beginning to sink in.

"About before…you know," Howard said tentatively.

"Yes?"

"Well. I wondered, are you sorry now that it happened? I have been thinking about it and I would hate for—"

Marina placed her glass down, staring passively at the elevator in which Molly had disappeared. "I know it's not going anywhere." She paused to look at him. "The sex is bloody good and it—"

He nodded, before she had chance to finish her sentence, he stood up. "Would you like a refill?"

"Actually, Howard, I'm quite tired."

"Sure." Howard tried to conceal his disappointment.

"But thank you for a wonderful evening. I've really enjoyed it," she added gratefully.

Howard saw Marina into the lift where she gave him a light peck on the cheek. He headed back to the bar and ordered another large scotch. There was no use analysing it. Marina would never be his again. She may want some loving from time to time but that would be as far as it went. He had to accept that, where Marina was concerned, his feelings ran very deep but it wasn't reciprocated. If he was honest nothing had changed, he didn't know her back then and he didn't know her now.

CHAPTER FOURTEEN

"Hold his head tighter please." Olivia scowled, as she hopped around, one foot on the ground the other wedged in the stirrup as she tried to mount Solvent, as the beast jiggled this way and that making it as awkward as possible. Carmen sighed before sending a blistering slap across Solvent's muscular chest; this sent him veering backwards in shocked horror, in turn making Olivia hop even more.

"He really is the most awful beast," Olivia wailed.

"No not really." Carmen made a feeble attempt to defend Solvent, who rolled his eyes dramatically. "He's just a spirited animal."

"Well I certainly don't seem to have much chance of getting on his back," she muttered breathlessly.

"Look he's standing now; perhaps I should give you a leg up." Carmen managed to push Olivia ungracefully up into the saddle, then led her slowly across to the paddock at Bramstone Hall. Once safely inside she let go of Solvent and turned to close the gate.

"Now be firm with him, Olivia. Lots of leg to keep him moving forward. Remember."

Olivia knew what to do. It didn't seem to work with Solvent though, he fidgeted constantly beneath her. Solvent had convinced himself there was some hidden terror lurking over to the right in the hawthorn hedge and every time they passed he spooked to the left.

"Be ready next time," Carmen bawled. "Keep that left leg on strong." After several loops of the paddock Solvent still insisted on being a pain.

Exasperated, Olivia pulled him up. "Here, you try!" She dismounted and gave Carmen the reins. Carmen pulled a face but accepted the challenge. Within five minutes he had reverted to a little lamb. "You see," she called across to Olivia. "Like I said, you need to use your legs more." Carmen rode back over to Olivia. "Now try again."

Half-heartedly Olivia got back in the saddle and rode a large circle. Solvent behaved marginally better and after a last brisk trot Olivia insisted on calling it a day, she'd had enough. Carmen readily agreed.

164

"Well that's it then."

"What?"

"I'll have to buy my own horse. Would you be kind enough to assist me in my purchase?"

Carmen nodded. "Of course I will," she replied.

Wondering in that moment if Olivia actually enjoyed riding. On the other hand, was it a vain attempt to impress Graham, who in her opinion wasn't worth it under any circumstances?

Carmen stopped to peer down at her bright red burnt and peeling shoulder scratching lightly at it. "Good horses don't come cheap you know, Olivia."

"I know. Graham paid a small fortune for him." She signalled across to Solvent who was now out in the paddock having a good roll in the dust.

"Well if you're sure." Carmen could see a nice earner coming her way out of this one. "I'll put the word out. See if we can find you something nice."

Olivia beamed. "Great, Graham will be shocked. Now I insist that you come in for a drink before you leave." Reluctantly Carmen followed her in to the house. She was only just beginning to trust her and believe that there wasn't some underhanded reason behind all of this.

Marina awoke; Brad hovered by the side of the bed with breakfast on a tray.

"Morning, darling, it's so good to have you home."

Marina yawned stretching her arms out in front of her then sat up. Brad placed the tray on her lap. "Looks good." She eyed the fresh grapefruit and muesli with freshly sliced strawberries. "Thank you, darling." She kissed his cheek.

"I hope that's all I'm not going to get." He gave a wicked grin.

"Just need to get over my jet lag first."

"Good idea. That's why you must stay in bed. I'll sort the horses today."

"Sounds good to me, honey." Marina placed the tray on the bedside table, and snuggled beneath the duvet again. The holiday had been a real turning point for her and Molly; she had every reason to feel quite pleased with herself. They wouldn't be seeing each other until the autumn now but she felt they had patched things up pretty well. As for Howard the guilt would pass. There were miles between them now. Marina had slept with him one last time. It had been on the last night, very raunchy and uninhibited; there was, however, no doubt in her mind that it was Brad she wanted and needed.

Jacob drove up the drive, returning from the village stores. It had been a hard enough sort of week at work, without coming home to be sent on shopping errands, which these days Isobel didn't seem to have time to do herself. He pulled the bag containing milk, sugar bacon and butter from the back seat, Simple basics that surely Isobel could find time to stock up on during the week. There was one good thing, Isobel had dropped her frosty attitude and he had to admit she seemed really jolly this weekend. They hadn't made love yet, but it had been a late evening round at the neighbours' last night, and it was definitely on the cards this evening, he thought.

Jacob put the groceries away and switched on the kettle. Edward appeared with an empty cup in need of a refill of juice. He waved it wildly in the air. Jacob looked down at him. He was really growing, all of a sudden shooting up; he reckoned he would probably be quite a tall lad.

Isobel was still in bed he took a mug of coffee up to her. "You're getting so sleepy." He prodded her playfully. Isobel let out a huge yawn then felt for the mug, which he thrust in her hand. She sat up to take a slurp of coffee. "Sorry I've been really busy this week."

"I noticed." He sat on the bed next to her. "Do you have a headache this morning by any chance?"

"No why?"

"It's just that you were knocking the drink back last night. In fact I don't think I have ever seen you drink like that before."

Isobel smiled. "I don't think I drank anymore than Graham." She looked quizzically at him.

He decided to leave it there. Standing up, he went over to the window and drew the curtains letting in the sunshine, which crept softly across the carpet covering the room in a warm inviting glow.

"So what's the plan for today?" He watched in fascination as Isobel rose naked from bed and padded softly to the bathroom. Isobel dived under the shower.

"Would you mind if I went riding this morning?" she shouted.

Jacob appeared at the shower door peering in through the steamy glass. "I should have thought the answer to that was fairly obvious. I mean I barely see you these days. I didn't buy the bloody horse to keep us apart you know."

Isobel scrubbed roughly at her skin. "Like I said I haven't had anytime to ride this week."

"Why fucking not!" He couldn't hold his tongue. Wondering why in hell's name he had he bothered to drive home.

Isobel emerged from the shower dripping wet. She looked across at him. Jacob had perched himself on the edge of the bath. "I thought it might give you and Edward a chance to have some quality time together."

"Perhaps, *we* should have some quality time together, had you thought of that?" He shrugged his shoulders then marched out.

"Don't you think I like some time to myself too?" she called.

He turned and came back. "What about Rita? I thought she had Edward a lot."

"She's been busy," Isobel lied, avoiding his gaze. "Anyhow don't bother." She turned and stomped over to the wardrobe.

Jacob watched her open-mouthed. What was becoming of them, fighting like cat and dog, it didn't seem possible they had always been so pleasant to each other.

Carmen entered the stable yard; it was strangely quiet. "Helllooo!" she yelled, disturbing the doves who flew in alarm from the barn. Brad looked over from one of the stables. "I thought it was you."

"You recognised my big gob you mean."

"Now did I say that? So what brings you here?" Brad went back to grooming Panther.

Carmen watched as he worked hard on the horse's silky black coat. "He looks well." Carmen ran a critical over the thoroughbred.

"Yeah he is a nice type." He gave the horse a hearty slap. "The owners are taking him to a show the other side of Marchwood this afternoon." He finished off with a flick of polish, wiped gently, with a soft cloth over Panther's quarters. He came out in to the sunshine to join Carmen. "Fancy a cuppa?"

Carmen followed him up to the house. "Where's Marina?"

"Still sleeping, I only picked her up from the airport late last night."

"How did it go?"

"Good I believe. They seem to be reconciled." He smiled. "Fingers crossed."

They sat down with a cup of tea. "I need you to look out for a nice, calm horse for me, Brad."

"What sort of money are you looking to spend?"

"Let me explain, but this is to remain top secret." Intrigued Brad sat back to listen.

When Carmen had finished he clapped his hands. "You're not going to believe this but I have just the horse you are looking for, and we can make a right killing on it too." It was a godsend; the stud badly needed an injection of cash.

"Now that's what I like to hear. So what have you got?"

"Jasmine, she has the sweetest temperament. Just the job, trust me." He was already counting the earner they could make in his head.

"Is she sound?" Carmen leant forward excited.

"Sound as a bell, if anything a bit overpriced."

"So what are they asking? I mean is there much to play with?"

"The owners want five grand."

"Wow, pricey." She drained her mug. "That's a bit steep for a riding horse."

Brad scratched his head. "Reckon we could get her for three and a half. What's Olivia willing to pay?"

Carmen rubbed her hands together. "I reckon I could get away with asking ten grand and settle at eight."

Brad leant forward planting a big smacker on her forehead. "Go for it, girl, if we pull this off it will be bloody fantastic."

Brad saw her out and hurried up to tell Marina the news. The stud could do with a good sale; they could put it through the books as one of the foals.

Marina had finally risen from bed and was drying off from the shower.

"I thought I heard Carmen, glad I stayed out the way." Marina had never been fond of Carmen; she was far too common. Sick of Brad jabbering on about Carmen, and the deal of the century, she silenced him by unbuckling his trousers and taking his mind completely somewhere else.

Jacob watched Isobel load the washing machine. He tried to make eye contact but she avoided his gaze. He hated this bad feeling. It was such hard work. It just wasn't like Isobel to be so pig headed. "Look." He placed a hand on her shoulder as she brushed by. "I'll make a deal with you. How about I take Edward in to town with me, you go and have your ride, and in return—"

She raised an eyebrow.

"And in return, well for a start you could lighten up a bit, and then we could put Edward to bed. So, just maybe we could have an early night." He smiled, pulling her close to him. Isobel forced a smile as she carefully manoeuvred herself from his clutch.

"OK, Jacob." She softened her tone, squeezing his arm lightly. "I'm sorry," she added.

Isobel took Edward upstairs, changed his clothes and washed his face. A few moments later, she stood on the front door step to see them off, planting a big kiss on Edward's cheek.

"I don't get one then?" Jacob hung his head, winking sneakily at Edward. Dutifully Isobel rose on tiptoe and kissed Jacob's furrowed brow.

"So how long do you think you'll be out riding?" Jacob asked brightly, without a hint of sarcasm.

"A couple of hours, I should think."

He checked his watch. "We'll get back for four o'clock then." He cocked his head to one side. "Will that give you long enough?"

"Plenty of time." Isobel nodded.

Once the car was out of sight she ran up to the stables. Hurriedly she put Quest's tack on, not even bothering to groom him first, as she normally would. Vaulting onto his back from an upturned bucket, she set off at a brisk trot across the fields, heading out towards the edge of the moors, slipping into an easy canter she surged on towards Dead Man's Copse, then down through the stream and up the bank into a large overgrown meadow smothered in the warm glow of buttercups. At the centre of the meadow there stood some ancient oak trees. As she neared the trees, she could see Adam sitting on a log kicking at the sun-baked ground, his horse tied to a nearby tree. As they approached the horse whickered welcomingly to Quest. Isobel pulled up beneath the shade of the trees and slithered down Quest's sweaty sides. Adam raised himself up from the log, stepping forward to take hold of Quest's head as Isobel loosened the girths, then Isobel took the reins from him and tied Quest over beside Adam's horse, a handsome bay he had borrowed from Carmen.

"You're twenty minutes late!"

"I nearly didn't make it at all," she wailed. She sat down on the log, on which Adam had been perched.

He sat down next to her. "Well you're here now. I was beginning to worry you know."

Isobel spied a flask lying on the ground. "What's in the flask?"

"Red wine, if you are up to it." He poured them both a cup full, before settling back and slipping a strong arm around her shoulders. "I haven't stopped thinking about you for the last forty-eight hours. It's been torture."

"What were you thinking?"

"Picturing your face, your smile and hearing the sound of your laugh, tasting your lips against mine." He leant over to stroke her cheek. "And more—much more," he added, wistfully.

169

Isobel turned kissing him firmly on the lips then smiled up at him. "I have missed you too, Adam."

"Not as much as I have you, you can't have done, it's been torture," he whispered.

Beneath the cool shade of the swaying oak branches they lay down on the soft bed of meadow grass.

"I need to make love to you, this time gently, taking time to explore you. I want to leave here today knowing every inch of your body." He gave a lustful sigh, she was thrilling, and he was smitten.

Blissfully unaware of anything around them, they rejoiced in their union and precious time alone. Curled together they lay naked, their burning skin cooled by the gentle breeze and gentle moist lingering kisses. Not even the restless snorting of the horses or the poignant cry of a young fox interrupted them. A shadow from behind the trees observed their union with mixed feelings. An emotional tear dropped to the soft grass, this time there was a memory, which hadn't been there before. They really had no idea of the countless pain they had suffered, these two souls joining on their endless quest for unity. The shadow lingered for a moment longer. After all, a moment like this only happened, once in every hundred years.

As they lay back in each other's arms Isobel began to cry. Tears of happiness rolled gently down her cheeks, she tried to conceal them.

"Hey, what's this?" Adam wiped the tears away with his fingertips.

"I'm happy, so very happy." She finally managed to croak, then gave a nervous laugh. "God this has never happened before." She wiped fiercely at her eyes.

Adam pulled her protectively closer. He really shouldn't but he was already dreading the moment she would leave. Leave and go back to her husband. He had never felt like this before, he knew it from the first time he had set eyes on her. He looked down at her. If she only knew, what, was going through his mind. What she had unlocked. He had waited his whole life for her.

Olivia slipped off her shoes replacing them with her smart new leather riding boots. Then she stood in front of the mirror to admire herself with childish glee. Oh, how much better she looked than Carmen did! Poor old Carmen, whose fat orange peel thighs showed painfully through her light beige jodhpurs. *Yes*, Olivia thought to herself, she looked quite the part. All she needed now was the darn horse, and even now as she stood admiring herself she had no doubt that Carmen would be working on that minor hiccup. In fact, she had already arranged for Olivia to attend a viewing on Monday at the Cobbetts', of all places. However if it was as good as they said it was, it would be worth the embarrassment. Carmen had promised that Brad would not utter a word to anyone.

Olivia heard a car pull into the driveway. She peered out of the window. Drat, it was Graham. Olivia hurried upstairs to change.

Graham arrived home, flung his keys down on the hallway table, and headed through to the kitchen for a glass of water. Frantically Olivia changed; she came down to find him sat at the kitchen table engrossed in the newspaper.

"Good day, love?" she enquired, as she leant over to place an affectionate kiss on his cheek.

He looked up at her. "Grand, things are just grand at the moment. We really are having, the most remarkable year."

"Oh that's good to hear." She poured herself a glass of water and sat down opposite him.

"Yes. It's great, seems more and more people are moving down to Devon. In fact." He gave a wicked grin. "I think those neighbours of ours have started a trend." He rubbed his hands together greedily.

Jacob left the farm a little after seven on Monday morning. He drove back to London feeling a lot happier than he had done a few days previous. Isobel had been much nicer to him this weekend, forgiving her wanting to ride out; still it had been nice for him to spend some time alone with Edward. He was missing out an awful lot on his childhood, what with only having weekends with him. He needed it to be like this, to enable him to deal with the week ahead.

As he negotiated the last stretch of country lane, he smiled, looking out at the beautiful countryside, then up to the clear sky overhead. It was going to be another beautiful day. While the weather was good, he really should take a week off. Spend more time with Isobel and Edward. In fact he would get Gloria to sort out a week in the diary, he needed a break and he needed much more time with his family.

Isobel had waved half-heartedly from the doorstep. She was feeling incredibly guilty. There was no doubt how hard Jacob was trying. She went back to the kitchen and fixed some scrambled eggs for herself and Edward. As they sat together she thought of Adam. He was so exciting he made her feel so alive. She looked across at Edward, he was so beautiful. How could she even begin to think of shattering his safe little world? Isobel put down her knife and fork, gazing wistfully across the kitchen. That was what she was considering though. It suddenly dawned on her, the enormity of it all. She had fallen in love with another man. She was considering leaving her husband and child. She wanted to spend all her time with Adam, it actually hurt to be apart, an intense pain, one she had never experienced, before. Not even with Jacob or Edward and she had thought she loved both of them more than anything, believed that she couldn't survive without them. She took a deep breath, of course she must love Jacob, he was the father of her son and he was a good man. Adam she hardly knew, but every part of her ached for him, it was exciting and frightening at the same time, but it was very real. Absently she watched Edward finish his breakfast. She pushed her plate away, suddenly feeling rather sick, a familiar feeling crept over her body, she shrugged it away, it didn't belong, yet she had felt it sometime before, it was strange, a feeling of loss.

Olivia collected Carmen in the Range Rover and together they drove up to the Cobbets'.

"You look very smart." Carmen said it genuinely, admiring Olivia in her new attire.

"Oh glad you like it." Olivia couldn't resist a quick glance in the mirror.

As they pulled up at the stables Brad appeared looking relaxed and tanned in a pale blue, checked shirt. Thankfully Marina was nowhere in sight.

"Morning, ladies, and what a fine morning it is." He leant and kissed both of them lightly on each cheek.

"Morning," Olivia replied briskly, whilst trying to appear businesslike. Even if, she really wasn't so educated on equestrian matters, she didn't want Brad to think he could pull the wool over her eyes.

"So you're looking for something sane and easy to manage?" Brad asked Olivia courteously.

"Yes. I'm not that brave, something safe for a novice such as myself."

Brad stopped to open a stable door. "Well this little diamond is certainly that."

Olivia peered in at the delightful grey mare, which whickered softly and looked at them with big brown eyes. The mare was pretty, if on the fine side; her coat was the softest shade of dove grey and her mane and tail were the colour of shiny steel. Cautiously Olivia approached her; the mare pricked her ears forward and looked attentively at Olivia. In turn Olivia immediately felt herself warming to the mare and her pleasant disposition.

Brad stepped forward. "Would you like me to tack her up?"

"Oh yes please." Olivia said it with a little bit too much enthusiasm.

Brad rode the mare first, putting her through her paces. Obediently she didn't put a foot wrong. She stood like a rock as Olivia mounted her. Carmen suggested that Olivia should do her own thing, to get a feel for the mare. Olivia rode in several circles, grim determination on her face. She glanced across at Brad and Carmen who it appeared were taking no notice, and were chatting and laughing with one another. She began to relax. Jasmine was most responsive. Whatever Olivia asked her to do she did with no fuss at all, forgiving any errors on Olivia's part.

"So what do you think?" Carmen yelled across at her. She rode over to where they were standing, giving a delighted thumbs up sign.

Brad smiled. "You like her?"

"Oh yes, she's a real poppet." Olivia slid down trying hard not to grin from ear to ear and handed Brad the reins.

"You know you're welcome to come back and try her again or perhaps you would like to take her out for a hack?" Remembering the pep talk she gave herself before leaving home, Olivia looked thoughtful.

"I want to go home and think about it." There she had said it! She let out a small sigh of relief; let them sweat awhile. That she was going to buy the mare there was absolutely no doubt, that they would make a profit there was no doubt either, so they could afford to wait a little longer.

On the drive back to Carmen's, Olivia evaded any pointed questions. She would go home, have a glass of wine, then ring Brad direct with her decision.

Brad had just finished down at the stables and was fixing a large gin and tonic for himself when Olivia phoned. After a lengthy conversation, Brad replaced the receiver grinning from ear to ear.

"Get dressed, honey. I want to go out and celebrate. Besides a nice little earner, Jasmine will be going to a first class home."

Marina emerged dripping from the pool. "Oh, so she wants her then?"

"You seem surprised, o yea of little faith! Jasmine's an exceptional little mare, she'd struggle to find better."

"Well I am a little. It had crossed my mind that she might be winding Carmen up."

"Well she seemed pretty certain to me. So get dressed and let's go."

"OK, honey." She draped a large towel around herself. "I need an hour to get ready. Anyway where are we going?"

"Feeling a little French this evening and I know just the place."

Isobel had planned this evening to the very last detail. She had a potential client with a barricade of work. Rita had, as she had anticipated, been very pleased to look after Edward in the circumstances and conveniently, Jacob was out for a business dinner this evening, as Gloria had earlier informed her. She would call around ten and leave a message on his answer phone, saying she had a headache and was going to bed, that way he wouldn't worry when there was no answer at home.

With her alibis in place, she checked her appearance in the mirror one last time. She drove to Adam's place, butterflies restless in her tummy. As she pulled up outside, she could hear the anxious thud of her heart. Isobel beeped twice. It had been Adam's suggestion that they go for a meal. It was risky in her opinion, but she didn't want to hurt his feelings. Adam appeared smiling cheerfully. He got into the car, kissed her neck tenderly whilst sliding his hand slowly along her bare thigh, causing her to whimper in delight.

"Mm, you smell good." They chorused in unison, and then giggled. Isobel struggled to follow Adam's haphazard directions. Each signal he gave her at the very last minute, causing them to overshoot the turnings on several occasions. They were certainly heading out in to the country, the middle of nowhere it seemed.

Adam watched Isobel's face as she drove along the winding country lanes; she was quite perfect, he decided. He was feeling slightly guilty that he hadn't had the arse or the time to tell Vanessa Coombs that it was over. Not that there's had been any sort of serious relationship, very casual really. Besides, Vanessa would have only just returned back to Britain from her parents' home in Geneva, so he couldn't have told her any sooner if he had wanted to, he placated himself. It was only fair that it should be face to face, he wasn't that much of an asshole. Isobel was unaware that he had been seeing someone, Adam had decided against telling her. It was complicated enough with her being married, Vanessa would only complicate things further he'd decided.

"That way!" He signalled frantically to the left, causing Isobel to brake violently nearly sending them both through the windscreen.

"A bit more warning would be nice," Isobel wailed, sticking the car in to reverse and taking the turn in a more orderly fashion. They turned into a rather grand gated entrance which led up to a large Georgian house.

"It doesn't look much like a restaurant." Isobel screwed up her nose at the imposing building in front of them.

"I can assure you it is." He squeezed her thigh playfully. "And I hear the bedrooms are awesome." He winked with a hopeful grin.

"Oh, Adam!" Isobel felt her cheeks flush then diverted her gaze back to the hotel in front of her. There didn't seem to be many cars parked outside. In fact there didn't seem to be much sign of life at all.

"It looks as if we may be there only ones here tonight. Oh well, at least it will be private." She looked grimly at him.

"What's wrong with that?" Adam frowned. "Now come on, I am ravenous."

Despite the pessimistic first impression, the hotel was indeed very posh inside. They made their way through to the cocktail bar, lots of foliage set off with bright lighting and there were deep, leather sofas. Adam ordered two vodka martinis, which they took through to the conservatory. Once seated, Adam handed her a menu. Isobel noticed another couple, fortunately, they hadn't acknowledged their arrival, so, Isobel with a sigh of relief, began to relax. She turned her attention to the menu, deciding, that she was far too excited to think about food. Snapping it shut, she placed it firmly down on the table in front of her. Adam looked at her in alarm. "Isn't there anything you fancy?"

Isobel giggled. "I have always wanted to say this." She took a sip of her martini; Adam looked at her expectantly.

She gave a smug grin. "You order for both of us."

Adam put on a clipped upper class voice. "Certainly, darling, if you're quite sure?"

Isobel nearly choked on her martini. Giggling more she elbowed him across the table. "Just get on with it, darling."

Adam placed his hand over hers. "No seriously I don't know all the things you eat. I might order something you absolutely hate."

"I'll risk it."

"OK, don't say I didn't warn you."

Isobel drained her glass; the thought had crossed her mind that he might purposefully set her up. If she had a few more martinis like that one, anything would be permissible. Well actually with the exception of snails, she thought.

The pretty waitress arrived to take their order, fluttering her eyelids at Adam. He gave her his cheeky lopsided grin and proceeded to order Moules Marinere for starter, followed by fillet of lamb baked with an herb crust served with herby fondue potatoes.

Isobel gave a small sigh of relief. "Great choice, thankfully I will eat all of that." She smiled across at Adam. "I was afraid you would order the snails in garlic!"

"Well if you would prefer?" He stood up to call the waitress back. Isobel pulled at his shirt sleeve. "No I'm happy with your first choice, really."

Adam sat back down. He leant across to bury his head into her neck, where he inhaled her warm, heady scent.

The waitress returned with Adam's choice of wine. Adam sent it back. It wasn't chilled enough. Apologetically the waitress returned with another bottle. Adam felt the bottle then gave her a wink. "Perfect. Thank you very much."

Isobel smiled to herself, as the waitress hurried off to put it on their table in the restaurant.

"I think she fancies you."

"Nonsense." Adam shook his head, avoiding Isobel's teasing grin.

The headwaiter arrived to show them to their table, in the oak panelled restaurant.

"Very private here, sir." The waiter waved his hands around, to emphasis the fact. Isobel felt her cheeks flush, feeling decidedly awkward. It was in fact, very private. Sat at the far end of the restaurant, they were concealed from the other diners by dense foliage of the tropical plants.

"Excellent." Adam nodded his approval. Smiling, the headwaiter nodded and left them in peace.

"How embarrassing was that?" Isobel squirmed in her seat. "What did you say to him?"

Adam chuckled. "Well you did say you wanted to be discreet." He poured them both a glass of wine. "Besides, relax, I just said it was a romantic celebration and that we would like a private table."

Isobel looked thoughtful for a while. "Of course he knows we're having an affair."

"So, what if?" Adam shrugged. "We love each other, don't we?"

Isobel looked wistful. "Yes, we do."

"And as long as you don't decide to bring your hubby here, well then it's not a problem, is it?" he said.

Isobel flinched at his remark. She was glad the starters arrived at that moment and she didn't have to pass comment. The food was delicious. Adam ordered another bottle of wine, from the waitress, as she cleared the empty plates away and made sure that Adam got an eyeful of her cleavage, as she leant over the table. Isobel chose to ignore it. Wherever she went with Adam, it would be like this. She guessed it would be something that she would have to get used to. Isobel excused herself from the table to go and use the phone. She best leave, Jacob a message on the answer phone. She was relieved when he didn't reply. It didn't even bother her if he was out with Elizabeth; in fact, they were welcome to each other.

They skipped dessert and opted for a glass of cognac. As the waiter set glasses before them and began to pour the aged brandy, Isobel heard a distinct laugh filter through from the other end of the restaurant. It made her blood run cold, she would know that laugh anywhere. Tentatively she peered between exotic palms, and then recoiled in horror. Adam, somewhat intrigued, watched her. Noticing the colour drain from her cheeks, he handed her the glass of brandy. "Have a slug of that, and then tell me who you've just seen." Obediently, she gulped back the warming liquid and looked back at him through eyes wide with fear.

"Oh, dear God, you're not going to believe it. But bloody Brad and Marina have just sat down."

"Oh shit. They didn't see you, did they?" he asked.

"Shush, no, but what are we going to do now?" Isobel's voice was barely audible.

"Well as I see it we have two choices."

"And what might they be, because right now I can't think of one?"

Adam gently took her hand. "First of all, don't panic," he soothed. "We can wait until they leave. Which if they've only just sat down may be quite a while. So perhaps, not the better option, although the brandy's very good," he said, eyes twinkling. Isobel gave an impatient shrug. Sensing her agitation, he continued. "Or we could brazen it out. Let them see us together," he said finally.

"How do we do that!?" Isobel wailed.

"Well didn't you say you were out with a client tonight?"

"Yes why?"

"I could be that client, couldn't I? I mean, you could be doing some secretarial work for me."

Isobel's heart fluttered and her stomach churned, there didn't seem to be a lot of choice really. Firstly, they may have noticed her car outside, and secondly she was in desperate need of the loo. She wouldn't be able to hang on until they left. Well not unless she wet herself and that would be far more embarrassing. No, Adam was right.

Her mind made, abruptly Isobel stood up. "I'll go first, you stay here. Pay the bill and then I will meet you out at the car." She drained the remainder of brandy from her glass, and without a backward glance raced through the restaurant.

Adam watched as she stopped briefly at Brad and Marina's table. There was a lot of waving hands and nervous snorts of laughter and then she left.

He settled up the bill and casually strode up to their table, planting a kiss on Marina's cheek and offering a friendly hand to Brad. He made polite conversation, recommending the lamb to them both, and left.

He found Isobel sitting grim faced in the car with the engine running.

"What about the room I booked!" he wailed, as he slid in beside her.

"Yes sorry about that, but there was no way I could stay!" She noticed him grinning at her. "What's so funny?"

"It's OK, I hadn't really booked a room. You want to see your face, Isobel, it's a picture."

She thumped his leg. "Well I'm glad you find it so amusing. I was absolutely wetting myself in there; I'm still recovering now." She wiped her sweaty palms together. "I could hardly breathe," she added.

Adam began to laugh. "Take it easy, babe. It all looked perfectly OK."

The farther from the hotel they drove, the more he saw her relax. When they finally pulled up at Adam's, she began to laugh. She wiped a tear of laughter from her cheek. "God that was close. I think they swallowed it though."

Adam placed a silencing finger on her lips. "I think they did, honey." He kissed her passionately on the lips until she began to giggle again.

"Oh come on!" He leant across and opened her door. "Let's go on up. The evening hasn't ended yet. Besides—" He guided her hand to his crotch and the huge bulge. Isobel felt giddy. Giddy with excitement.

"Besides, what?" she teased, unzipping his fly, turned on by the adrenaline pumping through her veins. What a dangerous game she was playing.

CHAPTER FIFTEEN

Usually by the end of August, the weathermen were keen to predict an Indian summer. It rarely materialised. It seemed this year, however, was to be a wonderful exception. The leaves on the ancient oaks changed their colour, to warm shades of amber and gold. The once lush paddocks were patchy and brown, starved of all vegetation by the stretch of good weather. The stream had dried up, barren of the abundant wild flowers that had once adorned its banks. There was a drought and in turn, the gardens at Bramstone Hall had lost their appeal, as the flowers wilted and the herbs turned brown, their leaves curling at the ends.

Olivia stood excitedly at the living room window, not even bothered by the fact that all her hard work was being spoiled by the lack of rain. She watched and waited eagerly for the horsebox, which would be delivering Jasmine, her long awaited surprise for Graham. They had been due to arrive over thirty minutes ago. Everything was in place.

As soon as Graham had left for work that morning, she had rushed out and energetically prepared the spare stable next to Solvent's. Brad had taken care of everything else. The mare had been checked over by the local vet, who had given her a clean bill of health and commented on what a lovely natured mare she was. Olivia was feeling incredibly smug. Brad had also had the mare kitted out with all the necessary equipment. She crossed her fingers, so far so good.

Olivia heard the truck trundling along the lane and ran out in to the sunshine to greet it. Brad jumped down from the cab. "She's travelled well despite the heat." He gave thumbs up sign. Marina hopped down from the other side and came round to join them.

"Would you like me to bring her down off the lorry for you?"

"No. Would you mind if I did it," she replied breathlessly.

Marina handed her the lead rope. Calmly Jasmine followed Olivia down the ramp and up to the stables, where Solvent stood ears pricked and neck arched. He snorted triumphantly at the little mare. Brad chuckled. "Don't think he can believe his luck, eh?"

Safely in the stable, Jasmine munched peacefully at her hay net, ignoring the rampant call of the stallion next door.

"She is adorable!" Olivia declared. "Now come down and have a seat in the garden. I'll fix you both a drink while the new arrival settles in."

Olivia brought out a jug of homemade lemonade and glasses filled with crushed ice. Brad and Marina stayed for over an hour, giving her lots of tips and advice, organised as ever, Marina had typed out some instructions for her to follow. Aware that Olivia was a novice, and Graham, she considered, not much better.

Olivia waved them off, and spent the remainder of the afternoon gazing happily over the stable door at the new occupant of Bramstone Hall.

Carmen received a call from Brad to confirm he had received the money, more importantly, her share of the profit. She whopped with joy, punching the air. The sleeping cats, alarmed by her outburst, scuttled off out of the cat flap.

Isobel saw off Jacob, as she did every Monday morning. These days, no longer with a heavy heart, more a sense of joy and freedom. Much to her relief neither Brad nor Marina had mentioned seeing her with Adam that night, so she hadn't brought it up. It was best left, besides, they were both so busy with the youngsters at the stud, and they probably hadn't given it a second thought.

Edward was to resume nursery this morning for the autumn term, much to her relief. With everyone out of the way, it would give her some much-needed space to think about Adam and the whole situation. Adam, the mere thought of him sent shivers down her spine. Jacob had taken the last week off, much to her annoyance, and she hadn't had chance to contact Adam. Besides he had gone to an exhibition in Birmingham and wasn't due home until tomorrow night.

Heading east, across the hard pitted earth; she picked up the old roman road which led to the designated bridleway. The sun beat relentlessly down upon them, as they headed toward the wood, it would be cooler there, she decided. The horse was becoming increasingly, agitated by the flies, shaking his head furiously, as they circled above him in a tiresome swarm, to escape them she pressed on ahead, in the shadow of the wood they would abate. At the woods edge, Quest stretched his neck thankful for the respite. It was quiet and peaceful, in fact there was no sound at all, not the song of a bird or the annoying buzz of a fly. Even the noisy rooks seemed to have disappeared.

Isobel rode peacefully along the curve of the trees for once it seemed quite welcoming. Her feelings hadn't changed, if anything they had grown in intensity. It would be hard but she knew the time had come. Jacob would be heartbroken and Edward distraught, but they would all have to get over it. She had to be with Adam. Could she really go through with it? She wasn't convinced that she had the strength.

Quest raised his head, pricking his ears with interest at something further ahead. Isobel couldn't see anything. She gathered up the reins and pushed the horse on with an encouraging squeeze. Suddenly a young woman emerged on the pathway, in front of them. Quest stopped dead in his tracks, jerking his head and pulling the reins through her fingers and taking a nervous step back.

"Steady now," Isobel soothed. She ran a comforting hand along his neck. He relaxed slightly and she managed to ease him forwards.

The woman smiled, as she approached.

"Hi there," Isobel called. Wondering what the woman was doing up here and on private land, Graham's land to be exact. The woman didn't respond she turned back toward the wood.

How rude! Isobel thought. Obviously, the woman hadn't planned on being caught trespassing. More fool her anyway, for going in there; it was more than she would dare do, all those tales of ghosts and witchcraft. No, she shuddered; she didn't fancy that at all.

Isobel rode the circumference of the wood; it wasn't that large, the woman couldn't hide in there forever. Staring in towards its depths, she felt a great sadness. This wood was a lonesome place.

A voice called out her name, in the stillness, shattering the tranquillity. Her breath caught in her throat, every nerve ending twitched, the horse sensing her fear, stiffened beneath her. It came from within the wood, more than a whisper. She looked around there was nobody about. Could it have been the woman she had seen earlier? It called again and this time Isobel was sure that she hadn't imagined it. It was most definitely real. Afraid, Isobel called out, "Who's there? What do you want?"

It was silent again, the breeze dropped. Isobel waited for some time but there was no further sound. Maybe she was imagining it; all this worry was driving her round the twist. She shrugged pulling Quest away from the wood, this time however, with an air of reluctance to leave.

Turning for home, Quest picked up pace glad to be heading back. The gentle breeze cooled her burning skin as they cantered back across the fields.

Olivia watched in eager anticipation, as Graham got out of the car. She listened for the front door, the jingle of keys. She rushed to meet him in the hallway.

"Good day, darling?" she asked.

"Not bad. Bloody hot in the office though. I could murder a cold drink, love."

Olivia fetched them both a glass of elderflower cordial. Graham slipped off his shoes. "How come you're not out gardening?" He looked across at her accusingly.

"Oh all done. Just have to water later."

"What's with the grin?"

Olivia sipped her drink daintily, hiding behind her glass as she managed to compose herself.

"Are you off riding this evening?" she asked casually.

"Thought, I might do." He peered at her over the rim of his glass. "Why was there something else you wanted to do?"

"Well I thought I might come out riding with you."

Graham stifled a chuckle. "I don't think Solvent would tolerate an extra passenger, love. And you certainly wouldn't keep up on your legs, as beautiful as they are," he added gently.

"OK, I know when I'm not welcome." Olivia shrugged, collecting up their empty glasses and taking them over to the sink. Graham watched her with mild amusement, scratching his head. She had obviously had too much sun today, bless her. As Graham sat idly flipping through the newspaper, Olivia sneaked upstairs changed and slipped out the side of the house. Jasmine welcomed her with a soft nicker. Breathlessly, Olivia saddled the mare and waited eagerly for Graham to appear, hoping she hadn't been too presumptuous.

Crouching in the depths of the stable holding Jasmine still, she heard Graham panting as he marched up to the stables, chattering to Ruffles.

Hardly daring to breathe, Olivia listened as he tacked up Solvent, muttering to himself as he did so. Finally she heard the stable bolt slide back. She opened the stable door and led jasmine out to fall in step beside Graham and Solvent.

Solvent let out a deep throaty grunt. Graham's head shot up and he wheeled round to face her, his jaw hanging to the floor.

"My God! Where did that come from?" He shook a finger at Jasmine.

"This is Jasmine." Olivia patted her neck enthusiastically. "My beautiful new horse, do you like her?"

"But you don't ride, Olivia."

"Oh yes I do." Olivia threw her head back, laughing. "I've been learning all summer. Are you pleased?"

"Amazed, actually! Is this a wind up?" He swallowed hard, flummoxed, at a loss for words. "Where did Jasmine come from?"

"From the Cobbetts actually, and before you say anything she has passed a veterinary examination."

"I don't know what to say, love." Graham stood in disbelief until Solvent gave him an indignant nudge, nearly taking Graham's feet from beneath him. He was visibly shaken, she smiled meekly, and it was, she supposed, rather a shock.

"I know it's a bit of a surprise, but a pleasant one I hope."

"You're not kidding." He gave a broad grin. "It's smashing, you're deadly serious, love, I'm overwhelmed, the best surprise ever."

"I knew you'd like it." She threw herself into his arms with joy. For once she had actually done something right and it felt amazing.

Jacob finished for the day, he felt good, lighting a cigarette and taking a large gulp of scotch, reserved for special occasions. He had finally clinched the Marshall deal after weeks of wining and dining the managing director, Jim Marshall. Turning the office lights out, he picked up his keys and headed for the door, surprised to find Elizabeth still busy at her desk.

"You're working late. You must be desperate for overtime," he teased.

She turned giving a faint smile, twisting her hair, around her little finger. "I just need to get on top of all this lot." She signalled to the overflowing tray on her desk.

"Great news!" Jacob beamed down at her. "We got the Marshall contract."

Elizabeth stood up, giving him a big hug. "Oh that's fantastic. Well done you!"

"I know, it's great, isn't it? Look I feel too excited to go home. Do you fancy joining me to celebrate?"

"I had been planning to meet up with a girlfriend." She looked thoughtful. "But as it's a special occasion I would love to."

"I don't want to interfere with your plans."

"You're not; I wasn't that keen to go. Give me five minutes and I'll be ready."

Elizabeth joined him outside the front of the building. Suddenly she felt apprehensive but the nerves soon subsided as Jacob slipped his hand into hers and led her along the busy streets, down towards the Thames. They found a small wine bar with great views. The place was heaving with tired, thirsty workers, fresh from the office. By sheer fluke Jacob managed to nab a table just as its occupants stood to leave. He promptly propelled Elizabeth into one of the vacant chairs still warm from the previous resident.

Elizabeth watched over her shoulder as Jacob stood patiently at the bar. He was so handsome. She wondered if he would ever notice how she felt. She needed to be more obvious, flirt a bit more; he was a man who needed a gentle push, she decided.

He arrived back at the table with a bottle of Cava.

"Best I could do." He shrugged. "It seems there's been a run on champagne this evening. There's not a bottle in the house, next best thing I'm afraid."

"We're obviously not the only ones celebrating." Elizabeth smiled up at him, her pulse quickened as Jacob held his glass toward hers.

"I propose a toast, to a long and successful association with Marshalls."

"I'll second that." Elizabeth took a sip of the fizzy Cava. "Well done, Jacob, you've worked so hard you truly deserve it."

The walk back to the office through the brightly lit streets, past rowdy bars and fashionable eateries went far too quickly for Elizabeth. Instinctively she slipped her arm through Jacob's. He unlocked the car; a shadow of concern fell across his face.

"I shouldn't really drive but it's not too far." He looked across at Elizabeth who nodded.

He fumbled with the key in the lock. "Would you fancy coming back to mine, for a few more celebratory drinks? I could call you a cab later," he added hopefully.

Elizabeth's heart soared but she remained calm. "Yes. Why not, Jacob." She checked her watch. "It's only just gone ten."

Relieved that Elizabeth had accepted his offer, Jacob drove back to the flat. Elizabeth was surprised as he held the door open for her and she sauntered in. It was very dowdy; purely functional, aged. Nothing like she had imagined.

Jacob opened a bottle of scotch. He looked across at Elizabeth. "Sorry it's all I have."

"Scotch is fine."

After a few drinks, Elizabeth heard herself telling Jacob about her childhood, not a wise move, one she certainly hadn't anticipated. A single tear fell to her cheek as she reminisced. Jacob noticed it, moving closer, placing a comforting hand on her shoulder. Perhaps it was the scotch or the euphoric feeling at clinching the Marshall deal. But his lips met Elizabeth's, who didn't seem to mind at all, reciprocating the kiss with fierce passion, taking him pleasantly by surprise.

Jacob had been snubbed so much by Isobel lately, it seemed only natural to take Elizabeth by the hand and lead her to the bedroom, he was feeling lonely and ignored. Carefully he undressed her. Starting at the top of her forehead, he worked his way down her gaunt body with light butterfly kisses. As they made love, there was a great need between them, mutual warmth. Elizabeth had finally achieved her goal. She was if she wasn't mistaken in heaven.

Elizabeth lay awake staring across the silent room towards the window, where a shaft of light from a street lamp, fell across the woven rug at the side of the bed. She couldn't sleep her mind was racing. Where would this lead to now? Was it wishful thinking or could she become Jacob's mistress. There for him all week, then taking time to pamper herself at the weekend ready for his return, from the country and his unloving, cold, wife.

She looked down at him, asleep beside her. He looked so vulnerable she was afraid to move for fear of waking him, even more afraid that the magic of tonight would be lost forever, she lay very still hardly daring to breathe, wondering what tomorrow would bring.

Isobel returned home, from dropping Edward at nursery. These days he couldn't wait to get there, possibly down to the fact that Mrs Wright, who ran the nursery, was looking after her sister's rabbit and took it to work with her to amuse the children.

Kicking off her shoes in the hallway, she stopped to stroke the dogs who greeted her enthusiastically. She called Jacob, he seemed grumpy, and instantly she wished she hadn't bothered.

"I only called to remind you that it's your mother's birthday. I wondered what I should buy for her, perhaps something for the garden."

"God I had forgotten all about it. What day is it?"

"Friday," she replied.

"Look perhaps you and Edward should come up to town for the weekend. We could take her out for lunch or something. Is there a remote chance?"

"Sorry, that's out of the question. I promised Rita that I would feed her animals while she's away."

"Oh I see, well leave it with me. I'll give it some thought and call you back later. I can easily pick up a present, besides there'll be more choice here."

She put the phone down. He had to get a little quip in, didn't he? Well it hadn't got to her, she stuck her tongue out at the phone and wandered through to the kitchen for some much needed caffeine.

Yesterday she had gone to see Adam, to tell him that it couldn't go on, to end the only thing she really cared about, apart from Edward of course. When she had arrived there, she had chickened out. She loved the man, she couldn't bear to say those words and end her happiness. It wasn't what she wanted to do in her heart, just the right thing. Instead they had made love, in the stock room on top of a new order of ludicrously expensive Italian designer wear.

Sitting absently at the kitchen table, the sleepy dogs by her feet, she forced herself to stop thinking about Adam. A walk was what she needed; it never failed to clear her mind. Grabbing the dogs' leads, she gave a whistle, eagerly they hurried behind her to the garden. Draping the leads around her shoulders, she set off across the fields. The dogs sped ahead their tails wagging. Isobel strode behind them, compelled to visit the wood once more. On reaching the edge of the wood, she found once again that there was an extraordinary stillness. The rooks were still absent. Serenity prevailed. Isobel felt no need to enter, but to be close to it. She sat down on an old log, to look back across the valley.

Isobel didn't hear a sound, yet she was aware of somebody moving around behind her, she didn't feel afraid as slowly she turned, to see the young woman, she had briefly encountered when out riding. Oddly she found that she wasn't surprised to see her. As the smiling girl came to join her, she noticed how strangely she was dressed. A simple grey cotton shift dress and much worn leather sandals on her feet. Her raven hair swept back from her face, tied with a faded yellow ribbon.

"Hello there." Isobel looked up with a welcoming smile; she didn't want to scare her off this time. As the woman came closer, Isobel, appalled by the paleness of her skin, tried not to stare.

"Good day." Nodding acknowledgement, the woman sat down next to her.

"Out for a walk?" Isobel asked, brightly.

"Just clearing my head, and you?"

"Much the same." She held out her hand. "I am Isobel Kadeer and you must be a friend of Graham and Olivia's?"

"I am called Isobel also, though I am known simply as Belle. I live down there." She pointed vaguely in the direction of Bramstone Hall. "I needed

186

some air and I figured you would be here too." She ignored the look of surprise on Isobel's face. "We need to talk. Would you like to tell me what's on your mind?"

"Excuse me!" Isobel snapped.

"Your eyes, they give it away. Oh, the eyes, they mirror your soul."

"Oh really, is that so? Why on earth would I want to tell you anything? I've only just met you. Besides if you're not a friend of the Pearsons, then you are a trespasser and that means you are breaking the law."

"I am not trespassing; I have as much right to be here as you have. You can tell me to mind my own business and if you like I will leave, but alas that will achieve very little and I really do think you need some good advice right now. As I said before, your eyes they give everything away. Call it a sixth sense, if you like. Now where shall we start, with Jacob or Adam perhaps?"

Isobel looked at the woman next to her in utter disbelief. Digging her nails deeply into the flaking bark of the log, she said, "I think you should explain what you mean." She looked pointedly at Belle, who stood up to leave. Isobel grabbed her arm; Belle looked down at the hand on her arm with raised brow. Ashamed Isobel released her grip. "I'm so sorry, how rude of me, perhaps we should start again."

"I think that would be a good idea." Belle sat down next to Isobel with a look of exasperation. For a fleeting moment Isobel recognised something about Belle's face, the mild irritation, in the way she held her jaw and the forgiveness in her eyes, then it was gone and she felt nothing. She had to share this burden, and as strange as it seemed, this was as good a chance as any.

Belle broke the silence. "What does your heart really desire, Isobel?"

Without a shred of hesitation, Isobel smiled. "Adam." She clasped her hands together looking down at the ground, giving a deep sigh. "Adam makes me feel complete. When I am with him my heart soars—" She gave a stifled sob. "But, I can't bear to break Jacob's heart, he is a good man."

Belle placed her hand lightly on Isobel's knee, resting it there with a comforting reassurance.

"What do you suppose they would like?"

"Me, I guess."

"Both of them, are you sure?"

Isobel sat thoughtful for a moment. "They both love me." She looked across at Belle with a frown. "You have the sixth sense, why don't you tell me?" she said gently.

"I would agree that they both love you, but one of them is very tired."

187

Isobel bit her lip, pondering Belle's answer for a moment. "Tired, what exactly do you mean, tired?"

Belle stood up ignoring the question, instead wrapping her arms around herself and looking across the countryside her eyes distant, she stood silently.

Isobel went to join her. "What should I do, please help me?" She looked pleadingly at the other woman. "Whatever decision I make will be the wrong one; I can feel it in my bones. Someone will end up getting hurt, and then there's Edward to consider. I can't bear to think what effect this will have on him."

Belle turned sharply towards her. "So you have decided, you're leaving Jacob then?"

Isobel frowned. "I didn't say that." She kicked at the hard earth. "I'm saying that I don't know. That I haven't got the courage to make a choice."

"So you would rather do nothing? You can't take the responsibility, so you would rather waste your life and take the easy path. You are a fool, Isobel." Her tone was mocking. Isobel was alarmed at her lack of compassion.

"That's not fair!"

"Dear Isobel." She turned to look at her, her face softened. "It is better to do something than nothing at all. You must follow your heart but you must listen." She clutched her hands to her chest. "You must listen to what is inside you. See past the Isobel that you know. Look to the other that lies within, your inner self and your higher self. This is the special element, which can see, beyond the restraints of time and has no fear." Her hands fell away from her chest and she relaxed. "I know this time, child; you will make the right choice."

Isobel couldn't make sense of her words; she brushed away the tears, only she could decide what to do there was no magical solution.

Belle came closer to give her a hug. "I must go now, look after yourself, Miss Isobel."

Isobel opened her mouth to protest, Belle held up her hand. "I must go, we will speak again soon, I promise."

"How can I contact you? I don't even know where you live."

"Don't worry I will find you." Belle gave a knowing smile. "Oh, something else, your house and the strange things, don't let them concern you." She looked at Isobel's puzzled expression. "Your son he sees her, don't be afraid. She is merely an imprint on time and she won't be around for much longer."

Before Isobel could reply Belle was gone, lost into the depths of the wood without a trace. Isobel rose to leave with one last longing look between the towering trees. She turned to walk back; there was no sign of either of the dogs. Belle's words were fading already, the memory of her face becoming a bleary haze. Had it been real, or was Belle a figment of her imagination? She shook her head sadly, not sure, what she should believe in any more. The wood seemed to cast its spell and no longer could she differentiate between what was real and what was not.

When she arrived back at the house she was relieved to see the two dogs dozing on the back step; they thumped their tails in a lazy greeting, looking at her through half closed eyes. Isobel let herself in. She poured herself a large brandy it soothed her trembling nerves. The light on the answer phone was flashing. She pressed the button and returned to her senses as she heard Jacob's voice, asking if she would mind, if he took Edward to London with him for the weekend. As she couldn't make it, he didn't see any need for Edward to miss out. She chose to ignore the sarcastic tone in his voice. He was bitter and in the circumstances it was to be expected, they hadn't slept together for weeks. She didn't mind Edward going; in fact, she was quite shattered. Fortunately, she hadn't told Edward that she would be feeding Rita's animals, so he couldn't play up over that. She called back, the lovely Elizabeth had great pleasure informing her that he was in a meeting.

Brad dropped Marina at the surgery. He decided, to wait in the car, he never could stand medical places. Just the smell turned his stomach. Marina had felt too weak to drive. Besides, he had bullied her, into coming. Marina found a spare seat in the waiting room. She felt so tired and very nauseous. The doctor smiled warmly as she entered his room.

"Morning, Mrs Cobbett. Just had a look at your notes, it's been over two years since we've seen you." He glanced at her over the rim of his spectacles. "So what brings you here today?"

Marina explained how terrible she was feeling. He made some notes then beckoned her to the couch for a physical examination. After a good prod on her stomach, he handed her a specimen jar, pointing her in the direction of the toilets. Marina returned to sit opposite him, after several minutes he smiled, and announced. "The good news is I know exactly what the problem is."

If it was supposed to be a lighthearted comment, Marina didn't smile, she felt too ill and she couldn't wait to get home.

The doctor cleared his throat. "Basically you are pregnant!" He paused to study her face, giving it a moment or two to sink in. "I take it from the look on your face that this pregnancy wasn't planned?"

Marina looked unwittingly back. Still trying to register what the doctor had just said.

"Are you using some form of contraception?" he asked.

"Yes." Marina put her face in her hands. "I'm on the pill, I get it from Redbridge Family planning clinic."

"Are you still taking it now?"

"Yes."

"You must stop taking them immediately. Have you had any sickness or have you taken a course of antibiotics in the last couple of months?"

Marina began to cry. She couldn't think straight. Normally she took her pill before breakfast every morning. Her lip began to tremble.

"I forgot a couple I remember now." Her chest began to knot.

The doctor stood up, perching himself on the edge of the desk next to her.

"That would have been about two months ago, is that right?"

"Yes." She began to chew at her fingernails. "It was when I was in America. I got confused, it was the time difference and—" Marina began to sob. The doctor placed a comforting hand on her shoulder, as he talked her sympathetically through her options. Marina wasn't really hearing him, as her body wracked by powerful sobs.

Brad saw Marina coming out of the surgery building. He hopped out to open the door for her, aware that she looked more ghastly than when she had gone in.

"So was it a bug, love?"

Marina managed a meek smile. "Yes, love. A bad bug but he thinks I'm on the mend."

"Oh that's good. See I told you that's what it was." He placed a comforting hand over hers. "Now let's get out of this place."

Jacob was feeling guilty about the message he had left for Isobel, but it was too late now.

It had annoyed him that she wasn't in; she was never in these days; annoyed that she had promised to do Rita's animals when she hadn't even consulted him. On reflection, he wondered now if he wasn't being selfish. After everything Rita had done for them. Perhaps it was the least she could do. Jacob hoped she wouldn't be too sore with him. Relations being strained enough as it was.

Jacob was trying to pretend it didn't happen but he was feeling lousy about his night with Elizabeth. It was wrong; half a bottle of scotch hadn't helped either. He had driven in to work the next morning with Elizabeth, both in silence. God only knew what was going through her mind. He watched her out in the office, sat at her desk. It should have been like any normal day but it wasn't. He had cheated on Isobel and he could never change that now. His phone rang, it was Isobel.

"Yes, Jacob, that will be fine for the weekend. Edward's really excited, I told him on the way to nursery."

"You definitely can't join us then?" he asked hopeful.

"No!" Isobel's voice was sharp. "I promised Rita."

There seemed to be no point in arguing. He arranged to drive down Thursday evening, and then they could leave early on Friday. Isobel was readily agreeable.

Jacob worked late that night, long after everyone else including Elizabeth had gone home. He let himself wearily into the flat just after midnight. He crawled into bed, without even bothering to undress. He just wanted the day to end.

Graham decided to take a few days off work, and with the weather surprisingly still good; it was a great excuse to ride out with Olivia.

Olivia was in the kitchen busily packing a hamper for their picnic. Smoked salmon, hard-boiled eggs, a crisp green salad and a bottle of Shiraz one of her favourites and Graham had brought some panniers to fasten to their saddles so they could ride unencumbered.

They loaded up and set off, their horses side by side, chattering away, in short sleeves thanks to the warm autumn day. They cantered up to the old railway. Olivia looked across at Graham grim-faced and clinging to Solvent's reins. It was glorious, why hadn't she learnt to ride years ago.

They rode for a couple of hours, choosing to stop at Branch Hill the highest point for miles. "This looks to be the perfect place for our lunch." Graham pulled Solvent to an abrupt halt. "Look we can tie the horses over there, under the beech trees. Not too close though we don't want Solvent getting his wicked way with dear sweet Jasmine, do we?"

Olivia unpacked, spreading a large rug out in a perfect position, to enjoy the fabulous view. They sipped the wine from plastic glasses, enjoying the warmth of the sun. Graham slipped his arm around her waist. "The best goddamn thing you've ever done you know, learning to ride."

Olivia smiled up at him. "I couldn't agree more."

"I was wondering. I mean we're up here all alone. Don't suppose." He smiled cheekily. "That you fancy riding your husband?" He tickled her playfully beneath the ribs.

Olivia nodded. "Only too happy to oblige." She threw her head back laughing.

A strong breeze picked up, cooling Olivia's pink cheeks as she sat astride Graham. He lay back, arms folded behind his head, with a grin spread the width of his face. Olivia felt her muscles tighten, as her breath rose, in tight rasps. She gave a deep moan, as her body flushed with ecstasy. Crying out like an injured fox, the sound echoed around the valley below. Graham held on to her tightly.

"At last," she squealed out in delight. "It's been too long."

Marina got up late the following morning. Doubled over in the kitchen, sipping ginger beer, thinking about her next doctor's appointment which was tomorrow morning, knowing she had already come to a decision. A termination was the only answer. All the arrangements could be made tomorrow. Nobody ever need know. Well apart from Isobel, she wanted to tell her. She would drive over later when the sickness subsided.

Edward's case was packed, everything ready to leave in the morning. Isobel zipped it up with a weary sigh.

Adam had called her to arrange to meet on Friday evening. Assuring her how much he had missed her and was aching for some time together. Isobel hated being apart.

As she pegged the last of the washing out on the line to dry in the sun, Marina pulled up. She got out of the car, immediately Isobel noticed that she was looking pale and gaunt.

"Hi there, stranger," Isobel called. She hugged her tightly, and then recoiled in horror. "God you're a bag of bones that must have been some bug. You have lost pounds."

Marina shrugged her face almost transparent. "I could murder a cup of coffee, if you have time?"

Isobel led her in to the kitchen. Marina plonked herself wearily down at the table, taking a deep breath as she did so.

"I'm not sick, Isobel, just two months pregnant, that's why I look so bloody awful, even though you're too kind to say it."

Isobel wheeled round from spooning coffee into two mugs. "Your kidding, Marina. How?"

"How do you think?" Marina gave a wry laugh. Then promptly bit her lip, afraid she might cry. Isobel noticed her trembling body. Dropping the teaspoon with a clatter to the floor, she rushed over to throw her arms around Marina's shoulders which crumpled on impact. Isobel held her close until the sobs subsided. Marina gave a hard sniff, looking up to face her and pulled a grubby tissue from her Jeans pocket, she dabbed furiously at her bloodshot eyes.

"I'm so sorry." Marina looked forlornly up at Isobel. Isobel looked back with concern at her friend.

"It doesn't have to be the end of the world," Isobel said firmly.

"Well I won't be keeping the baby." There was an air of defiance.

Isobel went back to making coffee. "To be honest, I would have been more surprised if you had said you were! I take it that Brad knows."

"No. And he must never find out. You're the only one that knows." Marina began to tremble, chewing nervously at her nails. "You see, Isobel, I doubt very much that it's Brad's baby."

For the second time Isobel spun round in disbelief, this time she sent the sugar bowl catapulting through the air, where it landed with an almighty crash in the middle of the kitchen floor, shattering into hundreds of tiny pieces.

"Oh shit. I hope you didn't want sugar, darling." Isobel hurried off for a dustpan and brush. "Dare I ask whose it is?"

"Howard, my ex, it was about that time. I just know it isn't Brad's."

Isobel took a large gulp of coffee. "When? I mean where?" She paused to stare in disbelief at Marina.

"In the States, on my holiday with Molly, stupid I know."

"So it really was happy families."

"Suppose you could say that. Anyway it's a long story. Even, if it was Brad's baby." She took a deep breath. "Well I still couldn't go through with it."

Isobel passed her the mug of coffee. Marina took it thankfully between both hands taking a large slurp. "My track history so far isn't exactly encouraging, is it?"

Isobel looked thoughtful. "I'm here for you whatever you decide. If you need me to cover for you or take you to the clinic, whatever."

"Thank you, Isobel, that means so much."

Olivia rode back to Bramstone, on the crest of a wave, glancing across at Graham, who was smiling to himself looking around at the beautiful countryside. Olivia smiled smugly. Everything was as near perfect as it could be now. How strange Carmen had entered their lives and nearly blown them apart. Yet in a funny sort of way she had actually saved them, repaired a massive flaw in their marriage. He caught her eye, smiling warmly back. "I love you, Olivia."

"I love you too," she whispered.

Edward was in a frenzy of excitement running to the window every five minutes, waiting for Jacob to arrive home.

"How much longer now, Mummy?" he wailed, for the hundredth time.

"Not long, honey." Isobel took his small sweaty hand and lead him to the living room. "Perhaps you could watch some TV until he arrives."

The weather report was on. Finally, the weather was set to change, rather spectacularly too. Heavy rain and high winds were forecast for much of the weekend.

The dogs began to bark, running around the hallway, their tails thumping with excitement. Edward screeched, leaping from the sofa. Jacob let himself in smiling.

"Hey that's a great welcome." He patted Edward's head then stooped to do the same to the whining dogs. Isobel watched them from the sofa.

"Shame Mummy's not pleased to see me too." He looked across at Isobel unable to resist the dig.

"Of course I am." She pulled herself lazily up and sauntered over to give him a light kiss on the cheek. "I'll make some tea." She headed for the kitchen, ignoring his questioning gaze.

"Actually I wouldn't mind a beer." He followed her through. "Suppose you haven't changed your mind about coming?"

Isobel gave him a vacant look as she took two beers from the fridge, poured them in to glasses and handed him one.

"Bit of a silly question really, you know damn well that I've promised Rita, don't you?"

"I thought you might swing it. I don't know perhaps ask Marina to help out or something?"

"Marina's been unwell. I have to be here, OK." She took her drink back through to the living room and sprawled across the sofa. Jacob sat in the chair opposite her and Edward clambered on to his lap with a trillion questions. Although Jacob was more interested in Isobel at that precise moment, he made a good job of pretending to be blown away by what Edward had to tell him.

Marina was feeling better that evening and insisted on cooking dinner. She was bored and wanted to take her mind off the pregnancy. Brad leant against the kitchen cabinet watching her every move.

"Are you sure you feel up to this, I can take over you know."

"Absolutely fine, really, stop looking at me that way." He eyed the venomous way in which she pulped the potatoes and held up his hands.

"OK you win; I'll leave you to it. Shout if you need me."

He switched the television on with the sound barely audible just in case there was a clatter from the kitchen or a cry for help.

Marina appeared a few moments later with two heaped plates of cottage pie. He eyed the amount on her plate with surprise. She must be feeling better, he had never seen her tackle such a large portion, and normally she ate like a sparrow. He insisted on clearing up. As much as Marina would have liked to argue she didn't have the energy. The appointment with Doctor Gerard preoccupied her mind. It would be hard, explaining the reason why she did not wish to keep the baby.

Brad appeared with a glass of apple juice. "You know what they say, an apple a day." He laughed. "We have no apples, so will this suffice." She took the glass draining it in one go.

"Gosh you were thirsty."

"Yes and tired too, I think I'll go up to bed."

"It's only eight-thirty!"

Marina rose from the chair. "I know it's pathetic but I'm so shattered." She stopped to kiss his head. It would be a few days yet before she was back, properly on her feet, he decided. Thank god, he hadn't caught whatever bug it was, too.

Isobel hugged Edward tightly, until he began to squirm. She looked deeply into his big brown eyes.

"Now you be a very good boy for Daddy and give my love to Grandma and Grandpa." Edward nodded beaming with eager anticipation. She brushed the dog hairs from the front of his sweater. It was going to be a real treat for him and Jacob's parents would spoil him rotten. Isobel helped him into the car then gave Jacob a quick hug, as it started to drizzle.

"Drive carefully. The roads will be extra slippery."

"We will don't worry." Jacob shut the door then gave her one last wistful gaze. "Look after yourself, and see you Monday night."

Isobel watched as they sped off down the drive. This would be the first time Edward had been away from home and her, since he was born. It felt unbearable already.

CHAPTER SIXTEEN

Marina had slept for over thirteen hours. However, she still managed to awaken feeling deathly tired. Her whole body ached and her throat was dry, she was feeling sick yet again. Throwing back the quilt, she swung her legs out of bed, feeling on the rug for her slippers. Successfully she dived her feet into their fluffy warmth then padded softly to the bathroom. Looking at her reflection in the mirror, she found she had puffy eyes with dark shadows. Her skin was waxy, her hair hung matted and greasy.

Wearily she turned on the shower, slipped off her pyjamas and stared with disbelief at the large red stain in her pyjama bottoms. Grabbing some tissue, she wiped herself, the blood was fresh and there was lots of it. Marina dived under the shower her mind whirling. Panic began to surface; she must get to the doctor's before Brad came back up from the stables.

Hurriedly she dressed, grabbing a handful of sanitary towels from the cabinet and stuffing them into her bag she drove to the surgery.

By the time she pulled in to the car park, she had begun to experience a low dull ache in her abdomen. The surgery waiting area was heaving. Groaning inwardly, she waited in the queue to speak to a receptionist, whilst a sea of blank faces briefly acknowledged her arrival then went back to staring into space.

The receptionist took her name, and then nodded in the direction of the only vacant seat in the entire waiting room.

"No. I can't wait." Marina hissed through gritted teeth. "I need to see a doctor now."

"Well is it an emergency?" the prim receptionist asked airily, as she looked, Marina up and down, haughtily. Why she couldn't just take a seat along with everybody else, she wondered.

"Yes it is. I can't wait out here."

Unperturbed the receptionist shook the papers that she held clasped to her chest.

"As you can see, madam, we are very busy. Can I ask what the problem is?"

"In a nutshell, no, it's none of your bloody business." Marina winced. "Believe me I need to see the doctor, immediately."

Looking down at her list she nodded. "OK if you would like to go on through to the treatment room, you can wait for the doctor there."

The kindly nurse she found in the treatment room was much more sympathetic, helping her up onto the bed, with a look of genuine concern.

"You're looking ever so pale, love. Are you alright?"

"No I'm in agony." Marina clutched at her stomach.

The door swung open, the doctor arrived looking frazzled. He apparently was not having a good morning either, judging by the expression on his face.

"I'm bleeding heavily." She looked at him weakly. The doctor patted the back of her hand gently. He frowned and shot a worried glance across to the nurse, who tried her best to smile encouragingly.

"It's OK you can say it. I'm losing the baby!"

He nodded his head. "It certainly looks that way. We need to get you to hospital and we need to run further tests. Is your husband waiting for you?"

"No. My husband is away," she lied. She laid back her head letting out a long sigh of relief.

"I have a friend, who I can call." She looked up at them hopefully. "She could be here in five minutes."

Marina gave the nurse Isobel's phone number and then lay back on the couch glad of the opportunity to rest and close her eyes. Hopefully it would all be over soon, and then she could get back to normal.

Isobel raced to the surgery, wondering why she had been summoned although she had a very good idea. If it was what she thought, it would be typical of Marina to land on her feet.

"God, darling, you look so pale." She winced at the sight of her, but managed a feint smile.

Marina raised her head to look at Isobel, gingerly she got up from the bed trying desperately not to show just how much agony she was in.

"So sorry dragging you out, Isobel, couldn't really call Brad."

"Don't be daft. Come on, sweetie, we need to get you to hospital." Gently she helped Marina out through the back entrance to the car. Marina tried not to make too much fuss.

"Is it agony?" Isobel asked with a pained expression. It was so weird to see Marina in this state. Isobel knew she had to be strong. No matter what Marina thought right now, she was still losing her baby, something she may actually come to regret.

The medical team at Marchwood General were great, whisking Marina off into their expert care. Isobel made her way to the waiting room, a bright apricot coloured room with two well-worn, shabby sofas, an ancient TV in one corner, a big box of toys and a small table with a selection of well-read magazines in the other.

It was very quiet. The odd nurse strode briskly past in the hallway. Isobel looked around at her surroundings, odd to think how many excited fathers had awaited here for news of their baby's arrival. It all happened here, including death, she shuddered, then took a deep breath. Impatiently, she checked her watch; Jacob and Edward would be in London by now. She hoped that Edward had travelled well. They would be wondering where she was, but she would call as soon as she knew how Marina was.

A nurse bustled in with a bright smile. "You must be Isobel?"

Nodding in reply, she stood up looking at the nurse who couldn't have been a day over 20.

"Marina is fine but we need to keep her in for a few days."

"How about the baby?" she asked.

The nurse shook her head sadly. "Bad news, I'm afraid. We need to take her down to theatre shortly but she's very keen to speak with you first if you wouldn't mind."

"Sure."

"I'll take you down, but before that, can I ask if Mr Cobbett has been informed about what has happened?"

With a start Isobel remembered Brad. Gosh what should she do? He would have to know if Marina was being admitted. The nurse stood patiently waiting for a reply.

"I'll try and contact him," Isobel managed to squawk, finally finding her voice.

"Good." The nurse smiled. "He needs to be here at a time like this."

When Isobel finally made her way out to the car, the drizzle had turned to heavy rain. Thick quarrelsome clouds hung heavily overhead, and the distinct rumble of thunder could be heard in the distance. Slowly she drove back toward Brad, to break the terrible news which would be all the more worse given that he had no idea that his wife was even pregnant.

As Isobel pulled in to the driveway, the front door flew open; Brad came out head bowed against the rain. The car was barely to a standstill as he wrenched open Isobel's door.

"Thank god, I've been worried sick. I've been trying to reach you," he panted breathless. "Do you have any idea where Marina is?" He peered at her helplessly. "She's gone missing. Not a word and she's been so poorly lately I have been terribly worried."

Isobel gulped, he was fraught with worry. She could barely look him in the eye, let alone explain this all to him.

"Yes, Brad, she has been taken poorly."

"I knew it, I knew it." He stamped his foot angrily, and then held his hands up to his face. "What's happened, it's nothing serious, is it? Where is she?"

"Marchwood General and she will be okay."

"Hospital," he shrieked. The colour draining from his face, as his lip curled back in horror.

"Look, please don't panic she's alright." Isobel spoke sternly, trying to gain some control over the situation but she was powerless. Brad was already fishing the car keys from his pocket and making a move. He looked shaken and the weather was appalling. "I don't think you should drive, Brad, I'll drive you." It was too late; already he was racing to the car. He jumped in and sped recklessly up the drive.

Isobel sat slumped across the steering wheel, watching guiltily. He had no idea. He hadn't given her a chance to tell him. God only knew what was going through his mind right now. She had tried but he wouldn't listen. Well it meant she had escaped lightly, all the way there she had been dreading telling him. Goddamn her for being such a wimp.

Slowly she drove home. The rain even heavier, the sky had turned black. As she put the key in the front door there was a flash of lightening she hurried in slamming the door behind her. The dogs crept, cowardly from the shadows, afraid and disturbed by the storm. Reassuringly she patted their silky heads. The telephone began to ring barely audible above the loud crack of thunder.

"At last, just wanted to let you know we had arrived, two hours ago in fact."

"Sorry." Isobel sat down on the bottom step, suddenly aware, how overwhelmed she felt.

Jacob softened his tone. "Ugh, well we're here now."

"Oh good, glad you're all there safe and sound. Edward travelled OK?" Isobel struggled to keep her emotions in check.

"Yeah he did, is anything the matter? You sound strange."

"Oh I'm fine, honestly. Shall I call you at your parents' tonight?"

"Yes please, love. Edward said to say hello too."

Isobel replaced the receiver. Sinking to her knees, she began to sob. Pulling herself into a tight ball, she lay motionless on the hallway floor. The storm echoed around the house, lightning ripped across the ebony sky. The dogs came to lie down by her side. It had been an awful morning. Poor Brad. He would no doubt be feeling perfectly beastly now. Poor Marina she would be feeling so ashamed. Isobel felt ashamed. Her life was a mess. Staring up at the ceiling, she began to tremble. The telephone began to ring she ignored it. Twisting over, she slung out her arm to protectively pull the dogs closer to her. Burying her head in Tarquin's warm, soft chest she sobbed until she fell asleep.

When she awoke, the storm had subsided and the dogs were eyeing her cautiously from the living room. Pulling herself to her feet, she went through to the kitchen where she poured herself a large brandy. Taking her drink through to the living room, she sat down on the sofa. Gingerly she sipped the brandy feeling it trickle warmly down her throat and settle comfortingly in her belly. Isobel checked the message on the answer phone just in case it was a problem with Edward. To her surprise it was Rita sounding very apologetic. She had been struck by a sickness bug which meant she would have to postpone the visit to her sister's. She hoped she hadn't ruined any plans. Isobel began to laugh. How ironic was that. There was no way she would tell Jacob she could hop on a train and join them, but then there was poor Marina. She guessed she had better be around for her, and Brad would probably need some support, that would be after he had had a bloody good go at her, for not telling him.

Carmen drove up to Bramstone Hall, her music blaring out of the car speakers. She had thought that it may be a good idea to look in on Olivia and see how she was coping. It was a bit mean to just dump her now. Arriving at Bramstone, she rang the doorbell. Hastily she brushed straw from her jumper.

Olivia opened the door. "Hi, Carmen. It's nice to see you. Please come in."

Carmen thought how well Olivia looked. Her skin was glowing, she was wearing pale grey slacks with a darker shade of grey lambs wool sweater, she looked stunning. Carmen felt a pang of jealousy, as she dared to look down at herself, in her faded denim shirt and her too tight black leggings. Olivia led her through to the kitchen.

Carmen froze, the smile wiped from her face. Graham sat to her right reading the newspaper. He peered over the top of it, scrutinising her for several seconds and managed a casual "Hi."

Carmen felt her cheeks explode and gave a nervous splutter. Olivia, on the other hand, seemed totally relaxed. "Please don't stand to attention. Take a seat."

"Thanks." Carmen sat down opposite Graham who continued to read the paper much to her relief.

"Fancy a tea or coffee?" Olivia bustled around the kitchen, smiling cheerfully to herself.

"Err coffee would be fine." She gave a quick sideways glance; Graham appeared to be engrossed in the paper and oblivious to her presence. As much as she hated to admit it she still liked him. Since they had split she hadn't slept with anyone else. He, as she remembered, had been a pretty good shag. Olivia placed a tray with a caffetier of coffee on the table in front of her.

"Would you be a love, Graham, and pour please."

"Certainly, dear." He closed the paper, folded it meticulously and placed it down on the chair next to him, glancing across at Carmen. Resisting a scowl, he handed her a cup. Keeping her eyes fixed firmly on the cup, she took it then averted her gaze back to Olivia.

"So, Olivia, how are you getting on with Jasmine?"

Olivia put her cup back down. She looked across at Graham. "Graham has taken the week off and we've been out riding every day, it's only the blasted rain that stopped us today. I've been doing really well and Jasmine is such a poppet. I can't thank you enough for finding her for me."

Graham sat watching the two women as they chatted. They were indeed worlds apart. Olivia sat straight-backed, elegantly sipping her coffee, while Carmen slumped like a bag of spuds with her wild hair and ruddy cheeks held her cup firmly between two hands taking long slurps. Carmen had been good in the sack but that was as far as it went.

Carmen drained her cup then stood up. She was keen to leave, uncomfortably conscious of Graham staring at her. She had definitely outstayed her welcome.

"Are you sure you can't stay for another cup?" Olivia seemed disappointed that she was going so soon.

"Positive thanks." She smiled warmly at Olivia. "I'm really glad that you're pleased with Jasmine and that everything's working out for you."

Graham stood up shaking the creases from his trousers with a waggle of his foot. "Let me see you out, Carmen."

Olivia waved goodbye as she began to clear the table. Carmen walked along the hallway, Graham hot on her heels. As they approached the front door, he placed an arm in front of her barring the way.

"Let's make this the very last visit, shall we?" he hissed in her ear.

Turning to face him, Carmen gave him a long thoughtful stare. "If I had known that you were here, I wouldn't have bothered calling in," she replied icily.

"You're not welcome, is that quite clear, never?" He opened the door, resisting the temptation to boot her up the arse.

Carmen strode out; head held high and didn't look back. "Piece of shit," she muttered under her breath. She slagged him off, all the way to the Cobbetts'.

To her disappointment there was nobody home, the place was deserted. Graham had pissed her off. She could do with a drink and catching up on all the gossip, anything to take her mind off that creep.

When she pulled up outside her place, she was surprised to see her father waiting. He stood, leaning against the paddock fence, smoking his pipe. He raised a hand in greeting.

"Daddy!" She flung her arms around him. "I didn't know you were coming to visit, why didn't you call?"

Her father returned the warm embrace then looked at her, his eyes sparkling happily. "I'm the bearer of good news, if somewhat surprising news."

"Really, oh how exciting, what is it?"

"Let us go in." Her father signalled to the house. "Besides I'm gasping for a cup of tea."

Carmen put the kettle on. She noticed the way her father frowned as he looked around at the kitchen.

"I know it's a mess, ever since I took the students on, I've precious little time to get everything done."

He shrugged. "It is your place, Carmen; I'm not here to pass judgement, quite the contrary."

Carmen sat down beside him. "So come on, put me out of my misery, what's this good news?"

"Firstly, it has come to light that your mother had a sister called Grace. I know…" He looked at her. "It was a great shock to me too, but I did warn you."

"How come we never knew? Mummy, wasn't the sort of person to keep secrets, was she?"

She thought of her mother, such a brilliant person, so kind and generous, so full of energy. In fact her mother had always wished for a sister, Carmen remembered her saying it, on more than one occasion. Carmen looked quizzically at her father.

"None of us knew, not even your mother. Apparently when your grandmother was sixteen she had a daughter, who she gave up for adoption." He looked across at Carmen. "Well you know how it was in those days? Your grandmother named her daughter Grace. Apart from her parents nobody ever knew about the baby, she never told a soul. Your grandmother never saw her from the day she signed the adoption papers."

"Oh how sad." Carmen thought about how painful that must have been handing over your baby then having to erase her from your life forever. Her father continued. "Grace grew up to become very successful in later life, but sadly she developed cancer, in fact, the same cancer as your mother."

Carmen hugged her knees to her chest, remembering the day her mother passed from the horrid disease that riddled her body; she looked across at her father, there was a tear in his eye. He cleared his throat. "At this point Grace decided, in fact became fanatical about tracing her real family, sadly to discover that her mother had passed away, the father wasn't named but to her delight she discovered she had a sister, your mother."

Carmen looked sadly at her father. "I suppose it was shattering then to find out she had died too."

"Yes indeed. But then she found out about you. And well to be honest she was that close." He held two fingers a small way apart. "To finding you, Carmen, when the cancer overpowered her and sadly she died too." He shook his head with disappointment.

"Oh how tragic, I wonder why she left it all so late?" Getting up from the sofa, she looked down at her father sadly. "It's a terrible shame. Mother would have been ecstatic to meet her long-lost sister."

Carmen poured boiling water into the teapot then brought it over and placed it down on the table in front of her father.

"So how do you know this entire story, Daddy?"

Her father leant forward his face animated. "Her lawyers contacted me. Grace made a will a few months before she passed away." He paused to put his hand over Carmen's. "She has apparently left everything to you, Carmen!" He smiled broadly at the look of surprise on her face. "She had no other relatives."

"Really, what do you suppose she has left?"

"Put it this way." He cocked his head to one side, giving her a coy smile. "The lawyers said it was a very substantial bequest." He stressed the word "substantial" just as the solicitor had to him the day before. Then he fished in his jacket pocket. "I have the card here." He pushed it across the table to her.

With shaking hands, Carmen scooped up the small gold embossed card, holding it anxiously between her chubby fingers she read aloud. "Rapkyn and Hayes, Winchester." She looked across at her father. He nodded. "That's right in Hampshire."

"Should I call do you think?"

"Most certainly or you will never find out what you have inherited."

Nervously, Carmen dialled the number. The receptionist put her straight through to Martin Rapkyn. After confirming her identity he went on to explain that she would need to attend at their offices for the formal reading of the Last Will and Testament of the late Grace Markham. Aware that she would be travelling up from Devon, and had a very busy life, they arranged a meeting for Monday morning at eleven.

As soon as she replaced the receiver her father looked expectantly up at her.

"So any clues, a cat, a family heirloom?"

"No, none at all I am afraid. I am to meet Mr Martin Rapkyn at his office in Winchester on Monday morning at eleven, when all will be revealed."

He patted her hand. "Of course I'll come with you. Perhaps I should make another cuppa, why don't you take a seat, let it all sink in."

Carmen sat down on the sofa. "I mean it could be anything, a draughty old haunted house complete with ancient emaciated cats, or a timber shack with no running water or electricity."

Her father sat down beside her scratching his head. "Yes it could be any one of those things. Exciting, isn't it?"

Carmen smiled to herself it most certainly was. And whatever it was she decided it was just wonderful that Aunt Grace had thought of her.

Isobel fiddled with her earrings in front of the mirror, smothering herself in perfume. She tried to ignore the butterflies performing dramatic somersaults in her tummy. It was a mixture of excitement and guilt, the norm, when she was due to see Adam. She would have thought she would be getting used to it by now, but every time was just like the first. Isobel took a deep breath and dialled Jacob at his parents'. His mother answered.

"Happy birthday to you." Isobel sang down the phone.

"Oh thank you, Isobel, but when you get to my age you'd rather not acknowledge them anymore." She giggled. "I must say however, it's wonderful having my grandson here to stay. He's such a happy little soul, a real credit to you both, my love."

"Yes he is great. I'm sorry I couldn't be there as well."

"Oh never mind I expect we shall see you soon. Now let me find Jacob for you."

Jacob sounded very relaxed and happy. Isobel decided not to ruin his mood and tell him about Marina.

"How is Edward?" she asked, wistfully.

"Great, getting spoilt rotten, as you can imagine." He laughed jovially. "He's helping Mother make dinner, as we speak. Would you like a word?"

"No don't bother him, if he's having fun."

"So how are you, Isobel?" he asked coldly.

She replaced the receiver a little hurt by his attitude. Isobel hated to admit it but she was being a complete bitch to him lately. It was exactly what she deserved if she was honest.

Tarquin and Sadie appeared excited, bustling into the room with their tails wagging. It was almost as if somebody had said the magic word, the one that starts with "W" and ends with "S."

Perplexed by their excitement she looked down at them both. "It's not really that time of day, guys." Then looking down at herself she decided if she stuck on her wellies and a large Mac perhaps they could squeeze in a quick one, it would make her feel a bit less guilty about leaving them for the night. The rain abated leaving the earth sodden. Pleased with themselves as their plan had worked the dogs ran ahead. Isobel pulled her collar up against the damp, pushing her hands deeper into her pockets.

She would walk as far as the stream then head back. There was something about this evening which reminded her of Sunday morning walks with her mother, maybe it was the smell of damp earth. How glorious it was being a child. No nasty distractions, no painstaking decisions.

Marina losing the baby had temporarily taken her away from her own problems for a while. It had been a welcome respite from the constant turmoil that had been haunting her mind; she wasn't a little girl anymore. She had to make choices and stick by them.

Letting out a long defeated sigh, she watched the dogs up ahead. They had ceased to frolic and were looking with increasing concern ahead across the fields. Sadie began to growl.

It was Belle. Isobel could just make her out swathed in a dark robe and hurrying purposefully toward the trees. Isobel called out but her voice was carried away on the wind. Belle disappeared in to the depths of the wood.

Curiously, Isobel wondered what she was doing. She should go and see Graham, to see if he could shed any light on her identity. She had asked around, the village and nobody seemed to have heard of her. Yet Belle had been most certain that she lived near Bramstone Hall. There wasn't really anywhere in walking distance. Isobel had wracked her brain and decided that when she next bumped into her she would be more assertive and find out more about her. After all it was only fair, Belle knew heaps about her. Turning for home, she whistled to the dogs who had resumed their boisterous play.

As they reached the rear terrace, the light was beginning to fade. Isobel was thankful that she had left the kitchen light on. Isobel fetched the dogs a bowl of water, then left them in the boot room to dry off. She went upstairs to comb her windswept hair. Brad called; he said Marina was fine and that she would be home on Sunday. He was, of course, gutted about losing the baby. However, in true Brad style, he laughed and made a comment about never really expecting to be a dad, there was an omissible quaver in his tone. As Isobel ended the conversation, she wondered if this loss would come to have a more profound effect on him, more so than Marina. It was very sad, she felt terrible for Brad. She tried not to dwell on it, as she climbed in to her car and headed to Adam's.

The rain began to fall again, gradually increasing in its intensity. Cautiously she drove along the winding country lanes, carpeted with fallen leaves, now made extremely hazardous by the falling rain. Turning on the radio, she smiled, as spookily, her favourite song the one which reminded her of Adam, was playing. It wasn't the first time this had happened, she wondered if it was a sign. If ever there had been a traumatic day then this was it. Isobel couldn't wait to get to Adam's and the safety of his arms.

Brad arrived home around seven, extremely weary. He trudged, rather begrudgingly, down to the horses. He didn't need this right now, he needed to go and bury himself away, with a good bottle of scotch. After endless filling of buckets and stuffing hay into hay nets, he finally locked up at nine. In the house, it appeared cold and uninviting. Peeling off his damp clothes, which he left in a pile on the floor, he dragged himself beneath the shower. Not keen to leave the soothing jets of water, he scrubbed aimlessly at his skin.

Losing the baby was tough. He would love to be a father. He had always taken it for granted that one day he would be. What hurt the most was the fact that Marina hadn't told him. He had a right to know surely. If he had known, he could have kept a proper eye on her and made sure that she had rested and then there would still be a child, his child.

The doctor had said it was just one of those things and that there was a multitude of reasons as to why it happened. That wasn't the case for Brad, he couldn't accept it. He wondered if he should call Molly. But what was the point in making her evening miserable as well. He would leave it until the morning. Besides he felt shattered, he could barely keep his eyes open. As he stepped out of the shower, there was only one thing he needed and that was his bed.

Isobel awoke in Adam's arms, she watched entranced as he slept soundly beside her. The rain lashed angrily, against the windowpane. Isobel shrunk further beneath the quilt.

Adam began to stir. She watched him wake.

"Your really still here?" he murmured. He pressed his body tightly, against her warm, silky skin.

"I wish I could stay here." She looked wistfully, around the bedroom.

"Me too, forever." He placed a lingering kiss upon her shoulder. Then pulling himself up on to one elbow, he looked longingly in to her eyes. "So, when will you leave Jacob? We should make plans."

Isobel knew the time would arrive, nonetheless now it had, and she wasn't prepared.

"Soon, Adam," she said softly.

"But you won't!" he said, smiling.

Isobel smiled meekly back she wasn't sure what to say. Searching for the right words, unable to find them, she remained quiet.

"It's OK, you don't have to answer. The mere fact that you would like to, is enough, for now. He paused. "Well for a little while longer." Gently he squeezed her hand.

Avoiding his gaze, she swallowed hard. Then wondered if he had any idea, just how much courage it would take to end her marriage. To have to stand face to face with Jacob and tell him it was all over. It was best really if she said nothing at all for now.

Adam was due to work, it was Saturday, the busiest day at the shop. After a quiet breakfast, she left for Orange Stream Farm.

The dogs had been left alone for far too long., so it came as no surprise to find that they had both had accidents on the floor. Isobel felt guilty, they were oblivious, just ecstatic to see her. Tarquin took her wrist gently in his mouth as Sadie bounced joyously at her heels. Once she had never dreamt of leaving them alone overnight but since she had met Adam the desire to be with him overtook all responsibility. Isobel went out to feed Quest. She didn't even bother to change her clothes. She turned him out in the orchard, to stretch his legs, the dogs followed close behind.

Adam called. Isobel was pleased, the sound of his voice, lifting her spirits.

"Look, Isobel, I'm really sorry about this morning." He didn't want to pressure her.

"No, you're right, Adam. I love you and I need to be with you." She stared hard at the chipped mug in her hand. "I'm going to tell Jacob tomorrow night, when he returns from London. It is only prolonging the agony."

Adam took a sharp intake of breath. "Are you sure you're ready for that, darling?"

"I know I can't go on living this lie. I know that the thought of losing you is totally unbearable."

"You know I will be there for you," he murmured. "I can support you and Edward."

"I know," Isobel replied, strangely confident. "I think you should come here tonight and we can talk it over."

Adam couldn't hide his surprise. "To your place, is that wise?"

Isobel laughed. "Why not, everyone will know soon enough, anyway."

Adam had to agree but he was uneasy about it. He would call in for a drink, but there was no way he would stay, that would be just taking it too far.

Isobel drained the remnants of coffee from her mug and looked out of the window. The sky was clouding over once again, the wind had strengthened and it rattled against the window. The weather was too rough to ride; besides, she would need all the energy she could muster to get through tomorrow night. Quest was rugged, so she decided to leave him out in the orchard. The dogs had settled and so for a while there was nothing that required her attention. She lit a fire in the stone fireplace. Both dogs made a dash for the woollen rug in front of it, Isobel left them sleeping, while she went for a soak in the bath, with her favourite oils. It was easy languishing in the warm scented waters, to forget what lay ahead and in the warmth of the cottage she could feel safe but a ferocious storm was approaching.

CHAPTER SEVENTEEN

Brad woke to a wet and dismal Saturday morning. Ever since he had been a young lad he had disliked Saturdays. This had to be one of the worst. After making a pot of tea he sat down at the kitchen table. Staring out of the window at the rain, absently he stirred his tea round and round in an endless circle. He wondered how Marina would be feeling this morning waking up in hospital. He knew how he felt, miserable and angry—angry at Marina for shutting him out, when it suited her. With great reluctance he slipped on his boots and went down to see to the horses. The previous day's events didn't mean a thing to them. As they caught sight of him they began to bang their doors whinnying and scraping with their hooves in eager anticipation of breakfast. Brad was so preoccupied he didn't notice their eager faces looking over their doors, the way he usually did or the fact that one was missing.

Following his usual pattern, he fed the mares first. Panther snorted in disgust kicking the stable door even harder, perturbed at not being first, it brought a feint smile to his lips, followed quickly by the realisation that Lizard was unusually quiet. Sauntering across to his stable, he whistled to get his attention, what was the git up to; he was normally one of the worst. Opening the stable door, he stopped in horror. The big athletic stallion lay on his side, his tongue hanging from the side of his mouth. Dropping the bucket of feed he was carrying, Brad rushed in feeling frantically at the horses sweaty sides. Sending a sharp slap across Lizard's quarters, he tried to encourage him. "Come on, big fella, up you get." He slapped him again harder and then again, he felt a wave of panic as the horse didn't respond. "Come on, for fuck's sake, get up," he sobbed.

His mind racing, he tried to physically push the lifeless beast onto his feet, but he merely moved him an inch. Interlocking his hands beneath Lizard's shoulder and chest, he pulled fruitlessly on the animal's leg, frantic now. He wanted to kick him hard in the ribs, anything to get a response. Hot tears stung at his eyes. "Get up, you bloody shit, move, come on." He was yelling now, blinking fiercely to see through the mist of tears. Dropping to his knees on the golden straw, he buried his face dejectedly in Lizard's silky mane. Sobbing hopeless tears, feeling useless, he let out a haunting scream, as he looked up to the heavens. "Why, oh why is this fucking happening? Please somebody help me."

Carmen arrived at the stables. She was excitedly making her way down to the stables when she heard Brad's bloodcurdling cry. Feeling her skin prickle and an overwhelming feeling of dread, she ran towards the direction from which it had come. Arriving outside Lizard's stable, she stopped transfixed in disbelief. Brad, straddled across the stallion, was crying uncontrollably.

"My god what on earth has happened?" Carmen dropped down beside the stallion's head, feeling his neck with urgent fingers for some sign of a pulse. Carmen let out a deep sigh shaking her head in disbelief. It was too late. Moving across to comfort Brad, she slipped her arms around him. He looked at her through swollen eyes.

"Is he dead? Is he dead, Carmen?" He began to cry again. She couldn't answer him, Brad fell sobbing in her arms.

Carmen held on to him. "Come on, love, let's go in." She helped him up onto wobbly knees and unsteady feet.

"I tried to get him up," he whispered through chattering teeth. "I tried so hard, Carmen, he just lay there. There was no spirit, his eyes they never flickered."

"I know, love. There's nothing you could do."

Carmen steered him out of the stable and back up to the house. "Does Marina know yet?" She looked tentatively up towards the house as they approached.

"No." Brad wiped at his eyes with the back of his hand. "She isn't here."

Surprised, Carmen sat him down at the kitchen table; she made them both a hot drink. Brad accepted it gratefully, staring at the wall; he set it down then snatched up the phone. "I should call the vet."

"Don't worry, I shall." Carmen took the phone out of his hand. "Let me call. You drink your tea."

He handed her the diary pointing out the vet's number. Carmen watched as he blew his nose then dabbed at his bloodshot eyes.

"I reckon it may have been a twisted gut. Was he colicky last night?" she asked.

Brad struggled to think back to yesterday, when he had arrived home from the hospital. "No he was fine early evening." He paused with a deep sigh. "I normally check them around bedtime but I didn't last night." He looked helplessly across at her. "I was so worn out." Brad cradled his head in his hands. "I wish I had now then maybe—"

Carmen interrupted, "You don't know that so don't even go there."

Brad looked across weakly at her, trying to gain some sort of composure. "I expect you're wondering where Marina is. Well she's in hospital. Yesterday she lost our baby."

Carmen gasped. "How awful. Oh, Brad, and now this on top of it. Oh, you poor, poor thing."

Carmen shuffled round to give him a hug. "Let me sort everything out. It might be a good idea if you go and have a lie down." She looked at her watch. "When is Marina due home?"

"Tomorrow morning, just as well really."

"Don't worry now, it'll be alright." She stood up. "I think we should both have another cup of tea while we're waiting for the vet to arrive and then you really should have a lie down."

Isobel woke up alone on Sunday morning. Adam had stayed late but hadn't wanted to stay overnight, she could understand why; she hadn't relished staying at his. She had to admit to herself it didn't seem right. She got out of bed then went over to the window. Parting the curtains, she peered out to see what the weather was like, dry at least, she murmured. Jacob and Edward were expected home after lunch, she had already made up her mind to go out for a long ride, clear her head ready for her heart to heart with Jacob this evening. That would be much later when Edward had gone to bed; she planned to make a special tea for Edward, having missed her darling son so much.

She wrapped up warm; it was chilly outside. The sun was already a distant memory. Slipping on her gloves, she hunted round for her riding hat, which seemed to have gone astray. She had always promised Jacob that she wouldn't ride without it. It wouldn't really matter today she would be taking it slowly. She decided to leave the dogs behind, she didn't need their distraction; she closed the door firmly behind her ignoring their look of disgust.

Turning a different way from normal, Quest jogged impatiently beneath her, pleased to be out, snatching greedily at the barren hedgerows as they passed by.

"Come on, greedy guts." Isobel laughed aloud as she leant forward to pull a stick from Quest's mouth. "I doubt that will taste very nice."

Pushing him forwards into a brisk trot, she rode down the large sloping eastern paddock until it met with the hawthorn hedgerow. Keeping to the same pace, they followed the natural curve of the hedgerow. She looked around at her surroundings with interest. It had been some time since she had been down here, then wondered why she hadn't as it was beautiful even this late in the year. Quest, enjoying the change too, took a strong hold, persuading her to give a little and move up to a steady canter. They climbed up towards a small copse. Quest picked his way expertly across the uneven, sodden ground. Urging him forwards faster his hooves squelched rhythmically through the wet grass. The strong wind picked up, blowing her hair into her eyes. Reaching the copse they slowed down, coming back to a walk. She leant forward to pat his strong neck, his ears twitched back and forth at the sound of her voice; she gave an indulgent smile, forgetting her worries for a few moments. She joined the stony track which headed west up to the wood. Isobel noticed the rooks had returned, circling their nests high up in the trees, the peace shattered by their constant cawing. Isobel turned right. To circle the wood the opposite way, settling Quest on the pathway, carpeted with decaying leaves. The wood had lost its tranquillity, it was back to being sinister. The cold scary place she had first encountered. The clouds moved rapidly joining ranks, as the sky darkened, the risk of rain increasing. Digging in her heels, she urged Quest on, to make it home before the downpour. She didn't fancy a soaking. Skirting the northern end of the wood, where the trees seemed more tightly packed and the path snaked sharply left they headed back towards home.

It happened very suddenly. She never really stood a chance. A cloaked figure emerged at speed, from the trees ahead of her, startling Quest who reared up onto his hind legs, spinning around terrified. The reins slipped from her hands as she crashed toward the ground. Then there was total darkness.

Slowly she emerged from the darkness. It was growing lighter but her vision was blurred. She found she was sitting on the sofa in her living room; two faces peered curiously down at her. A sharp, stabbing pain at the base of her neck felt unbearable. The haze shrouding her eyes began to soften. Slowly, she recognised Graham and Olivia, who were looking intensely at her. She opened her mouth to speak; it came out with a croak. "What's happening?"

Olivia leant further forward. "Are you OK, love? We've been in two minds whether to take you to hospital or not."

"Mm, indeed." Graham rubbed his chin. "You've had a nasty fall by the look of things. We found your horse first. Stood there he was trembling, with his bridle half hanging off, and you, love, in a crumpled heap, a little further along the pathway. Don't know what happened but you must have had a terrible tumble."

Isobel went to speak, but Olivia held up a silencing hand. "It's alright, we've checked him over and he's in his stable safe and sound. We are more concerned about you; you gave us both quite a fright." She looked at Graham, who nodded in agreement.

Instinctively she placed her hand to her aching neck, thoughtful for a while. Vaguely she could remember. It was very vague, but the veil of blackness began to descend again, blotting out what little she could remember. Slowly their faces disappeared; everything went quiet until there was nothing except the ever-descending darkness.

Edward sat singing happily to himself at the breakfast table. He had enjoyed his time with his grandparents but he had missed his mummy and was looking forward to going home. Jacob patted his shoulder then smiled indulgently as he watched his son dipping his toast soldier into the boiled egg.

Jacob's mother came into the kitchen. "He reminds me of you when you were that age."

Jacob turned to kiss her cheek. "Thanks for a great weekend, Mum."

"It's been a pleasure, darling. Now promise me when you get back you and Isobel will sort out all this silly nonsense."

Jacob shook his head. "I can only try, Mum." He shrugged. "If she won't talk then, what can I do?"

She looked across at Edward. "That boy needs his parents together." Her eyes welled with tears. "Marriage is hard, son, but you two—well you were made for each other, you have to work harder at it."

Jacob felt a lump in his throat. He loved Isobel he didn't want to lose her. They would talk tonight; whatever he had to do, he would win back her love and respect.

Brad took a slow drive to the hospital. It was another dreary day, which mirrored his mood perfectly. He had come to the decision that he wouldn't tell Marina about Lizard today, it was too soon after her losing the baby. Entering the ward, he found Marina was dressed and sat on the side of the bed with her packed case beside her.

"I've been discharged, so let's get out of here." She slipped her hand in his.

Brad hadn't really been sure what to expect, how this happening would affect Marina. To his dismay all the journey home she chatted gaily as if nothing had happened. He went along with it not sure how to handle it. Not once did either of them mention the baby.

Marina felt good being back home, never had it seemed more welcoming. She sat on the sofa while Brad made her coffee. She was desperate to put this whole episode behind her as quickly as possible. At some point Brad would look to her for some answers. She had decided that she would cross that bridge when she came to it, for now she would shut it out and concentrate on getting her strength back.

As he placed a cup of coffee down in front of her, Brad wondered what on earth was going on in her mind. He would leave it for today, but tomorrow some questions would need answering.

He sat down next to her, hugged her to his chest, and softly kissed her hair. A silent tear rolled down his cheek. He wiped it savagely away.

Rita sat in her kitchen watching the rain with a deep feeling of unease. When the weather improved, she would pop over and check up on Isobel. It was not like her, not to return her call, but there again in all fairness, Isobel probably didn't feel obliged to come round after Rita had mentioned she had had a bug. Not that Rita had really had a bug at all; she had used that as an excuse not to go. She had fully intended to visit her sister, had nearly packed a case and all. She took a sip of the herbal infusion, grimacing at the sour taste. No she had been all set and looking forward to it too, then she had had a vision and it had worried her, but she was at a loss to interpret its meaning. Scratching her head, mystified, she remembered the balloons floating through the sky and wondered what this meant.

Rita went over to the dresser, shaking her head in disbelief at what she was about to do. She took a glass down from the top shelf; fishing inside it, she pulled out a key. Rita held the key up to the light, then running a trembling finger along its edge; she turned it over and laid it in the palm of her hand. She hesitated for a second before ambling over to the larder. Opening the door, she walked inside. On the back wall hung a small violet coloured curtain. She pulled the curtain back to reveal a small wooden door with a lock. Standing on tiptoe to reach it, her hands trembling, she took a deep breath and inserted the key. With one quick twist, the door opened. She stretched inside to pull out a black tin box. Carefully she carried the box in both hands and placed it in the centre of the kitchen table. She went over to the cooker, and feeling along the top of the mantle found a box of matches, then went about the kitchen lighting the candles that stood dotted here and there, the kitchen soon bathed in a warm glow. The candles began to flicker casting restless shadows along the wall. She picked up a blanket, threw it around her shoulders, then sat down at the table with her eyes fixed firmly on the box before her.

Isobel blinked profusely against the intense piercing light, as it engulfed the entire room. It was unlike any other light she had experienced before. It was brilliant, pure, white light, consuming everything around it. It appeared to be dragging her in towards its core, she felt powerless to fight it. As quickly as the light had enveloped her, it disappeared, giving way to a sense of peace and calm, and the overwhelming feeling of being weightless, if she wanted to float, she could she was sure of it.

Opening her eyes, everything was different, things weren't as they should be, she gave a gasp as she moved her hand and it swam effortlessly through the air before her eyes. It didn't feel as if it were part of her body. In that, bizarre moment she became aware of how many cobwebs clung to the old oak beams. It seemed like a century's worth. Isobel looked below her, the dogs were sleeping soundly, blissfully unaware that she was floating high above their heads. It was then with a gasp of disbelief that she saw herself, curled up on the sofa asleep. Curiously she watched, fascinated by the chance to observe herself, how peaceful she looked, but oh so pale. What followed was an overwhelming feeling of love, for her physical self, lying there below, but yet with an air of detachment. Instinctively she knew the time had come to say goodbye, her spirit was ready to leave. The intense buzzing, so loud it hurt her ears, knocked her backwards, she began to fall, she tried to stop, desperate to stay where she was, but the force was too strong. With a violent jolt, she opened her eyes to look but this time up at the ceiling.

There was a continuous rapping at the door. She tried to ignore it, stunned by what she had experienced it but whoever was there was relentless. Rising gingerly, unsure of her capacity to walk, she hobbled over to the window. It was dark outside; she had absolutely no idea of the time. Rain lashed against the windowpane, she shivered hugging her arms around herself, as she pressed her forehead against the cold glass. The gentle beam of a car's headlights shone in the driveway. The person at the door banged impatiently again and again. Clasping the handle with shaky fingers, she threw it open, and the driving rain blew in, refreshing on her face. Two policemen stood towering in the doorway.

The more portly of the two stared at her then stepped forward. "Are you Mrs Isobel Kadeer?"

Isobel nodded, taking a step back, as the other policeman removed his helmet.

"P.C Reynolds and Sergeant Woods." He signalled to the other man. "Would it be OK if we come in, we need to talk to you." He raised an eyebrow at the weather and looked past her inside. Isobel stood aside to let them pass, they turned to face her and the sergeant gave a comforting smile, sensing her apprehension.

"I'm very sorry to have to inform you that there has been an accident."

PC Reynolds stepped forward his eyes full of compassion. "We believe it is your husband and son."

Isobel didn't hear him finish the sentence. Her throat tightened, her head began to throb her sense of hearing deserted her, she was afraid she may faint.

"What has happened? Are they hurt?" Her eyes pleaded with the policemen to tell her everything was fine. "Are they OK? Please tell me they're OK."

"It happened on the M5. I'm afraid they were involved in a serious RTA involving—"

"Are they alright?" She held on to the banister for support, the colour drained from her face. She just needed an answer.

"Please sit down, Mrs. Kadeer. I'm so very sorry to have to tell you the accident was fatal, is there someone we can—" The policemen stepped forward just catching her as she slivered towards the floor.

Isobel opened her eyes to a misty haze, as it cleared she recognised Graham. He was standing alongside the two policemen. They all turned to peer at her. Graham lunged forward to take her hand which had begun to shake uncontrollably.

They didn't really need to tell her that her husband and son had both been killed instantly. Their faces said it all. As they went on officially informing her of the details, trying to appear sympathetic, Graham squeezed her hand tightly. She clung to his hand for support as their voices became distant and distorted until there was no sound at all and then the terrible blackness prevailed once more.

The day seemed to drag endlessly. Marina had flicked with little interest through every magazine that Brad had thoughtfully brought and left lying on the coffee table for her to find. She would never appreciate how Brad had painstakingly vetted every magazine in the shop first, to make sure there were no articles on miscarriages or babies dying.

Snapping the final magazine shut and throwing it down, she stood up, smoothing her hands down her denims. She needed to get back to normal. The smell of her favourite dish filtered in from the kitchen, where Brad was frantically chopping herbs and stirring a sauce. He wanted to make Marina happy; he also needed to keep busy, he looked up from his béchamel sauce as Marina entered the kitchen.

"How are you feeling, love?"

"Extremely bored, I thought I make take a wander down to the stables."

"No!" Brad dropped the metal spoon with a clatter on to the floor with a look of horror.

Marina arched an eyebrow questioningly. "I'm not a total invalid you know."

"I know that." Brad shot her a mutinous glare. Then softening his gaze smiled. "Leave it until the morning, eh, babe? Besides, dinner is nearly done."

Shrugging her shoulders nonchalantly, she padded back through to the living room swinging her legs up onto the sofa, she lay back beginning to settle until a familiar "Hi, folks" echoed from the hallway. Marina gave a smile of delight. Oh goodie it was Isobel. Isobel would cheer her up, she could fill her in on all the gossip. She sat up expectantly, waiting for her to breeze in as she did. It was all quiet apart from the grind of the nutmeg mill in the kitchen. Marina stood up and went across to peer in to the hallway which was empty; she looked out of the window, surprised that there was no sign of Isobel's car. How strange. She shivered. She could have sworn she had heard her.

"Brad, did you hear Isobel?" she called out to him.

Brad appeared looking hot and bothered. "Nope, didn't hear a thing." Then he scurried back to his spoiling dinner.

Marina hugged herself in a comforting embrace. It must be the painkillers; the doctor had warned her they were strong. Perhaps she would give Isobel a call anyway. There was no reply; she let it ring for ages, finally replacing the receiver with a sense of disappointment.

Brad appeared with two steaming plates. "Dinner is finally ready, come on let's eat."

Carmen had planned to have an early night; the first train was leaving at six a.m. Her father nodded as she left him downstairs watching TV. She paused halfway up the stairs to look down at him. "I am getting nervous about tomorrow you know."

"I am not surprised, not knowing what to expect, isn't it?"

Carmen looked quizzically at her father. "She may have left me a heap of debt to sort out."

"It's a possibility but I very much doubt it. The solicitors wouldn't be so keen to see you. Don't worry, love, it will be fine."

Carmen found it hard to sleep. She hadn't been able to share her news with anybody yet. Poor Brad and Marina they had their own problems, it was hardly the right time to tell them her curious news. Maybe it was for the best, she mused. After all, it could turn out that Aunt Grace had the last laugh, at her expense. Carmen tried counting sheep to no avail. The night seemed endless as she tossed and turned this way and that.

Marina was finding it hard to sleep too. She wanted desperately for tomorrow to be normal, but she knew it would be a battle with Brad. He seemed to be intent on treating her with kid gloves. In a way, it should all be forgotten. It was for the best. Marina had been angry that he had told Molly. There hadn't been any need for her to know. The worst thing was that Molly would have told her father by now. Marina just hoped, he hadn't put two and two, together. On second thoughts knowing Howard he would have done. Well at least apart from Isobel, nobody around the village knew. She wouldn't be able to stand all those pitiful glances when all she wanted was a can of coke or a loaf of bread from the village shop.

Restlessly, she pulled the quilt around her. Brad was breathing deeply beside her and she was insanely jealous, He looked so peaceful. Marina leant across to kiss his forehead and he didn't stir. It would be another couple of weeks before she could ride. Lizard would be as fresh as a daisy, by the time she finally got back in the saddle. She wondered if Brad had reduced his feed now that he wasn't being ridden. Marina smiled to herself. Of course, he had! Brad remembered everything.

CHAPTER EIGHTEEN

The air felt damp and cold from the earlier downpour, slowly Isobel made her way through the mud up towards the wood, determined that today, she would go inside its eerie depths. It was finally time to overcome her fear. The light was beginning to fade, but it was darker still as she approached the veil of towering trees.

The dogs skittered around to her left; their noses pressed hard to the damp earth. The rain had washed away any exciting scents. With a quick backward glance across her shoulder, she strode confidently into the wood. The dogs did not dare to follow her. Once she had entered the wood the pockets of fear, which had held her back, seemed to disperse. The trees seemed to shrink back in a defeated sense of welcome. Confidently, she held her arms up to the branches and the grey sky yonder to acknowledge their change. Instinctively she raised her arms up above her head to embrace the earthy feeling of calm that caressed her.

Isobel came across a narrow pathway. Intrigued she followed its twists and turns between the massive trunks, which steadily appeared to become denser. As she picked her way along, the darkness began to turn to light; gentle warmth filled her body, it appeared to amplify the further she walked towards the warm pinkish glow that lay ahead. Unexpectedly filled with a sense of excitement of what she might find, swiftly she moved on, noticing that the grass which carpeted the ground ahead looked so lush and green, not anything like you would expect to find in the depths of a wood where the sun struggled to filter through the obstructive oaks with their gnarled boughs and far reaching branches. She looked above, mystified as to why there was so much light and surprised that the trees had healthy green leaves as if it was summer here. Unperturbed Isobel pushed on filled with an insatiable urge to find the central point of the wood, feeling no need to digress from her path, even though she had passed several turnings that lingered temptingly between the trees. There was a whisper of a sound, more of a gentle vibration, she felt centred by its melodic hum as it filtered into her ears. The path rose steadily uphill, passing between two sentry oaks, solid and imposing. At the top of the hill, to her utter amazement, the dense forest gave way to a beautiful meadow. It was almost as if she had come through and out the other side of the wood. Isobel had circled this wood many times and knew that this meadow did not exist. From this certainty she could only conclude that she was in fact, still within the confines of the wood itself.

Yet here was a meadow of such beauty, so vibrant and intense, filled with flowers that were so striking and colourful, ranging from the palest lilac to the most powerfully intense orange she had ever witnessed and some were of colours not of this world. A wide stream ran across the meadow. She could hear the soft chortle of its waters that flowed and bubbled, rushing in a torrent between its banks. It felt warm here, there was a sense of peace, much like one felt on the most perfect summer's day, but the cloudless sky that prevailed above was a muted shade of pink creating a dusky glow. There was no sun or clouds but the air felt fresh and comfortingly familiar.

"Isobel."

She turned to look around at the sound of her name, the voice gentle. She had taken it for granted that she was alone, the only person witnessing this incredible scene. Isobel let out a gasp at the sight of Belle. Belle stood smiling, dressed in a vibrant gown looking radiantly across at her, her face alight with beauty, yet tranquil, not awed by her being there.

"Belle, what are you doing here, did you follow me?"

Belle came towards her gracefully with her arms outstretched, her eyes sparkling magically, drawing Isobel towards her. Isobel looked at her, she drew in breath, mesmerised by her beauty.

"I'm here for you, Isobel. This is going to be confusing for you, but we really must talk." She beckoned for Isobel to accompany her; Isobel followed to the shelving bank of the stream gazing around at her surroundings in wonderment.

"It's so beautiful here. I had no idea it existed."

"Indeed it is." Belle looked around and then turned back to Isobel to smile knowingly. "Do you know why you're here, Isobel?"

"I have no idea, I just followed the path. I think the wood wanted me to come in today. It has always shut me out in the past."

"Yes it did." Belle placed a quietening finger on Isobel's lips. "Isobel, you must pay attention to what I tell you, we don't have much time." Belle leant forward to squeeze her hand tightly. "You are here at the transitional stage."

"What do you mean transitional?" Isobel asked bemused.

221

"You are here because you should be. It has been allowed. Normally you might only get to see this when you are on your journey back home to source. Today you rest here with me, your eternal guide."

Belle searched Isobel's face for any sign of recognition. She had been here before, albeit over 150 earth years ago and her job would be easier if Isobel could remember. Not the slightest hint of recognition flickered within her eyes, Belle gave a sad sigh.

Isobel threw back her head laughing. "What's all this stuff?" She raised an eyebrow. "Are we in Heaven? Because if we are it's as beautiful as they say it is, and when you say eternal guide, what do you mean?"

"No we are at the transitional stage. As I told you, and I am your guide, the guide to your soul, the very essence of you, and the part that you so easily forget here on earth. Poor Isobel, you forget so much. Alas I can only guide, the rest is up to you." Belle took her hand. "Come to the stream, and I think it would be simpler for me to try to show you."

Silently they knelt together at the water's edge, two women worlds apart yet connected in the most miraculous way. Isobel gazed wondrously at the pretty shapes and soft colours of the intricate stones, lodged on the stream's bed. The crystal waters began to cloud over, slowly a picture emerged in the running waters. Squeezing Isobel's arm encouragingly Belle whispered. "Watch carefully, it will make your future path much smoother."

Isobel watched the waters closely, giving a gasp in astonishment at the strange occurrence. There amidst this beautiful haven, in the crystal waters she saw herself as a child. She was happy, smiling at something. Isobel caught her breath it was her mother. They were walking together hand in hand. In addition, her mother looked so young, the love radiating from her eyes directed at Isobel who skipped happily at her side. Isobel felt a lump in her throat, her bottom lip quivered and her eyes began to well up, suddenly painfully aware of how much she missed her mother.

In a moment the vision faded, leaving Isobel bitter with disappointment, only in the next instance for another picture of her to emerge, this time with Jacob. He was grinning at her boyishly, as he always did. He looked down at the thing she held nestled lovingly in her arms. It was Edward so tiny and fragile, not more than a few weeks old. Isobel looked across to Belle, bewildered, what did this mean? Bell nodded with a reassuring smile, tilting her head back to the water, indicating for Isobel to keep watching as the memories flooded back, bringing with them a torrent of emotion. Adam was there, he looked pleased and she bent to look closer at the water's surface. He was smiling at her. She was there. Isobel gasped, she looked so beautiful, animated but older.

"We look so happy, so in…." She broke off.

"In love you mean." Belle looked pleased with herself. "Yes you do. Adam is very important to you; I think that much at least you've figured out. You have been together through many lifetimes." Belle sat up drawing her eyes away from the stream; she gave a sigh of frustration. "There is much love between you, love, that has lasted lifetimes." She gave a restless shrug. "All I can say is that you both have so much work to do. You never succeed and Adam is dependent on you. Without you completing this cycle, he will be brought back time and time again and alas poor Jacob too."

Isobel watched Belle, closely, there was sorrow and pain, what did it all mean?

"Are we soul mates, is that what you're trying to tell me? I mean if we are, then why didn't we find each other years ago? Why did I fall in love and marry Jacob?"

"Yes soul mates, I believe that's what you call it. But remember it is never easy." She nudged Isobel's arm. "Watch the waters please."

A small girl, about five or six, with the most amazing green eyes, sat astride a beautiful white pony. She was giggling as she flung her arms around the pony's neck which she showered with sweet kisses. She was so delicate. The prettiest child Isobel had ever set eyes on. She looked across at Belle who gave an encouraging nod.

"In time, in time, you'll see."

A vision of Jacob danced on the surface of the water. He was crying, lost and forlorn. He was looking up and the pain etched on his face was unbearable. Isobel winced, turning in alarm to Belle. "What's happening, why, he is so upset? I can't bear it."

"I can't really help. I know that sounds silly. Just trust that you will discover all." Belle smiled encouragingly, but there was an air of sadness which she could not conceal.

Isobel watched in silence as the dream that had haunted her for so many nights, played like a silent movie on the waters before her. She winced at the pain and turmoil, and she felt helpless as she watched Adam die in her arms, recoiled at the sight of herself sobbing uncontrollably, as she looked down at her bloodstained palms and Adam's lifeless body. For the first time she noticed the anguish on Jacob's face. Saw the hatred which turned to pity, the power which turned to defeat. She watched herself wilt like a dying flower.

Moreover, for the very first time she saw three globes of golden light rise into the sky above their heads and join to form a ball of such intent light that shone down on the sea of agony below it.

Belle turned to her, her voice steady. "You are so lucky, not everybody gets to see this."

Isobel raised a brow, her voice heavy with sarcasm. "Well, lucky me. I have no idea what's going on. I just don't understand, but can we just quit the guessing game?" She signalled with a wave of her arm around them. "What is the point of any of this if it's going to turn out to be one big riddle? How am I supposed to know what all of this means? I feel you want me to do something. I can't change the past, let alone from a life I don't even recall."

Belle glared her words scornful. "There is no room for your earthly ways here. This is life, Isobel. Nobody knows the answers when they are on earth, that's why you are here to learn. If you are wise you won't make the same mistake again. Only the foolish trade their contracts and sell their soul to the darker forces." She threw her head back defiantly. "You are a great spirit, from a higher plane and yet you shake off your responsibility so easily. You rely on me for all the answers and if you but knew, mine is by far the hardest job. Century after century I have had to watch you make the same seemingly tiny mistake, over and over again. Each time we leave home to embark on this trip to earth, you are sure of your path, eager to move forward, keen to be done and return home."

"Sorry." Isobel dropped to her knees as tears sprung to her eyes. Overwhelmed she buried her face in her hands and began to weep. Belle placed a comforting arm around her shoulders.

"It's good to cry, very healing for the soul." She patted her arm. "There is no riddle, Isobel. If you look into your heart, you will find the answer." Belle sat motionless for a few moments. "I've said enough already. I have my part in this too." She scrambled to her feet, looking down, sympathetically at Isobel. "Your family need you. You must leave now. It's time for you to return."

Isobel looked up pleadingly. "Please let me stay here a bit longer, it doesn't feel right to leave yet," she asked, afraid what faced her when she left the peace and tranquillity.

Leaning over, Belle placed a kiss on Isobel's tear-stained cheek. "It will be a while before we meet again. Yet, I will be right by your side, in spirit. It would be wise to remember that." She looked up at the sky and frowned. "There is one, when you go back, who has knowledge. One person who can help you more than I am able to. One who also loves and cares about you. One with whom you share the same realm, for you are my child, from the same soul group."

Defeated, Isobel stretched out on the soft grass. She had no idea who Belle was referring to at all. If she told anyone about this place, the stream and Belle, they would think she had completely lost her mind. She didn't want to go back and face this insurmountable task. She just wanted to remain here a little longer, she thought, as she lay back and closed her eyes feeling ever so secure.

Rita laid the cards out before her, trying to remain calm. This was the first time she had handled them since her husband's death. She tried to control her trembling fingers. The cards lay face down on the table, inviting her to seek their knowledge. Her understanding of the tarot was immense. She had read these cards so many times with astounding accuracy, even surprising herself with the depth of knowledge they unearthed.

Two days before her husband had died they had told her what was to be. She had felt sick to the pit of her stomach. Even though he had been ill for a considerable time it had been a shock and she had hoped with all her heart that for once the cards would be wrong, that she had made a mistake.

She brushed a tear from her eye at the memory of that day and the fateful reading. Yet here she was about to question the cards once again, and why? Quite simply Edward! She felt herself go cold at the prospect of their meaning. She had known that there was something tragic to befall the family. From the very first day she had seen the family arrive at Orange Stream Farm she had known. Her sixth sense told her that Edward would be okay, that he would come to no harm. But the latest vision had worried her, causing alarm bells to ring. Somehow Edward would be caught up in the tragedy and she prayed that she could save him.

With a determined grunt, shrugging off the inward fear which threatened to surface, she turned the first row of cards. Her breath caught in her throat, where it stayed, her whole body tense as she looked down through eyes wide with fear, at the card which sat in the centre of the first line—*the reaper!*

CHAPTER NINETEEN

Carmen stared out of the of the carriage window. The countryside passed in a flurry before her eyes. She turned to look at her father, who had his head buried in the newspaper. Carmen felt for his hand squeezing it tightly. He looked up, giving her an encouraging smile.

"It will be alright, love. Trust me."

Carmen smiled back nodding. It was a strange feeling, a mix of heady excitement, tinged with a nagging doubt. Here she was, heading to the office of a well-to-do firm of solicitors, to find out what she had inherited from an aunt she had never known. It was like a scene from a movie.

As the train pulled in to Winchester station, she clasped her father's hand, as she often had done as a little girl, whenever she was feeling apprehensive. They climbed into a vacant taxi; Carmen pressed her forehead against the window, staring out with interest, as they meandered through the early morning traffic.

The offices of Rapkyn and Hayes were just outside the city centre, in a smart office block, shared with several other companies. She paid the taxi driver. "Keep the change," she said.

They headed up the steps; Carmen glanced at her reflection in the smoked glass doors, pausing to smooth her linen skirt which had creased on the journey. She cursed softly, wishing she had worn something else. Her father gave her an encouraging nod, then taking her by the arm marched her in before she had time to change her mind.

Martin Rapkyn, much to Carmen's surprise, was a bit of a dish. A tall, lean man around forty, she guessed. He had heavy lidded, brown eyes not unlike a jersey cow, she thought, trying not to stare at them. He had a good tan and his hazel hair glinted beneath the strong lighting. He seemed genuinely pleased to meet them, taking both their hands, in turn, with a warm positive shake.

"Did you have a good journey up? Trains aren't the most comfortable form of transport."

"Yes it wasn't too bad at all," Carmen replied, smoothing her skirt, yet again.

"Good, I guess you left Devon early; we must find you both a drink." He picked up a large folder from an adjacent desk. "Please, follow me." He led them to a large conference room. In the centre stood a circular table, at which were seated two gentlemen and an older woman. Martin introduced them as the two senior partners, one obviously his father, with the same heavy eyes and there was Jackie, his personal secretary. Carmen began to tremble. It must be quite important for them all to be here. She gave her father a sideways glance, he didn't seem alarmed, and she took a seat between him and Mr Hayes.

Martin Rapkyn winked at her; it was a friendly gesture, meant to put her at ease.

"Please don't look so alarmed," he said.

Carmen tried to ignore the flutter of her heart. The journey was worth making, just to set eyes on him. She fidgeted nervously in her seat, hoping it wasn't too obvious that she found him very attractive. He dropped his gaze, to the folder on the desk, in front of him.

"Let's begin." He looked around at each of them in turn and began to read. He was most professional. Carmen could not help but be impressed. She watched intrigued, sidetracked from what he was saying, by his sultry mouth and the sexy voice. He put down the papers, to look across at Carmen. She looked back eagerly. The corners of his mouth eased into a friendly smile. "As we understand it, Carmen, you never got to meet with your aunt. Grace Markham was a lovely woman and quite a character." He paused. "In fact you are of the same colouring." He cleared his throat and continued. "She has left a trunk, which we have here, full of information and photos. We have been instructed to pass this on to you. I believe she was very keen for you to get to know her. Even after her death."

Carmen felt a lump in her throat, what a wonderful idea. She would be able to discover her aunt and learn who she was, if only her mother was here now. It would be like opening a treasure trove. Tears pricked at her eyes, afraid she may cry she gave a short cough, and turned her focus to the pile of papers scattered before Martin Rapkyn.

"Your aunt was a very wealthy lady, as you will see. You are the sole beneficiary to her estate." He rose from his chair, and coming around the table, he handed her some papers. "It would probably be easier if we go through it together, so you can see the details on paper."

Her father looked across at the papers she held in her trembling hands. Carmen couldn't read the writing her eyes were beginning to well up, it was becoming a blur.

"If you take a look at page four please. There is the named property, Crofters Farm, which was her main residence. A 17th century farmhouse along with agricultural outbuildings and approximately fifty-seven acres of land, plus two farm workers cottages, these are currently let. Then we have Bowen Lodge. This property situated in Gloucestershire; it comes with a couple of acres. I believe this was your aunt's bolthole when she wanted to escape from the farm."

Carmen couldn't really take it all in. She was aware of her father's gasp in astonishment, as Mr Rapkyn read. Aware that this exceeded her wildest dreams and that it didn't feel real, things like this didn't happen to her. When Martin had finished reading the will, he suggested that she may wish to extend her visit. Indeed, it would be a good idea to see the properties and discuss at length how she would like to precede. A most interesting proposition, she thought, especially as Martin would be working alongside her.

Martin took them to lunch, a quaint pub in a neighbouring village, with a cosy inglenook fireplace and a roaring fire. Carmen felt too shell-shocked to eat, settling instead for a large whisky. Her father talked excitedly at her prospects, asking Martin's advice between mouthfuls of hunters' pie.

Martin sensed Carmen's shock; he thought it best if they returned home and let today, sink in. They could schedule a meeting for next week. Carmen smiled with relief. There was certainly a lot to think about and more importantly, she wanted to get the chest home and discover whom her aunt was. Until she had done that, she couldn't think about touching one single, solitary, penny of her inheritance.

Isobel woke, the room felt strange, almost three-dimensional. The weird nightmare had made her toss and turn restlessly and her neck ached terribly from the twisted position she had held it on the pillow. The dogs stormed into the room from the hallway where they had been cowering, as Isobel had cried out in her sleep. Pleased now that she was awake they bounded in jumping onto the bed. Isobel sat up wedging a supporting pillow behind her head. She shuddered at the memory of the nightmare; it had seemed so real.

There was a light knock on the door; she looked up surprised to see Olivia who peered cautiously round the door at her.

"I guessed you were awake, I could hear the dogs leaping around." She looked at Isobel's confused expression. "I assume you remember what happened?"

Isobel looked blank. "No I'm not sure I do."

"Oh, dear, in that case, I wonder whether we might have a mild case of concussion on our hands." She sidled closer to the bed, to frown at Isobel. "Do you know what day it is?"

"Yes, it's Sunday, and what's all this about concussion, Olivia? I think you need to explain."

"Yes I will, but just hang on one moment." Olivia went back to the door and called along the hall. "Graham, Graham, get up here please."

Isobel pulled the sheet tightly round herself with a shiver.

"Graham, what's Graham doing here?" she asked, bewildered.

"In which case, you really don't remember." Olivia wagged a finger at her as Graham sauntered in with a look of concern. Isobel looked up at both of them.

"Will somebody please explain what has happened before I scream?"

Graham perched himself on the end of her bed. "We found you up by the wood, you had taken a terrible tumble from your horse, and before you ask, yes the horse is fine, but we have been ever so worried about you."

Olivia's eyes rose in despair, she butted in. "If Graham had listened to me we would have called the doctor straight away. I knew it."

Graham held up a silencing finger at Olivia with an authoritative glare. He turned back to Isobel with a smile. "We brought you back here and you seemed to be okay, but then you blacked out. We were going to call the doctor but then you came round again, and you seemed perfectly all right. You started chatting and you were telling us about Edward visiting his grandparents. I fixed you a large brandy which seemed to revive you dramatically."

Isobel couldn't remember anything; it was a total blank.

"How are you feeling now?" Olivia sat down beside Graham and looked at Isobel through squinting eyes.

"I feel fine, but I have to admit I can't remember anything of what you have said, but I feel okay."

Olivia and Graham raised a brow in unison.

"No, really I do."

Graham stood up smoothing his hair. "Well you came up here for a nap and you've been asleep hours, I guess it's fairly safe to assume there's no long-term damage."

Isobel nodded and suddenly she recalled her nightmare and sat up in alarm "What time is it?"

Graham looked at his watch. "It's just gone half past three."

"What time did you find me?"

Graham glanced across at Olivia. "About 10 o'clock this morning, wasn't it?"

She nodded in agreement. "Yes, love, around 10ish, and you've been asleep for over four hours, Isobel."

Isobel threw back the sheet, leaping naked from the bed. Graham, shocked, turned away; Olivia quickly passed Isobel her dressing gown.

"Shit, I have to call Jacob. I have to go to London, now, please. God! Don't let them have left yet." She raced for the stairs, Olivia and Graham following closely behind her.

"What do you mean, why have you got to go to London? I don't think you're in any fit—"

Isobel spun round to face them her face ashen. "The nightmare, it was awful, trust me. I must leave and soon."

Scratching his head, Graham turned towards the kitchen. "I think I should go and make us all a cuppa. We could all use one right now."

Olivia followed Isobel through to the study. "What is all this nightmare nonsense and why all the urgency?"

"Oh, Olivia, you don't understand, it was Belle. She was trying to make me see something. I'm not even sure I understand myself, and then there was the terrible accident, and the meadow, and being on the ceiling and it's all so crazy."

Olivia sat perplexed in the armchair. "None of what you're saying makes any sense, my love. I still think you should have a check-up, you're rambling on about a load of old nonsense."

At that moment, Graham came in with a tray. "Maybe that's not such a bad idea, love." But Isobel had picked up the phone and was dialling Jacob's mother's number.

"Shssh, everyone, please…" She scowled at them both. Sheepishly they grinned back.

"Jacob, it's me, I'm so glad that I caught you."

"Oh, Isobel, we were just about to set off, is something the matter?"

"Yes, I mean no, it's just…" She paused. Was she acting crazy, had she finally flipped? "It's just I thought I would come up to London for a few days."

"Really, that would be great, Rita's back then?"

"Yes, I thought I would catch the train up. I could be with you late this evening."

"Brilliant. Mum and Dad will be really pleased to see you. Thanks, Isobel, it would mean such a lot to me."

She replaced the receiver with a feeling of dread. She couldn't explain it, but she had to go. The nightmare had been so real. They mustn't travel back today; she would have to go to them. With a heavy heart, she thought of Adam. Darling Adam, she would have to tell him, it couldn't be put off any longer.

She looked across at Graham and Olivia, who were sipping their tea. "I know you think I have concussion or some bloody thing, but I'm positive that I'm absolutely fine. I need to get to London to be with my family. I don't mean to be rude but I really must get ready."

Graham set down his cup. "Okay, point taken, we'll be out of your way. There's a train for Waterloo at six this evening, at least let me come back and drive you to the station."

Isobel ushered them towards the doorway. "Yes, okay, thanks, Graham, that would be most kind." She let them out and then closing the door stopped and lent against it to take a deep breath before dashing upstairs where hurriedly she dressed.

She set off to Adam's house, her pulse racing and her stomach in knots. He would be upset. Goddamn it, she was upset, she adored him. Right now though, she had to be with Jacob and Edward. Too much was at stake.

Much to her frustration Adam wasn't home, she needed to speak to him face to face. She sat on the step holding her head in her hands, hot salty tears of frustration trickled down her cheeks. There was nothing she could, do except leave a note, until she could meet with him and explain her sudden change of heart.

Letting herself back in at Orange Stream Farm, she picked up the phone to call Rita, to ask her to look after the dogs, whilst she was away. Rita was feeling much better and Isobel cursed herself, for not phoning before to enquire about her, she had been so wrapped up in herself. She was marginally surprised that Rita so readily agreed, not even asking her, why she was leaving for London at such short notice.

Isobel looked out of the kitchen window, nursing a steaming cup of coffee between her cupped hands. She looked out toward the wood. It had featured so strongly in her nightmare. Perhaps it was haunted after all, there was certainly something sinister about it. A shiver coursed her spine. Dragging her eyes away from the dark wood, she glanced up at the clock, it was quarter past five; she needed to pack a case. She didn't intend to stay in London for long, just a couple of days. She needed to pull herself together a bit. There was a terrible queasiness in her stomach. Yesterday, her mind was clear and there was no question about her decision and now some awful nightmare had made her doubt herself. It was Adam she loved. She was sure of that. Her need for him was overwhelming and she had no doubt about how much he loved her, but she had a duty.

The train was packed, for most of the journey she was sandwiched between the window and a fat middle aged lady, who stunk of garlic, making Isobel want to retch unsettling her already churning tummy. The woman was insistent on telling Isobel her life story. Isobel resisted the temptation to yawn, instead smiling sweetly and pretending to be mildly interested despite her thumping head and the overwhelming nausea.

Edward and Jacob stood hand in hand on the platform waiting for her. She pulled Edward into her arms, squeezing him tightly until he cried out in pain and wriggled from her grasp. For the first time in months, she hugged Jacob, overwhelmed by her emotion. They caught a taxi back to the flat, where Jacob put Edward to bed, he was exhausted and his weekend in the city had tired him out. Isobel sat at the side of his bed until he fell asleep.

Jacob opened a bottle of Chardonnay, she didn't feel like having a drink but equally she didn't want to offend him. She was feeling shattered herself and was struggling to keep her eyes open. It had been the right decision to come, even if she had harboured some doubts and as she fell asleep she wondered what may have been if she wasn't here with her family right now.

There would be plenty of time to explain to Adam, he would have got the note she had left him by now. In it, she had promised to meet and talk, on her return. Jacob snored softly beside her; she turned to look at him, how exhausted he looked, so drawn with dark circles beneath his eyes. Sadly, it was the first time she had cared to notice.

Adam hadn't slept well; he had lain awake half the night worrying about Isobel. It was going to be terribly hard for her ending her marriage. He would need to be there with lots of love and support. He would show her how serious about the relationship, he was.

The wind had picked up outside, he sat up to take a sip of lukewarm tea, she would have told Jacob by now, God he hoped it had gone alright, that

Jacob hadn't gone mad at her. Jacob's world would have been torn apart and for that he felt sorry for the guy. Isobel would be facing an intense grilling for much of the day and at this point there was nothing that he could do. Today, tomorrow or maybe next week, at least she was coming, that was all that mattered.

Outside the wind grew in strength, picking up the fallen leaves, tossing them high in to the air, taking the handwritten note along with them, through the air and across the sodden fields. It was gone in a few moments, with no evidence, that lodged, between the empty milk bottles; it had ever been there at all.

Elizabeth climbed shakily from bed, she clutched at her stomach, it must have been the prawns in the curry her mother had prepared last night. She sat on the side of the bed, taking deep breaths; it was no good she had to throw up. Running to the toilet, she leant over the seat, just in time. Once she started, she couldn't stop. When it finally subsided, she sat down on the edge of the bath holding a cold flannel to her face, mopping gingerly at the corners of her mouth. Slowly the colour began to return to her cheeks and she started to feel a bit better, in fact she felt starving.

Slipping on her dressing gown, she went down to the kitchen, her mother was up and dressed and busy. In the middle of cooking a fry up, much to her delight. Her father was sat at the table reading the papers. He looked up. "You're up late. No work today?"

Elizabeth shrugged, looking up at the clock. She should have left ten minutes ago. Sitting down, she grabbed a slice of hot toast from the rack, which her mother had just placed on the table. Just this once she would be late, besides her mother's breakfast was far too good to miss.

Elizabeth heaped her plate full, she didn't notice her parents exchange puzzled glances. Elizabeth always picked at her food, paranoid, about putting on weight, this was an extremely rare sight, and her father raised a quizzical eyebrow.

Edward held on to his parents' hands, as he skipped along the pavement, they were heading for the toy shop after breakfast, he had five pounds in his pocket from Grandpa and he couldn't wait to spend it. They had got up late, Isobel hadn't been surprised to find there wasn't anything to eat or drink at the flat. Edward was whining that he was hungry and she was feeling rather empty, her stomach growled hungrily. Jacob had suggested they head for the

233

River Café for breakfast, if Edward was good and ate all his food they could go to the toy shop he had promised. The café was crowded; it took a long time to be served. Isobel was feeling lightheaded; she couldn't remember when she had last eaten. Edward moaned about the lengthy wait, fidgeting restlessly on his chair. Jacob was becoming increasingly irritated with him, Isobel smiled to herself, he had only been in charge of him for a few days and already the novelty was wearing off, but today it wasn't irritating, she was glad that they were here altogether, safe and sound.

As they left the café, the heavens opened. They hurried around the corner, deciding to take refuge in a charity shop, until the worst of the downpour had passed. Feeling guilty, Jacob decided he should buy something, after all, it was for charity, and Edward had his eye on a small soft koala bear. He looked longingly up at Jacob.

"Ah, look, Daddy." He held the koala aloft. "Jo Jo wants to come home with us to see the doggies."

Jacob gave a hearty laugh. "Does he indeed, well I suppose we better take him then." He winked at his son, thrusting his hand in to his pocket and pulling out a handful of change. Edward gave a satisfied smile hugging Jo Jo tighter, looking up at his mother in delight.

They left the shop with the newest member of the family, huddled beneath Edward's coat. The heavy rain had begun to ease, now a light drizzle. People began to re-emerge on to the street. There were still quite a few tourists, sightseeing, despite the weather. Isobel pulled her Mac more tightly, around herself. It was chilly and she began to shiver, she couldn't imagine wanting to sightsee in weather like this. She thought longingly of Orange Stream. The cosy living room with its roaring fire, oh, what she wouldn't give to be curled, in front of it now. Jacob nudged her arm as Edward skipped along in front of them.

"Thanks for coming," he said gently.

Isobel smiled, squeezing his arm. "I'm sorry it's taken me so long, a lot has happened this last year, I think maybe there are things that we should talk about—" She broke off at the look of horror on Jacob's face, following the direction of his horrified stare. Edward had strayed from the pavement and was standing in the middle of the road looking up at a bunch of colourful balloons. They were gently swaying in the wind, the end of their strings clutched by a street trader, as he crossed from one side of the road to the other. A car was travelling down the road straight towards Edward who was oblivious of anything else around him. His eyes were set eagerly on the balloons. Isobel heard herself scream out his name. Edward turned to look at her as she lurched forward in to the road, her arms extended to push Edward onto the pavement out of the path of the car. She was conscious of Jacob moments behind her, the weight of his body toppling over hers, the sickening screech of breaks and the sound of tyres skidding on the wet road. She felt her neck click; there was a loud roaring in her ears, she screamed as pain shot through her head and neck. The cars headlights were inches away as she clawed with her fingers to reach Edward. Clasping a handful of his anorak, it slipped through her wet fingertips. Then there was nothing.

Adam watched the ducks on the pond. He had braved the weather to clear his mind and somehow he had ended up here. A lonesome figure huddled on a park bench, watching the ducks bobbing up and down, on the choppy, muddy waters. The sky overhead was grey, threatening more rain. There was a feeling of unease in the air, it hung heavily all around him even the ducks sensed it. Taking a deep breath, he looked across the lake to the bleak sky shrouding the horizon. He twitched nervously. He had felt this before, long ago when he was younger. It had worried him then and it worried him now. It was a strange feeling, one of foreboding; his great-aunt had called it a sixth sense. To him it was just an unwelcome feeling, one he had no desire to feel, but it always preceded some dreadful news.

He took the hip flask from his jacket pocket, taking a large gulp of whisky, he tried to blot it out, he should be happy, after all he was about to get the one thing he wanted with all his heart. The clouds bubbled up overhead, stealing the light. The ducks along with the moorhens began to screech, flying from the lakes surface to the safety of the rushes at the water's edge. There was the distant rumble of thunder, followed by a crack of lightening which ripped through the sky. Adam stood up, tucking the flask back in his pocket; the rain would be along shortly. A feeling of panic swept his entire body. Shivering, he plunged his hands deeper in to his pockets and headed home.

Rita let herself in; the dogs ran to meet her, they were panting with their tails tucked firmly between their legs. They seemed afraid; she bent down on to one knee, to fuss them.

"There now it's OK. Good things you are." She stood up to close the door. That's when she felt it. Their presence hung heavily in the air all around her. She took a deep breath, so the time had come. It was what she had feared all along, known from the day she had set eyes on Isobel. That was one of the unfortunate things about her gift, you saw the bad as well as the good and you were powerless. Slowly she closed her eyes and took a few deep breaths, clearing her mind from the everyday clutter, drawing her attention inward.

She gave a thankful smile, mouthing the words, "thank you," as she did so. Her efforts had not been in vain, they hadn't let her down.

She let the dogs out into the garden for a run and sat down at the table. The wise council had been here, along with the guides, a meeting of great importance cast. No wonder the poor dogs were half-scared to death. Mind you that was the beauty of this place, it was powerful and in turn Mrs Jackson had finally found the light and been taken into God's care. With a satisfied sigh, she grinned. At last, this place was free. One day, when the time was right, she would explain all about this place and the sacred ground it stood on, the magical ley lines that led to the holy site and the secrets it held within its walls. The dogs bounded in, their tails wagging, their lips crinkled in greeting. The last of the energies left, out the door, to be absorbed into the earth's vibration. Already this house seemed different, alive with positive energy, eagerly awaiting the arrival of its new owner.

CHAPTER TWENTY

Six Weeks Later

It seemed to go on forever and ever; Isobel looked ahead at the spiralling tunnel. Belle's voice sounded sharply in her right ear. "I really think we should go now." There was a hesitant edge to her voice.

Isobel swallowed hard. It was just like Belle to spoil her fun. It's what she always did. Why did she have to be so practical all of the time? Besides she was tired, all she had wanted was a rest. Belle shook her right arm violently. Isobel turned to look at her, shocked at the alarm on her face. "Time to say our goodbyes then, I want you to know, Isobel. You can be darned hard work." Isobel gave a cheeky grin. Poor Belle, what had she done to deserve her.

Belle moved away from her, turning back to wave. Isobel went to raise her arm but she was paralysed. No longer smiling, she looked at Belle with distaste. It was not amusing anymore; she'd had enough of her games. Isobel found herself rooted to the spot, as Belle was distancing rapidly away from her. Alarmed Isobel looked back over her shoulder, the light behind was blinding. As the distance between herself and Belle grew ever larger, the light behind was advancing rapidly. She felt afraid, waiting to be engulfed by it. All she could do was wait and watch, as Belle smiled serenely from a distance. But now there was somebody beside her, another woman flanked her side. She was about the same height as Belle, her raven hair braided into a ponytail and her skin was dark. She looked past Isobel expectantly, the serenest smile caressing her lips.

"Isobel, look to the light behind you." Belle's words were distant, barely audible. Isobel struggled to hear them. She wanted to turn to look but still she was unable to move. The roar intensified, a shadow fell across where she stood as it passed at speed overhead, for just one second blocking the brilliant light. Belle and her companion outstretched their arms, smiling joyously. The shadow and the light passed, she watched as a figure joined the path just ahead of her, blocking her view of Belle. It was a man; he walked away from her. The light gathered around him, swirls of energy enveloped him. She looked further ahead, who were all those people behind Belle and the other woman, so many people, all of whom smiled holding out their hands welcomingly. As he reached the others and turned, she saw him clearly for the first time. He grinned boyishly at her, and she knew instinctively, it was for the last time.

"Jacob?" The words hadn't surfaced. She found herself flying backwards further and further until they were just specks on the horizon. Small black specks, that somehow joined and became one black mass.

Marina came in from the stables. The loss of Lizard had been a terrible blow for the stud. She watched from the terrace as his only son frolicked in the meadow. He was simply stunning; as he raced across the wet grass, kicking up his heels then swerving just before the fence to race back to his playmates. Marina watched him proudly. It would be a good three years before she would be able to sit on his back. Looking at him now, even at this young age, she could tell he would be as good, if not, better than his father.

Brad crept up behind her making her jump. He wrapped his arms around her waist. "He is stunning, isn't he?"

Marina nodded a tear in her eye. "Out of something bad there's usually something good to follow."

Brad squeezed her arm. "You're not getting all sentimental, are you?"

"Trying not to," she sniffed.

However, it was hard; the last couple of months had been so eventful. Brad pulled her toward him, rubbing his hands up and down her spine. "Try not to be sad, we have an awful lot to be thankful for."

The telephone rang from indoors, nervously they exchanged glances, he pulled away to go and answer it, she caught his arm. "Thank you, Brad, you've been a tower of strength. I don't know what I would have done without you." He nodded, winking at her, before hurrying into the house to answer the phone.

She watched the colt, closely. Subconsciously she was holding her breath; it was like this every time he answered the phone. She had stopped answering it weeks ago, afraid of hearing bad news. Marina felt her nerves twitch, as she heard him come back out on to the terrace behind her. "Marina, darling—" He took hold of her shoulders and turned her around to face him. His eyes were misted. She felt the knot in her stomach tighten.

"Marina, darling, she's awake. It's a miracle. Adam just called, she's back with us, darling. Isn't that wonderful?" Marina hugged him tightly; her whole body began to tremble, tears of relief sprung to her eyes. Engulfed by a powerful surge of emotion, she began to weep, burying her head into his chest. Brad struggled to hold back the tears too, as he softly, stroked her hair. Marina looked up at him through puffy eyes. "Has he told her yet?"

"No, honey, not yet! Later I believe," he said. Then he pulled her protectively back towards his chest.

Carmen arrived back to her shabby, untidy house, the house she loved. No matter what, she wouldn't be leaving here, this was her home, and all her friends were here. Her father helped her drag the large chest into the centre of the living room. Carmen knelt down beside it running her hand along its gnarled surface, tracing each knot with her fingertips.

"Are you going to open it?" Her father looked expectantly at her. She shook her head with a secretive smile.

"I don't want to offend you but—" She took a deep breath. "I would like to do it alone, if you don't mind."

He smiled, trying to hide his disappointment. He had been rather looking forward to it.

It had taken her six weeks to collect it from the solicitors and still she was reluctant to open it. He wasn't daft, he knew her too well and he knew that once she did her life would change forever. Change wasn't something she coped with. Carmen had lived her whole life without knowing Aunt Grace. A few more days wouldn't hurt. Besides it was time he got off home himself. Life for Carmen had been hectic these last few weeks; she could really do with some time alone.

Carmen kissed her father goodbye, giving him an emotional hug on the doorstep, she watched him leave. Then she turned and went back inside. She sat on the worn sofa, looking intently at the chest, her fingers trembled in anticipation. Carmen sensed her mother's presence, smelt her musky scent in the air. "Here goes, Mummy." She smiled heavenward. The telephone rang! Tearing her eyes from the chest, she hesitated for a moment, before going to answer it, the moment spoiled for now.

"Hi, Carmen, how are you? It's Martin." There was no mistaking the deep sexy voice, she smiled coyly to herself.

"I was wondering if you were coming back up to Winchester this weekend." He took a deep breath. "I thought that maybe we could go to dinner?"

Carmen felt her spirits soar. A warm glow alighted in her tummy. For a moment she was unable to speak. "I think that would be lovely." Hugging the receiver to her chest, she looked upward and mouthed, "Bless you, Aunt Grace. Bless you."

Isobel stared lovingly at Adam through red-rimmed eyes. He sat pale faced at the side of the bed, holding tightly on to her hand. Shakily, she found her voice, trying not to tremble.

"They want you to tell me the bad news, don't they? The nurse has been avoiding my questions all day." She squeezed his hand encouragingly. "It's OK I can face it, I have to know."

Adam looked into her eyes, he gave a sad nod. "Yes they have, Isobel." He tightened the grip on her ice, cold hand. "There was nothing they could do," he added, helplessly.

Isobel held back the tears. Instead she focused hard on Adam's face.

"Have they had the funerals yet?"

Adam looked at her confused, unsure how to react. As far as he was concerned, she knew nothing. The doctors had decided it was best for him to tell her. Apart from Edward he was the nearest thing to family she had now.

"What do you mean funerals, Isobel, I don't understand?" He saw the glimmer of hope in her eyes. Isobel took a sharp intake of breath.

"The car accident, the policeman, he told me Jacob and Edward—"

Adam stood up; he leaned over her and said. "Isobel, my sweet, precious darling, Edward's fine he's with his grandparents. It's Jacob, I thought you had realised that at the time of the accident, how foolish of me." He paused, it didn't seem right for him to tell her this news. The medical staff had insisted, and Jacob's parents were obviously too distraught. "Jacob was killed; he was trying to save you and Edward from being hit by a car in London. Do you not remember anything of it?"

Isobel shook her head. Tears began to roll down her cheeks. "I have to see Edward, please bring Edward to see me."

Adam sat back down. He pushed a tendril of hair back from her cheek.

"Edward is on his way here to see you. Dear Isobel, it's been touch and go, whether you would pull through this." He shuddered, as he signaled to all the wires and equipment she had been attached to for the last six weeks. He took a few moments to compose himself. "Everybody has been praying. Edward's been in a terrible state, to lose one parent is bad enough but both."

Isobel looked up at the ceiling. Poor Jacob, he had saved Edward, he had succeeded where she had failed.

It was in her mind, behind layers of disbelief. She turned away from Adam, thoughtful for several moments and then it hit her, suddenly apparent. That's why Jacob had been there with Belle, he had entered the tunnel, whereas she had been unable to. Isobel hadn't dreamt this, any of it, it had all been real. Unwittingly she had carried out the work that Belle spoke of. Belle had been unable to tell her the truth, that day at the meadow. What was that truth? Now it seemed quite simple.

Willing to sacrifice her love for Adam, she had solved the final piece of the puzzle. The piece that she now realised would have been so important, many lifetimes ago. The lesson had been letting go. It seemed so trivial, but wasn't that what Belle had hinted at, from their very first meeting? It was just as Rita had said, that day in her kitchen. Isobel thought back to her words. "Think of it, much like going to school. It's what you learn that's important." And so it was. Isobel saw it all made sense now, in a funny sort of way. The nightmarish dreams had been memories, memories from another lifetime. Back then, it seemed she didn't have the courage to do anything at all. And then when she had progressed to make a decision, it had been a selfish one, and she had, or rather poor Adam had paid the price. She looked at him now, why didn't he remember any of this? Was it purely her lesson to learn? Is that why both he and Jacob had had to keep returning, always alongside her, until she got it right? Like Belle, loyal and committed to the path of their spiritual progress. Like the globes of light, they joined; united to help each other's souls ascend?

Isobel shuddered, but she had lost Jacob this time, and in a strange way he had seemed relieved, at peace finally. Is that what he had been waiting for, to return home?

Adam examined her closely; this was all such a terrible shock. Waking up, after being locked in a coma for weeks and to such awful news. Her face was deathly pale, almost translucent, her eyes heavy with sadness. He felt utterly useless. As if reading his mind she felt for his hands, taking hold of them gently, managing to smile, despite the intense, heartache. Slowly she moved up the pillows to a half sitting position, to look deeply at him. A sparkle crept to her eyes.

"Do you know it's a beautiful place?" She gave a knowing smile. "Heaven, quite unlike anything you would ever imagine?" Adam looked back at her, his heart aching with love and admiration. He bent over, to gently place a kiss on the bridge of her nose.

"I love you with all my heart, Isobel. I love you so much it hurts. I can love Edward with all my heart too." He stopped to wipe away a tear. "I can never

241

take away your pain, but you have my word that I will never let you down, either of you.”

The tear slid down his cheek, it fell softly on to her outstretched palm, staining her skin for eternity, and slowly she traced its mark with her fingertips.

“I love you, Adam, it sounds silly I know, but this is the first time this has ever happened.” She took a deep breath, resting her head back against the pillow. “You’re still here with me. For once you’re still here.”

He looked up at her. “I don’t understand, Isobel.”

She shook her head. “I’m only just beginning to understand as well.” Through her pain she managed to smile. “I will explain it to you, as best I can.” Unfolding her clenched fist, she showed him the palm of her hand. “Where there was once blood there’s now a tear.”

He looked confused. “I don’t know what you—”

“Dearest Adam, love of all my lives.” She closed her hand around his. “I will explain it all, even though you must know, somewhere, deep inside. For wasn’t it you who said, this time you will not fail!” And she smiled, for one day he would realize. He would remember.

Printed in the United States
80758LV00003B/124-195